MURD[illegible] OXFORD LANE

A gripping mystery full of suspense

TONY BASSETT

THE BOOK FOLKS

Published by The Book Folks

London, 2022

ISBN 978-1-913516-21-5

www.thebookfolks.com

Murder on Oxford Lane is the first title in a series of mysteries set in the Midlands. Details about the other novels can be found at the back of this one.

Chapter 1

It had been no surprise to Harry Bowers to learn that someone was sleeping with his wife. He had known about it for several weeks. He even knew who the man was.

But it had come as a great shock to discover that the shameless creep had been bold enough to pay occasional visits to his wife at their family home. He'd learnt this through a chance remark made by his young daughter.

Tonight, for the first time since he learned of these visits, the two men were due to meet again. They could hardly avoid it. They sang beside each other in the church choir.

As he travelled home in his car from the railway station, Harry vowed to remain calm and see how the evening developed. For the present, he would say nothing to his wife. After twenty minutes following country roads, their imposing Georgian mansion loomed up before him in the twilight.

The black, two-metre-high gates to the estate, just outside the village of Norton Prior in Warwickshire, swung open. He put his white Audi into gear and the car swept up the driveway, past the tennis court and the pink rhododendron bushes. The neatly trimmed conifers stood like sentinels, casting eerie shadows across the gravel.

At last, he came to a halt by the stone steps that led to the red, colonial-style front door. The thirty-nine-year-old property tycoon strode past the two white gothic pillars standing on either side and turned the key.

'Must get a move on,' he muttered to himself. 'Choir practice starts at seven fifteen and I was late last week.'

The house seemed quiet as he pushed open the door and walked in.

'Maggie, are you here?' he asked, his deep voice echoing round the vaulted reception hall.

'Of course, I'm here. I'm always here,' came the reply. Margaret Bowers strolled from the kitchen, looking as stern as a sultan's mother.

'I saw the credit card statement this morning,' he announced.

'I wondered when you were going to bring that up.'

'You've gone a bit mad at the sales, haven't you? We've hardly got Christmas out of the way.'

She rolled her eyes and adjusted the long, dark-brown hair she'd tied behind her head. 'I don't have to account for my spending. I needed some new clothes.'

'We should've discussed it first,' he insisted.

She scowled. 'You've never got time to talk about anything.' She then climbed the oak stairs and disappeared from view.

Harry hurriedly cooked himself a microwave meal. The days of cosy family meals round the table had long since passed.

After bolting down his pasta, he raced upstairs and took off his grey suit. He pulled on his blue jeans before returning downstairs and snatching his hymn lyrics from the writing bureau in the living room. He looked at his watch. It was nearly a quarter to seven.

'I'd better get moving,' he told himself, glancing in the mirror to comb his short, dark hair. After slipping into his dark-blue trainers and pulling on his black overcoat, he rushed out into the bitterly cold January air.

It was a clear night with a slender crescent moon and stars visible in the sky. Leaves, brittle with frost, crunched beneath his feet as he made his way along the Worcester Road towards the church.

He passed two black-and-white cottages and then a row of trees, tall and thickly clumped together. He darted in and out of their shadows on the pavement as he walked. Above the rumble of the traffic, he heard the church bell in the distance toll seven times. He quickened his pace.

In his mind, he rehearsed the hymn they were due to perform at Candlemas in just over three weeks' time: *'Of the Father's love begotten, ere the worlds began to be, he is Alpha and Omega, he the source, the ending he, of the things that are, that have been, and that future years shall see, evermore and evermore!'*

Within ten minutes, he had reached the churchyard, which stood on the corner of Oxford Lane, enclosed by a solid stone wall. Behind the monuments to the dead stood the floodlit Norman church of St John the Martyr, rising like a beacon in an ocean of darkness.

Harry turned into the lane, passing the pair of terraced cottages on his right, and was pleased to see the lights were still glowing at the village newsagent's, Norton News, housed on the ground floor of an Edwardian villa.

'Another cold one, isn't it?' he muttered to the shopkeeper as he climbed the three steps into the shop. Harry undid some of his coat buttons, reached into an inside pocket and handed over a pound coin.

Smiling, the proprietor passed him a packet of mints and his change. 'Cold enough for snow,' came the reply as Harry refastened his coat and left.

He had only gone a few steps when he noticed the very man who was sleeping with his wife, James Hockley, walking slowly up the pavement towards him.

Harry crossed the lane and waited by the dark, timber lychgate. Taller than Harry and with dark, ginger hair, Hockley glared when he noticed his fellow tenor.

Harry had never intended to be confrontational. He had wanted his rival to admit to the affair and promise to end it. But now face to face with him, his anger erupted and dominated his emotions. There was something about his rival's swagger that antagonised Harry.

'You can wipe that smirk off your face!' he bellowed.

Hockley, a PE teacher who kept himself extremely fit, quickened his pace as he approached, his face incandescent with rage. He was cursing Harry, calling him 'an old drunk'.

'Are you going to wipe it off for me?' he hollered. 'Come on then.'

He lunged at Harry, his punch engaging with his face. The blow sent him flying backwards so that he struck his head on the churchyard wall. He lay almost motionless on the frosty ground, moaning.

The teacher looked around to make sure there were no witnesses to the assault. Then he regained his composure and proceeded along the lane towards the church hall, acting as though the event had never happened. He hadn't thought of the consequences of his actions until that moment. Now it occurred to him that Harry might recover and stumble into the hall, battered, bruised and berating him. What would happen then?

While the choir began rehearsing their fifth-century hymn inside the small, brick-built hall, Hockley remained uneasy. He tried hard not to worry about Harry making a sudden appearance and concentrated on the lyrics. Nearly half an hour passed. Surely his fellow tenor should have recovered by now and joined them?

He continued feeling unsettled and, when the practice was over at a quarter past eight, he didn't linger to exchange gossip with other choristers. He was keen to return to the scene in Oxford Lane.

He was relieved to find the businessman was no longer lying by the lychgate. There was no blood by the wall or on the leaf-strewn ground. There was no sign that any skirmish had disturbed the peace of the night.

So where was Harry? Had he slunk off home? Had a passer-by attended to his wounded head? Had he been rushed to hospital? There was no clue and no one to ask.

He pulled out his mobile phone and dialled a familiar number. Within a minute, Margaret Bowers answered.

'James. Is everything all right?' she asked. She had not been expecting him to call.

'I know this might sound strange but is your husband there?' he asked.

'No. He goes to the church hall on a Tuesday.'

'I know,' said James. 'I saw him in Oxford Lane before the choir practice started, but he didn't show up at the hall. I'm just wondering what's happened.'

'Not like you to worry over Harry,' she muttered.

'I know, but this is a real mystery. Look, I may as well tell you. We had an argument…'

'Oh, here we go…'

'We had an argument just a few yards from the hall. I'm sorry to say, I lost my temper and hit him.'

'I'm sure he's survived worst.'

'I hit him probably a bit harder than I should've done. I left him on the ground.' A sudden urgency crept into his voice. 'He was all right. He was still moving. Just a little dazed. That's all.' He paused for breath before adding, 'I can't understand why he failed to show up for choir practice and there's no sign of him in the lane. I'm wondering if he's gone to hospital.'

'Unlikely. They'd have phoned me if he'd been taken in. Look, don't worry, James. He'll turn up. He always does, more's the pity. But I expect, when he does, he'll be baying for your blood.'

Chapter 2

Detective Sergeant Sunita Roy was in the ground-floor ladies' washroom facing a row of basins when her phone rang. She made sure there were no eavesdroppers before answering.

'You took your time,' said her sister, Tulika.

'What do you want? I'm late for work,' replied Sunita, inspecting her long, dark hair in the mirror.

'Sunita, you really are the limit. You haven't called Mummy and Papa for months. And don't tell me you've been too busy.'

'You know why I haven't phoned them. They haven't forgiven me for defying Papa's wishes.'

Tulika, a trainee solicitor with a Birmingham law firm, sneered. 'That's no reason to act like you have. It's as if you've disowned them. They're both concerned that they haven't seen you or even heard from you.'

'Tulika, I'm trying to build myself a future. I've turned my back on my old life.'

'For God's sake, why don't you at least find the time to give them a call,' said Tulika, raising her voice.

'If you're going to shout at me, I'm not going to carry on this conversation,' said Sunita as she hung up. She sighed before glancing back at the mirror and tidying her hair. She cared for her parents, but they had upset her more than she could admit to her sister.

She smiled as a young, uniformed constable emerged in the doorway.

'Good holiday, Sarge?' the constable asked.

'Wicked time, but strange for me. Like being in a foreign country as I was brought up in England.'

'Bloody hot, I'd imagine.'

Sunita nodded. 'I love the buzz of Kolkata and seeing the relatives, but I missed England and, in a way, I'm glad to be back. Anyway, it's time for the reckoning.'

'Don't worry – he's in a good mood,' came the reply.

Twenty-five-year-old Sunita slipped past her colleague and climbed the stairs to the CID section. She hurried to her desk and began scrolling through her computer messages.

* * *

'Sunita, have you got a moment?' The deep voice with a rich Birmingham accent rang out across the open-plan CID office.

The young sergeant, who was slim and five feet seven inches tall, picked up her small, black notebook and hurried across the beige carpet to her boss's room – the last of four private offices partitioned off at the side.

DCI Gavin Roscoe was standing in his open doorway, casting his eyes round the office, as she reached him.

'Yes, sir?'

He smiled. 'Good holiday?'

'We really enjoyed ourselves, thank you, sir. I know it was awkward, needing time off so soon after starting here.'

'No problem. I hear you sorted out some drunk on the flight back?'

'Yes, sir.'

'You'll have to tell me all about it. Right now, I want to brief you and Brett Dawson about a job.'

He was still trying to make up his mind about his new sergeant. She always dressed smartly and sounded intelligent when she spoke. But she lacked practical knowledge. Would she really fit in at Heart of England Police after her three years with the West Midlands force?

He beckoned to the young constable by the drinks machine.

'Dawson, could I have a word?' he yelled.

PC Brett Dawson approached like an errant schoolboy summoned to the headmaster's study.

Sunita and Dawson nodded at each other and made themselves comfortable in black vinyl chairs as Roscoe returned to his desk and answered his ringing phone.

'You'd better knock on a few more doors,' he was saying. 'We've just got to get more evidence... That sounds like a good idea. Oh, and, Omar, give me a call when you've done that. We might think about arresting that lad from Kenilworth.'

The young pair glanced round the room as their boss continued his briefing. Sunita listened with interest to the way he spoke. She realised he was a few inches taller than her, of medium build and with ruddy cheeks. His demeanour reminded her of a harassed uncle she knew in India.

'Sorry to keep you waiting,' mumbled Roscoe as he ended his call. 'A boy of fifteen's been stabbed. But I've got one of our best men on the case.'

He leaned back on his black executive chair and gazed out of the window at a children's park across the road.

'Now I've got an important job lined up for you two. We've had a report of a property tycoon who's gone missing. Name of Harry Bowers.'

Sunita began writing in her notebook.

'It's all right. I've got a print-out here,' said Roscoe. He leaped up and plucked a sheet of paper from the tray of his printer before handing it to Sunita.

'It's from a constable at Queensbridge called Underhill. Very reliable guy. Bowers' wife Margaret called in at the station yesterday and reported him as missing.'

'Do we know when he was last seen, sir?' asked Sunita, as she took the print-out from him.

'Last seen? Let me see. January 8th outside the church in Norton Prior. That's a village three miles west of Queensbridge. All the information's here. You've got wheels, haven't you, Sergeant?'

'I'm sorry, sir. My car's still being repaired.'

'What about you, Dawson?'

'Yes sir,' the constable replied enthusiastically. 'I've got my car with me. We'll get there in no time.'

'No need to break the speed limit,' said Roscoe as he resumed his seat behind his desk. 'Look, this could be something or nothing. You get a lot of these mispers, as you know, and they usually turn up sometime or other, but we've got to look into this with some urgency. Bowers is a close friend of the Assistant Chief Constable.'

* * *

'This one's a bit of a mystery, isn't it?' Sunita muttered as they left St James Street police headquarters in Dawson's red Ford Focus for the twenty-mile journey to the town of Queensbridge-upon-Avon.

'How do you mean?' said the amiable constable, who was four years younger than her.

'Well, it says in the boss's print-out it took a week before the wife told police.'

'Maybe he's one of these men who's always going off without telling his family,' said Dawson as his car left the busy M42 motorway and headed past Redditch. 'Most of these missing people turn up in the end. If you ask me, we're probably wasting our time.'

She glanced again at the CID report. It began by saying that Heart of England Police, which covered Warwickshire and parts of Worcestershire and Birmingham, were growing increasingly concerned for the welfare of 'a thirty-nine-year-old man from Norton Prior'.

She began reading out loud: 'Mr Bowers was last seen at approximately 19.00 hours on Tuesday, 8 January while walking to St John's church hall in Oxford Lane for a choir practice. Officers are appealing for the public's help in tracing Mr Bowers as he failed to return home and has not been seen since.'

'What's the description?' Dawson asked.

'The guy's white, five feet eight inches tall with dark hair and hazel eyes. He's of medium build and originally from Solihull. At the time of his disappearance, he was wearing blue Levi jeans, a thick black coat, and navy-blue trainers.'

'He wasn't taking any chances with the weather.'

'My flatmate told me that week was exceptionally cold,' Sunita asserted. 'Anyway, how're we going to play this? I suppose we should go and see the wife first.'

'Yes. Underhill, the force liaison guy, says a team have already been out in the streets where he was last seen. They've done some house-to-house. They've also searched the river and woods.' Dawson glanced at her for a second while he ruffled his spiky blond hair.

'Someone mentioned the boss owns a tea shop down this way,' he said, changing the subject. 'I expect we'll be passing it in a few minutes.'

'It's in the town's main street, so I don't think it's on our route.'

'I thought it might be interesting to drive along the high street and see if we can spot it.'

Sunita shrugged and sighed. 'It's your petrol,' she said.

They entered the bustling Warwickshire market town of Queensbridge, which straddled the River Avon. The car swept along the high street before passing the red-brick police station and some black and white Tudor cottages.

'That's the Roscoes' place,' said Dawson as he checked his rear mirror and drew to a halt beside the kerb. They looked across. The words 'Apollo Tearooms' appeared over the doorway of the quaint seventeenth-century building. A waitress in a black and white outfit with a white maid's hat could be seen flitting between tables.

'So his wife runs it?' Sunita asked.

'That's what I've been told. Looks an interesting place,' Dawson remarked before driving off again.

After passing through open countryside, they reached Norton Prior, an affluent village with period properties and an 'Old England' appeal.

Sunita had read somewhere that, centuries before, the village had served as a stopping point for drovers herding flocks of sheep from the Welsh borders to London markets. It was now a popular village for Midlands commuters.

Sunita rummaged in her black handbag for her mobile phone.

'I'll just have a word with the force liaison guy and see if there's any update,' she muttered.

As they drove through the village, she phoned through to the station and was fortunate enough to find PC Underhill was available to take her call.

'Got a few questions. That OK?' she asked.

'Of course. Fire away,' said the twenty-seven-year-old constable.

'Well, first of all, have you got a photograph of Mr Bowers?' she asked.

'Yes. I'll email it over in a couple of seconds. You haven't seen the note, have you?'

'What note?'

'The wife found a handwritten note which said, "I just can't take any more. I have gone away. Don't bother trying to find me." I'll email a copy of that over as well.'

'How bizarre.'

'I know. His bank account hasn't been touched and we can't find his phone.'

'I was wondering – is he actually Harry or Henry?'

'He was christened Henry but he's always been known to family and friends as Harry.'

They passed the village green before the light-grey stone church of St John the Martyr with its ninety-foot tower loomed up on the right.

'He's married, isn't he?' she asked.

'Yes, he's got a wife, Margaret, and a young daughter, Rachel, who are obviously distraught. Everyone says this vanishing act is completely out of character.'

'What did he do for a living?'

'He ran a large property business in Birmingham.'

'Does he have a brother or sister?'

'His parents are in Solihull. I'm not too sure about any other personal information. They just give us the basics,' the constable said.

'Any relevant hobbies?'

'I'm told he's a regular at Birmingham City. That's all I know.'

'That's football, isn't it?' she asked.

'That's right. Football,' the voice on the line assured her.

Underhill told Sunita that a team of officers and volunteers had been searching woodlands and fields around the village for a few days.

'So you don't think he's going to turn up alive?' she asked.

The officer thought for a few seconds. 'He's not been suffering from depression or been made homeless. He doesn't fit the usual profile of a missing person.'

After she ended the call, Dawson glanced at her.

'You've never been interested in soccer then?' he asked.

She shook her head.

'So, no sense in me asking if you'd like to watch Villa play Stoke next month?'

'I'd rather watch my uncle's iron gate rusting in the rain,' she replied.

Eventually, Dawson stopped the car outside a walled property with a pair of large metal entrance gates. A brass sign said, 'Heathwood House'. Sunita opened her window and shivered. Temperatures appeared to have plunged.

'We could be in for some snow,' she said, eyeing the grey clouds in the sky.

The pair gazed into the grounds. The long, straight driveway led to an imposing house. She pressed a buzzer on the right-hand brick pillar. An educated female voice asked what they wanted.

'Police,' Sunita replied. 'We need to talk to Mrs Bowers.'

At once, the gates began to creak open, allowing Dawson to begin the journey up the drive.

Harry Bowers was obviously a successful man. The family's front garden resembled a small park. It was laid to lawn with a number of pine trees on either side of the drive.

Behind trees and bushes, she caught a glimpse of tennis courts beside the main house, to the left. As they reached a circular turning area in front of the house, Dawson brought the car to a halt.

Just a few yards from the front steps, they could see the burnt-out remains of a garage annex or stable block. Sunita at once got out. She walked over to the charred ruins. Part of a burnt-out car was visible beside the blackened walls. An acrid burning smell faintly lingered. She stood alone for a moment, staring at the ruined building in shocked silence.

Chapter 3

After overcoming their surprise at seeing the burnt-out building, Sunita and Dawson walked to the front door of the house. Sunita climbed up the steps and pressed the bell. She was almost expecting a maid or butler to respond, but instead a slim, attractive woman with dark wavy hair appeared.

Margaret Bowers was smartly dressed in a red cashmere roll-neck jumper, black and white tweed trousers and a pair of stylish ladies' boots. She was holding a fawn coat as though she was about to leave the house. Her eyes were red. The sergeant wondered if she'd been crying.

'Mrs Bowers?' Sunita began. 'Heart of England CID.'

The homeowner nodded. 'What do you want now?' she complained.

'We need to ask you a few questions about your husband, if that's all right.'

'I've told the constable that came everything I know.'

'I'm sorry,' said Sunita. She didn't want to admit they'd only just been assigned to the case.

'There are some gaps in our information,' Dawson suggested tactfully.

'Very well,' said Margaret, stepping back from the doorway. 'You'd better come in.' She crossed the vaulted reception hall until she reached the foot of the oak stairs.

'Rachel, dear!' she yelled. 'Mummy's got some visitors. I'll come up and see you in a minute.'

Then she led the pair into a beamed sitting room with a huge open stone inglenook fireplace. It was furnished with two large brown leather three-seater settees and two matching armchairs. An oval dining table with six chairs stood close to the Georgian-style windows. The corner of the room was occupied by a Steinway piano.

'Did they show you the note?' she asked as the pair sat down on one of the settees.

'Is this the one you mentioned in your statement to PC Underhill?' asked Sunita.

'Yes, the officer took it away.'

'We haven't seen it yet.'

'It was just a brief note in an envelope addressed to me, saying he'd planned to leave.'

Before she could stop herself, Sunita said, 'Is that why you took so long to...' Then her words petered out.

'Look, I know it seems strange I didn't report him as missing straight away. I'll be frank with you, as I was with the policeman. Harry and I hadn't been getting on and we'd been talking about splitting up. He's only really been here these past months for the sake of our daughter.

'As the days passed, I felt I ought to bring in the police. I read the note again and worried he might do something silly, like harming himself.'

'Do you have any idea where he might've gone?' asked Sunita.

'None at all. Wherever he is, I hope he's safe and well, naturally. He's the father of my thirteen-year-old daughter. I wouldn't want any harm to befall him.'

Sunita was inwardly surprised by how cold Mrs Bowers seemed in her attitude towards her husband's disappearance, despite her sympathetic-sounding language.

'How long were you married?' she asked.

'I first met Harry at university eighteen years ago. He was a really good-looking guy – you know, broad shoulders, a strong jaw and a confident charm. By the time we left uni, we were married and I had Rachel a year later. I didn't realise it at first, but Harry's a workaholic and he became more and more absorbed in his business. The rows began soon after we moved here six years ago and we gradually drifted apart.'

'When did you last see your husband, Mrs Bowers?' asked Dawson.

'Well, I last saw him sometime on the Tuesday evening,' she said.

'January the 8th?' asked Sunita.

'That's right. He'd been up to his office in Birmingham and travelled back to Queensbridge. He got back here in the car a few minutes after six. Then he had a bite to eat and went off to choir practice. We didn't speak much. Then later he didn't come home. But, you know, that's not unusual. He often stayed out. The next morning the choirmaster phoned, asking why Harry hadn't been to choir practice.'

'You say it wasn't unusual for Harry to stay out?' asked Sunita.

'We've been living separate lives for some time.'

Dawson leaned forward and interrupted her. 'We couldn't help noticing the burnt-out building near the front of the house.'

'Yes. There was a fire in October. It was just one of those things. Luckily, no one was inside at the time.'

'It was a garage block, was it?' he asked.

'Yes, my husband lost his two classic cars.'

'How did the fire happen?' Sunita asked.

'I'm not sure. Just an accident, I suppose.'

Sunita found her response unhelpful but decided to let the matter lie. 'Well, I think we'd better go,' she said, as she rose to her feet.

'All right,' said Mrs Bowers. 'I'm sorry if I don't sound more concerned, but my husband is a man who can look after himself. I'm inclined to think that, when he learns police are looking for him, the old dog will probably turn up, wondering what all the fuss is about.'

Sunita walked slowly and thoughtfully down the stone steps of Heathwood House. Margaret Bowers had been unemotional – almost indifferent – while discussing her husband's disappearance. She and PC Dawson had both been shocked by her attitude.

'She's a strange one,' Sunita observed as they slipped back into the car. 'I can't get over the way she took a whole week to report her husband as missing.'

'Maybe it's one of those part-time marriages,' he replied as they drove down the drive and set off towards the village green. 'They clearly hadn't been getting on.'

'I know, but it's not just that. She comes across as very blasé and very detached.'

On arriving in Oxford Lane, they spent fifteen minutes knocking on several front doors at the lower end of the street, but none of the householders was in.

'It's the wrong time of day,' Dawson muttered. 'They're all at work.'

Sunita noticed the blue sign above the newsagent's shop, Norton News, across the road from the church and a short distance from the lychgate.

'Let's try here,' she said. 'This is where he was last seen.'

Edward Bailey, the newsagent, was serving a customer when the pair climbed the three stone steps to enter the premises. They waited until the customer had left and then approached the counter.

'Mr Bailey?' Sunita asked.

The shopkeeper, who was dressed in a striking purple shirt and dark-blue trousers, nodded. She showed him her warrant card.

'Heart of England Police,' she said. 'Sergeant Roy. This is PC Dawson. We wanted to ask you about the missing man.'

Mr Bailey looked at them for a moment.

'Oh yes, Mr Bowers. Nice guy,' he said. 'He often comes in here to buy a newspaper or packet of mints.'

'So he came in here on Tuesday evening last week?' Sunita asked, as she glanced absent-mindedly at the front of the local newspaper, the *Queensbridge Gazette*, which was stacked in three piles on the counter.

'That's right, young lady. I was just thinking of closing and he came in.'

'What time would that have been?'

'It must've been a few minutes after seven because I'd just heard the church bell sound the hour.'

'How did he seem?'

'Oh, normal self. He was well wrapped-up because it was a cold night. He was a keen member of the choir and wanted a pack of mints. He gave me the money and left.

He just said, "Another cold one, isn't it?" and that was it. I assumed he'd gone to the church hall.'

'He never turned up apparently,' said Dawson.

'I know. Strange, isn't it? If I had my life again, I'd have looked out of the shop to see where he went.'

Sunita nodded. 'And he was wearing...'

'Blue jeans and a black coat, as far as I recall,' said the shopkeeper. 'There was just one thing that surprised me.'

Sunita stared at him. 'What was that?'

'Well, choir practice starts at a quarter past seven and he's often late,' he went on. 'It's usually about ten past seven when he calls in here. That night he was a little earlier, so maybe he was meeting someone.'

Before they left, she bought a copy of the Gazette, which had come out that morning, and was surprised to find no mention of the missing man on the front page.

However, as they returned to the car, she found a three-column piece on page three. It was headlined, 'Police appeal to trace missing Norton Prior man'. The report said, 'Police have launched a hunt for a missing property tycoon who's not been seen since leaving his home nine days ago. Harry Bowers, aged thirty-nine, has not been seen since he set off for choir practice in Oxford Lane, close to Norton Bridge.' The report included a comment from the rector.

> *Revd Peter Hughes, Rector of St John's, told the Gazette: "Harry's a much-loved and respected member of the choir and the congregation. His family and friends are anxious for news of his whereabouts, and I'd urge anyone with information to help the police. We need to get him reunited quickly with his family."*

The pair stopped for lunch at the village pub, the Coach and Horses, a former fifteenth-century coaching inn on the edge of the green.

'Might pick up some gossip,' Dawson muttered as he drove into the pub car park.

But the pair were disappointed when they eased the stout black, wooden front door open and gazed inside. There were only around a dozen customers taking lunch beneath the oak-beamed ceiling of the main bar. A sign outside had mentioned facilities included a skittle alley and a rear garden.

'I'm a bit whacked, to be honest, Sarge,' the constable muttered as they walked towards the bar. 'I was at a pub quiz in Dudley last night and I've been on the go for hours this morning.'

'A pub quiz? Sounds like fun.'

'Not really. We got beaten. We seemed to go to pieces after a question about the Battle of Waterloo. The quizmaster asked what words Wellington used to rouse his troops. The answer was the well-known "Up guards and at 'em!" But all we could come up with at the time was "Fill your boots!"'

She laughed as a balding, heavily built man in his mid-fifties emerged behind the counter after clambering up the steps from the cellar.

'Sorry to keep you waiting,' he said with a smile. 'What can I get you?'

'Just an orange juice for me,' said Sunita as Dawson waved a ten-pound note towards the bar.

'A pint of QB Bitter for me,' said her companion, who had developed a taste for the locally brewed ale. 'And can we see the menu, please?'

'I take it you're the landlord?' Sunita asked as he shook a bottle of orange juice, took off the top and poured it into a glass.

'Yes, that's right, young lady. Brian Porter's the name. Ice?'

Sunita nodded. 'We were just wondering if you knew the Bowers family?'

He smiled as he poured the beer.

'What are you – Old Bill? I thought so. You're too smartly dressed to be the press. I'm afraid I can't help you.'

'You didn't know them?'

'They never came in here for food or drink,' Mr Porter added. 'I've seen police searching the fields behind the pub and I heard they were bringing an underwater search team to inspect the Avon. But there's been no gossip.'

'Can I leave you my phone number?' she suggested. 'Maybe you could let us know if you do get any information.'

'Of course,' he said, leaning against the counter and twisting the card round in his stubby fingers. 'If I hear anything, I'll be in touch, young lady.'

Chapter 4

Gavin Roscoe was in high spirits as he drove to work on Friday, 18 January. His wife had revealed during the evening that she had bought tickets for them to see *Timon of Athens* in Stratford.

He was humming a tune to himself as he arrived at St James Street Police headquarters, which was a few miles south of Solihull. Unfortunately for him, the celebratory mood would be short-lived.

As soon as he reached his desk, he received a call from Chief Superintendent Nicola Norris, his superior. She wanted to see him urgently. With some trepidation, the DCI climbed the stairs to the second floor and made his way to Norris's office. He knocked and waited before her voice roared, 'Enter!'

Roscoe, who was smartly dressed in a navy-blue suit, murmured, 'Morning, ma'am,' as he stepped across the beige carpet towards the large oak desk.

He hardly noticed the photographs of police awards ceremonies on the wall behind the chief superintendent or the picture of the Queen. He had seen them so many times before. He was more concerned with the troubled look upon his boss's face.

Norris, whose head was topped with neatly combed, mid-length grey hair, was sitting in her wheelchair at the front of her desk. She had been seriously injured in a horse-riding accident and had lost the use of her legs. The prospect of an early retirement on health grounds was beckoning, but she intended to remain in post for a while until a successor could be found.

She peered across at her visitor with the air of a hospital matron, ready to upbraid any well-meaning subordinate for the slightest misdemeanour.

'Gavin, what's the latest on this missing man?' she demanded. 'I promised to find out for the Assistant Chief Constable. People go missing all the time – domestic problems, accidents, suicides – I know that, but this one's a bit different.'

'I've read your email,' remarked Roscoe as he drew up a chair and sat down. 'The missing man, Bowers, has done extremely well in property with his firm, Heathwood Property Group, hasn't he? Bought a lot of land cheaply and threw up lots of flats.'

Norris nodded. 'That's right. Well, do you remember that man from HMRC who used to tip us off?'

'Oh yes. I know who you mean – Irish guy, O'Connor.'

'Yes,' she said, wheeling herself along the carpet until she was in her usual place behind her desk. 'Well, he called me about Bowers yesterday and we had a long chat. Looks like Bowers may have done a bunk and skipped off somewhere – possibly out of the country.'

Roscoe looked astounded. 'You mean he might've faked his own death?'

'That's right,' she said. 'HMRC have launched an inquiry into Bowers' business affairs. There were several suspicious deals and they claim he owes them up to a million pounds. So I want you to give this case top priority.'

Roscoe looked blank and shook his head. 'This doesn't have the hallmarks of an ordinary missing person search,' he said thoughtfully.

'No. What checks have been made so far?'

'Early inquiries reveal his bank account has not been touched. No CCTV footage. Something serious has happened to our Mr Bowers. You know about the strange "goodbye note"?'

'Yes. Have forensics looked at it?'

'Yes. They only found a print from his wife Margaret's index finger, but as she opened it and read it you'd obviously expect that. We can't work out if it was written by him or someone trying to muddy the waters.'

'Has Bowers' mobile phone turned up?'

'He left it at home when he went to the church hall. His wife handed it to the constable from Queensbridge who first interviewed her.'

'His message and call log have been checked?'

'I've got our new sergeant, Sunita Roy, going through his phone records. She and PC Dawson have interviewed the rector, the choirmaster and every single member of the church choir except two. One's away on holiday and the other's never at home when we call.'

'What about credit and debit cards?'

'They haven't been used.'

'You say there's nothing on CCTV?'

'Only one camera in Oxford Lane, which didn't pick him up. We've got him on CCTV in Worcester Road at around seven o'clock heading towards the church hall, but there's no sign of him walking back later on.'

She cupped her right hand round her lower face.

'He could be anywhere,' she said with a frown. 'Anyway, please get moving on this case, Gavin. I want this Harry Bowers found – and quickly.'

* * *

Roscoe's blue BMW 3 Series saloon glided into the quiet rural lane on the outskirts of Queensbridge. The detective turned off the engine.

It had been another busy day in the CID office. How much longer would he be able to cope with the twenty-mile journey each way? The stacks of emails? The long hours? The new procedures and the heavy demands of the job?

The work had its compensations, he realised, as he gazed across his lawn towards the front hedge. Especially when his team cracked a difficult case or their efforts were rewarded in court. But the wheels of justice often seemed to turn so slowly and he wondered, from time to time, how his life would've turned out if he'd remained a bobby on the beat.

He had risen rapidly through the ranks. He had been appointed a detective inspector six years before and DCI a year ago. But he often thought he might have been happier if his life had followed a different course.

Would he ever become accustomed to being woken at all hours of the night by news of some major crime?

After locking his car in the garage, he walked past the leaded light windows and opened the front door of the 1930s detached house.

'Helen!' he called as he dropped a pile of papers on the hall table. 'Do you know where my map of Norton is? I couldn't find it at work.'

'Have you looked in the top drawer of the hall table?' came a voice from the kitchen.

'No. I'll look now,' he said. He tugged the brass handle and there, at the top of the drawer, was the small black and white map he needed.

'Did you find it?' asked Helen as she emerged wiping her hands on a light-green teacloth. Her long blonde hair swayed to the side as she reached up and kissed her husband on the cheek. The couple had first met when

Roscoe was a young Birmingham constable and Helen had just completed her Geography course at university.

She had been helping her father, who at the time was the police canteen manager, by working part-time shifts in the kitchens. She and Roscoe exchanged banter and, after dating for a year, got married. Their son George, who was now nineteen, arrived a year later and daughter Melody a year after that.

It was when the children enrolled at secondary school that the Roscoes bought the Apollo Tearooms, which Helen now managed – assisted from time to time at the tables or in the kitchen by family members, including her husband.

'George gave us a hand at the tearooms today,' she explained as he took off his jacket and hung it in the cupboard beneath the stairs. 'Gavin, he really made me laugh. Just before we closed, old Jim Carter called in, asking if anyone had seen his umbrella. A moment later, George emerged from the kitchen brandishing a purple parasol decorated with tiny white rabbits. "This isn't yours, is it, Jim?" he asked with a chuckle. "There's a matching rainhat with it." Old Jim says, "No, you cheeky young blighter." Then a customer in the back part of the restaurant, who knew Jim, shouted out, "There's a purple scarf in here that would set off the whole ensemble!" There weren't many customers around by then, but everyone was in hysterics.'

'Old Jim's a lovely fellow,' said Roscoe.

He wandered into the dual-aspect living room, which was around ten metres long. The smell of fresh paint lingered in the newly decorated room which had cream walls and a red patterned carpet. A painting of sunlight emerging from behind a mountain stood above the open brick fireplace, where it captured the attention of every visitor. Patio doors led to a back garden which was mainly laid to lawn and a small swimming pool at the side, which had been covered over for the winter.

'Have you got someone working on the Harry Bowers case?' she wondered aloud, following him into the room where the television news was on.

'Yes, darling. Why do you ask?'

'Oh, I don't suppose it's important. George was on the bus with someone who was on their way home from a midweek football match. Apparently they made an announcement at the match to say he was missing.'

'I suppose all publicity helps,' said her husband, dropping down onto the leather settee. 'Was it a Birmingham City game?'

'I think so.'

'It makes sense. He was a regular there.' At that moment, heavy rock music began booming from a room upstairs.

'Can't a guy get a moment's peace round here?' Roscoe said.

'It's all right. I'll go and tell her,' said Helen, stepping towards the hall.

'Stay there,' said Roscoe. 'You've had a hard day at the tearooms, I expect. I'll tell her.'

He marched to the foot of the stairs and yelled for Melody to turn the music down. When the racket continued unabated, he stomped up the stairs and thumped on her bedroom door.

'Melody!' he yelled. 'Turn it down.'

His daughter peered round the door, her curly blonde hair tumbling across her shoulder.

'Is there a problem, Dad?' she asked.

'Mel, your music's loud enough to wake the dead.'

'Sorry, Dad,' she said with a grin as she went to turn the volume down.

Chapter 5

The doorbell rang at the flat Sunita shared with her university friend Rupa.

'Are you expecting anyone?' Sunita shouted through the bathroom door to her friend, who was taking a shower.

'No. But I'm waiting for a parcel,' she replied. 'Maybe they left it with one of the neighbours.'

'There was no delivery note left. There's usually a note,' said Sunita, as she walked through the hallway and entered the living room. She gazed through a gap in the venetian blinds at the garden path which was glistening in the glow of a streetlight following some rain.

The figure of a man was shrouded in darkness by the door. He was staring up at the upstairs windows. She couldn't see his face, but something about him seemed familiar.

Against her better judgement, she cautiously opened the front door. It was the face of a man she'd once known. A face she'd hoped never to see again.

'Sunita!' he began, beaming at her from the rain-soaked path. 'I hope you don't mind me dropping by. I've missed you so much.'

'Arun! What are you doing here? I've told you it's over between us.'

'I can't stop thinking about you, Sunita. Don't I deserve another chance? We're so right for each other.'

She peered out at him as he stood smiling in the cold January air. He was short with unkempt black hair, black moustache and beard and a broad, toothy smile. What could ever have attracted her to him in the first place? she wondered.

'I'm sorry, Arun. I've moved on with my life and I suggest you do too. I'm working for the police now. And can you stop sending me text messages? We had a relationship but it's over now.'

'Why though? Why?' he wailed.

She felt sorry for him, standing alone in the darkness, begging to be readmitted to her life. But she knew she must stand firm. Arun Halder, whose family, like hers, had come to England from India, was no more than a relic from the past.

'Because we've nothing in common,' she insisted. 'Now, if you don't mind, I'm going to close the door.'

'No, no, don't close it,' he stammered. 'I've got to talk to you. We had a life together. We can still have a life together.'

'No, Arun,' she continued. 'We were friends for a couple of months – that's all. Then I chose not to see you anymore. I made it quite clear to you. You'll have to learn to get over these things and get on with your life.'

A voice behind her said, 'What is it, Sunita?' It was Rupa, her flatmate, who was now dressed and staring over Sunita's shoulder at the stranger on the doorstep. She had heard the raised voices and wondered if Sunita was in some kind of trouble.

'It's an ex-university friend. He's just going,' said Sunita as she closed the door in her visitor's face.

'What was he doing here?' whispered Rupa, who was twenty-six, shorter in height than Sunita and with medium-length, black hair.

'He's a pest,' she replied in an equally low voice as they moved back from the entrance door. 'I don't know how he's found my address.'

The doorbell rang again.

'Go away!' yelled Sunita. Then, to Rupa, she whispered, 'He doesn't seem to be getting the message.'

'Doesn't he realise you work for the police?'

'He knows, but it doesn't seem to make a difference.'

Rupa gestured for Sunita to move into the living room. 'Let me have a go. You go and sit in there,' she insisted.

Drawing back the front door with a flourish, Rupa glared out at Arun.

Summoning up as much ferocity as she could muster, she shouted, 'If you don't leave, I'm going to dial 999. And don't you dare come back here again.'

The strident voice seemed to have an effect. The unwanted guest sidled off up tree-lined Cateswell Road, in the Birmingham suburb of Hall Green. Rupa watched his every move as he unlocked a silver car parked twenty yards away and appeared to drive off.

'I think he's gone,' Rupa informed her friend while closing the door.

'I hope he doesn't come back,' said Sunita. 'He's been annoying me for a few weeks with phone calls and texts.'

'Phone calls? What does he say?'

'Sometimes he just says my name. Other times I just hear him breathing. He's also been writing to me. Look at this.' She marched to a cabinet in the living room which stood beneath a colourful Kalighat painting of five Indian women with sickles, *Villagers Harvesting Crops*. She searched in a drawer and returned with several sheets of paper, which she handed to her flatmate.

Rupa read the first part of the letter out loud:

> *My dearest darling Sunita, I think about you all the time. We had such a happy time together in Manchester and I'm so unhappy being apart from you. I have to be part of your life again. We were destined at birth to be together.*

'He rambles on in a similar way over three pages,' Sunita remarked.

'He lives in Staffordshire?'

'I think that's his parents' address or maybe his brother's.'

'Why haven't you mentioned this before,' said Rupa. 'Something could've been done about it.'

'I just thought he would get bored and give up. Now, somehow, he's discovered where I live and I've got an idea he's going to try to cause trouble for me.'

'Maybe you should have a word with your boss.'

'I don't like to. He's got enough to worry about right now.'

'He ought to be concerned for you, Sunita. Considerate bosses care about their staff.'

'Maybe I will – if Arun comes back.'

'No, do it anyway. He doesn't sound like the kind of guy who's going to give up easily.'

* * *

Two hours later, Sunita's phone rang. She picked it up with some trepidation, but quickly relaxed as she recognised the caller's number. Her boss's voice boomed down the phone.

'Sunita, I'm very annoyed with you. What's this about a fire at the Bowers' house? Dawson's been telling me about it, but there was nothing about it in your memo.'

'I'm sorry, sir. I didn't think it was that important.'

'Not that important? A millionaire's gone missing and, a couple of months before, there's a suspicious blaze at his home which wipes out his collection of classic cars?'

Sunita shrugged her shoulders. 'Mrs Bowers said it was an accident, sir.'

'Dawson tells me you didn't probe her about the fire. You simply got up and prepared to leave. Luckily, he realised the importance. I've got him checking the files with the fire brigade.'

'Sorry, sir. It was just one of a number of avenues of inquiry open to us. I believed our resources would be better employed following up other leads.'

He sighed. 'All right. We'll say no more about it for the moment. Now I'd like you to accompany me on Monday. I thought we should go and see Bowers' parents to begin with and then we'll go and see Margaret Bowers together after that – if there's enough time.'

'That sounds sensible, sir.'

Chapter 6

As he parked outside police headquarters the following Monday morning, the DCI noticed a slim, dark-haired woman leap from a bus and hurry towards the building, which was next to a car showroom.

The frenzied figure ran diagonally across the car park, her beige coat flapping in the breeze.

'Sorry, if I'm a little late, sir,' she murmured.

Roscoe smiled and walked towards her. It was a cold day and it had been raining.

'You're not late, Sunita!' his voice boomed as she clambered up the brick steps.

Then, clearly to her intense embarrassment, she slipped and tumbled onto the concrete surface. She glanced up to find her boss towering over her.

'Are you all right?' he asked, stooping to help her up.

'I'll be fine,' Sunita insisted as she found her feet. She examined her grey jacket and skirt. 'My hem's a bit damp. It'll soon dry.'

'I've just got to brief DC Khalid on something and then we'll be off,' he said.

Roscoe had been disappointed by her failure to grill Margaret Bowers more thoroughly over the garage fire. He expected colleagues to give greater attention to detail. In his mind, she was on probation. If she slipped up again, he'd have to reconsider whether she could remain part of his team.

Half an hour later, these thoughts were set aside as they embarked on the ten-mile journey to visit Harry Bowers' elderly parents. As they reached the traffic-clogged streets of the Birmingham suburbs, they passed rows of terraces, semi-detached houses and shops.

Roscoe glanced around, recalling the days he patrolled these same streets as a young constable. There had been subtle changes in some of the homes since the hardship of the post-war years but they were clearly recognisable as the streets he'd known – *his* streets, he thought.

'How did you get on with the phone records?' he asked Sunita.

'A lot of calls to his business partner, Rashad Mahmood,' she replied.

'That's interesting. There's a suggestion Bowers might've been in financial trouble. I've got Tom Vickers, our acting DI, working on that side of things.'

After around fifteen minutes, the car reached the wider, tree-lined streets to the north of the prosperous market town of Solihull, eight miles south-east of Birmingham city centre.

Joseph and Sheila Bowers lived in a five-bedroom modern detached house in one of the streets off Blossomfield Road. The retired banker and his wife had kept their home in an immaculate condition. The front garden was mainly laid to lawn, but, at the rear, the couple enjoyed well-stocked, south-facing landscaped gardens.

Roscoe's car swept up the drive until they reached a circular flowerbed in the middle of a turning circle, close to the blue front door. Sheila Bowers clearly had heard the car arrive. She was standing in the doorway, watching as they stepped out.

'This is so terrible. So terrible. My poor boy!' she muttered while ushering the two detectives into a spacious living room with a feature stone fireplace and antique furniture. Through double-opening patio doors, Roscoe could see a large, paved patio area, shaped lawn, flower borders, shrubs and evergreens.

Joseph Bowers, who was balding and about the same height as his son, was standing by the fireplace.

Roscoe smiled sympathetically. 'Let me introduce myself. I'm Detective Chief Inspector Gavin Roscoe. My colleague, Sergeant Roy.'

'It's good of the police to show interest at last,' said Joseph.

He eyed them as if he were assessing them for a loan and then shook their hands. His sixty-four-year-old wife, a former bank secretary with greying hair, suggested they should sit down, but they both decided to stand.

'What do you think has happened to your son, Mr Bowers?' Roscoe asked.

'As we said in our police statement, we don't know what to think. Nothing like this has ever happened in the family before.'

'He's your only child?'

'No. We've also got a daughter, Kelly, whom he was very close to when they were growing up. She's married and lives in London.'

'Is it possible he's gone to stay with her or another relative or friend?' asked Sunita.

'We've called everyone,' said Joseph. 'All we can think is that he must have had some kind of breakdown and gone away on his own for peace and quiet. Perhaps he's staying in a hotel somewhere. I don't know.'

'What were relations like with your daughter-in-law, Margaret?' Roscoe asked.

'Not very good,' he admitted.

'They were always at each other's throats,' sobbed his wife, who was now sitting down on their white leather settee.

'They've had a few rows over money,' Joseph continued. 'My son was a wealthy man thanks to property, but he despises extravagance and thought Margaret was overspending. They also rowed about their daughter and his long working hours. I suppose they were drifting apart.'

He paused and glanced down at the light-green carpet.

'In one of our last conversations, he mentioned he'd been to the doctor for some antidepressants. He'd become really down, which wasn't like him at all. He threw himself into his work rather like an ostrich burying his head in the sand. Maybe he thought everything would work out for the best in the end.'

'Police have been shown a note, saying he'd gone away,' Roscoe remarked.

'Yes, so we've been told. Somehow that doesn't seem quite his style.'

Sunita noticed some travel brochures on a glass table a few feet from where they were sitting.

'Have you been planning a trip, sir?' she asked.

'We got them for Harry,' said Sheila. 'Towards the end of last year he suddenly took an interest in visiting South Africa and Australia for business reasons. I was going to show them to him...' She burst into tears.

Her husband moved towards her and put his arm round her shoulders consolingly.

'There, there, love,' he said. 'Try not to upset yourself. Our Harry might walk through the door any time.'

As the two detectives left, Joseph praised them again for showing concern at their son's disappearance.

'Thank you both,' he said. 'You're welcome to call us any time.'

Sunita walked towards the car, but Roscoe was contemplative and walking more slowly, looking downwards at the gravelled forecourt. He glanced back. Joseph had retreated into the house, but Sheila remained in the doorway, watching them. He walked back.

'I sense there's something you've not told us,' he said in a low voice. 'If we're to find your son, you've really got to be completely frank with us, Mrs Bowers.'

'Of course, Mr Roscoe,' she replied.

He glanced towards Sunita, who was gazing at him, before handing Sheila a card.

'This is my private number,' Roscoe said. 'Call me any time. I'm determined to find your son and bring him back to you.'

Chapter 7

A few minutes passed. The pair left the salubrious, leafy suburbs behind and followed the Stratford Road towards the M42 motorway. Then Roscoe's phone rang. He pulled in at the side of the road. As he stopped the car and answered, he heard Sheila Bowers' gentle voice.

'I didn't mean to be reticent,' she said.

'I quite understand,' said the detective.

'It's just that things are difficult right now,' she went on. 'I don't really know how much I should say. I don't want to upset Joseph, but your kindness deserves a response, Mr Roscoe.' Her voice sounded distressed.

'Mrs Bowers, we need to know everything to stand any chance of finding your son alive,' he said. 'Please take your time.'

'Joseph didn't want me to call, but I must tell you the truth, Mr Roscoe. I've had my son crying on the phone to me.'

'I'm very sorry to hear that, Mrs Bowers,' he said.

'His wife's taken a lover.'

Sunita glanced across. She was listening intently.

'Do you have any idea who?' Roscoe asked.

'No. No idea at all. He broke down after he told me. He was in the habit of calling me late at night if he was distressed.'

'When did he tell you this?'

'I'm sorry, Mr Roscoe. My husband's calling. I've got to go.' Then the line went dead.

As they resumed their journey back to police headquarters, Roscoe was engrossed in thought. He felt the case was becoming far more complicated than he'd envisaged. There were so many possibilities – so many loose strings. The man could've had a breakdown, harmed himself, been harmed by another person or fled abroad.

'If asked publicly about a case, we often say we're keeping an open mind and not ruling anything out,' he complained to Sunita. 'That statement really does apply here.'

'I'm starting to realise that, sir,' she replied, as the car drew into the police car park. 'But the longer he's missing, the greater chance he's dead.'

'Come on,' said Roscoe. 'I want to have a closer look at the note Mrs Bowers handed in.'

He led her to the newly opened extension at the rear of the building which now housed the forensics department. They passed through double doors and then negotiated their way through a maze of corridors.

The new extension was the province of thirty-eight-year-old senior forensic scientist Dr Alice Ling. Roscoe had got his sergeant to alert her in advance that they wished to see the note and its envelope. The two items, still inside see-through plastic evidence bags, had been placed on a worktable for them to study.

'The fingerprint people have examined them, but there was just one print from Mrs Bowers,' Dr Ling explained.

Roscoe studied the note carefully. It had been written with a blue ballpoint pen on what appeared to be plain white writing paper. Roscoe read it to himself: 'I just can't take any more. I have gone away. Don't bother trying to find me.'

'As you can see, the envelope was simply addressed to "Margaret",' Dr Ling said.

Roscoe concluded that the writer was a person of intelligence. The note was neatly written with correct spellings and punctuation. Some of the letters sloped to the left and others to the right – sometimes indicating muddled thinking – and four of the letters – the *j*, *y* and two *g*s – had larger than usual loops that swept back up and nearly touched the preceding letter in each case.

The letter *g* on the envelope had been written in the same style as on the note. They'd have to call on the services of a handwriting expert, he decided. Sunita pored over the documents.

'I think we should get copies of Bowers' writing from both his home and his office to make sure it's written in his hand,' she said.

The DCI nodded.

* * *

After lunch in the police canteen, the pair made the fifteen-mile journey from St James Street to Norton Prior in less than thirty minutes. Roscoe knew where Heathwood House was, but he'd never seen the property itself as the main house was some distance from the road and hidden behind tall leylandii trees.

Sunita used the intercom to introduce herself. The electric security gates opened, and they travelled up the drive.

After parking beneath the Georgian-style windows, Roscoe climbed the steps and pressed the doorbell. He glanced around, impressed by the way the Bowers had transformed the house into a magnificent family home. But, like Sunita and Dawson, he was shocked to see the charred remains of the former garage block.

A minute passed before Margaret Bowers came to the door, accompanied by a young, ginger-haired teenager.

'Yes? Have you brought any news?' she asked.

'Mrs Bowers, we're very sorry to bother you,' he said solemnly. 'I'm DCI Gavin Roscoe and you'll remember

Sergeant Roy from her visit last week. Could we come in?' He presented his Heart of England Police identity pass.

The attractive, long-haired brunette seemed more ebullient than Roscoe had expected. Here, he thought, was a confident woman who showed little sign of being traumatised.

Margaret bade her daughter, Rachel, go upstairs while she led the pair into the spacious living room. A single log was burning on the open hearth in the inglenook fireplace. The pleasant aroma of burning wood wafted round the house.

'You're lucky to find me in actually,' Margaret remarked, strolling over to the table by the window. She turned one of the dining chairs round and sat down, facing them. 'I was just about to take my daughter riding. It's a diversion for her.'

'Mrs Bowers,' said Roscoe, 'I'm afraid we don't have any news. Teams have spent hours searching woods, fields and waterways in the area, but all to no avail.'

'That's a shame.'

'We need to ask a few more questions,' he continued as he made himself comfortable on a brown leather settee. Sunita remained standing. 'How long altogether have you known your husband?'

'For eighteen years,' she said, casting her eyes down at the red patterned carpet. 'It all began on my first day at Birmingham University.'

Margaret, a thirty-eight-year-old farmer's daughter, described how they'd met at a student union dance. The twenty-year-old banker's son with dark hair and hazel eyes had been studying accountancy and she was studying fashion.

They married shortly after graduating and she gave birth to their daughter Rachel a year later.

'But as I explained to your sergeant, Harry became more and more absorbed in his burgeoning Midlands property business and, since buying Heathwood House, I'm afraid we drifted apart,' she said.

Just then, there came the sound of her daughter's footsteps rushing down the stairs. Margaret looked towards the door into the hall.

'I won't be long, Rachel. Get ready to go out,' she called.

'Madam,' said Roscoe, bringing her attention back. 'May I ask what you argued about?'

'Money, his long hours, his trips away and Rachel's education,' Margaret replied.

It sounded to Sunita as though she was reading from a well-rehearsed script. In her mind, she appeared to be consoling herself with the thought 'Now Harry's gone, there'll be no more arguments. He's left me before. Now he's gone for good.'

'I'm sorry I have to ask this. Did these arguments ever lead to violence?' Roscoe asked.

'No, he always stopped short of hitting me. Divorce was mentioned several times.' She glanced through the French doors that led to the rear garden. Rachel was swaying to and fro on a garden swing.

'By you or by Mr Bowers?' asked Sunita, who sat down next to the DCI.

'By us both.'

Roscoe followed her eyes out towards the rear garden. The sun was struggling to emerge from behind the clouds.

'When did you last see your husband, Mrs Bowers?' he asked.

'Early on the Tuesday evening,' she said.

'January the 8th?'

'That's right. He always went to choir practice on a Tuesday.'

'Presumably, he'd been to work that day?'

She nodded. 'He'd been to Birmingham and got back here just after six.'

'What sort of mood was he in?'

'His normal selfish mood.'

'So you argued?'

'Yes. Over money,' she said. 'He found out I'd spent more than a thousand pounds on clothes in the New Year sales. He'd just received his credit card statement. He was very tight with money. It wasn't as though we can't afford it.'

Roscoe frowned. 'So he stormed out?'

'Yes.'

Roscoe stared thoughtfully at the floor. 'Mrs Bowers, I want to get the timings right. How long would you say it takes your husband to walk from here to the church hall – ten minutes?'

'Yes, I'd say so. Maybe a little more.'

'He never drove?'

'No. It's only down the road.'

'A shopkeeper near the hall saw him at three minutes past seven. So what time did he leave here?'

'I've no idea. He just stormed out and the next day I found a message on the table.'

Sunita looked Margaret in the eyes. 'Did he put the note on the table himself?' she asked.

'Well, I don't know. How would I know? I imagine so. He just walked out and the note was on the table the next morning. It was a complete surprise. I don't know if Harry'd placed it there earlier and I'd simply not noticed it or if it was pushed through the letterbox and someone put it on the table.'

The DCI wondered to himself why Harry Bowers would have written a message to his wife and then posted it through his own front door. Why did he not simply leave it for his wife somewhere inside the house? Why leave a message at all when he could explain himself to her face?

'Who could've placed it on the table?' he asked. 'Could your daughter have found it on the doormat and put it there?'

Margaret nodded. 'I suppose that's possible – or the cleaner.'

'It seems strange to me if he returned to the house just to post a note through the letterbox, Mrs Bowers.'

'I think he must've decided on 8 January that he didn't want to see me again. As a last-minute thing, he must've returned just to post the note through or got someone to deliver it for him.'

Roscoe leaned forward. 'Mrs Bowers, could we have a quick word with your daughter about this? I take it she knows about her father's message?'

Margaret nodded again. 'Yes, of course. I'll call Rachel.'

She opened the French doors and called the child who, seconds later, came bouncing into the room as excited as though it were an Easter morning. Then, seeing the two detectives, she appeared embarrassed.

'Rachel,' her mother explained. 'This lady and gentleman are from the police. They just want to ask you about something.'

'Is it about Daddy?' asked Rachel, her eyes becoming as wide as saucers. Her mother nodded and placed her arm on the child's shoulder.

Roscoe smiled down at the little girl. 'Rachel, you know your daddy wrote a note for Mummy? Did you pick it up from the doormat and put it on the table?'

'No,' she said. 'I never saw it till Mummy showed it to me.'

Roscoe shrugged. 'OK, that's fine.'

'Are you going to find Daddy and bring him home?'

'We're going to do our best to find him,' Sunita said. 'Your mummy will be the first to know when we find him.'

The answer seemed to reassure her.

'OK.'

'Run along and play. I won't be long,' said her mother.

Rachel returned to the garden, jumping back onto the swing.

Turning to Margaret, Roscoe asked, 'What's the cleaner's name?'

'Tessa Griffiths,' she said.

Roscoe immediately recognised the name. She was a girl who had worked at the tearooms on a few occasions as a waitress.

'We'll have to speak to her,' he said. 'Just to clear up this riddle about how the note arrived on the table.'

'I can give you her address, but she doesn't work for us anymore. She wasn't a good time-keeper and I had to sack her.'

Roscoe quietly sympathised. She'd let Helen down twice and they no longer employed her either. Sunita was eager to steer the conversation round to her husband's business affairs.

'Mrs Bowers,' she said. 'Did your husband have any business rivals or any enemies connected with his work?'

'I've been asking myself that question. I don't really know,' she said. 'But it's possible he had enemies here in our village.'

Roscoe leaned forward in his seat.

'We noticed the burnt-out building,' he said.

'Yes. Don't know how the fire happened.'

'You told me it was an accident,' said Sunita, rather indignantly.

'Well, I wasn't sure what to say to you. I'm sorry. It may have been an accident or someone might've started it deliberately.'

'Could you tell us about it?' asked Roscoe.

'It was one of the most frightening moments in my life. I'll tell you what I remember.' As she began her account, her mind drifted back to that horrific afternoon in late October.

Chapter 8

The two visitors felt genuine sympathy for Margaret Bowers after hearing her harrowing account of the fire. They were concerned to hear her gardener and two firefighters risked their lives by searching the blazing annexe for her daughter. In the end, the teenager was found safe in her bedroom.

They were also intrigued to hear the senior fire officer had found traces of an accelerant, indicating arson.

'It must've been so upsetting, not knowing where your little girl was,' said Sunita, giving Margaret a reassuring look. 'You must've been so relieved when you found her.'

'Yes, I was,' Margaret replied.

But Roscoe felt there were further questions that needed answering.

'Why didn't you tell us this before, Mrs Bowers?' he asked.

'I didn't think it was relevant. It can't have anything to do with my missing husband.'

'We'll be the judge of that. Look, there must've been an investigation by police and fire brigade, Mrs Bowers,' he said. 'We can check the records ourselves, but do you happen to know what the outcome was?'

'There was a brief investigation by Queensbridge police, but nothing came of it,' she said.

'Do you have any idea who might've been behind the arson attack?' Roscoe asked, as he made a mental note to run a check on police files.

'None at all. We get on with everyone in the village.'

She looked as if something was on her mind. Roscoe noticed the change in her facial expression.

'You didn't have a problem with any of your neighbours?'

'No.'

'I see.' He stood up and took a few paces towards Margaret. 'Right, Mrs Bowers,' he said. 'We've taken up a lot of your time already but, before we go, we ought to see your husband's passport and bank statements. Oh, and does he have an office or study here?'

Margaret shook her head. 'I can't find his passport. The officer who spoke to me before – was it PC Underhill?'

'Yes, PC Derek Underhill,' Roscoe confirmed.

'He asked me last week to search for it, but I couldn't find it,' she said. 'But you're welcome to see his bank statements. They're in his study upstairs. Would you follow me?'

Margaret led them up the wide oak stairs to the first floor. Harry Bowers' study was a large room near the top of the stairs. There was a long desk with a computer on one side of the room with filing cabinets and cupboards containing documents on the other. In the middle stood the businessman's high-back leather office chair.

A Midlands map, a world map and shelves full of books covered the wall above the desk. There were also colour photographs of Midlands housing developments. A window at the far end overlooked the rear garden and the dark-green hills beyond.

'Do you mind if we check the drawers?' asked Roscoe.

'No, of course. Go ahead,' she said, watching the detectives' every move.

Most of the documents the pair uncovered in the study related to planning applications. There were also solicitors' and Land Registry letters. There were maps of South Africa and Australia, together with some British Airways travel guides.

Sunita seated herself at the desk, where she found bank statements which showed various accounts in credit. She informed her DCI, who was hovering over her left shoulder, that the most recent statement ended on 7 January.

Roscoe glanced at Margaret, who was watching them from the doorway. She didn't have a hint of sadness in her face. She appeared worried lest the pair left any item out of place in the study, but there was no note of concern in her voice and no sign of emotion. Perhaps she'd had time to overcome the shock of her husband's disappearance. Or perhaps, in a way, it was a relief that he was no longer there – a relief from the constant arguments she'd described.

Sunita, who had been poring over documents, switched on her phone after deciding she would take some photographs of some of the papers. She was shocked to find she had sixty-five messages from her ex-boyfriend, Arun Halder, as well as twenty-four missed calls.

Roscoe noticed the shocked expression on her face as she stared at the screen of her phone.

'You all right, Sergeant?' he asked.

Gathering her composure, she quickly replied, 'Yes, I'm fine,' before proceeding to photograph some of the documents.

As he stood over his seated sergeant, Roscoe asked, 'Mrs Bowers, have you been on holiday recently?'

Pointing to her pale, untanned face, she said, 'Do I look like a lady who's just returned from sunning herself in some exotic country? No, I've not had a holiday for two years.'

'I thought not,' said Roscoe. 'So did your husband go off on his own at all? I mean, do you think he could be abroad? Do you have an overseas home?'

'No,' she said, becoming slightly irritated by the line of questioning. 'We don't have a home abroad.'

'So you don't think it's possible he's left the country?'

'Well, anything's possible. I really have no idea. I don't want to speak ill of him as he's my husband, but I don't have a clue. He could be anywhere.'

'It's just there are travel brochures in one of the drawers here.'

'I think you'll find they've been there for some time. I don't think he's gone off to overseas like the train robber Ronnie Biggs, if that's what you're implying.'

Five minutes later, Sunita seemed to have fully recovered from her ordeal at finding the missed messages and an idea was forming in her mind. It was as if a switch had been flicked inside her head, flooding her brain cells with light and energy.

'Mrs Bowers,' she said. 'Do you by any chance have a piece of paper?'

'Why yes, of course,' she said. 'You want to take a note of something?'

The sergeant nodded. 'I wonder. Here's my pen. Could you draw me a map of the village, showing the precise location of your house and the route your husband would've taken on the night he disappeared?'

'Yes, OK,' she said, standing by Sunita's right shoulder. 'I'll have a go, but I studied fashion – not town planning.'

Margaret took Sunita's place in her husband's leather chair and proceeded to sketch the streets near the family home. Her map showed Heathwood House, the main street, the village green, the church and the church hall. Looking over her shoulder, Roscoe noticed that she used the words 'church,' 'river,' and 'church hall'.

He said, 'I wonder. Could you add "St John the Martyr" before the word "church" and mark the main road? While I think of it, could you also write in the words "railway line".'

Margaret turned to Sunita mischievously and said, 'He doesn't ask for much, does he? You'd have thought the police could provide their own maps!'

After a few minutes, she handed the sketch to the sergeant, who folded the paper without looking at it and put it in her pocket.

'Thank you,' she said.

The pair took details of the maid's address and then said goodbye to Margaret at about five thirty.

As they drove back towards St James Street, Roscoe stopped the car by the side of the road to take a phone call. While he spoke to Tom Vickers, Sunita used the opportunity to remove the piece of paper from her pocket and study it.

'That was some good news from Tom Vickers,' said Roscoe as he started the engine and took to the main road again. 'You haven't met my DI, have you? Excellent detective, although he wouldn't win a best-dressed man competition. He was just bringing me up to date with an arrest.'

Sunita nodded. 'Anyway, sir, what do you make of Mrs Bowers and her missing husband?'

'There's something very strange about her,' said Roscoe as their journey took them through open countryside. 'She seems to have taken her husband's disappearance far too well.'

'There's something strange about the note also,' said Sunita. 'I've been studying her handwriting. I wouldn't be surprised if she wrote that note herself.'

Chapter 9

Rupa Chakrabarti stumbled bleary-eyed from her bedroom. Her straggly dark hair was hanging loosely round her neck.

'Sunita, what time is it?' she asked as she stood on the landing in her lacy, white nightgown.

'Half past nine,' said Sunita, emerging from the kitchen. 'I thought you'd left for work already. Sorry, I would've called you.'

'No, it's all right. I've got the day off. I could say the same to you. Shouldn't you be at work?'

'I've got a job for my boss nearby. I'm just about to leave. I've got to call on the missing man's business partner. He's only a couple of miles from here, so it wasn't worth me going into the office.'

'You be careful, won't you?' said Rupa, taking a few steps towards Sunita. She had been concerned about her flatmate since Arun Halder paid them a visit four days earlier. 'That guy might be around.'

'He's been sending me more texts and trying to call me all through the night,' Sunita admitted as she walked back into the kitchen where she'd been doing her laundry. She brandished a black T-shirt she'd bought in India which bore the slogan 'Amar Kolkata'.

'Do you like it? I bought it from a market while on holiday,' said Sunita.

'That's wicked,' said Rupa. 'Sunita, hasn't your detective boss got any advice for you about stalkers?'

'I haven't told him yet.'

Rupa glared. 'What? Why not?'

Sunita shrugged. 'I'm in enough trouble with him already. He's accused me of not being thorough when I first visited the missing man's wife. I can hardly tell him an ex-boyfriend is causing trouble for me. He'll probably take me off the team.'

'You'd have thought someone in his position would be more understanding.'

'I know, but he's very demanding. He expects all his team to give a hundred per cent. He told me at the interview he won't put up with "slackers". He certainly doesn't want anyone being distracted by some emotional baggage to do with an ex-boyfriend.'

'He sounds a nightmare.'

'It's just the nature of the job, I suppose.'

'But, Sunita, everyone says you're very conscientious. You've only been in the force five minutes and yet you're already a detective sergeant.'

'I know. I've just got to prove myself with him. That's all. I'm sure he'll come round in time. It's just that, for the moment, we're not seeing eye to eye.'

'Look,' said Rupa as Sunita walked into the hall to fetch her grey coat. 'You must promise to tell your boss about Arun as soon as the time's right. The guy's obviously not giving up on you. The chances are he'll be back, so please be careful.'

'Don't worry. I will!' Sunita assured her as she opened the front door and headed out into the street.

Harry Bowers' property business had an office in a parade of shops in the Birmingham suburb of Acocks Green, just over two miles from Sunita's flat.

As she set off on foot along the busy, urban streets, she kept her eyes open for a small silver car – in case her ex-boyfriend was out hunting for her. But her walk was uneventful.

* * *

Bowers' premises were located on a wide pavement beneath a blue sign proclaiming 'Heathwood Property Group'. An equipment hire shop traded on one side while a day nursery operated on the other.

Two men and two women were sitting at desks when she walked inside the shop, which resembled an estate agent's office. They were all engrossed in conversations with one another and didn't appear to be doing much work. Finally, one of the women broke off from her conversation to ask, 'Can I help?'

'I'd like to speak to someone in authority, please?' she said.

The woman disappeared into a back room and returned moments later followed by an immaculately dressed man.

'I'm Rashad Mahmood. How can I help?' the man asked.

Sunita took her warrant card out of her small black handbag. She said, 'Heart of England Police. I'm making inquiries about Harry Bowers.'

Mr Mahmood was taken aback. He wanted to know which department of the police Sunita represented.

'CID,' she replied tersely.

He seemed relieved once he had established she was from a major crime unit handling murders and serious offences – not financial matters.

Now in a more relaxed mood, the blue-suited businessman led her into a small but well-lit back office containing two desks, four high-back chairs, a filing cabinet and three chests of drawers. Daylight streamed in through a large sash window at the rear.

'My dear sergeant. We were all shocked to hear about Harry,' said Mr Mahmood, indicating a chair for his visitor. 'So how can I help?'

As the director tidied a few items on his desk and sat behind it, Sunita took the opportunity to assess her host. Rashad Mahmood was a bearded, grey-haired man in his early fifties. He was about five feet eight inches tall and rather corpulent. He spoke in a concise, articulate voice with a slight accent betraying his Pakistani parentage and Birmingham upbringing.

'So when was the last time you saw Mr Bowers?' the sergeant asked.

'Well, let me see. He was here on January the 8th. Yes, that's the last time. He left early that day – at about half past four. The last thing he said going out the door was, "See you tomorrow. Let me know if there's any news about Coventry."'

Sunita frowned. 'Coventry?'

'Yes. We're waiting for news on a development in north Coventry. He wanted me to call him if I received any fresh information. I just nodded and waved.'

'I see. How often did he come into this office?'

'Sometimes he works at home and sometimes he comes here. It varies. On the day we're talking about he came into the office at nine o'clock and was here all day.'

'Was it a normal day at the office? There were no incidents?'

'My dear sergeant, it was a perfectly normal day.'

'Why did he leave early?'

'He had choir practice. They were rehearsing something for Easter.'

'How did he seem in himself?' Sunita asked.

'I'll be honest with you, Sergeant,' the director said. 'He's not been his normal self. I think he had a bad Christmas – personal problems.'

'How do you mean – with his wife?'

'Yes. I've known him for ten years and he confided in me a little. But he was the kind of man who'd generally try and keep his troubles to himself. He certainly didn't want anything to affect the business. So this is a major inquiry now?'

'Yes,' said Sunita. 'We're becoming more concerned as time goes on. We've carried out large-scale searches around West Warwickshire and now the operation's being extended. Can you think of any reason why he might've gone away?'

'No, as I say, all I know is he wasn't a happy soul of late,' Mr Mahmood said.

'Is that his desk?' the detective asked, pointing behind Mr Mahmood. 'Can I just take a look?'

'Hang on a minute,' said Mr Mahmood. He leaped up and quickly examined papers stacked in the centre of his partner's desk.

'Yes, I've got no problem with that,' he said, thumbing through documents. 'But I don't think you'll find any clues to his disappearance.'

She noticed he'd removed several pages from a folder with his right hand. He had then put these papers in a drawer.

'Our latest project's involved getting planning permission for a large tract of land on the outskirts of Coventry to build new homes,' he mumbled. 'I can't think that that can have anything to do with him going off the radar.'

The sergeant flicked through the documents on the desk and rummaged through the drawers. She couldn't find anything that could assist the investigation, but she was annoyed Mahmood had snatched a few items away. She hardly wanted to face a second accusation from her boss that she was not being thorough enough.

'What are those pages you put away just then?' Sunita demanded.

'My dear sergeant, they were just documents to do with our planning application. It's just that they haven't become public yet.'

'Mr Mahmood, do you want me to call my boss and get the whole team here, have you arrested and have your premises searched from top to bottom?' she demanded. 'I'm being fairly easy with you at the moment. But things could get really tough – believe me.'

Mahmood grudgingly changed his attitude and handed her the documents he'd been so eager to hide. One was an email from HMRC demanding more than a million pounds in unpaid tax. The other, a few weeks later, outlined action they were planning to take against the company. She looked him in the eyes.

'You haven't got the means to pay this bill, have you?'

He looked down to the floor like a wayward schoolboy who'd been caught out by the headmistress.

'No,' he admitted. 'We haven't decided what we're going to do. It was one of the matters I was planning on discussing with Harry. Like everyone, we have our ups and downs with the taxman. I'm sure we'll find a way of paying it, although, without him, it's hard to sign off paperwork.'

'Can you give me copies of both those emails before I leave?'

He nodded.

'How long have you been a director here?' she asked.

'Harry set up the business ten or so years ago, as you probably know, and I joined him a few years later. I became a director two years ago, concentrating on the marketing side.'

'How long have you been in these premises?' the detective asked.

'Two years. We've got seven very loyal members of staff.'

'I only noticed four out there?'

'Three have got the day off.'

Sunita nodded. 'I think that'll be all for the moment. But perhaps you'd let me know if anything else occurs to you?'

'Of course, my dear sergeant,' Mr Mahmood said. 'And if there's anything else I can do, please don't hesitate to ask.'

'Well, there is just one thing,' the detective said. 'Could you let me have a sample of your handwriting?'

'Handwriting?' Mr Mahmood repeated back to her. 'Whatever for?'

'We just want to eliminate something from our inquiry.'

'Well, I've got my shopping list here. Will that help?'

'Perhaps you could write… I don't know. Here goes. How about "My property group's trying for planning consent."'

'Always pleased to help the police,' Mr Mahmood said, before writing the exact words requested on a piece of notepaper.

After handing over the paper, he went to the photocopying machine in the main office and produced print-outs of the HMRC emails. Then he accompanied the detective back through the main office and to the entrance door.

'I'm so sorry about our little disagreement a few minutes ago, my dear sergeant,' he said. 'I was probably being oversensitive.'

'Goodbye, Mr Mahmood,' Sunita said. 'You'll be hearing from us.'

She walked slowly back to her flat, believing the DCI would be more than happy with her discoveries. She had confirmation in her hand that the missing man's business was in financial trouble. She smiled to herself as she reached Cateswell Road and began taking the final steps towards her home.

But as she approached within a hundred metres of her front door, she heard shouting and realised to her horror Arun Halder had returned. He was yelling and screaming at Rupa, who was waving her hands at him in exasperation in the doorway.

Sunita was on the point of running towards them when she thought better of it. If she made an appearance, it could only exacerbate the situation, she thought.

Instead, she cast her eyes around until she spotted a silver car. It was a five-year-old silver Ford Fiesta, which, she was almost certain, must be Arun's car. She took out her black notebook and jotted down the registration number.

Then she noticed a public footpath between two houses and hid there in the shadows, peering out into the street.

A few minutes passed. Arun walked over to the Fiesta, jumped in and drove off.

Sunita made sure the vehicle was out of sight before she went home.

'Rupa, what happened?' she asked as she stepped into the hall.

'That man's been back,' Rupa replied as she emerged from the living room. 'Sunita, he's been making threats against you. He's nuts.'

'Calm down, Rupa. It's all right. I can take care of myself. I've been on a martial arts course.'

'Oh, I know that. You told me what happened on the plane back from Dubai when you overpowered a man with a knife. But Arun is seriously crazy. He claims to own you and says something terrible will happen if you don't become his girlfriend again. You've got to do something. You've got to tell your boss what's happening.'

Chapter 10

Gavin Roscoe gazed out of his bedroom window towards the trees at the foot of the garden. Clusters of naked twigs and branches, flecked with frost, swayed in the breeze, while the lawn glistened like a silver carpet beneath the grey morning sky.

It was barely eight o'clock on Thursday morning, 24 January, and something – possibly a chorus of birdsong – had roused him from his sleep.

He stomped his way downstairs and greeted Helen with a kiss on the cheek, while gently caressing her shoulder.

'Good morning, my dear,' he said. 'You're up early.'

'Yes, I'm sorry if I woke you, but we've got a cake delivery at the tearooms in an hour's time, so I'm in a rush. I'm so annoyed with the new delivery firm. They've changed the time again.'

'You might consider going back to the previous firm.'

'There were problems with them as well.'

'I'm beginning to wish Tom Vickers was still my sergeant,' said Roscoe, as he sat down on a kitchen chair.

'Why? What's the problem with your new girl Sunita?'

'Oh, I don't know. I want to give her a chance to settle in, but I'm not sure how it's going to work. She doesn't seem to show much initiative.'

'Give the girl a chance. It's early days. How long's she been with you – two weeks?'

'Yes.'

'Listen, George heard something last night that might interest you.'

'What's that, dear?' he asked as he spread the morning newspaper across the table and began to read a frontpage story predicting Britain faced five weeks of unusually low temperatures.

'He was doing a shift at the pub and one of the customers playing skittles was a bit drunk.'

'You mean, the Coach and Horses at Norton Prior?'

'That's right. His friend, Ryan, the landlord's son, was also working. The guy causing a fuss was ranting about Harry Bowers.'

Roscoe put down his newspaper. 'Is George about?'

'I think so.'

Roscoe found his son listening to music in the living room.

'No college today?' he asked.

George removed his headphones. 'I've got a class this afternoon,' he replied.

'How did you get on with the careers advisor?'

'I've got to make my mind up whether I want to go into farming or the hotel trade,' said George as his father sat beside him on the beige settee.

'I don't want to interfere. You've got to reach your own pathway in life. But remember I'll always be here to guide you, as a father should.'

'Thanks, Dad. I appreciate it.'

'What's this about a neighbour of the Bowers' causing a scene?'

'Yes, you know David Harrington?'

Roscoe nodded. 'The farmer?'

'Yes. He'd had a skinful last night and was giving his opinion on the Bowers.'

'That's interesting. Go on.'

'Well, apparently, there's been a long-running dispute between Harrington and the Bowers over their boundary. Bowers somehow managed to get planning approval for a new garage building on land that Harrington claims is his.'

Roscoe's mind at once flashed back to the conversation with Margaret Bowers in which she told of the devastating fire.

'The new building burned down three months ago,' Roscoe said.

George nodded. 'Yes. The Bowers are thought to have pulled a few strings to get planning approval and Harrington was furious about it. The cops never found any evidence to charge Harrington with arson – he was on holiday in Spain at the time of the fire – but there was a lot of gossip in Norton. Last night, he was drunk and accusing the Bowers of stealing the land from him.'

Roscoe was deep in thought. He recalled a similar dispute years before when he'd been a young policeman in Birmingham. A row between neighbours over the position of a fence had led to an assault and the case went to court. How do these ostensibly minor matters have such major consequences? he wondered.

George went on, 'The disputed strip of land is on the edge of a field belonging to Upper Norton Farm, which has been owned by the Harrington family for generations. Harrington went down there at some stage with two men and put up wooden posts on the boundary. They've also blocked a path that the Bowers sometimes used when cutting leylandii trees on the edge of their grounds.'

'So, what was Harrington saying, exactly?' Roscoe asked.

'He was effing and blinding and saying the Bowers were thieves.'

'That's a bit tasteless, considering Harry Bowers has been missing for two weeks.'

George nodded. 'Oh, he didn't hold back. He was saying, "Maybe the bastard's dead." Some of the regulars were annoyed with him and I thought there was going to be a fight, but luckily, after he'd been ranting and raving for a while, he left of his own accord.'

Just then, Helen put her head round the door and told them she was leaving for the tearooms. The pair waved and wished her a good day before Roscoe continued talking to George about the incident at the Coach and Horses.

* * *

Later, on arriving in his CID office, Roscoe made a phone call to Warwickshire County Council's planning department and was assured that the Bowers' garage application had been successfully approved. A planning official told him the building plans had gone out to public consultation and confirmed David Harrington as the only objector.

He then phoned an official at the Land Registry. She assured him that the plot of land where the new garage block was built was within the grounds of Heathwood House. She added that Mr Harrington had been causing a nuisance, making numerous calls to the council and sending a string of angry letters about his grievance. However, the council's view was that the building had been properly erected on the Bowers' land.

He called Sunita into his office.

'We're going to pay this farmer, David Harrington, a visit later today,' he told her. 'It seems he's got a long-standing grudge against the Bowers. He's got questions to answer.'

* * *

The short, brown-haired girl tapped timidly on the glazed door.

'I'm afraid the shop's closed,' called a croaky voice from within the premises.

'I've come about the job,' said the girl, who had no coat and was shivering.

Humming quietly to himself, Edward Bailey walked unsteadily towards his shop door and fumbled in his pocket for the key. After a few seconds, he found it, turned it in the lock and the door creaked open.

'Are you Julie?' he asked.

'Yes,' said the shy girl in the red, patterned pullover and dark trousers.

'You were meant to be here at a quarter past five for the interview.'

'I'm sorry. The bus from Queensbridge was late,' she replied.

'Never mind. You'd better come in. Excuse my husky voice. I've got a cold.'

He led Julie past the counter displaying newspapers and packets of sweets, past shelves laden with groceries and two upright refrigerators filled with drinks. She found herself in a dimly lit, cluttered back room. More shelves were crammed with tins and packets of food, and bundles of newspapers were stacked to the ceiling.

In the centre of the room were two old, well-worn, dark-green armchairs. The newsagent, who had short, dark receding hair, sat in one and invited Julie to take the other.

'So, you're interested in the position of part-time retail assistant?'

'Yes, Mr Bailey. I'm afraid I haven't much in the way of experience. I've only just left school, but I'm a quick learner.'

'How old are you?'

'Seventeen. I'll be eighteen in October.'

'What are you like at maths?'

'Well, I got a GCSE in it – grade 5, which the teachers call a strong pass. By the way, you probably know my grandfather, Jim Carter.'

'Late seventies? Retired farm worker? Yes, I know him. Bit of a character.'

She laughed. 'Yes, Grandad Jim's definitely a bit of a character.'

'The job's mainly selling papers and groceries. We pay the minimum wage. It's twenty hours a week with a month's notice either way. Hours are seven to eleven. Look, I'll take a chance on you. I know what it's like at your age. All the shops say they can't give you a job without experience, but you can't get experience unless someone gives you a job. Can you start Monday?'

'Yes, Mr Bailey. Thanks very much. That's absolutely terrific. Can I ask something? Is it just you running the shop?'

'It's me and Mrs Bailey. We've also got a newsstand at Stratford station. She's over there most of the time.'

'I think I've met her. Is she a blonde lady? Khaki coat with a fur collar?'

'Yes. You've seen her then?'

She nodded. 'I was with my grandad in Stratford yesterday when he stopped to buy a paper there.'

'You see a lot of your grandad then?'

'About once a month. I called on him yesterday and took him shopping while Mum and Dad were helping in the search.'

'The search? Oh, the search for Harry Bowers.'

'Yes, they were traipsing through woods and streams around Upper Norton Farm. They found two supermarket trolleys and an old television in the river, but nothing much else. Dad's furious. He reckons the police should search Biddington Woods, but they say they haven't got the manpower at the moment.'

'Yes, they're overstretched.'

'Dad said they ought to check the CCTV cameras.'

'There's only one round here – just by the shop – but there was a voltage drop and it picked up nothing on the night of the choir practice.'

'Oh.'

'What do your folks do?'

'Dad's a maintenance man in Queensbridge. Mum's a carer. I like your wife's coat.'

'Her coat?'

'Yes, your wife's khaki coat.'

'I got her that for her birthday. She loves it. But she's not been her usual self. I think we both need a holiday.'

'This cold weather gets us all down, Mr Bailey.'

'You're right. You seem like a very sensible young lady.'

'So I've definitely got the job then?

'Yes. I'll see you Monday. I'm here from just after six, but I'd like you at seven.'

'That's cool. Thanks so much. It's been so hard trying to find a job. My dad's been on at me for ages.' Julie got up and walked back through the shop.

'I'm so thankful, Mr Bailey. I won't let you down,' she said while waiting for him to unlock the door. She ran down the lane to the main road, waving to him as she went.

Bailey was pleased with his new recruit. He believed Julie Carter would meet expectations. It had taken him several weeks to find a suitable morning helper. Now he could focus on trying to save his marriage. He knew he'd not always been a perfect husband. He and the woman he called 'Princess' had had a difficult few weeks. He loved her deeply and would be devastated if she ever left him.

Chapter 11

Three times on Thursday, 24 January, Gavin Roscoe attempted to leave the CID office and set off for David Harrington's farm. But each time his phone rang as he went to collect his coat and he was called back to his desk.

But eventually, just before half past two, he and Sunita set off together in his car for the twenty-mile journey.

'Sorry about this morning, Sunita,' said the DCI. 'There was a shooting at a post office in Crows Wood. Two men with a gun got away with twenty thousand pounds.'

'I hope no one was hurt.'

'The sub-postmaster's mother, who used to run the post office, tried to play the hero and got shot in the shoulder. She's having an operation at Queensbridge General.'

'Let's hope she's all right.'

'She's seventy-seven, so it's touch and go. I've got Tom and Omar Khalid onto it.'

The pair continued their journey for a moment in silence. Then they passed Norton Prior's village green.

'By the way,' said Roscoe, 'you did well getting that tax letter from Mahmood.'

Sunita smiled. 'He was reluctant to let me see it.'

'I bet he was. So we've got a few leads to follow now. Bowers' neighbour had a grudge and, on top of that, Bowers and his partner were billed for more than a million pounds before he went AWOL.'

'People have taken their lives for less money than that,' Sunita murmured.

Roscoe nodded.

Although Harrington was the Bowers' neighbour, the entrance to the farmhouse at Upper Norton Farm was nearly a mile from Heathwood House. It was reached along a winding country lane.

Roscoe wanted to avoid getting mud on his car wheels, so he parked thirty metres away from the main farmhouse on a piece of tarmacked land. The pair noticed an old green Land Rover parked outside one of several outbuildings as they stepped out into the chill air of the afternoon. They then followed the stony, mud-strewn roadway that led to the farm's front door.

Sunita's phone beeped. She viewed the screen and then turned it off.

'Got a message?' Roscoe asked.

'It's nothing, sir. It'll keep,' she replied.

A dog began barking the moment Roscoe pressed the doorbell and, at first, it appeared the farmer might be out. But after more than a minute, the door opened and a lively black Labrador came bounding towards them.

'Oscar, come here!' a grumpy voice called out from inside the house. 'Oscar!'

The friendly dog raced up to the two detectives, sniffing and wagging his tail. But, on hearing his master's voice, he turned round and bolted back inside.

Moments later, sixty-eight-year-old Harrington himself emerged in the doorway as the detectives detected the scent of burning wood coming from inside.

He was about six feet tall, heavily overweight and scruffily dressed in a green, moth-eaten pullover and mud-splattered black trousers. His most striking feature was his mop of white hair. Gone was the aggressive attitude he'd apparently displayed in the village pub. Instead, he appeared to be in a cheerful mood.

'What can I do for you?' he asked, staring intently at Roscoe before adding, 'Haven't I seen you somewhere – the tearooms in Queensbridge?'

Roscoe nodded as he displayed his warrant card. 'It's a family business. You might've seen me there in the summer. Mr Harrington, Heart of England Police. I'm DCI Roscoe and this is Sergeant Roy. May we come in?'

'Yes, of course,' Harrington said, ushering the two detectives through the porch of the stone farmhouse, which was part-seventeenth century in construction, and into a large living room.

The visitors noticed a wealth of original features, including some ancient oak beams and a log-burning open fire.

'If it's about the Land Rover, the cheque for the road tax is in the post,' he said as he stood in the centre of the room.

His Labrador ran over to Roscoe and jumped up, looking for affection. Sunita stepped backwards nervously.

'Get down, Oscar,' the farmer demanded. 'Calm down! Sorry, folks, he's a bit mad like me.'

'You farmed here for long?' asked the DCI, glancing at the wood blazing in the grate.

'My family's been here for generations.'

'How well do you know the Bowers?'

'Oh them. Not very well. They're relative newcomers. They've only been here six or seven years.'

'How would you describe your relationship with the family?'

'Don't see much of them.'

Roscoe frowned. 'Apparently you've got some very strong feelings about them.'

'Says who?'

'You've been heard making threats against them.'

He broke into a smile. 'Oh, I'm afraid I had a little too much to drink in the Coach and Horses. I said one or two things that, in the light of day, I probably shouldn't have said.'

Roscoe walked over to the fire and warmed his hands as the dog sat down at Harrington's feet. Sunita joined her boss at the fireside, all the while wary of the dog's presence.

'So what actually is your problem with the Bowers?' asked the DCI.

'Well, that family have stolen some of my land.'

'Not according to the council,' Roscoe said.

Almost at once, their host's tone and demeanour changed. He glowered. He appeared to be struggling to curb his temper.

'They've got their bloody facts wrong,' he claimed. 'That bottom field has always belonged to the Harringtons, right up to the trees.' He scowled. 'There's something fishy going on. The council refused me planning permission for a new building down that end of the field five years ago, but the Bowers got permission for their building almost straight away – no arguments – and part of the site is on my bloody land.' He bent down to stroke Oscar.

'Mr Harrington, there was a serious fire at their new garage block last October,' Roscoe said.

'Yes, so everybody keeps telling me, but it was nothing to do with me. As I told the police at the time, I was abroad when the fire broke out. I was as shocked as anyone when their garages burned down.'

'Surely, sir,' interrupted Sunita, 'when you heard about the fire, you must've felt the Bowers had got their just desserts.'

'Not at all.'

Roscoe glanced down as flickering flames crackled up the chimney and sparks spurted out. He found the farmer's attitude at odds with what George had told him.

'Mr Harrington,' the DCI continued. 'Can you account for your movements on the night of Tuesday, 8 January?'

The farmer stroked his chin. 'Can you remember what you were doing two weeks ago? I was probably watching television after sorting out the sheep or spreading slurry.'

Sunita, who was gradually overcoming her concerns about Oscar, asked him, 'Do you keep a diary or have some other way of recollecting what you did that evening?'

'No, I don't keep a diary. Hang on, though. I've got a calendar. I'll go and see if I wrote anything down for that day.' The farmer ventured into the kitchen and returned a moment later.

'As I thought, I'd been spreading slurry that day,' he said. 'But there's nothing down for the evening, so I was probably here.'

'Do you live alone, Mr Harrington?' the DCI asked.

'There's only me and my son, Michael, since my dear wife died three years ago.'

'Is your son here right now?' Roscoe asked.

'No, he's in Queensbridge.'

The DCI handed him a small white card with his direct line phone number.

'Ask your son to call me sometime this week,' he said. 'I need to talk to him.'

'Maybe you're thinking I bumped old Harry Bowers off?' the farmer said.

'Did you?' asked Roscoe.

'No, of course not. It's a life sentence if you murder someone.'

Roscoe nodded.

'Look, I'm not going to pretend I didn't have a grievance against the Bowers family, because I did. That family have got the cheek of the devil taking my land and I've been thinking about going to court over it. But I've certainly got nothing to do with him disappearing. If anything, his going missing has complicated matters for me. If it does go to court, everything could get delayed because of it.'

'All right,' said Roscoe. 'We'll be going now, but mind you, ask your son Michael to phone me. Thank you for your time.'

He took a few steps towards the hallway, but Sunita had become distracted. She had noticed a twelve-bore shotgun, propped up in the far corner of the room. She pointed it out to Roscoe.

'I take it you've got a licence for that shotgun, Mr Harrington?' she asked.

'Naturally,' said the farmer. 'We always need a gun on the farm for pest control.'

The pair trudged back to Roscoe's car. The DCI was engrossed in thought as he unlocked the car.

'Everything all right, sir?' Sunita asked.

'Sorry,' he murmured while squinting across the huge expanse of open fields and hedgerows in the fading light. 'I was just wondering what on earth could have happened to our property developer. The case bears all the hallmarks of a murder investigation – except without a corpse.'

'Yes, it's a real puzzle, sir.'

'I'm not discounting our friend the farmer, but there's no evidence he's had anything to do with the disappearance. I'm wondering now whether Harry Bowers suffered some kind of breakdown and ended his days out among the hedgerows – after perhaps collapsing into a ditch or valley shrouded by trees, lost and forgotten to the world? Or has he fallen foul of some enemy and forfeited his life in an act of spite?'

Sunita sighed. 'This place is a haven of secrets,' she muttered.

Roscoe unlocked the car and the pair got in.

'I'm glad you spotted the firearm in the corner,' he said.

'First thing tomorrow, I'll check with PC Underhill that he's got a licence for it,' she replied.

He turned towards her. 'Sunita, is anything wrong? You've been rather quiet this afternoon. Is there something on your mind?'

She looked solemn. 'Well, to be honest, sir, there is. I wasn't going to tell you, but the situation's become worse.'

'What situation?'

'Well, to be totally frank, an ex-boyfriend's giving me trouble.'

'What kind of trouble?'

'Well, he keeps coming round to my house. He's stalking me.'

'He's stalking you?'

'Yes.'

'I don't like to hear about any member of my team having problems. Tell me about it.'

Sunita took a deep breath. 'I knew him at university. His name's Arun Halder. He's started turning up at my door and he's sending me dozens of messages every day.'

'Saying what exactly?'

'This is awkward.'

'I've been in the force for nearly thirty years. I'm sure I must've heard everything by now.'

'Just saying he wants to be with me, sir. Now twice he's turned up at my door in Hall Green. He's upsetting me and my flatmate, Rupa. Last time he made threats against me, saying something terrible will happen if I don't become his girlfriend again.'

'I don't suppose you've got a recording of him making these threats?'

'No, sir. I was out and he made the threats while speaking to Rupa, but I've got his car number.'

'I'm very sorry to hear about it, Sunita. No one should have to go through this. You can't deal with it yourself since you're the victim. But I know just the man who can sort this out – Tom Vickers, your predecessor as my sergeant. Just as soon as he's finished dealing with the armed robbery, I'll get him to have a word with you and take on the case. Make up a report for him and I'll give you his email address. How does that sound?'

She smiled. 'Sounds great, sir,' she said as Roscoe's phone began ringing

'Roscoe,' he announced as he raised his handset to his ear.

'What time was it?' he asked the caller. 'Three o'clock? Where exactly? OK. We're on our way now.'

He turned to Sunita, who was fastening her seatbelt.

'There's been a development in the Bowers case,' he said. 'They've found a body.'

Chapter 12

It was a boy of fourteen, Barry Fisher, who first spotted an object floating in the river at Queensbridge just before three o'clock. He and his family had been staying with relatives in one of the moored boats.

Barry raced along the footpath that runs beside the pebbly shore to inform his parents. They, in turn, alerted Tyler Brown, who was in his office at Queensbridge Marina. Within seconds, he was reporting the sighting to PC Underhill at the police station.

During the second week of January, Gavin Roscoe had called in police frogmen to assist local volunteers in searching the Avon. But the force had concentrated on the stretch of water closest to Norton Prior, believing it unlikely his body would have found its way as far downstream as the market town.

Underhill immediately went to the scene, where boat owners helped him haul the body onto the riverbank. He examined it for signs of life, but the man was clearly dead.

He quickly took charge and called for back-up. Within a short time, a team of officers had assembled and the whole area was cordoned off by half past three that afternoon.

The marina was situated on the western side of Queensbridge, about a mile from the town centre and three miles from Norton Prior. It was one of the largest marinas on the river with around two hundred metres of river frontage. Four pontoons stretched into the water from the bank and there were many established quayside moorings.

Dozens of narrow boats and motor cruisers of various shapes, sizes and colours moored there – one of the most picturesque havens for boats in Warwickshire. In the summer, spectators admired the views across lush green fields on the far side of the river extending to the hills beyond. Branches from willow trees, deeply rooted in the bank, drooped gracefully over the water's edge.

The corpse was spotted bobbing about, face-down in the water, between two moored boats.

Less than half an hour after its discovery, Roscoe was clambering down the concrete steps to the quayside, his dark-blue coat open and flapping in the breeze. Sunita scurried behind in her navy-blue trouser suit, struggling to keep up. They found the forensic team had installed a white canvas tent over the body and a police photographer was inside taking pictures. PC Underhill immediately recognised Roscoe.

'Good afternoon, sir,' he said.

'Good afternoon, Derek,' Roscoe replied. 'You haven't met my new sergeant, have you?'

After the pair had shaken hands, the constable introduced them to a stout man in his early sixties who was standing a short distance away in a grey anorak and jeans.

'This is Tyler Brown, the marina owner,' Underhill explained. 'He's the one who first called the police.'

'Pleased to meet you,' said Roscoe, shaking the hand of the smiling, bearded man.

'Doesn't your wife run the tearooms?' Brown remarked.

'Yes, she does.'

'Delightful place.'

'Finding this body must've come as a bit of a shock, sir.'

'Too right, it did. Just sorry we couldn't save his life,' said Brown. 'But it looks like he'd been in the water a while.'

'Could you explain what happened?' asked Sunita.

'A boy called Barry saw something unusual in the water and went for a closer look,' said Brown. 'He called for help when he realised what it was. Barry's father came and held onto the man's coat while Barry ran to the office to find me. Barry and his dad were obviously upset. I used a rope to secure the body by the pontoon until police arrived.'

'You've acted entirely properly,' she said.

'I presume this must be the missing man, Bowers?' said Mr Brown. 'I feel very sorry for his wife and family.'

'It looks that way,' Roscoe admitted. 'We may not know for some time though.'

The marina owner then walked away to his office, a black timber building on the bank. A sign above the door said 'Royal Avon Marina'.

'Looks as though our search for Harry Bowers is over,' Sunita remarked.

'Yes. It looks that way. I don't expect we'll have to wait long for it to be confirmed.'

The pair returned to the DCI's car and put on some white protective clothing that Roscoe kept in the boot. Then, together, they walked back to the edge of the shimmering water where the body lay.

Since the photographer had completed his task, Roscoe ducked his head beneath the canvas and stooped over the corpse. He had seen many dead bodies over the course of his career and this one yielded few surprises. The man had long, black, straggly hair. His face was white and swollen. Roscoe gazed up and down the heavy black coat wrapped around the victim before emerging from the tent.

As he stood back on the grass, delighted to be gulping in some fresher air, Sunita too drew back the canvas to take a glimpse. She quickly recoiled. The stench seemed worse than rotting fish in a Kolkata street market.

The sound of loud footsteps along the path at that moment signalled the arrival of portly, middle-aged Home Office pathologist Dr Silas Reynolds. The doctor, an amiable Cambridge University medical graduate, had arrived at the waterside suitably dressed with a green waterproof apron over his brown trousers, a green pullover and rubber gloves. He had black rubber boots on his feet for wading in any mud.

As Roscoe emerged from the tent, the newcomer greeted him heartily.

'Roscoe, old fruit!' he said, peering over the top of his horn-rimmed glasses. 'I haven't seen you since that double murder in Coventry. I thought you were more of a desk man now?'

'Someone at HQ has got a particular interest in the Harry Bowers case.'

'Sorry. I haven't heard that name. Been too busy looking at corpses.'

'He's a businessman from Norton who went missing a fortnight ago. I'd be grateful if you could help us decide whether this is his body.'

'I'll do my best. And who's this delightful young lady?'

'Sorry,' said Roscoe, breaking into a smile. 'This is our new sergeant, Sunita Roy. Sunita, meet the most cantankerous, disagreeable pathologist you're ever likely to meet.'

The fifty-eight-year-old doctor immediately gave the DCI a playful punch in the stomach. Then he placed on the ground his brown leather 'murder bag', containing a thermometer, syringes, a handsaw, sterile swabs, a small torch and a camera.

'Pleased to meet you, sir,' Sunita remarked. 'I know when the boss is joking.'

'Good. You'll need a sense of humour to work with him, my dear,' said Dr Reynolds. 'I'm used to his cheek. I've been around too long. Right, let's have a look at what we've got, shall we?'

The detectives waited patiently for more than five minutes as the pathologist examined the body. Finally, he emerged from the tent.

'We don't know a lot at this stage,' the doctor said. 'We'll have to take the body away for a full range of tests. It's partially decomposed and obviously been in the water for some time. It's bloated and bruised. I've checked the man's watch, which is broken and stopped at just after eight o'clock. It's more than likely it stopped at the time of the man's death, which could be the time when the body entered the water.'

Roscoe and Sunita continued listening intently as the doctor peeled off his gloves.

'There are minor injuries to the face and hands, but it's possible they occurred as the body was buffeted about in the river and knocked against objects, such as rocks and the boats here,' he said. 'Aquatic life has led to his lips and nose being partly eaten away and we may have problems taking fingerprints. We've got bloating of the face and abdomen with marbling of veins and peeling of the outer layer of the skin on hands and feet.'

Roscoe leaned backwards and folded his arms. 'Silas, this missing man, Harry Bowers, is about five feet eight inches tall with dark hair. He's of medium build and was wearing blue jeans, a black coat and trainers. Could this be him?'

The pathologist nodded. 'Everything fits. Certainly, it's a black coat and he's about that height. Anyway, have a look at this.' He lifted the tent flap and the detectives peered through the gap at the victims' hands, which were pale and heavily wrinkled.

'That's a sure sign of a long immersion in water,' the doctor said. 'Especially look at the fingertips and the backs of the hands. As you know, it'll be hard to work out whether this is accidental or a case of murder for some time. But it's fairly clear he drowned because there's froth present in the mouth.'

'Sir, do you think we might need dental records to identify him?' Sunita asked.

'Correct,' said the pathologist, before adding, 'Once the coroner's given permission for the body to be moved, I'll make arrangements for it to be taken to the mortuary at Queensbridge General for a full post-mortem.'

After Dr Reynolds had left, Roscoe and his sergeant spent a few minutes talking on the riverbank as they watched the coroner's officer and two of his officials place the body in a black van and drive away.

Both were inclined to believe it was Harry Bowers' body but it was frustrating having to wait for a positive identification to be made. No other man had been reported missing from the Queensbridge area of late and the presence of the black coat pointed strongly towards the body being that of the property developer.

'We could be looking at a suicide here,' the DCI muttered. 'That big tax bill would've driven anyone to the brink.'

Sunita, however, was keeping a more open mind.

'We can't rule out foul play, sir,' she insisted as she stared into the gently flowing river. 'Disposing of a corpse in water's a common trick adopted by killers. It's a convenient way of concealing the body. It could well be a case of murder.'

Chapter 13

Chief Superintendent Norris was hunched over her desk and busy writing when Roscoe knocked on her door and walked in, early on Friday 25 January.

'I was informed five minutes ago you wished to see me, ma'am.'

She looked up without expressing any greeting. 'Gavin, what do you know about this body in the river?'

'We've so far been unable to identify the man,' he replied. 'But I'm going to be talking to Dr Reynolds later today with a view to obtaining a positive identification.'

While speaking, he glanced through the floor-to-ceiling window behind the wheelchair. Norris's office was twice the size of his and had a far more extensive view across the park.

'Let me know as soon as you hear anything,' continued Norris who, at fifty-nine, was eleven years older than the DCI. 'I've had a call from the missing man's parents. They're desperate for any news and say you promised to keep them updated.'

'At present, there really isn't anything to tell them,' Roscoe replied. 'Progress has been slow.'

'Let's hope we get a quick resolution to this whole matter. It's very worrying having someone like this vanishing off the face of the earth. What's Tom Vickers doing these days?'

'He's tied up with the Crows Wood robbery.'

'Well, as soon as he's free, get him involved in the Norton case and see if we can't get it all wrapped up.'

She glanced at the front pages of some of the national newspapers, which were strewn across her desk. 'How's that new sergeant settling in?'

'Sunita Roy? She's fine. I had some concerns about her the other week. She didn't seem too meticulous when she interviewed Bowers' wife. I was thinking that, although she's got a wonderful university degree, her lack of practical experience might hold her back. But since then she's shown promise. I think she's going to fit in quite well.'

'Good to hear that, Gavin. I've had some good news. They've started the process for my successor. They haven't given me a leaving date yet, but things are moving in the right direction.'

'Pleased for you, ma'am.'

'Right, don't let me hold you up, Gavin. Let's get cracking!'

* * *

Once he'd returned to his first-floor office, the DCI looked around for Sunita before remembering she was due to visit Tom Vickers. He then spoke to Omar Khalid about possible drugs charges to be made against three suspects who were in custody.

He was on the point of making himself a coffee when the switchboard operator informed him there was a clergyman on the phone who wished to speak to him.

'You'd better put him on,' said Roscoe.

The caller introduced himself as the Reverend Peter Hughes, rector of St John the Martyr Church in Norton Prior.

'Who am I speaking to, please?' asked the rector in an educated voice.

Leaning back in his chair, Roscoe explained who he was.

'A few days ago, I spoke to a lady sergeant from your force,' Revd Hughes explained. 'I'm afraid, although I'm a man of the cloth, I wasn't totally frank. I've got some information that may be useful to your inquiries. I wondered if I could speak to you confidentially?'

Roscoe frowned. 'Look, thank you for your call, Mr Hughes. If you've got information about the Bowers case, I think I should come down and have a chat with you face to face. Are you free at the moment?'

'Yes, of course. I've got to go out at three, but I'm available until then.'

'Good. There are several matters I want to discuss with you anyway. How does midday sound?'

The rector assured him he would be at the rectory in Oxford Lane at that time.

'See you later,' said Revd Hughes. 'God bless.'

* * *

Half an hour earlier, Sunita Roy had left the CID office through the double doors and started searching for Tom Vickers' office. She came to a halt by the stairwell.

'Now where?' she asked herself. 'Do I go straight on?'

Just then she heard footsteps coming up the stairs and saw the familiar face of PC Dawson approaching. He looked furtive.

She frowned. 'What have you been up to?'

'Just been outside for a crafty fag, Sarge.'

'OK. Listen, could you help me? I need to find DI Vickers' office.'

'Just walk straight ahead and it's the first room on the left,' said Dawson. 'You can't miss it. No news on that body in the river?'

Sunita shook her head.

'No, not yet,' she assured him as she followed his directions.

She stopped at the door marked 'Acting DI, Tom Vickers' and knocked. Within seconds, Vickers flung open the door and welcomed her in.

'Won't keep you a moment,' he assured her as he rushed back to his desk at the far side of the room. 'Just finishing something off.'

As he resumed a phone conversation, Sunita looked around. It was a medium-sized room containing four desks, a filing cabinet and some video equipment. The inspector and a young female detective, who was sitting near the door and seemed engrossed in her computer screen, were the only occupants. Daylight flooded in through two floor-to-ceiling windows.

After two minutes, he ended his call, beckoned her over and found her a chair.

'Sorry about that,' he remarked as she sat down. 'Would you like tea or coffee?'

'Tea, please. Just a dash of milk.'

'We've got dried milk, but no sugar or sweeteners and no biscuits, I'm afraid.'

'Dried milk will be fine.'

'Yes, sorry about that. Welcome to our world. I expect Wendy will have a tea. She normally does,' he said.

Sunita had previously only glimpsed the inspector from across the office. Now, while he put the kettle on and searched for cups, she was able to view him properly for the first time. He was around five feet ten inches tall, slightly overweight, with short brown hair and a moustache. What she noticed most was that he was rather scruffily dressed in a blue check shirt and blue denim trousers that badly needed pressing. Otherwise all she knew was that he was aged thirty-two and originally from Wolverhampton. She'd heard he was warm-hearted and had a good sense of humour.

He glanced round. 'Have you met Wendy?'

'No. I haven't,' replied Sunita.

He quickly introduced her to DC Wendy Hopkirk, who was in her early twenties with long, dark hair. Much more smartly dressed than her inspector, she grinned and shook hands with Sunita before returning to her computer.

After handing out the drinks, the inspector settled down at his desk and said in a low voice, 'I thought this would be a good time to discuss your troublesome ex-boyfriend. I've already got West Mids working on it.'

'Because the offence occurred in their area?'

'Exactly.'

Sunita looked unsettled. Vickers glanced at his computer and then his gaze returned to her. 'There's a DS due here in half an hour to talk to you about it. You might know him – DS Nigel Martin.'

'Vaguely.'

'They've agreed I can act as liaison.'

'I'm surprised wheels are rolling already. I only mentioned about it to the DCI yesterday afternoon.'

Vickers smiled. 'The DCI doesn't hang around – particularly when one of his team's having problems. He's upstairs at the moment, isn't he, with Niggler?'

She frowned. 'Niggler?'

'The Chief Super's real name is Nicola Norris, but some bright spark nicknamed her "Niggler" a few years ago because of her pettiness and the name's kind of stuck. She once left a young policewoman in tears for tipping coffee over her and a new recruit was nearly sacked for dropping cake crumbs on her desk. Anyway, thank you for the report you filed late yesterday. They've been to see your Mr Halder.'

Sunita looked up at him. 'Already? How did they trace him?'

'From the car number.'

'I expect he denied everything.'

'Of course. After you've been interviewed later today, they're planning to revisit him and they're likely to give him a harassment warning.'

'Thank you so much for taking an interest,' said Sunita. 'This whole experience has been so draining. I've gone from being a fairly confident person to someone who's nervous and irritable. As I mentioned in my report, he's made threats on my life.'

'Yes, I read that. It must make it difficult for you to concentrate on your CID work.'

'Do you know something? I've become completely absorbed in the Harry Bowers case. Despite my personal problems, I'm absolutely determined to find out what happened to him.'

'Good. That's the attitude we like to see. Getting back to your stalker, the DCI says we need to see some evidence. Chummy hasn't put any threats in writing. They were only spoken to your housemate and you haven't got a voice recording.'

'That's right. I realise now we should have tried to record him. If he comes back, I'll definitely try and do that.'

As they were speaking, Sunita saw an address had been scrawled across a police report form which was lying on the inspector's desk. Although it was upside down, she believed one of the words was 'Ellfield' and the other 'Leicester'. He noticed her studying it and moved it out of view.

'Are you able to give me his address?' Sunita asked.

'I don't think that's appropriate, given the circumstances,' the inspector continued. 'But rest assured, we'll be keeping an eye on him from now on, and, if you have any further concerns, here's my direct line.'

He handed her a card with his name and phone number.

'Call me any time,' he insisted. 'Oh, by the way, did I mention that your Mr Halder is married?'

Chapter 14

Just before midday, Gavin Roscoe's blue BMW drew into the short driveway outside the Grade II listed St John's Rectory. He turned off the engine and got out.

During the half-hour journey, his thoughts had turned to the man in the river. It was gradually dawning on him that the corpse may not be Bowers. He had only been missing for seventeen days. The state of the body indicated it had been in the water for far longer and had steadily begun to decompose. But if the corpse in the mortuary wasn't Bowers, who was it – and where was Bowers?

Roscoe gazed at the impressive frontage of the late Georgian building with its five multi-pane front windows.

Finished in mellow brickwork, there was a Palladian-style porch leading to a blue, wooden front door. A modest garden containing three cherry trees lay at the front.

Revd Hughes, who'd been appointed by the diocese to take charge of the Norton Prior parish along with two other rural parishes five years earlier, must have heard the car arriving. He opened the door and offered a warm welcome.

He firstly insisted on showing Roscoe round the four-bed house. The detective admired the sweep of the oak staircase, the oak panelling, the oak floors and the marble fireplaces.

Then, after his housekeeper had made them both tea, he invited Roscoe into his first-floor study and, sitting behind an antique desk, the rector gave him a brief history of the parish.

The detective sipped his tea patiently while sitting on a brown leather settee, surrounded by piles of documents and newspapers. He found himself waiting for an opportunity to interrupt the sixty-two-year-old rector and apply himself to the main purpose of his visit. Some of the details he already knew. The congregation now numbered around three hundred and fifty – he'd read that somewhere.

'But if I see sixty people in church on Sunday, I consider it a triumph,' Revd Hughes was saying.

'I'm sorry, Mr Hughes,' said Roscoe. 'You were saying on the phone you hadn't been entirely frank with us.'

'You're quite right to bring me to the matter in hand,' the churchman said. 'I take it there's no news, Chief Inspector?'

'No, sir. Not yet, I'm afraid.'

'Poor Margaret,' he said. 'Look, as I say, I haven't been entirely forthright when I was asked about Mr Bowers. I'll keep this as brief as I can. Harry's been a keen member of our choir for two years since Gerry Davies took over as choirmaster. There are about twelve women and eight men in the choir and he was one of the four tenors. We've been preparing a choral presentation for Candlemas on 2 February. Are you familiar with the Christian calendar?'

Roscoe shook his head. 'Sadly not,' he said, wondering how knowledge of this ancient Christian feast day would aid his investigation.

'We've been practising the fifth-century hymn "Of The Father's Love Begotten",' he said. 'Well, I've got to tell you, I don't think this is my imagination. Around Christmas, I sensed some ill feeling between Harry and another of our choristers, Mr Hockley. He's a sports teacher at West Warwickshire Academy.

'I saw them exchanging words on Christmas Eve as they came out of church. There was also some jostling – pushing and shoving. It wasn't the kind of behaviour we expect at a time of great rejoicing over the birth of our Lord. I don't know what was said, but they scowled at each other. That's all I know. I just thought I'd mention it. They'd once been such great friends.'

Roscoe looked at him with interest. 'Did either of them say anything?'

'Yes, they were arguing. It was mainly Harry holding forth. He was clearly annoyed about something. Maybe it was just a quibble over their harmonies. Choir members get very obsessive about their singing.'

'Do you know where this Mr Hockley lives?' Roscoe asked.

'Yes. It's James Hockley, by the way. He lives in one of the new houses up Norton Hill. I think it's a development called Tree Tops, but I don't know the house number.'

Roscoe had feared he might have had a wasted journey. Now he was glad he had come. This new piece of information – details of a disagreement concerning the missing man – could lead the inquiry in a new direction.

However, he was annoyed. He could see that the rector was a man of duty and devotion, but he had held back information from the outset and this continued to trouble him.

'Thank you for mentioning that. Is there a chance I could have a look at the church hall where the choir practice is held?'

'Certainly.'

The pair walked out of the drive, turned left and strolled up Oxford Lane past the village car park until they reached the hall. It was a single-storey, red-brick building with a tiled roof. A row of Victorian terraced houses lay beyond.

'Why don't the choir practise inside the church?' he asked.

The rector smiled. 'They used to, but we've had some building work going on and there's a lot of dust, so they decided they'd prefer to use the hall for the time being.'

'Did you visit the hall yourself on the night Harry disappeared?'

'No. I don't tend to get involved with the choir very much. The choirmaster's got a free rein.'

'So on 8 January, the choir held their practice as normal?'

'Yes. As I understand it, there was a full turn-out – apart from Harry, of course.'

'Nothing was said about his absence?'

'No,' the rector said. 'The choirmaster just assumed he'd been unable to make it.'

'Nothing else unusual happened during the practice?'

'No, not that I'm aware of. By the way, would you like to take a peep inside the church, Chief Inspector?'

Roscoe had little interest in religion or churches but he was loath to upset him and wished to remain on friendly terms in case he needed his help later in the investigation.

'Yes, that would be interesting,' he said.

The pair strolled back down the lane. They passed into the rectory grounds before Revd Hughes led Roscoe along his private path into the churchyard next to St John the

Martyr Church – which, like the rectory, was Grade II listed.

Instead of showing him into the vestry, the minister took the detective to the main entrance because he wanted him to see the Norman arch that had survived rebuilding work over the centuries.

Despite having private reservations, Roscoe was impressed by the tranquil beauty of this country church. The main path from the village was shaded by twelve lime trees, each planted in honour of one of the apostles. Inside the building, he admired the craftsmanship of the sixteenth-century font, which gloried in a series of stepped layers of carving giving it the appearance of an inverted wedding cake, and some of the church's magnificent stained-glass windows based on New Testament themes.

Before leaving, he asked the rector for the names of all choristers and the choirmaster, which he intended to check against the names Sunita had compiled. Revd Hughes smiled in agreement.

'Yes, of course. I'll email it over to you. Thank you for coming round, Chief Inspector, and I'm sorry I wasn't more forthcoming before. I very much hope we see Harry again soon but, whatever his fate, I shall pray for him.'

* * *

True to his word, the rector said a prayer for the missing man at morning service the following Sunday. In the middle of the service, he read the banns for a forthcoming marriage between a Daniel Green and Vanessa Wright. He then asked the congregation of around fifty parishioners to kneel in prayer.

He said, 'Please remember in your prayers Graham Cruickshank, who was taken ill this week and is currently in Queensbridge General Hospital. He's the widower of Daphne Cruickshank, who was buried in our churchyard at the beginning of January.

'We should also mention in our prayers the family of Harry Bowers, a well-loved member of our congregation who sang in our choir. Members of our community have been shocked at his disappearance and have been helping the police to search for him. Margaret and Rachel are in our thoughts and we hope the family are soon reunited.'

Chapter 15

To the casual observer, Dr Silas Reynolds' laboratory in Kings Heath, Birmingham might appear to be a cold and clinical place. It had grey tiled floors, fluorescent lighting, desks cluttered with microscopes and computers along with a room containing plain white tables for dissecting bodies.

Gavin Roscoe never felt at ease there. He told Helen the atmosphere always reminded him of childhood trips to the dentist. But for Dr Silas Reynolds, who had spent eight years at medical school and attended countless forensic medicine courses, this space at the rear of an NHS building was like a second home. It was his sanctuary where he was often to be found contentedly examining, cutting, testing, and conferring with colleagues.

The following Tuesday morning, Roscoe put his misgivings to one side and agreed to meet the pathologist there, accompanied by his new sergeant.

Dr Reynolds had pointed out in an early morning phone call that he had made some important discoveries which were best explained in person.

Shortly after arriving at the lab, the pair found themselves staring blankly at a rack of test tubes filled with different samples of brown river water.

'Gavin!' Reynolds yelled as he marched towards them, smiling and breathing heavily. 'Listen, I'm afraid this fellow we heaved out of the Avon isn't Harry Bowers.'

The DCI groaned and sat down on a stool beside the test tubes. Sunita remained standing.

'Go on,' he pleaded.

'River Man's about the same height and has a similar dark coat, but this isn't your property developer,' said the doctor as he took a stool next to Roscoe.

The DCI had been quietly hoping the body from the river would prove to be that of Bowers so that the case could be quickly concluded. But this news was devastating.

'This very morning, I performed further tests on biological samples taken from the body and from water samples taken from various locations along the river between Norton and Queensbridge,' explained the doctor, who was dressed in white overalls. He scrambled around on a nearby desk for his horn-rimmed glasses and clipped them round his ears before resuming his seat.

He smiled. 'Be lost without these. Now, first of all, we haven't made a positive identification of this fellow from the Avon. The body's still at the mortuary in Queensbridge. But we know it's definitely not your Harry Bowers. I obtained Bowers' dental records from a dentist in Queensbridge. His teeth are different. Bowers' teeth are in a better condition with fewer fillings and only one crown. The teeth in the body have been heavily filled and there are four crowns.'

Roscoe and Sunita listened with interest like two undergraduates absorbed by the eloquence of a university professor.

'It's an older man's body. I'd say he's between fifty-two and fifty-four. Height: five feet ten inches or 1.77 metres. Weight: twelve stone seven pounds or 79.4 kilograms. He's Caucasian with poor personal hygiene. He's unshaven, balding and has dirty fingernails, although that dirt could be river mud.

'The signs are he may have been living rough – perhaps as a tramp. He was wearing black trousers, a white shirt and black coat, but it's surprising he wasn't wearing more clothes as it's been so cold. There was no personal identification on him. In his pockets were string, some tobacco, matches and a small amount of money. No wallet or keys.'

Roscoe frowned. 'He's a rather different man from Bowers. For one thing, Bowers is five feet eight inches tall.'

'Precisely. Also, this man's got long, black hair and he's much slimmer than Bowers. I should also mention this chap's got a tattoo on each arm – a scorpion on his lower left arm and a lion rampant on his lower right arm. As you know, drowning deaths are among the hardest to investigate. Was it immersion in the water that led to the death or did the man die earlier and have his body dumped in the river?

'Well, I've carried out extensive tests using what scientists call diatoms. These are microscopic algae found in all water sources which are a real boon to the pathologist. They're often inhaled and swallowed during drowning. They travel round the body and get deposited in a number of organs – including the lungs, brain and bone marrow.

'We can take samples from various parts of the river and compare these tiny algae with those found in the human organs. If there are none in the body, it suggests the victim's death wasn't caused by drowning. Well, these algae *were* present in this poor fellow's body, which suggests the cause of death was drowning.

'We're still trying to calculate whereabouts the body may have entered the water and how far it could've travelled over a certain period of time. All we can say reliably at the moment is that it was in the river for at least a month. I can tell you one thing with certainty though. This poor chap's been murdered.'

The two detectives glanced at each other.

'What makes you say that?' Roscoe asked.

'Gavin, there was a piece of rope tied round the left leg. I didn't mention this to you at the scene because it was unclear whether the rope had been purposefully tied to the leg or whether it had simply become entangled round the leg while the body was being buffeted around in the river. But I've examined the nylon rope and it's tied with a couple of reef knots.

'I'm firmly of the belief that, at the time he entered the water, a heavy weight was attached to him with the aim of keeping the body submerged. The rope was rather frayed in places and it's snapped off – possibly during some of the storms that have swelled the river in recent days.'

Sunita was contemplating all the hard work that lay ahead. 'We need to get divers in, sir,' she remarked. 'We need to make a thorough search of the riverbed for a weight – a rock or something – that's got a length of rope attached to it.'

Turning to the pathologist, she said, 'Dr Reynolds, do we have any idea at all at what point the body might've entered the water? Presumably, the killer got rid of the body upstream? It wasn't simply dumped in the water at the marina?'

He nodded. 'That's right. I'd have thought it could've entered the river somewhere west of Norton. Of course, for a time, if it was weighted down, it might've remained in one place. But once the rope broke, it could've travelled freely downriver for miles. Searching the water thoroughly can be a daunting task, my dear, but one that may pay dividends.'

'Silas, could you tell us about marks on the body?' asked Roscoe.

'He'd got bruising around the body and cuts to his head. A violent attack cannot be discounted as there are many minor injuries to the body,' he said. 'Some of these injuries, of course, are likely a result of the victim being knocked against rocks and boats and other objects in the water.'

He added that the body had now been frozen to prevent further decomposition after discussions with the senior Warwickshire coroner.

Roscoe looked solemn as he rose from his stool. 'Has the coroner asked for a toxicology report to see if there were any alcohol or drugs in the victim's body?' he asked.

Dr Reynolds nodded. 'Yes, but as you know, this can take up to eight weeks.'

'Right,' said Roscoe. 'Before we do anything else we'll have to let Mrs Bowers know that the body isn't her husband's – in case she's heard about its discovery.'

Chapter 16

'How long has Arun Halder lived in Leicester?' asked Rupa as she and Sunita relaxed in their living room. It was a chilly, blustery night. The heating had been on for an hour and Rupa was still suffering from the cold.

'No idea,' said Sunita, who was lounging on their grey, three-seater settee. 'I'm just amazed that he's married.'

'Doesn't sound as though his marriage is going very well. Where did you say she's from again?'

'Well, her family are originally from Durgapur, but her grandparents came over to England in the 1960s. Apparently, she's twenty-two and called Rani.'

'So a policeman traced him through the car?'

'Yes, it was registered at his address on a housing estate. The detective from West Mids went round and interviewed him.'

Rupa, who was sitting opposite Sunita in an armchair, frowned and swept a few strands of black hair away from her eyes. 'What? In front of his wife?'

Sunita shook her head. 'No, he got him to step outside first. Arun denied knowing who I was and said they'd got the wrong man.'

Rupa shrugged her shoulders. 'What sort of place was it?'

'A ground floor council flat. A bit untidy,' said Sunita while thumbing through a fashion magazine.

'Really? Doesn't sound like Arun is doing very well, despite his degree in computer science.' She paused and then said, 'Do you think this Rani realises her husband is obsessed with you?'

Sunita groaned. 'How do I know? She probably doesn't even know I exist. I'm hoping the inspector has warned him off and we won't see Arun again.'

'For your sake, I hope that's true. But you say you're still receiving text messages?'

'Yes. He sent ten today and he's trying to message me through Facebook. I don't feel safe walking to and from the station, but thankfully I should get my car back from the garage tomorrow – so I'll have wheels again.'

'You can take care of yourself,' said Rupa. 'You've had personal safety training.'

'I know, but that doesn't help too much if you're taken by surprise. Anyway, let's see if the inspector's warning has done the trick. Maybe the messages will stop and he'll take heed of the advice.'

But, despite her hopes that Nigel Martin's journey to Leicester would've deterred Arun, Sunita was infuriated when the doorbell rang half an hour later and she realised her tormentor had returned. A glance through a gap in the venetian blinds was enough to confirm it. She immediately pressed the 'Record' button on her phone and placed it on a small table in the hallway.

Then, bristling with indignation, she switched on the light and threw open the front door to find him smirking at her from behind his beard.

'You've got a nerve coming here again!' she bellowed. 'You've been warned off.'

'I've decided to forgive you for sending the cops round,' he told her as he paced around in his blue jacket and blue jeans by the door. 'Here. These are for you.' He brought out his hand from behind his back clutching pink, purple and yellow tulips.

'You can take them away right now!' boomed Sunita.

But instead of leaving, he slipped past her into the hall.

Rupa, who had been lurking in the living room, dashed towards him.

'Why don't you go home to your wife?' she cried. 'She must be wondering where you are.'

'I'm afraid I made a mistake when I married her,' he replied. 'I don't love my wife. It's you I love, Sunita.' He thrust the flowers towards her.

Sunita, now concerned that Arun had managed to sneak inside the house, backed away. So he placed the bouquet on the hall table close to the phone that, unknown to him, was recording every word he said.

'Let me back into your life, Sunita. We were good together.'

'We weren't, Arun. And you've got to learn that when a woman says no, she means no. It's over and you've just got to accept it.'

His smile faded. His tone changed. 'I can make life very difficult for you, Sunita,' he said. 'I know some very heavy people who could make you disappear. No one would know where you were. You'd never be found.'

'Don't threaten me, you bastard. Leave our house right now! And don't come back!' Sunita yelled.

'It doesn't have to be like this, darling Sunita,' he whined. 'We can go back to how we were…' He reached forward with his hand in order to clutch her right hand.

But, in a split second, Sunita sprang into action. Using a self-defence move she'd learnt from a police trainer, she grasped Arun's fingers with her other hand and then swung her right hand up, forcing his arm towards the ceiling.

'Let me go!' he screamed.

She then grabbed the back of Arun's wrist with her right hand and forced his extended right arm downwards, leaving him sprawling on the carpet.

Finally she forced his arm behind his back and frogmarched him out into the street.

'You'll be sorry for this!' he shouted. 'I'll make you very sorry.'

Just then a police car drove slowly along the road. He watched for a few seconds as the patrol car's brake lights came on twenty metres down the road. Then he walked to his car and drove away.

* * *

Gavin Roscoe called Sunita into his office as soon as he arrived in work the next morning on Wednesday, 30 January. They were no closer to unravelling the Harry Bowers mystery, but the revelation that the man in the river had been murdered – and possibly in the same location where Bowers had disappeared – was an intriguing development.

The dead man appeared to have been a tramp, but he was obviously somebody's son and possibly somebody's husband or lover. Maybe he was somebody's father. And whether he was a tramp or not, he still had the right to have the case of his murder dealt with as robustly as any other.

Yet why would a tramp be murdered? And why would someone go to such lengths to attempt to hide the body in the River Avon? All these questions were swirling through Roscoe's mind as he waited for his sergeant to end a phone call.

'Good morning, sir,' she said with a smile as she knocked and walked in. 'The diving team have started work near Norton Bridge. PC Dawson is with them.'

'That's not what I wanted to talk to you about. Take a chair,' he replied.

Her eyeliner was slightly smudged because she had earlier been crying, but Roscoe failed to notice. He was too preoccupied with details of the tramp's murder.

'What I'm wondering is why anyone would kill a harmless tramp,' he said.

'Unless he wasn't harmless,' Sunita suggested. 'Perhaps he knew more than was good for him.'

'That's possible,' he said. 'Whoever killed him most likely drowned him in the river and then weighed the body down so it wouldn't be found.'

'Yes, sir.'

'In that case, there would've almost certainly been signs of a struggle on the riverbank somewhere – marks in the mud, that kind of thing.'

'Yes, sir. But it would be hard to find the exact spot. We don't know if the body entered the river from a public place, such as a bridge or woodland beside the river, or from private land.'

'It's so difficult,' said Roscoe. 'There are miles of riverbank to cover and, at the end of the day, there might not be any clear signs. This killer might've taken the trouble to cover their tracks. A riverbank search would be such a challenge. Our time would be better spent checking out the main access points to the river and on looking for the second part of the rope.

'Look, Sunita, while I'm arranging that, could you have a word with this guy James Hockley, the choir member who had a row with Bowers?'

'Certainly, sir. My transport problems are over now. I've just picked up my car from the garage.'

'What was wrong with it?'

'Gearbox trouble. They've had it for nearly a month, but it seems all right now. Sir, you know PC Dawson and I had a brief chat on the phone with Hockley two weeks ago when we were interviewing all the choir members?'

Roscoe nodded. 'I know, but we're more interested in him now. He had a row with Bowers on Christmas Eve. So can you see him in person?'

He handed her a scrap of paper on which he had scribbled down Hockley's address. 'Let me know as soon as you've got anywhere.'

Chapter 17

Sports teacher James Hockley closed the book he had bought in the pre-Christmas sales before placing it down on the brown leather settee beside him.

In the fading light, he stared out of his front window past the solitary birch tree that stood in the centre of his newly cut lawn. He gazed across at his neighbours' neat, twee little gardens. The novel had seemed intriguing when he flicked through the first few pages in the shop in Queensbridge. Now he was unable to sustain any interest in it. All he could think about was the attractive, dark-haired woman he'd recently met in the town.

His life had been rather lonely and unexciting until that moment when they met. His previous relationship had ended because they'd been unable to agree on so many things. This new relationship was rich with promise. That first encounter with her in the high street could have come straight from a novel.

She'd dropped some of her shopping and, to her amusement and great appreciation, he'd stopped to help her pick everything up. They'd chatted for a while.

Then, a few days later, another chance meeting had arisen in one of the town's cafes. They'd talked and laughed together in a corner and time had sped by. After exchanging phone numbers, he'd taken her to a restaurant for a meal and their relationship had blossomed. She'd begun visiting him at his small, two-bedroom house situated in the middle of a new housing development on the edge of Norton Prior. Training youngsters to be proficient at sport and games had once been his principal concern. Now life was different. Now there was a new dynamism about him, a new joie de vivre, a new purpose.

The minutes ticked by. She was due to arrive at half past four that Wednesday afternoon and it was only a quarter past. He felt both excited and nervous at the same time like one of his young gym stars, waiting expectantly beside the school stage to receive an award from the headmaster.

He whiled away some time by tidying the front room at his home, which was tucked away at the back of a private estate on the edge of the village. He dusted the books on his bookshelf, wiped the mantelpiece with a damp cloth and vacuumed the wooden floor, moving the two-seater settee and armchair out of the way as he did so.

He thought, later that week, he should give the whole house a thorough clean. Like many people, he believed in spending a few hours preparing the home for the forthcoming year in the quiet days following Christmas. When the temperatures plummeted and the cries of children playing in the street were no longer drifting in through the windows, he knew it was the right moment to launch into his spring-cleaning drive.

He looked at his watch. He still had at least another five minutes to fill. He walked upstairs to the second bedroom, which he'd turned into a home gym. He gazed with pride at his exercise bike, rowing machine and the set of weights for body building. He was just beginning to arrange them in a neat fashion together at the far end of the room when the doorbell rang. It was her!

Hockley dashed downstairs, opened the door and he almost dragged her in. Her face was wreathed in smiles as their eyes met. He threw his arms around her and they kissed passionately. Hockley took her fawn coat and hung it at the bottom of the banisters with her purple headscarf. She gazed longingly at him and her fingers sought out his hand. Then she turned round and led him up the stairs to the main bedroom.

The medium-sized room contained two double wardrobes, a dressing table and mirror, and two maple bedside cabinets, one on each side of the king-size divan. A small, vintage, three-tier chandelier hanging from the centre of the room added some style.

'I just couldn't wait to see you again,' she murmured.

'Me too!' he whispered.

The woman fell onto the bed's thick white duvet and pulled the teacher down with her. Again they kissed, aware only of each other. It was as if they were alone in the world and nothing else mattered.

Slowly she reached down and removed her black leather boots. They fell in turn to the floor with a thump, as the teacher kicked off his shoes and undid his shirt.

Hockley slipped his left hand behind her back and unbuttoned her blue, floral-patterned dress. He unclipped her white bra, reached down and kissed her warm shoulders. In the distance, he thought he could hear a sound. Mesmerised by the woman's beauty and sensuality, hypnotised by the exquisite aroma of her perfume, he chose to ignore the ringing noise. The woman began to remove her tights, but there it was again. It must be his doorbell.

Cursing silently beneath his breath, the teacher put his shoes and shirt back on before climbing halfway down the stairs. Through the misted, half-glazed door he could discern the outline of a medium-sized woman in a grey trouser suit. He wondered for a moment if he could ignore the caller and return to his lover. But curiosity overcame him. He headed towards the door, vowing to send away whoever had the temerity to disturb him. After examining himself in the hall mirror and straightening his hair, he drew back the door.

* * *

Sunita had only just collected her white Peugeot 208 from the garage that day. She was rather reluctant to use it for a long journey knowing the gearbox had only just been repaired. She was uncertain whether the problem had been fully resolved.

However, she decided she had little choice. So she set off on the twenty-two-mile journey and reached the Tree Tops housing estate at the top of Norton Hill after three quarters of an hour. Luckily, her car performed well.

She felt safe to assume as soon as she arrived outside James Hockley's house that he was at home. A small blue Toyota car was positioned in front of the attached garage. There was a green Volvo estate parked a few metres away, which she assumed belonged to a neighbour.

While strolling up the short drive, she thought she detected the sound of voices coming from within the house. So she was surprised when, to begin with, no one came to answer the door.

But finally her persistence paid off. She pressed the bell a second time and the door opened.

'Mr Hockley? James Hockley?' she asked.

'Yes?' the teacher replied cautiously.

'We spoke on the phone briefly two weeks ago. I'm DS Roy from Heart of England CID.'

Hockley frowned. 'I've told you all I know.'

'I'm sorry, sir. Some new information's come to light. May I come in?'

'It's a little inconvenient,' he said. 'Will it take very long?'

'Just a few minutes. We need to clear up something.'

'I'd rather you came back another time.'

'We can do this down the station if you prefer, sir. This is a major missing person inquiry.'

Hockley's manner changed. He believed he might be able to dispense with the caller quickly and return to his guest.

'OK,' said Hockley. 'I can spare a couple of minutes, I suppose.'

The teacher, who had dark, ginger hair, was at least six feet tall and he appeared to be physically fit. He was thirty-four, spoke with a slight Bristol accent and he was broad-shouldered with a muscular frame. Before embarking on a teaching career, he'd helped in his father's timber merchants, sawing wood for customers and handling timber deliveries. Waiving the chance of succeeding his father in the timber trade, the sports lover turned to teaching. He'd spent six years teaching sport in Gloucestershire before moving to teach at West Warwickshire Academy five years ago.

As she stepped into the hallway, Sunita noticed a woman's fawn coat and a purple scarf draped around the banister post but said nothing. Hockley led her into the living room and the pair remained standing as they spoke.

The teacher was amiable but seemed on edge. He looked for a moment like an errant schoolboy. 'It's a real mystery what could've happened to Bowers,' he muttered. 'I suppose the police have checked abroad?'

'All avenues of inquiry are being explored,' said the detective, relying on a standard police response to such a question. 'Mr Hockley, you knew Mr Bowers quite well at one time, didn't you?'

The teacher shrugged. 'Well, he's one of several friends I made since moving to the village. We're both in the choir, so I spent a lot of time singing with him. Nice chap. Good tenor voice. We've had a few drinks together.'

'So what led to you falling out with him?' she asked.

'I haven't fallen out with him, as far as I know,' said the teacher. 'Look, if you don't mind, I'm quite busy this evening.'

The sergeant persisted. 'I understand you had words with him on Christmas Eve while coming out of church.'

'Someone's been yakking–'

'You were seen arguing with him.'

'Who says? Some village gossip?'

'The rector, Revd Hughes,' said Sunita.

'When's this meant to have happened?'

'Christmas Eve'

'Christmas Eve? Let me think. Now you come to mention it, I've remembered. Bowers might've been a little bit annoyed about the way I was singing one of the carols. I'd had a little too much of the Christmas spirit, I seem to recall. He had a go at me. That's all it was. A discordant note among the choristers, you might say.' Then the teacher paused. 'You're not suggesting I'd anything to do with his disappearance, are you? Listen, Miss...'

'Sergeant Roy.'

'Sergeant Roy, it was just a silly argument over a Christmas carol. It was nothing more. We parted as friends.'

'The rector says there was some jostling as you emerged from the church. Some pushing and shoving.'

'Probably a bit of festive high jinks.'

Sunita raised an eyebrow. 'High jinks?'

'Yes, you know. I was looking forward to Christmas, I expect.'

Sunita made her way towards the front door.

'I won't take up any more of your time, sir. It's just that we've got to consider everything connected with events that occurred before Mr Bowers disappeared,' she said. 'His wife and family are worried sick. We need to find out everything that happened before he went missing. Even the slightest detail could be significant. I'm sure you understand.'

Chapter 18

Gavin Roscoe drew back the light-brown curtains in his bedroom and gazed out across the back garden on the first day of February. A light sprinkling of snow coated the ground.

The vast open fields beyond were as yet untouched by the plough's blade after the ravages of winter. But mauve crocuses and snowdrops near the house were beginning to burst through the soil beside the yellow jasmine, bringing the tantalizing promise of spring.

Although it was only eight o'clock, he had already decided to visit Margaret Bowers again – this time alone. He had no meetings planned at work. But as he was about to get dressed, his phone rang and the ensuing conversation put all thoughts of a leisurely trip to Heathwood House out of his mind for a while.

As he stood shivering in his dressing gown and slippers in the hallway, he realised from the screen of his handset that the caller was Dr Reynolds.

'Roscoe?' he said. 'You took a long time to answer.'

'I've only just woken up,' he confessed. 'Isn't it cold!'

'Listen, Gavin,' the doctor said. 'I've made an interesting discovery about the body in the marina. We've been examining water samples from the river. We can't be completely certain, but it appears he didn't drown in the Avon.'

The DCI looked bemused. He took his phone into the living room and sat on the settee.

'The microscopic particles found in the body aren't a match for those found in the samples collected from the river at precise locations between Norton and Queensbridge,' the pathologist continued.

'You mean he drowned elsewhere and then his body was dumped in the river?'

'Exactly, old fruit. This means he was drowned in a different river or water source and his body was then placed in the Avon – possibly in order to confuse poor mortals such as us.'

'So, to be absolutely clear, your theory is that the man drowned in one place and afterwards there was an attempt to conceal the body in a watery grave elsewhere?'

'Precisely, old fruit.'

The phrase 'one body, two crime scenes' was reverberating in Roscoe's mind. It might prove even harder to find the killer now, he thought.

As he thanked the pathologist and ended the call, Roscoe felt it was more vital than ever that he should re-visit Mrs Bowers.

Roscoe frowned. She had not been completely honest with the police. She told them about the fire and traces of petrol being found, but she'd been slow to admit the feud with her neighbour. She claimed to have no idea who was behind the arson attack and had no enemies. He had to probe deeper. He had to find out why she had been rather obstructive.

He also decided to hold a press conference to raise the profile of the case. Hopefully, as a result, a witness or two with valuable information might come forward. Mrs Bowers would be invited and, if she failed to show, that would be incriminating in itself. He was beginning to suspect that she was somehow involved in her husband's disappearance.

The sun emerged from behind a cloud as the DCI left his home and set off on the four-mile journey to Heathwood House. A grey-haired man in a green coat whom he didn't recognise was pruning the wisteria and rose bushes as his car drew up outside the front of the property. He concluded that he must be Jeff Williams, the gardener.

'Is the lady of the house in?' he asked.

'Yes, as far as I know,' said the man as Roscoe pressed the bell.

'Won't you come in, Chief Inspector?' said Margaret, who was dressed plainly, as she opened the door. 'Any news?'

The DCI frowned. 'I just wanted to tell you that I'm planning a press conference and I'd like you to attend.'

'Oh, er... Would it help that much if I came along?' she asked. 'I'm not much good at public speaking and the whole business is so upsetting.'

'Yes, you should definitely come,' said Roscoe. 'There'll be a few reporters and photographers – mainly local press and folk from Birmingham, I'd imagine. But you don't need me to tell you how important this is. I know you could face a few intrusive questions from the press. But we desperately need some publicity. Time's getting on and we need help from the public to find your husband.'

Margaret looked down at the hall's tiled floor. Her expression changed and her mood lightened. She shrugged. 'Yes, of course, Chief Inspector,' she said. 'Something like that might help to find him, although I do feel he may not want to be found.'

'*You* want him to be found though, don't you?' said Roscoe, feeling slightly irritated by her manner.

'Yes, yes, of course. To end the mystery, if nothing else.'

Roscoe adopted a more solemn expression. 'Now, Mrs Bowers. You've not been entirely truthful, have you?' he said.

The woman appeared startled. 'What do you mean?' she gasped.

Roscoe shook his head. 'When we were here before, we asked you whether you'd any enemies. You failed to tell us about the dispute with your neighbour, Mr Harrington. We've been to see him.'

'I'm... I'm sorry,' she said. 'He's not really an enemy. It's just a planning dispute. He was annoyed with us because he tried to get planning permission for his own building and he was turned down.'

'A number of witnesses have spoken to us about his feud with you and your husband and you must've known how angry he was. Didn't you think it important enough to mention that to us? It's very remiss of you.'

'Harrington was in Spain when the fire happened,' she said. 'So we decided he couldn't have had anything to do with it.'

'You don't think he might've paid someone to carry out the arson attack for him?'

'Who knows? Anyway, the whole thing was months ago. We received insurance money and one day I'll have it rebuilt. Life moves on.'

As Roscoe left her, he promised that, later in the day, he'd phone her and provide her with full details of the press conference.

* * *

After he'd gone, Margaret heard the doorbell ring and found Jeff Williams, waiting outside.

'Will that be all then, Mrs Bowers?' he asked as he stood at the foot of the steps. 'I've pruned the wisteria and roses and tidied up the greenhouse.'

'Yes, that's fine,' she said. 'Here's the eighty pounds I owe you for this week. See you next Wednesday?'

'Yes, I'll be round just before nine as usual.'

'That's cool, Jeff, and thanks for all you've done,' she said. She stood watching while he collected his bicycle from the side of the house and pedalled slowly away down the drive.

As she watched him depart, she thought about what an odious time she'd suffered since her husband performed his vanishing act. Fortunately, her bank manager had been very understanding. She'd managed to transfer funds from her husband's account to the new personal account she'd set up a year ago.

While she had no problems paying household bills, paying the mortgage had proved more troublesome. Building society staff had been concerned to learn the main breadwinner was no longer around and wanted her assurance she could afford the monthly instalments on her own.

After long discussions, they refused to remove her husband's name from the building society roll but said they'd accept payments from her for the time being.

However, her husband's co-director, Rashad Mahmood, had proved extremely difficult to deal with. So, as a result, she'd decided to leave him, for the moment, to run the company single-handed. Every now and then, he'd send her a document in the post for her to examine and she'd file it in her husband's study.

She sometimes had to stop and question her own behaviour. Shouldn't she be more concerned about her husband's desertion? How could she deal with matters of the day so coolly?

Luckily, the family's finances were in a robust state. The company's main project had involved building new homes at a site in Solihull. But they'd also bought a piece of land in Knowle with ramshackle buildings; gained planning consent for homes; and then quickly resold the land at a far higher price.

This meant she had sufficient funds in the bank to last for a while. If money became tight, there was always the joint life insurance policy she'd taken out with Harry, although it might be a long time before he could be officially pronounced dead and she could make a claim. Thank God he'd thought of their future when they took out that policy ten years before.

Good old Harry! She could hardly say she missed him. He'd been a self-obsessed, quarrelsome, hard-hearted husband. But he'd been a great provider. She began to walk up the oak stairs and then suddenly remembered the promise she'd just made to the chief inspector. She'd agreed to attend a press conference in Queensbridge.

'Bloody nuisance!' she muttered to herself.

* * *

After his morning visit to the Bowers' house, Roscoe began planning the rest of his day. He needed to speak to Tom Vickers. He'd also decided to send his sergeant to visit the Bowers' cleaning lady, Tessa Griffiths.

But before heading off to police headquarters, he had to make a brief detour to his home to pick up some documents.

He had hardly walked through his front door when Melody called out to him from her bedroom. She hurried downstairs, beaming like a politician with a state secret.

'Dad,' she said. 'I've got some interesting information for you. I couldn't help overhearing you yesterday when you were talking to Mum. The name of one of my teachers came up – Mr Hockley.'

Roscoe turned towards her. 'You know I often seek your mother's opinion on a case. Anyway, go on.'

'Well, I thought I'd better tell you that Alex saw Mr Hockley with a particular woman in his car.'

'Alex – that's your new boyfriend?'

'Dad, he's just a friend. I've only been out with him twice.'

'Where was this?' her father asked.

'It was at Oxford Park on Saturday,' she said.

The park consisted of more than thirty acres of open fields, ancient woodland and wild-flower meadows. The Avon meandered through the centre of the park, which contained two sports pitches.

Melody went on, 'This is the first chance I've had to tell you. Alex is in a soccer team run by Mr Hockley. He saw the teacher arrive in a small blue car. When the training was over, Alex noticed a woman standing beside the car.'

Roscoe was listening intently. 'I guess she was waiting for him.'

'Yes. Alex had changed out of his soccer kit and was standing at the nearby bus stop. After a few minutes, Mr Hockley left the changing room and ran to the car. He unlocked it, they both got in and they kissed.'

'How long was she waiting for him?'

'Only about five minutes.'

'What kind of car was it?'

'A blue Auris.'

'How can Alex be so certain that was the make?'

'He's been thinking of getting one himself when he passes his test.'

Roscoe hesitated before asking, 'What kind of kiss was it? Was it a peck on the cheek or a long, lingering kiss?'

'A long, lingering kiss,' Melody said. 'Alex was some distance away. After that, the bus came and he got on.'

Roscoe nodded. 'Did he see the car drive off?'

'No, he didn't see anything else,' she said. 'He was more concerned about getting home. This could be important, couldn't it, Dad?'

'Yes, it certainly could be,' her father said. 'Does Alex have any idea who the woman was?'

'He thinks it was Mrs Bowers.'

Chapter 19

It took Sunita Roy more than three quarters of an hour to drive from her home in Birmingham to Norton Prior on the Friday morning. She followed the main A435 road past Redditch through flat countryside until she reached the Roman town of Queensbridge.

Finally, after a further three miles in her white Peugeot 208, she reached Norton Prior's village green – a circular expanse of common grassland which had served as the centre of the community's life for centuries.

After parking by the roadside, she stepped out of the car and gazed around. Four majestic oak trees stood at the edge of the grassed area by the main road. A diverse selection of more than forty houses and bungalows curled round the far edge of the green.

She set off on foot at a steady pace, looking out for door numbers, until, after a few minutes, she reached the address the DCI had given her for Tessa Griffiths – number thirty-one, The Green. It was an address twenty-two-year-old Tessa had given Helen Roscoe two years earlier when she did some shifts as a waitress at the Apollo Tearooms.

Sunita had also been given a mobile phone number for Tessa, but this no longer appeared to be operating.

The sergeant found herself staring up at a semi-detached council house. After opening the wooden gate and walking up the tarmacked path, she pressed the doorbell and waited. No one seemed to be at home. She peered through the letterbox of the red-bricked house and could see a pile of letters and magazines strewn across the hall floor.

'Damn!' she said to herself.

She decided to try the house next door. Fortunately, someone responded almost immediately at number thirty-three when Sunita knocked.

A faint female voice from inside asked, 'Who is it?'

'It's the police, madam,' she replied. 'Sergeant Roy.'

'What's it about?' A small dog began barking at the far end of the house.

'I'm trying to find your neighbour,' she yelled through the door. 'Have they moved?'

'OK, hang on!' said the voice.

A middle-aged lady with a slightly hunched back wearing an apron and curlers and a healthcare uniform opened the door a fraction.

'Hello, dear. I'm worried about the dog getting out. What is it you want?'

Sunita held up her warrant card. 'Just wondering what's happened to Tessa next door?' she asked.

'Oh, she's gone,' the woman said. 'I don't know where. She had a lot of her grandmother's furniture and it was all taken off in a huge removal van. She lost one of her jobs and was worried about paying the bills. It's been a bit of a struggle for her.'

Sunita groaned. 'That's a nuisance.'

The woman pressed her finger to her nose. 'You could try the council or maybe the Bowers. I think she worked for them.'

Sunita thanked her and walked slowly away down the path. Once she had returned to her car, she called CID, hoping the DCI could help her decide her next course of action.

But instead of hearing Roscoe's deep voice, the phone was answered by the strident Black Country accent of Tom Vickers, who had been placed in charge of the DCI's office while a meeting was going on upstairs. She explained her predicament.

'You've got a problem there, Sunita,' he told her. 'Griffiths is a very common name. But we've got a genealogist in Brum who's an expert on family trees. Here's his email address. He's fairly quick. He should be able to dig out the names of Tessa's parents in no time.'

She also explained about Arun Halder's latest visit and he promised to ask DS Martin if regular patrols could be set up around her home.

Sunita used her smartphone to send an email to the family researcher, giving him the sketchy details she had for Tessa Griffiths. She knew Tessa had been born in about 1993 – probably in Queensbridge – and that she had a sister. While waiting for a response from him, she also put in a call to Warwickshire County Council, and gas, electricity and water utility staff in the hope someone might have a forwarding address for her. Unfortunately, since Tessa had only just moved house, no one was able to help.

Through online research she discovered there were twenty-five Griffiths households in Queensbridge and surrounding villages on the Police National Computer.

She was becoming discouraged. But soon afterwards she checked her inbox and was delighted to find the researcher had succeeded in tracing family details.

Tessa had been born not in Warwickshire but in Aldershot, Hampshire, the researcher informed her. Her birth was registered in June 1993 with the mother's maiden name given as Treherne. After examining the marriage records, he'd found a marriage in 1991 between a Gordon Alan Griffiths and a Sarah Anne Treherne.

The email also revealed that Tessa's sister Sally was born in 1995, and she also had a brother called Richard, born in 1996. He knew they were children from the Griffiths-Treherne marriage because the mother's maiden name of Treherne was listed beside all three birth entries. In addition, there was a G.A. Griffiths listed as living at 67 Oakdale Road, Queensbridge. Sunita immediately set off for that address with the aim of finding Tessa's parents.

She quickly realised she might be visiting a military family. Aldershot was known throughout the world as 'the home of the British Army' and Queensbridge was less than twenty miles from the headquarters of the Royal Warwickshire Regiment's base at Budbrooke Barracks.

The Griffiths home was a large Victorian terraced house close to the railway station in a quiet street which sloped down from the high street. Sunita rang the doorbell twice, but there was no reply and she learned from neighbours that the family were away in the Canary Islands.

However, she was not prepared to give up. She had thought of one final way of tracing the cleaner. She returned to the neighbour's house at the village green which she'd visited earlier and rang the doorbell. This time the entrance had been firmly locked from the inside and it took the occupant a few minutes to open up.

The same middle-aged lady said, 'So you're back again, young lady. I often lock my door these days. There are so many crooks around.'

'Yes, I quite understand,' she told her. 'I was just wondering… do you by chance recall the name of the removal firm that moved Tessa's belongings?'

'No, I'm sorry,' she said. 'I didn't take much notice. I've got my old man poorly in bed upstairs. I was seeing to him a lot on Tuesday.'

Sunita frowned. Then, in one last attempt to gain information, she asked, 'Do you recall the colour of the removal van?'

There was a pause. Then the householder said, 'Well, funny you should mention that. There was no mistaking it – it was purple, so it stood out a bit. You couldn't miss it from either of the front bedroom windows.'

'Thank you,' said Sunita. 'That's very helpful indeed.'

'Well, I can't see how. But you're very welcome,' the woman said as she returned inside and relocked the door.

Sunita was delighted to find out that the removal van was purple. She had noticed during her time in this part of the Midlands that there was one firm that had a fleet of purple removal vans, Harrington and Sons of Queensbridge, which she believed might be linked to the family of the farmer, David Harrington. She at once returned to her car and phoned the company.

The managing director, John Harrington, was in the office at the far end of the town when she called.

'You're working for old Gavin Roscoe, are you?' Harrington's voice boomed down the phone. 'I've known him for years. Pass on my regards, won't you? Yes, Tessa Griffiths. That was only the other day. If you hold on, I'll get the details.'

After a few minutes, he came back to the phone.

'She's moved to Worcester to be with her sister,' he revealed. 'It was a very pleasant, easy journey for us of about twenty-five miles or so. Here's the address: Sunnyside, Main Road, Upper Wick.'

Chapter 20

The roads around Worcester were crammed with homebound commuters when Sunita Roy approached the city that evening. Words of praise from her boss were still ringing in her ears.

'Good bit of work,' he had told her. 'When you find Tessa, ask whether she's got any knowledge of the note, obviously, but also see if you can get a sample of her handwriting. And guide her gently into talking about relations between Harry and Margaret Bowers. Perhaps we'll be lucky and she'll let slip some clue as to what was happening in that house.'

It was nearly half past six by the time she arrived in Main Road, Upper Wick.

The dark street contained a hotchpotch of buildings. There were old commercial premises at the start of the street. Then came a variety of Victorian terraced houses with occasional infills of modern houses and flats.

Towards the end were semi-detached houses built in the 1950s and 60s.

She was forced to stop and speak to several pedestrians before discovering that Tessa Griffiths' new address was one of these semis, set back a few metres from the highway. Each home had rounded bay windows and small front gardens shielded by high hedges. She was encouraged to see that lights were on at Sunnyside.

While clambering out of her car, Sunita noticed a small, black Mini Countryman with muddy tyres was parked in the drive. It appeared the occupants had undertaken a major clear-out. An old mattress, an old suitcase and several bundles of newspapers were piled up next to two dustbins close to the gate.

Shivering a little in the cold evening air, she walked up the short driveway, past the Mini, and strode up to the white front door in the twilight. It was opened almost immediately by a young woman in her early twenties. She was about five feet five inches tall, had mousy, medium-length hair, and was of average build. She was wearing a crisp white T-shirt and pink jeans.

Sunita smiled. 'I'm looking for Tessa – Tessa Griffiths?'

'Yes,' said the woman, whom she later learned was Tessa's younger sister, Sally. 'Who shall I say…?'

'I'm from Heart of England Police. It's all right. She's done nothing wrong. We just need help with some information.'

For a few moments, Sunita was left staring at the flaking paint on the partly open door as she waited. Then Tessa herself emerged.

She was slightly taller than her sister – about five feet seven inches in height. She had long, blonde hair and was slimmer. Some might have considered her prettier than her sister. She greeted her visitor with suspicion.

'If it's about the money I owe…' she began.

'No, you're not in any trouble. Just need to ask you about your employment with the Bowers family.' Sunita displayed her warrant card.

Tessa looked as relieved as a shipwreck survivor who has spotted a rescue boat.

'Of course. Mr Bowers is still missing, isn't he?' she said while leaning against the doorpost. 'Do you want to come in?'

'I think you know my boss, the DCI,' remarked Sunita as she entered a narrow hallway.

'Oh, Mr Roscoe. Yes. I used to work at the tearooms in Queensbridge. So, what's your name?'

'Sergeant Roy,' said Sunita.

'Well, you'll have to excuse the mess,' said Tessa. 'I've only just moved here. By the way, I hope you don't mind me asking. How did you find my address? I haven't told no one – not even my parents.'

As she led the sergeant into a dark, cluttered front room, Sunita explained, 'Your removal firm – Harrington and Sons – gave me the address.'

'That's clever of you,' she said.

Cabinets, tables and chairs were stacked on top of a green, three-seater leather sofa to the right of the door and also covered a matching armchair in the bay. A large mahogany table in the centre was covered in curtains, books and newspapers while bundles of clothes were spilling out of black refuse bags on the floor.

Sunita noticed a rolled carpet, a dog kennel, a TV, a guitar and a filing cabinet had all been crammed into the medium-sized room. There was just a space near the doorway where they could sit on a pair of dining chairs.

'Is there anywhere else in the house where we can chat?' Sunita asked, wary of holding a conversation in what was virtually a storage unit.

'I'm afraid not,' Tessa said. 'What it is… I've just moved in with my sister. I had a lot of me grandmother's furniture. We've got to start sorting things out.'

Sunita knew she'd have to make the best of it. She removed her black notebook from her pocket. 'We're trying to solve the mystery of what happened to Mr Bowers.'

'Strange business, innit?' Tessa said. 'He's just vanished off the face of the planet. Why d'you come to see me then?'

Sunita took out photocopies of the handwritten note found at Heathwood House and the front of the envelope that contained it. 'Do you recall this note?'

Tessa studied them both.

'I've never seen that before. But then I don't suppose it was intended for me,' she said. 'Let me look more carefully at the envelope. Yes, I remember. A note like that was on the doormat when I turned up at the house. As it was addressed to Margaret, I dropped it on the living room table for Mrs Bowers to see.'

Sunita looked into her blue eyes. 'Do you remember what day in January this was?'

'More than likely January the 9th.'

'How can you be so certain?'

'I remember because my brother Richard, who's a gravedigger, suddenly got took bad the day before and had to go home early from work in the middle of his job. It turned out it was flu.'

'Mrs Bowers says she dismissed you from your employment.'

Tessa looked as embarrassed as a maiden aunt at a lap-dancing club.

'No,' she said. 'I left of me own accord. This business with the note – it happened on one of the last days I worked for the Bowers. I'd been thinking of giving it up for some time. She was always telling me off. I was a little bit late a few times. I was off sick twice. So what? It wasn't my fault really. I just have a problem getting up in the morning and getting lifts to work. Other people are always letting me down. I was late for Mrs Roscoe a couple of times.'

'Oh I see,' said Sunita, recalling that the DCI had mentioned Tessa had proved unreliable.

'The Bowers were always like cat and dog,' she explained. 'They once had a full stand-up row in front of me. It wasn't a pleasant place to work and, to top it all, Mrs Bowers sometimes changed the times she wanted me to work.'

Sunita nodded her head, believing Tessa might open up if she acted sympathetically. 'Who started the rows?' she asked.

'Either of them could start. It would begin over something trivial like whether a household bill had been paid or whether the daughter should go for a riding lesson. Then it would just build up from there.'

'Was there ever any violence used?'

'Well, I never saw nothing, but the words they used sometimes implied violence. Do you know what I mean? There could've been violence when I wasn't around.'

'You never saw any black eyes or bruises on either of them?'

Tessa shook her head.

'What made you decide to move here with your sister?' Sunita asked.

The young woman thought for a moment, then said, 'I wasn't managing that big house on me own. It'd been me grandmother's council house and, when she passed on, I carried on living there. The council wanted me out because my name wasn't on the tenancy.

'It was all right while me boyfriend were living with me, but I split up from him and couldn't manage the bills. Sally let me move in. It's only for the time being – till I get to stand on me own two feet again.'

Sunita had been casting her eyes round during the conversation. She stood up and reached for a piece of paper that she'd noticed on top of the table. She asked, 'This your shopping list?'

'No. It's a note for the milkman I forgot to put out.'

Sunita sat back on her chair and read the note, which said, 'Dear Milkman, Pleese leeve two pints of semy-skimmt Wednesday and two Friday. Also an orange joose and six eggs on Friday. Tessa.'

Overlooking the atrocious spelling, Sunita realised this scrap of paper could assist them in eliminating Tessa as being the author of the note.

'Do you mind if I take this away?' she asked. 'We're collecting samples of handwriting from a number of people.'

'Be me guest. I don't need it now. It was for last week,' Tessa said.

Sunita stood up and grinned. 'Right, well, you've been very helpful, Tessa,' she said.

As she walked back to the car, she studied Tessa's handwriting under a streetlight and compared it to the writing on the Harry Bowers note.

'The writing's completely different,' she told herself. 'There's no way she could've written the message and I can't think of any reason why she would've. Still, I suppose it was important to rule her out.'

Sunita often listened to the car radio while travelling. But this evening, as she headed back to Hall Green, she chose not to turn it on. She was absorbed in thought. Tessa Griffiths' words kept drifting through her mind – about the rows at Heathwood House; the phrase 'got took bad'; and the girl's spelling mistakes. There was no doubt in her mind that Tessa Griffiths had not written the note found at Heathwood House. All the evidence seemed to point to Margaret Bowers having written it.

Chapter 21

That evening, after Sunita returned home from visiting Tessa Griffiths, she leaned over the first-floor banisters and called out to her flatmate.

'Rupa, have you been in my room?'

'No,' said her friend rather indignantly as she stepped into the hallway and gazed up. 'Why do you ask?'

'I always close the door behind me. It was open when I arrived home five minutes ago. I just wondered if you might've wandered in – you know, to check the radiator was on or something.'

'No, I haven't been upstairs since I came home. That's strange, isn't it? Can I ask you something? Did you leave the kitchen window open when you went to work, Sunita?'

'No. Why?'

'Come and have a look.'

Sunita quickly finished changing from her work clothes into a white kurti and blue jeans. Then she hurried down to join her friend, who was pointing at the window by the sink. It was wide open.

Sunita frowned and examined the frame. 'I didn't leave it like that and the edge of the wood looks damaged. Have we had a visit from Bill the Burglar?'

Rupa looked blank. 'I hope not.'

The pair went into the back garden and examined the window. Part of a muddy footprint could be seen on the ledge outside.

'I hope the landlord doesn't notice the damage to the frame and charge us,' moaned Rupa.

Both women rushed back in and began a thorough search of the house. But, after half an hour, nothing appeared to be missing.

Rupa looked her flatmate directly in the eyes. 'You don't think…?' she began.

'You mean, Arun?' said Sunita. 'He's the only person I can think of who might do something foolish like this. But if nothing's been taken...'

Rupa sat down at the kitchen table and stared at the window.

'Sunita, this situation is really starting to worry me.'

'If it *is* Arun that's behind this.'

'Who else could it be?'

'Maybe the landlord came round.'

'And left his footprint on the ledge, failed to shut the window and snooped in your room?'

'Well, I think we should give him a call – just in case he came round or sent someone round.'

'He always said he'd give us notice of any visit.'

'Maybe he forgot to let us know.'

'Sunita?'

'What?'

'You've got to face facts. Arun's been round, and you've got to sort this out or we may have to consider moving. Can't you have a word with your inspector friend?'

'Maybe I should.'

'You definitely should. Didn't you play him the recording of Arun saying he knows some "very heavy people" and he could make you disappear?'

'Yes, he's got a copy of what Arun said.'

'They ought to pay him another visit and lay things on the line. They should give him a harassment order.'

'Yes, you're right. I'll speak to the inspector tomorrow.'

* * *

When Gavin Roscoe arrived home that same Friday evening, rock music was blaring from his daughter's bedroom. He tore up the stairs and banged on her door.

'Mel, turn it down!' he yelled.

'Sorry, Dad!' she replied.

For a while, the sound levels were reduced.

'Don't be too hard on her,' said Helen, as she emerged from the kitchen with an apron round her waist and kissed him on the cheek. 'She's had a tiring week.'

'*She's* had a tiring week?' said Roscoe. 'How about the rest of us? You've been busy, haven't you?'

'Yes, dear. Actually, I was going to mention something to you. Let's go in the kitchen.'

Helen began peeling potatoes over a water-filled saucepan.

'Listen, we had a guy in for tea and sandwiches this afternoon called Mahmood. I thought he must be something to do with Harry Bowers because he had a credit card with the words "Heathwood Property Group" on it.'

Roscoe raised an eyebrow. 'Go on.'

'Well, he tried to pay with this card but it was rejected twice for some reason. In the end, he had to pay cash.'

'That's very interesting. Did you speak to him at all? You know, did you try and find out why he was in Queensbridge?'

Helen nodded. 'He just said he was visiting someone in the area.'

'He's probably been to see Margaret Bowers about the property company. Thanks for mentioning it.'

'There was also some excitement in Norton Prior today, according to some of the customers. Someone's dog unearthed some bones in Oxford Park. People were wondering if someone else had been done to death, but they turned out to be animal bones.'

Her husband nodded his head. 'Now you mention it, I remember reading something about that online.'

‘There are a lot of worried people in Norton at the moment. Every customer that comes from the village is talking about the Bowers family and the tramp. There are lots of rumours going round.’

‘I know you’re sensible enough to pay no attention to rumour.’

‘Yes, of course. Oh, while I think of it, Gavin, could you do me a favour? Can you spare me an hour at the shop on Monday morning? I’ve got that new sideboard arriving. I could do with a bit of muscle.’

‘Couldn’t your chef help you?’

‘We need a few guys. You know, if you’re not too busy.’

‘We’re always busy. You know what they say? Crime and tide wait for no man.’

‘It’s *time* and tide, as you well know. So can you help on Monday? Yes? I knew you wouldn’t let me down.’

* * *

An hour later, Roscoe was relaxing on their settee in the living room watching a news programme when Melody burst in, playing music on her MP3 player. On noticing her father, she quickly turned it off.

She gazed at him and smiled. ‘Dad, I wanted to ask you something. You know Valentine’s Day is coming up?’

He nodded.

‘Is there… is there any chance I could go to the Coach and Horses that night? Alex’s rock band is playing live.’

‘Is it a school night?’

‘Yes, it’s next Thursday night.’

The question had taken the detective by surprise. But he didn’t need to think long about it.

‘I’m afraid not,’ he said. ‘You know your mother and I think you should only go out at weekends until your exams are over.’

‘Please, Dad. Have I got no chance at all?’

'Put it like this. There's more chance of Ed Sheeran and the president of Russia cycling past the house in a sponsored race singing "Una Paloma Blanca" than you going to see a rock band on a school night – Valentine's or not.'

Chapter 22

Queensbridge was bustling with activity on Tuesday, 5 February as journalists and television crews arrived for the morning press conference at the police station. Without realising it, Gavin Roscoe had arranged the event on the town's market day.

Shoppers and tourists were vying for parking places in the high street with reporters and photographers from London and the Midlands. Liveried vans from the BBC and Sky were parked outside the building's entrance – some partly on pavements – an hour before the 10.30 a.m. briefing was due to begin.

The DCI had commandeered the station's incident room, which was around twelve metres long and five metres wide, and set up three trestle tables at one end. Six large posters headed 'Missing' and showing a head-and-shoulders photograph of Harry Bowers were displayed on the wall behind.

At the foot of each poster it read, 'Can you help? If you have any information regarding this man's whereabouts, please contact any of the telephone numbers below.' Phone numbers for Heart of England CID and the incident room at Queensbridge police station followed.

Roscoe had arranged chairs for up to thirty reporters and photographers in the centre of the room. Space had been set aside at the back for TV camera crews, who were among the first to arrive at a quarter to ten. Crews began setting up lighting equipment and installing microphones on the tables at the front.

At a quarter to eleven, the event finally got under way. The DCI, in a smart navy-blue suit, calmly walked in. He was followed immediately by sullen-faced Margaret Bowers, dressed soberly in a grey cardigan and blue dress. She took a seat near the windows, furthest from the door. She had the look of a woman who would rather be receiving root canal treatment at the dentist than basking in the media spotlight.

Roscoe ensured she was as comfortable as possible before taking the chair beside her. They were joined at the tables by Detective Inspector Andy Chadwick, who'd travelled from Stratford-upon-Avon; PC Underhill; and Sunita, who sat closest to the exit door.

'Well, good morning, ladies and gentlemen. I'm sorry we're a little bit late starting,' said Chadwick as he took his seat in the centre of the group. 'This, as you know, is a press briefing related to the disappearance of one of our local residents, Mr Bowers. Without further ado, I'll ask DCI Gavin Roscoe from Heart of England CID, who's heading the investigation, to say a few words. DCI.'

'Good morning,' Roscoe began as cameras flashed and the air was filled with the sound of camera shutters clicking. 'I called this briefing because four weeks have now passed since the disappearance of businessman Harry Bowers.

'We've had a lot of information from the public during this time, but unfortunately it hasn't led anywhere. Quite frankly, we need some publicity to help us either to find him or to find out what happened to him.

'Mr Bowers is a property developer whose business is based in south Birmingham and lives just a few miles from here in Norton Prior. He's got a wife and daughter who are frantically missing him and are desperate for news. We need to do all we can to reunite him with them.

'We've made inquiries with other forces, the Salvation Army, port and airport authorities and Interpol – all in vain. We've also carried out searches of woodlands, fields and waterways in Norton and surrounding areas to no avail. We've had dozens of phone calls of possible sightings, but nothing's come of those either.

'Now we're privileged to have Mrs Bowers here with us today. She's obviously been distressed about the disappearance but has, nonetheless, kindly agreed to come and answer a few questions. We know how you ladies and gentlemen of the press operate. You have your jobs to do, like everyone else.

'I'd just ask you to respect the fact that she's faced a lot of upset and upheaval in her life because of this disappearance and to treat her with your customary courtesy.'

Turning to her, he said, 'Perhaps you'd like to say a few words, Mrs Bowers?'

At this point, cameras flashed again towards ashen-faced Margaret, which added to the discomfort she was already experiencing at the prospect of having to discuss her husband.

'What do you want me to say?' she whispered to Roscoe.

'Just tell them you miss him terribly and we need information about what happened on 8 January,' he whispered back.

'OK,' she said, remaining seated but attempting to raise her voice. 'Well, as you know my husband came straight home from work on 8 January and, after having something to eat, he went to choir practice as he always does. He's not been home since. His family, particularly our daughter Rachel, miss him so much.'

Close to tears, she added, 'I just wish all this would end.'

As she came to a pause, Roscoe decided he had better continue speaking on her behalf.

'All we know for certain is that Mr Bowers arrived in Oxford Lane at around seven o'clock on the eighth,' said the DCI. 'But he failed to attend choir practice and he's not been seen from that moment.'

Sensing Margaret Bowers was unlikely to say more, Roscoe invited questions from the journalists.

Adam Bunyon, announcing himself as chief reporter at the *Queensbridge Gazette*, asked, 'Is there any reason why he might've disappeared? Were there any problems?'

Margaret looked towards Roscoe, who gestured towards her with both hands upturned that she might like to answer the question rather than him.

'No, there were no problems,' she said.

'Your husband left a note, didn't he?'

'That's right,' she agreed. 'The note said he'd gone away.'

The DCI glanced at Margaret and then said, 'We're not sure what was intended by the note. So don't concern yourselves with that for the moment. The fact is that he's missing and there's no evidence he ever left the village.'

Bunyon, in his thirties and wearing a crumpled brown suit, continued, 'I've heard your husband might've had financial worries.'

'No, nothing like that,' Margaret insisted.

Gazette reporter Susan Ellis-Jones, a tall, slim blonde, interrupted to ask Roscoe, 'Chief inspector, as time goes on, do police fear that some harm may have befallen Mr Bowers?'

'Yes,' said Roscoe. 'Obviously, we're hopeful of finding him alive – even after all this time. However, this is quite out of character for the man and we're becoming increasingly concerned for his welfare. Just to remind you all, he was wearing a white shirt, blue Levi jeans, a black coat and navy-blue trainers when he vanished.'

A voice near the back declared, 'John Singleton, Midlands Television. Mrs Bowers, we've heard rumours of a dispute with a farmer over some land and we understand one of your buildings burned down. Could that have anything to do with the disappearance?'

'There was a planning dispute which the farmer lost,' Margaret replied in a quiet voice that many found inaudible. 'And there was a fire. But I don't believe that's got anything to do with my husband going off.'

Tall, dark-haired Singleton continued, 'Can you tell us about his hobbies and pastimes. Did he play any sport?'

At this question, Margaret seemed to become distressed. She turned to Roscoe and, in a low voice, said, 'I think I've done enough here.'

With that, she stood up looking extremely upset, and said, 'Sorry, I've got to go!' and hurried out.

She was quickly followed by PC Underhill, who tried to offer some comforting words. Sunita pursued the pair. A hubbub of loud conversation filled the room.

Chadwick shouted, 'I'm sorry, ladies and gentlemen. It appears the challenge of facing a press conference has proved too much for Mrs Bowers and she's decided not to answer further questions. Now I understand our DCI's got a short announcement.'

Roscoe nodded. 'Yes, thank you, Andy,' he said as the noise abated. 'The police haven't released this information before, but as you're all assembled here now, this seems a fitting moment.

'As has been reported in the press, a man's body was discovered in the River Avon at Queensbridge Marina twelve days ago. It had been in the water for some time after travelling downstream. Our forensic people and the Home Office pathologist and his team have been working extremely hard ever since to try to identify this man.

'Unfortunately, we've so far failed to get a positive ID, but we're certain he's not Harry Bowers. Rather it appears he may have been a tramp or rough sleeper. We've not yet been able to find him through dental records either.

'I can reveal today for the first time this man was murdered.'

The room at once fell silent.

'He was drowned somewhere away from the river. Then his body was brought to the river and some form of weight attached by rope to his left leg. We believe this was done by someone in a feeble attempt to try to prevent the body reaching the surface and being discovered.'

Several of the excited journalists suddenly began firing questions at him. Were police linking this murder to the Bowers case? How long had the body been in the river? How far could the body have travelled down the river? Had other police forces with missing persons appeals been alerted? Had the man been subject to a violent attack before he died? Why hadn't police announced before that they were treating this as a murder case?

'Gentlemen, ladies!' Roscoe said. 'One at a time, please. Mr Bunyon?'

'Yes, sir,' said the chief reporter. 'I was asking whether police are linking this murder to the Bowers case?'

Roscoe sighed. 'I'm afraid I'll have to give a fairly standard police response to that one, Adam. We're keeping an open mind about any possible link with the disappearance of Bowers. We believe we could be dealing with a cunning individual who goes to extreme efforts to hide his crimes.

'Our team of trained officers have spent hundreds of hours probing every minute aspect of this case, and yet we've drawn a blank. This has proved an extremely challenging month. What we're hoping for now is some publicity so we can flush out this killer and resolve both cases.'

The DCI said they had trawled the river in search of any weighted object to which the body may have been attached at some stage but had so far failed to find anything significant.

'I should add that a twenty-thousand-pound reward is being offered for information that leads us to finding Harry Bowers.'

Afterwards, as the room began to empty, Susan Ellis-Jones approached the chief inspector.

'We were surprised at the way Mrs Bowers left so suddenly…'

Roscoe nodded. 'You people don't realise what an ordeal it can be for someone who's not used to dealing with the press. You know, to be suddenly confronted by people with cameras, lights and notebooks. It can be quite intimidating. She obviously found it too much.'

Chapter 23

The following morning, Gavin Roscoe was feeling rather pleased with himself as he drove towards his office. Tom Vickers had just arrested a second man over the Crows Wood post office raid and hundreds of calls had been flooding into the incident room as a result of the press conference.

After parking his car in his reserved space, he walked across the forecourt and climbed the headquarters steps with a little more vigour than usual. He greeted the reception desk constable with a cheery 'Good morning!' before taking the stairs to the CID room. However, he wasn't the only person in CID in a buoyant mood.

While he made his way up the stairs, Sunita Roy suddenly realised she had left her mobile phone in her car outside. In an excited frame of mind, she dashed across the main room towards the exit. She failed to see the DCI arriving and collided with him as he thrust open the double doors.

'Oh sorry, sir!' she said, battling to regain her composure.

'No harm done,' said Roscoe. 'Have you had a chance to speak to Michael Harrington?'

'Yes, sir. I had a long chat with him. I've produced a memo for you. His alibi for 8 January seems solid. He was at a Young Farmers' Club meeting.'

Roscoe stroked his chin. 'All right. Can you come to my office in half an hour? I need to talk to you.'

'Yes, sir.'

The room was the scene of vibrant activity, with detectives on the phones, scanning computer screens or chatting about crimes, except in one corner. DI Vickers was hunched over one of the desks and appeared to be asleep.

Roscoe frowned. 'Good morning, Tom.'

The slouched figure failed to stir.

'I said, "Good morning, Tom!"'

Gradually, faint signs of life began to emerge from the crumpled heap and the inspector raised his left hand – as if to signal he could recognise sounds, if nothing else. Slowly, he raised his head and, with a husky voice, mumbled, 'Good morning, guv.'

'You've not been here all night, have you?' Roscoe asked as he unlocked the door to his room.

'I'm sorry, guv,' said Vickers. 'I was manning the phones till two, so I decided to kip here. Hope you don't mind.'

Roscoe frowned. 'No harm's done. You'd better have a wash and tidy yourself up.'

He was just collecting his newspapers from the post room nearby when a flustered PC Dawson hurried towards him.

'Sir, there's a shopkeeper from Norton Prior on the phone. He's got some information about Harry Bowers and asked for you by name.'

Roscoe smiled. 'Well, done, Constable. I'll take the call in my room.'

Moments later, the chief inspector found himself listening to the croaky voice of newsagent Edward Bailey.

'Are you the detective in charge?' he asked.

'Yes, this is DCI Roscoe. How can I help?'

'Listen, there's been something on my mind since your sergeant came to see me in the shop a month ago. After I saw the appeal on Midlands TV last night, I decided to give you a call.'

The chief inspector leaned back in his chair. 'Very good of you, Mr Bailey.'

'Yes, that TV report pricked my conscience, you could say. I think you ought to know, Mr Roscoe, that there's been a lot of bad feeling between that Mr Bowers and a local resident called Hockley.'

'James Hockley?'

'I think that's the fellow's name. Look, it's not like me to speak behind the back of one of my customers, but when I saw that Mrs Bowers in tears on the TV, I just had to call you. You see, I've gradually got to know Mr Hockley. He's often in the shop, buying bottled water or picking up a copy of *Runner's World*. We're both into sport and fitness and, over time, he's told me one or two things about Harry Bowers.'

The chief inspector sat forward in his chair. 'What sort of things?'

'Well, that he mistreated his wife, tricked people into selling land to him cheaply – that sort of thing. It's not for me to say, but he had some deep grudges against Harry. He disliked the man intensely. I just thought you ought to know.'

Roscoe was glad Mr Bailey had phoned. His remarks supported the rector's disclosure of disagreement between the two choristers. He gazed out across the park where five children were clambering up a climbing frame. Another pair of children who'd reached the top of a slide were struggling with each other for the chance to slither down first.

'All right, Mr Bailey. Thank you very much for calling.'

'I should have told your lady sergeant, but the Hockley fellow's been a customer for a while. I don't like to speak bad of my customers. Do you see what I mean?'

'Definitely. Mr Bailey, if it's all right with you, I'll arrange for one of our team to come down later today and take a fresh statement from you.'

'Yes, that'll be fine, Mr Roscoe. Always happy to help the cops.'

Later that morning, the chief inspector found time to leaf through his pile of newspapers.

'Hunt for maniac in murder village', read a headline in one national daily, while another devoted a whole page to a report headed 'Police search for murder fiend'.

But worse was to come when he turned on his desk computer and browsed the online edition of the *Queensbridge Gazette*. Beneath the headline 'Queensbridge Marina man was murdered, say police' came a report alleging detectives were struggling to make progress with their investigation.

Then he glanced through a report from PC Dawson, informing him three hundred and eighty-three people had so far called the incident room, claiming to have information about Harry Bowers. Around three hundred claim to have seen him. He's been spotted in Scotland, Manchester, the Isle of Wight, the South of France and on the Spanish Costas. Bizarrely, he'd been seen working on a roof in Hertfordshire, serving drinks in a nightclub in Leeds and walking a dog in Norwich.

He left his seat and opened his door. He stood there for a moment watching as his staff toiled at their desks. He found it sad so many callers had been women searching for missing husbands or partners.

Roscoe sat at his desk, quietly contemplating. He knew it was only a small proportion of husbands or boyfriends that abandoned their families totally. But any relationship break-ups – even when the family continued to receive financial support and partial contact – left shattered lives behind.

Walking away from an unhappy relationship might solve one problem but it often created another.

His thoughts were interrupted by a knock on the door and Sunita Roy's smiling face appeared.

'Come in, Sergeant,' he said. 'Do you remember the shopkeeper you interviewed in Oxford Lane last month?'

'Mr Bailey?'

He nodded. 'Yes. Just had him on the phone. Called after seeing Mrs Bowers on the news. Claims Hockley had a grudge against Harry Bowers. Anyway, I'll tell you about it later. First of all, what happened with Mrs Bowers after the press conference?'

'A load of photographers were trying to take her picture,' said the sergeant as she made herself comfortable on a chair in front of his desk. 'She was in no mood to pose for them. She jumped into Derek Underhill's car and I slipped in the back with her. Then we drove off.'

'Did she say much on the way to Heathwood House?'

'No, sir.'

'How would you describe her mood?'

'Angry, sir.'

'Strange woman, don't you think? She's lost her husband and you'd think she'd want to help find him.'

She nodded.

'Great work on Tessa Griffiths as well, Sergeant. Meanwhile, can you book us a couple of train tickets to London for Friday morning? We had a call last night. Omar Khalid took it. It's a woman in London who claims she was a close friend of Harry Bowers' and she's got something important to tell us. She's very eager to speak to us.'

'I'll get two seats booked straight away, sir.'

She moved towards the door. Then she looked back.

'There's something I've been meaning to tell you, sir. When I visited Mr Hockley in Norton Hill, I spotted a fawn coat on his banisters. I'd obviously called round while he'd got female company. I realise now where I've seen the coat before. It belongs to Mrs Bowers. She was wearing it in the car yesterday.'

'Well spotted! That fits in with some information I've picked up about the possibility of those two having an affair.'

* * *

Two hours later, Roscoe received the call he'd been dreading. Chief Superintendent Norris wanted to see him. He strode through the CID room to the stairway and climbed the steps to the second floor.

Norris yelled, 'Come in, Gavin!' as the DCI knocked and entered. She glared at her visitor as Roscoe crossed the carpet. It was amazing she could inspire such concerns among her staff.

'Have you seen the headlines?' Norris demanded as she thumbed through the same newspapers Roscoe had been reading.

'I'm not very happy,' she admitted. 'The Queensbridge paper says police are struggling. It's not the publicity we want. You're quoted as saying "Our team of trained officers have spent hundreds of hours probing every minute aspect of this case, and yet we've drawn a blank. This has proved an extremely challenging time."'

Roscoe sighed and slumped down into a chair in front of his superior. 'That journalist's taken my words completely out of context,' he asserted. 'I began by saying we were keeping an open mind about any possible connection between the two cases. The press has put two and two together and are trying to turn this into a hunt for a serial killer, which isn't the case. We don't even know for certain Harry Bowers is dead.'

Norris tutted. 'I suppose we must expect this sort of thing from the press. There's something else I wanted to speak to you about, Gavin. We've had a complaint from a man named James Hockley. Does he have a connection with the Bowers case?'

'There was some ill-feeling between Hockley and Bowers around Christmas. I sent Sergeant Roy to see him.'

'He wasn't very happy at receiving a visit in his home. He claimed the sergeant was rather pushy.'

'We were only doing our job, ma'am. He's a person of interest.'

'Yes, I know. I think he knows some high-ranking members of the force and might try and cause trouble.'

Chapter 24

Sunita Roy was smiling broadly as Gavin Roscoe arrived to meet her at Stratford railway station just before nine o'clock on the morning of Friday, 8 February. Wearing a smart grey trouser suit and carrying a light-brown raincoat, she had agreed to meet him by the ticket office. Dark clouds hovered malevolently overhead.

Within a few minutes, she spotted the DCI with his neatly trimmed, short, black hair walking towards her in the distance. He was wearing a dark-blue suit with a yellow patterned tie and carrying an umbrella, which he waved as he approached.

'There was a light shower earlier,' he said with a smile. 'You can't be too careful!'

'Good day for a train journey, sir.'

'That's right! Let's hope the weather clears up by the time we reach London.'

Roscoe realised he just had time to visit the newspaper kiosk next to the station entrance before their train left. He bought two national newspapers from an attractive blonde woman in a khaki coat with a fur collar that he seemed to recognise. He decided he might have seen her while shopping in Queensbridge.

As they boarded the train nearly fifteen minutes later, Roscoe began to divulge some additional information about the woman they were going to see. Her name was Gillian McLeod. She lived in the King's Cross district of Central London. She was thirty-two, worked as a marketing manager for a major construction firm and lived in a third-floor flat in a mansion block.

She'd met Harry Bowers at a property exhibition in Munich three years earlier and they'd struck up a friendship. Eventually, they had become extremely close, and he'd visited her several times at her flat while on business in London.

She'd been made aware of his disappearance from the press publicity and was keen to help police find him. The detectives were due to visit her at midday.

The train was packed with passengers, but Sunita had managed to book them seats opposite each other in one of the middle carriages and they made themselves comfortable for the next two hours.

'How are you finding life with us now?' Roscoe asked as the train drew out.

'It's cool, sir,' Sunita replied as she took out her mobile phone.

'I think you're fitting in very well,' Roscoe said. 'You've been very helpful on this current case.'

She smiled. 'I just do my best.'

'Was your father in the force?'

'No, he was a lawyer for the first part of his life. Later he started a guesthouse business in Birmingham with my mother. She used to be a nurse.'

'I expect they're proud of you,' said Roscoe.

She smiled but was reluctant to speak more about them. She was embarrassed. She hadn't spoken to either of them for nine months and didn't know if she ever would again.

'My own dad worked his way up to superintendent,' Roscoe disclosed. 'There was never any other job I considered. I left school at seventeen, went to training school and, like you, started with West Mids.'

'Did your father look like you?'

'Yes, he did. He died last year unfortunately.'

'Oh, I'm sorry.'

'Yes. He was only sixty-five. It was a bit of a shock.'

'Is your mother still with us?'

'Sadly not. She passed away a few years before him.'

'So sorry.'

Their journey passed along the tree-lined rail route that runs through the towns of Leamington Spa and High Wycombe. Roscoe caught up with the day's news in his newspaper, while Sunita responded to some friends' posts on Facebook.

A few minutes later, Sunita looked up. 'I don't know if Brett Dawson's mentioned it, sir, but we've now spoken to every choir member except one.'

'And who's that?'

'It's a retired teacher, a Mrs Thomas.'

'Stick with it,' said Roscoe as he leaned back in his seat. 'We need to cover everything.'

At High Wycombe, some of the passengers sitting near them left the train. Roscoe then felt more at ease discussing police matters with her.

'Sunita, could you do me a favour? Could you go through with me again what you learned on your first visit to Norton Prior – including what Mrs Bowers told you?'

Over the next fifteen minutes, Sunita recalled in a low voice as much as she could of her visit to Heathwood House and Oxford Lane on 17 January. Roscoe listened intently and jotted down details in a notebook.

Then, as the train reached Ruislip, the green pastures and rolling hills gave way to the endless residential streets that are typical of the London suburbs. Thereafter, the train carried them through a section of dark tunnels and past high-rise flats, which heralded their arrival in the capital.

The rain had stopped and the sun was shining as the pair descended from the train at Marylebone station. They hailed a taxi for the two-mile journey to the busy, tree-lined street near King's Cross where Gillian lived. The driver stopped directly outside the address.

The impressive Victorian building was stucco-fronted with ornate cornicing, but it was built mainly from red brick. Like many structures in Central London, the design of its facade had been inspired by the classical architects of Greece and Rome.

The pair headed towards the wide entrance, which had a stone pillar on either side, and were directed to the lifts by a uniformed concierge sitting behind a desk who looked as pompous as a doorman at the Savoy. They made their way to the third floor flat, where Roscoe pressed the doorbell.

An elegant woman with dark hair and blue eyes came to the door and invited them in. Gillian McLeod was an attractive, well-educated, rather buxom woman with a welcoming smile and an easy manner. Roscoe produced his warrant card.

'DCI Roscoe, Heart of England CID,' he said.

'Pleased to meet you.'

'And this is Sergeant Roy.'

She beamed at them both. Roscoe shook her outstretched hand.

'Won't you come in?' she said.

They found themselves in a large, light and spacious room with high ceilings and a white period fireplace on the left. The flat had a solid oak floor, large sash windows with fawn curtains and contained a gold-coloured three-piece suite. A large landscape painting of an English cavalier on a horse had a commanding presence above the fireplace.

'Won't you sit down?' Gillian asked.

'We should apologise,' Roscoe remarked. 'We're about twenty minutes early.'

'That's no problem at all,' she replied. 'I'm eager to do all I can to help.'

Roscoe and Sunita sat together on Gillian's three-seater settee as their hostess remained standing. Roscoe smiled up at her. She somehow reminded him of a psychotherapy patient desperate to unburden herself of her troubles.

'Can we ask how you got to meet Harry Bowers?'

Gillian looked towards the windows. Sunlight was streaming in.

'I was at a trade fair in Germany,' she recalled. 'He was passing our stand and we started talking. We were both interested in new trends in the construction business and we must have chatted for half an hour. Eventually, I had to speak to a potential customer and he wandered away. Later he returned and invited me to come for a light meal at a nearby restaurant. We found we'd a lot in common. We both came from the Midlands. We both studied accountancy at university and we both had fathers in banking.'

'You eventually embarked on a relationship with him?' Roscoe asked.

'Yes,' she said with an embarrassed look. 'He didn't tell me he was married to start with. Then he eventually admitted he was. Of course, I felt bad to begin with – knowing he was married. But it became clear to me it had become a very unhappy marriage. They were arguing all the time. I gather his wife was a difficult woman. He came down to London whenever he could to see me. He could be a very kind, considerate man. He took me out for meals, to the cinema and to the theatre. He told me he suspected his wife was seeing another man. It was a bit of an open marriage.'

Roscoe nodded. 'You read in the press about his disappearance?'

Gillian lost her composure a little.

'Yes. I was shocked when I saw his photograph and the headline about his wife appealing for information,' she said. 'I called the police immediately to see if there was anything I could do to help.'

Roscoe asked whether she had any idea what could've happened to him.

'No,' said Gillian, who was standing next to a brown Victorian antique table. 'He had no enemies, as far as I knew.'

'Were there any people he spoke about or places he longed to visit?' Sunita asked.

'He said he'd always wanted to visit Italy,' she said. 'But he only mentioned that a couple of times during our three years together.' She looked down at the table and picked up some photographs. 'I don't know if these'll help. They're photographs of me and Harry, and Harry on his own. Do you need to take any of them?'

Roscoe nodded again. 'Perhaps we can have a look at those in a moment. Can I ask... when did you last see Harry?'

'It must have been last October,' said Gillian.

'So you've not seen him for over three months?' said Roscoe.

'That's right,' she said.

Gillian had gradually been turning away from them and looking towards the painting above the fireplace. A few seconds later, she turned towards them again and the two visitors could see there were tears in her eyes.

'We had an argument,' she said. 'We'd decided to have a break from each other.'

'What brought that about?' Sunita asked. 'You'd been so close.'

'Yes, I know,' Gillian said. 'The thing is... I found a love letter from another woman.'

Roscoe realised their conversation had taken its toll upon her. He stood up and urged her to take a seat on the settee. She wiped away her tears with a handkerchief and sat down while Roscoe remained on his feet.

As she looked up at him, Roscoe asked, 'Are you all right?'

'Yes,' she said. 'Talking about it has brought it all back. A letter slipped out of his pocket. It must've meant something to him – for him to have carried it round with him.'

'Have you still got it?' asked Roscoe.

'Yes,' she said. 'It's on the table with the photographs.'

'May I?' Roscoe asked.

She nodded and he walked over to the table.

The unsigned letter had been written on paper torn from a writing pad. It appeared to have been written in haste and some of the words were unintelligible. After a few moments spent studying it, Roscoe managed to decipher the illegible words. He read it out loud to the two women.

> *My Darling, How wonderful to see you again and spend time with you. Thank you for your charming gift which I shall treasure forever. I watched you with love from afar for so long. I'm so happy that you feel the same way about me. Sincerely hope it's not long before we meet again. Sorry this is so brief, but I wanted to say how much I love you. Every moment with you is cherished. Loved you on day we met in Stratford. Have loved you madly since year dot.*

A cross, representing a kiss, had been squeezed in after the word 'dot'. But the writer had only just managed to squash the words in on the last line before reaching the paper's ragged edge.

Roscoe turned to Gillian, who had by now become embarrassed as well as distressed.

'You must've been extremely upset to find he was carrying on with another woman,' the detective remarked.

'I was devastated,' she said. 'It just fell out of his pocket onto the floor next to where I was standing. I'm not sure he even realised to start with. I picked it up and straight away read "My Darling" and although he'd written in a similar vein to me in the past, I didn't recognise the handwriting and knew immediately I wasn't the "Darling" on this occasion. For one thing, I've never been to Stratford.

'You can imagine how I felt. I was apoplectic. He tried to invent an excuse, but his little secret was out. We had a furious row and he caught the train back to the Midlands shortly afterwards. Over time, I tried to forgive him, but I knew deep inside it was over. He phoned me a few times, but I let his calls go to voicemail. I couldn't face talking to him.'

'You're over it now?' Sunita asked, sounding sympathetic.

'I don't know if I'll ever get over it,' Gillian said. 'I loved him very much. Perhaps I was foolish to get involved with a married man who, if the press are right, was something of a philanderer. But to begin with I didn't know what he was like and I just got more and more involved.'

Roscoe smiled at her. 'Well, it was very good of you to contact the police anyway.'

'I felt I had to do something,' she said. 'I wouldn't like to think any harm's befallen him.'

Roscoe glanced towards Sunita. 'Do you think we should make a move?'

She nodded.

Turning back to Gillian, he asked, 'We'll need to take this letter with us.' He carefully placed it in his jacket's inside pocket.

Gillian nodded as she stood up. 'Of course. I don't need the wretched thing. I don't know why I kept it. He'd demanded it back, but I was so angry at the time I locked it away and refused to return it to him. Now you're welcome to take it.'

Roscoe patted her on the arm consolingly. 'Thank you. I think we'll leave the photographs for the moment. Mrs Bowers gave us several.'

'That's up to you,' she said. 'If you need them, you know where they are.' She paused and then added, 'Mr Roscoe, do you think you're making headway?'

'Yes, I think we're making a little progress. But I don't want to give you any false hope that Harry Bowers will be found alive. I'm afraid it's looking increasingly likely that he's been murdered.'

Chapter 25

After bidding Gavin Roscoe goodbye at Stratford station on their return from London, Sunita waited for ten minutes and then, just before half past four, caught a train back to Hall Green. She was looking forward to a hot meal and then watching television. If she felt up to it, she decided she might visit the Shree Krishna Mandir in Leamington Spa, a Hindu religious centre, over the coming weekend.

During the forty-minute journey from the Warwickshire town, she phoned Rupa, who worked as a teacher at a nearby school and normally arrived home before her.

'I should be back at a quarter past five,' she told her friend.

Light was fading as Sunita arrived at Hall Green station. She walked up the short approach lane that led to the busy Stratford Road. Three children were playing by a bus stop, stamping in puddles that had formed after the rain. It brought back memories of how she used to play in puddles as a child with her sister Tulika and cousin Daniel.

As cars and lorries thundered by, she turned right, took a few steps along the main road and then turned right again at the tyre depot. She was tired after her long day visiting the capital.

As soon as she began the long walk along Cateswell Road, she was plunged into darkness. Her only guide was the orange glow from the lamp posts and the occasional shafts of light from the semi-detached houses.

For no apparent reason, she felt uneasy. She glanced back, but all she saw were shadows formed by trees swaying in the streetlights. A man in a hooded jacket shuffled towards her along the pavement, his face as pale as the winter sky. A young woman with long blonde hair also scurried past, her unbuttoned dark coat swaying from side to side in the cold night breeze.

Then she was disturbed by a noise behind her. Someone's footsteps perhaps? Or the sound of her own shoes, clattering on the pavement?

Then she heard the sound again. This time there was no mistake – footsteps close behind. She glanced round. A short man with tousled black hair was running towards her. He held something in his hand. It was Arun.

'The time for games is over, Sunita,' he said. 'You must do exactly as I say.'

Sunita glanced down in fear. He was holding a small Beretta pistol.

'Arun, you're making a big mistake. Go home to your wife. There's no future with me. Hand me the gun!'

'No, you're coming with me and, if you don't, I won't hesitate to use this.'

She then opted for a gentler approach in an effort to defuse the situation.

'Look, Arun, let's not get too hasty,' said Sunita, who was only a few metres away from the safety of her home. 'Maybe we can sort this out. Maybe we can have a chat in the house.'

But this failed to placate him. She realised he was in earnest.

'It's too late for that, Sunita. I've been making plans.'

He marched her to his Ford Fiesta which was parked close to her house, unlocked it with the remote and ordered her to climb in.

'Help me! Please help me!' she screamed at the top of her voice as he pressed the nozzle into her back.

'Shut up, you bitch!' he hissed as curtains twitched in a nearby house. 'Get in! I said, get in!'

She did as he instructed and he then slammed and locked the door.

'Where are you taking me?' she demanded as he walked round to the driver's door and got in.

He ignored her question. He looked around apprehensively in case anyone had heard Sunita's cries. But no one rushed out. Whoever heard the screams no doubt blamed the noise on juvenile horseplay.

Arun placed his gun in the map pocket of his car door and drove off.

She found they were travelling in a north-easterly direction towards Yardley.

The journey continued until they reached Tyseley railway station, Sunita realised they were heading towards the A45 Coventry Road.

Traffic was running smoothly, but these were always busy urban streets. She expected they would meet snarl-ups ahead as they approached South Yardley and thought she might have a chance to jump out if Arun was forced to stop at traffic lights.

Her phone rang. Rupa's face appeared on the screen.

'Don't answer that!' Arun snarled.

'It's my flatmate. She'll expect me to pick up.'

'Leave it!'

The phone rang out for more than fifteen seconds. Finally it went to voicemail. He snatched the phone from her hand.

'I should've taken care of that earlier,' he said, opening his window and throwing the handset out into the street.

'I was due home more than ten minutes ago,' Sunita informed him. 'She's under strict instructions to call the police.'

It was a lie which she felt Arun might believe, but she noticed no change in his countenance as he drove on.

She had to escape – no matter what. Arun must have had some kind of mental breakdown, she surmised. She had no idea where he planned to take her or what he planned to do. But she was determined not to be around long enough to find out.

As they passed through the bustling streets of south-east Birmingham, she kept looking for traffic lights ahead. In her personal experience, they always turned red as her car reached them. Now she longed with every fibre in her body for them to do just that so she might have a chance to escape – but they were defying her. Every set was showing green and Arun sailed through.

After they turned right into Coventry Road, Sunita began seeing signs for Birmingham Airport. The road was wider now. Ash, beech and oak trees rose up on both sides of the highway. Suddenly she felt as though someone had switched on a light, illuminating the deepest recesses of her mind.

'Arun, are you taking me to the airport?'

Still he refused to answer.

'Where are we going? Are you taking me to your relatives in India?'

Silence.

'How can you take me? I haven't got my passport.'

At last, he spoke. 'I've got your passport, Sunita,' he said. 'We're going to India to begin a new life together. We'll be married, have children and do all the things other people do.'

She glanced at him. 'No, Arun,' she said softly.

'Sunita, we used to have such happy times together and the happy times will come back. I made a mistake when I married Rani. I thought I could maybe recreate with Rani what I had once with you. But I was wrong. It was you I wanted all along. I thought I could get over you, but I can't. I can't stop thinking about you. People make mistakes. It happens in life. We have to realise our mistakes and move on. I made a mistake with Rani. You made a mistake when you told me you didn't want to see me anymore.'

The gravity of the situation was gradually becoming clear to her. It was Arun who had broken into their house. She and Rupa had initially been of the opinion that nothing had been stolen, but they must've been mistaken. He must've found her passport in one of her bedroom drawers. Now he was going to try to use it to spirit her out of the country. And through the same airport she had travelled into just three weeks earlier.

'Arun, the police know your car number,' she pointed out. 'My friend will have called them by now. Maybe one of our neighbours heard my shouts. We'll be picked up on the traffic monitoring cameras. They'll be onto you before you know it.'

'We'll be on the plane before they're out of the station yard,' said Arun with an impish smile.

'Arun, why have you got a gun? You never used to have a gun.'

'It's my insurance, Sunita.'

'Your insurance?'

'Yes, it's to make sure you comply with my wishes. Since you joined the police, you've become very handy with the unarmed combat they've taught you. It's to make sure you toe the line.'

Several minutes passed. They were nearing the airport. Arun turned down a slip-road and passed two roundabouts before entering the airport approach road. He stopped at the yellow barrier and reached across to take a ticket.

Sunita considered jumping out and running away but maybe not yet. She needed to choose the right moment.

From the distance, she thought she could detect the sound of a siren. Perhaps Tom Vickers had been alerted or Nigel Martin. Perhaps they were on their way to rescue her.

Her captor was driving towards an NCP multi-storey car park where the charges were more than eleven pounds for a two-hour stay. Then another thought crept into her head. He wasn't going to pay it because he wasn't going to be coming back. He was dumping the car, so it didn't matter how high the parking charges were.

Arun found a space on the ground floor and cut the engine. He groped around for his pistol and, as soon as he had retrieved it, stepped out of the car.

'Come on. Let's go,' he ordered as he came round to unlock her door and pointed the gun at her.

Hesitantly, she climbed out and shut the door. Then she walked to the rear of the vehicle. Arun was collecting some luggage from the back seat.

'I'm afraid this is as far as I'm going with you,' she told him. He dropped his two cases on the ground as she approached him.

'How do you mean?' he asked, aiming the gun at her.

Sunita ducked her head to the left as she bravely grabbed the barrel of the gun with her left hand. Then, remembering the words of her self-defence instructor, she immediately chopped his wrist with her right hand and wrapped that hand round the gun's handle.

'Let go! Let go!' he yelled.

With both hands clutching the gun, she wrenched it out of his grasp and then trained it upon him.

He glared at her. 'You bloody little fool!' he shouted.

As he stepped towards her, she kicked him hard in the groin. He fell back, clutching his crotch and screaming. The situation had changed in an instant. Sunita was now calling the shots.

She was vaguely becoming aware of two vehicles behind her making their way towards them with lights flashing. She was also aware that Arun's shouting had attracted a small audience of vehicle owners who had no doubt seen the gun and were watching events from a safe distance.

As her anguished ex-boyfriend writhed in pain, Sunita glanced at the gun she was holding and laughed.

'The safety catch is on, you idiot,' she said.

'I know. I never really wanted to hurt you,' he insisted as he began to recover from the agonising blow. He heard a click.

'It's off now,' she announced.

Then a male voice behind them in a familiar Black Country accent broke in.

'Doesn't look like we're needed after all!' the man said.

Sunita glanced round to find the smiling face of Tom Vickers in his crumpled shirt and trousers. She was so delighted to see him that she wanted to hug him, although she knew that was ruled out by police etiquette.

'You've done a bostin' job here, Sarge,' he said. 'Now you'd better let us take over.'

Chapter 26

Gavin Roscoe had a host of important matters on his mind as he set off for work early on Monday, 11 February. It was a bitterly cold morning and, after parking in his allocated space outside the headquarters building, he sprinted up the steps and through the entrance doors.

He had heard at the weekend that the sub-postmistress who tackled two robbers at Crows Wood had died as a result of her injury. So the two men Tom Vickers had arrested now faced a murder charge.

They seemed no closer to finding Harry Bowers and, to add to their burden, his sergeant had been abducted at gunpoint. He had spoken to her over the weekend. She hadn't needed to go to hospital and seemed fine after her ordeal, but he remained concerned about her.

As soon as Sunita and Tom Vickers arrived, he called them both into his office.

'All right, Sunita?' Vickers asked her as the pair drew up chairs in front of the DCI's desk.

'Yes, Tom. I've got over it now.'

'Good. Got a new phone yet?'

'It's being delivered tomorrow.'

Roscoe interrupted. 'I was very sorry to hear what happened. Do you need any time off?'

'No, I'd rather carry on working, if that's all right, sir. It'll help take my mind off what happened.'

'That's the idea. Good. Tom, what's happened to the young man involved, Arun Halder?'

'He appeared in court this morning, guv, charged with abduction. I just came back ten minutes ago. He's been remanded in custody.'

'He's looking at a long stretch,' remarked Roscoe.

'Definitely. I haven't mentioned this before, Sunita, but his brother appeared in the dock with him. We caught him at the airport later on Friday evening.'

'Ashok?' asked Sunita.

'Yes, Ashok Halder. He was at the airport to assist his brother with your abduction and he's been charged as an accessory. We believe the pair would've ditched the gun before going through departures and the brother had drugs on him, which they would've used to subdue you.'

Roscoe shook his head. 'A delightful pair. Hope they throw the book at them.'

'I feel so sorry for Halder's wife,' murmured Sunita. 'This must've come as a huge shock to her.'

'Well, thank you for bringing us up to date, Tom,' said Roscoe. 'So now you're off to see our robbery suspects?' He glanced down at some written notes. 'Messrs Dennis Bachelor and Joseph Donaghue?'

'That's right, guv,' said Vickers as he stood and moved towards the door. Turning to Sunita and tapping her arm, he said, 'If there's anything else you want to discuss, you know where I am.'

'Yes, Tom,' she said. 'Thank you very much for all you've done.'

After the inspector had returned to his own office, Roscoe began discussing the visit to London to see Gillian McLeod. But seconds later his mobile phone rang. It was Helen.

'Could you bear with me a moment, Sunita?' he asked as he moved his chair back towards the window.

'Yes, dear?' he said, after pressing the answer key.

'Gavin, have you forgotten something?' his wife asked.

'Sorry, dear. I don't think so. Why? I've been very tied up this morning. One of our sergeants–'

Helen promptly ended the call.

'I sometimes think I'm married to a strange woman, Sunita. Now, where were we?'

* * *

When Roscoe returned home that evening, he could hear the dishwasher sloshing and gurgling like a geyser about to erupt. He wondered later if he should have recognised this as a sign of trouble ahead.

As he walked into the living room, George rose from the settee and said in a low voice, 'Mum's in a foul mood,' and then brushed past.

Roscoe looked confused. 'Do you know why?'

'Something about a sideboard,' whispered George as he disappeared upstairs.

Suddenly Roscoe remembered. He'd promised Helen he would help her shift some furniture earlier that morning.

He found Helen putting some plates away in the kitchen. The atmosphere was frostier than a Siberian winter.

'Helen, is everything all right?' he asked.

'Of course.'

'I haven't upset you in any way, have I?'

'No,'

'It's just that George mentioned you'd seemed upset.'

'No.'

All the signs were there that he'd annoyed her – the tone of her voice, the staccato replies, the refusal to make eye contact. He'd seen his wife react in this way several times before. She was the kind of woman who allowed her resentment to build up slowly like a simmering cauldron. Eventually, her angry feelings would explode.

'Well, if there's nothing I can do to help…'

'You've got a nerve,' she said out of the blue.

'How do you mean?'

'You promised faithfully you'd help me at the tearooms first thing. I had to ask the guy next door to lend a hand instead. Then I had a party of tourists. The children and I have been rushing round like cats with their tails on fire.'

Her husband shrugged. 'I'm sorry, dear. I've been worried about our new sergeant. As I told you over the weekend, she was kidnapped at gunpoint on Friday night.'

'Well, I'm sorry but your family are important as well.'

She slammed a cupboard door and stormed off upstairs. Five minutes later, she burst into the kitchen again.

'Mel is annoyed as well,' she revealed. 'She's been moaning because you barred her from a Valentine's Day party.'

Roscoe looked apologetic. 'I'm sorry. Perhaps it was rather a snap decision. Look, Helen, I'll make it up to you and Mel.'

He recognised that he needed to build bridges with his family. After mulling the situation over, he walked upstairs and found Melody doing some homework in her first-floor bedroom.

'Mel,' he said. 'I've been thinking about the party night at the Coach and Horses. Are you still interested in going?'

'Oh, Dad. I'd so like to go,' she said.

He smiled. 'OK. Perhaps I was a bit hasty before. You can go this time.'

'Thanks so much, Dad. Alex is their tour manager. It's one of their first gigs. They've been finding it hard to get bookings and I so want to be there.'

Chapter 27

The sun streamed past the curtains into Bethan Thomas's bedroom. Its rays flickered and danced across her uneven oak floor. Its patterns disturbed her sleep. Then came the faraway sound of birdsong, followed by the much closer noise of a lorry thundering along the road outside.

Mrs Thomas, a grandmother of three and a widow, was for a moment unsure exactly where she was. Was she still in her friend's four-bedroom chalet just to the north of Verbier in Switzerland? As her head remained on the pillow, she thought for a moment. Or was she back home at her cottage in Norton Prior?

She raised her head above the sheets. She could see her two large, unopened suitcases at the far end of the room and her skis propped up against her pine wardrobe. She remembered. Without doubt, she was in Norton Prior after arriving back at Birmingham Airport the night before.

Mrs Thomas, a sixty-two-year-old newly retired teacher, had been away for just over a month, skiing with a group of friends. It had been a once-in-a-lifetime opportunity to hone her skills on the piste. Now she couldn't wait to be reconciled with her partner, the sixty-four-year-old owner of Queensbridge Marina, Tyler Brown.

She was also eager to hear all the gossip about her friends in Norton and Queensbridge that had been circulating since she'd gone away.

Mrs Thomas, originally from South Wales, had taught domestic science and home economics in a school before retiring. She now spent her time cooking, gardening, playing bridge with friends and singing in the church choir.

She was a slim, dark-haired woman who was about five feet eight inches tall. She'd been renowned for attractive looks in her younger days but was now relying more and more heavily on cosmetics to maintain them. She lived in the last house in Oxford Lane – a detached, eighteenth-century oak-beamed cottage abutting fields and woods.

Mrs Thomas had a large sitting room with an inglenook fireplace, which had been created from having two rooms converted into one. The cottage had three bedrooms. She didn't need the space, but it was convenient whenever her daughter and grandchildren came to stay. She also had a newly fitted kitchen where she liked to produce her own puddings, pastries and jams.

French doors led from her living room into her large garden, which contained a pond, a shed and a wood store. For her three grandchildren, she'd had a swing, slide and sandpit installed. She and her partner liked to sit out on the brick patio on summer evenings, drinking wine and gazing across the meadows.

It was a Friday. As Mrs Thomas rose from her bed and got dressed in a white top, green cardigan and green skirt, she remembered the *Queensbridge Gazette* would have been published the day before with all the latest news and gossip. She'd just walk down the lane to the shop and buy a copy so she could catch up on events.

She felt she'd benefitted greatly from her holiday. Tyler Brown, who had his own house in Queensbridge but often stayed with her at the cottage, had at first been annoyed when she mentioned she'd been invited on the group holiday to the Swiss resort.

He'd been unable to accompany her for business reasons and he'd been brusque with her for several days. But, with time, his attitude had mellowed. Their relationship had survived and she was looking forward to seeing him again later in the day.

After a breakfast of muesli and black coffee, she put on her brown coat. Then, as the time on the kitchen clock approached nine o'clock, she left through the front door, stepped down the path past her rose bushes, and set off on the half-a-mile walk to the other end of the lane.

The primroses will soon be out, she thought to herself. After fifteen minutes, she arrived at the newsagents, Norton News, opposite the church. Although there were two people serving – the shopkeeper, Edward Bailey, and a teenage girl she'd not seen before – there were five other customers before her. They'd called in to buy milk, stationery and greetings cards. She had to wait a few minutes to be served. When she finally reached the counter, Mr Bailey greeted her warmly.

'I hear you've been skiing, Bethan,' said the shopkeeper.

'Yes, just got back,' she said. 'Very cold, but a lot of fun. Just the local paper, please, Edward.'

As he lifted a copy of the *Queensbridge Gazette* from the counter in front of her, she asked about his wife.

'Dorothy's fine. Moaning about the weather, like all of us!' he said, watching her more closely than a dog watching his food bowl.

She paid eighty pence and began reading the main headline. It said, 'Public assist police over body in Avon'. The report revealed that the police had received several calls from the public following a press conference.

She stepped outside the shop and nearly bumped into David Harrington, who was in his normal garb of a green pullover and mud-splattered trousers. He'd parked his shabby green Land Rover across the road, next to a small blue car, and had called at the shop to buy cigarettes. He greeted her with a cheerful 'Morning, Bethan!'

'Hi, David,' she said. 'I've only been away for a short time and the world seems to have gone mad.'

'Yes,' he said. 'First Harry Bowers. Then the man in the river.'

'Harry? What's happened to him?'

'Oh, it's been all over the papers. He's gone missing. His bank account's not been touched,' Mr Harrington replied.

Mrs Thomas was shocked into silence as if a plane had just crashed into her house.

At that moment, a familiar figure, neatly dressed in his black clerical shirt, white dog collar and grey trousers, emerged from the rectory. Revd Peter Hughes crossed the road and walked smartly towards them.

'Good morning, Bethan! Good morning, David!' he called before going through the shop's open doorway. He reappeared on the pavement seconds later clutching some milk and joined the gathering.

'Good holiday, Bethan?' he asked.

'Yes, thanks, Peter. It was.'

'You've been away a long time.'

'Yes, I'm very lucky. A friend of mine owns a chalet in Switzerland.'

'Sounds lovely.'

'Had a terrific time. There was a group of us, you know. My friend has invited us all back next year as well.'

She paused to gather breath. 'But I seem to have missed all the drama. What's all this about Harry?'

Revd Hughes looked solemn. 'He's not been seen since the first choir practice of the year. He failed to show up at the hall that night and no one's seen him since.'

'Well, that's strange because I saw him that night,' she said. 'January the 8th, wasn't it?'

'What do you mean, you saw him?' Mr Harrington asked.

'I saw him near the lychgate with James Hockley,' she said. 'I was late for the choir. They were having a fierce argument. James was wagging his finger and shaking his fist. And when I spoke to him in the hall later, he said Harry must've gone home.'

'What time did you see them arguing?' the rector asked.

'Well, Gerry likes to start prompt at quarter past seven, as you know, and I was rushing because it was just after that.'

Revd Hughes frowned. 'I think you'd better speak to the police about what you saw. I've got a phone number for their DCI Roscoe. He's the detective in charge of the case. Are you going home now?'

She nodded. 'I'm going straight back to the cottage.'

'I'll call you in a minute with his direct line phone number,' the rector said. 'I think he'd be interested in speaking to you.'

'That's not all I saw, either. There was somebody lingering in the shadows,' she said mysteriously. 'They were holding something. It could've been the handlebars of a bicycle. Maybe I need to tell them about that as well.'

After Mrs Thomas set off home with her newspaper, Revd Hughes returned to the rectory, where he searched for his address book. Why was nothing in the place where one expected to find it? Eventually he discovered the book beneath a pile of his past sermons. He tried to call Mrs Thomas's landline at the cottage to give her Gavin Roscoe's direct number at St James Street police headquarters. But, although she'd told him she was going straight home, there was no reply to her phone.

That's strange, he thought to himself. Maybe she's called in to see someone on the way back. Or maybe she's gone to report directly to the police station in Queensbridge. Anyway, I'll try her again a little later.

* * *

Contrary to what the rector thought, Bethan Thomas had gone straight home. She spent a few minutes gazing through the French doors, watching a robin feeding on her garden bird-table. Then she put her coat and handbag down on an armchair by the doors and went to the kitchen to make herself a cup of tea.

Since talking to the rector, she'd felt a sense of unease. She may have witnessed the final moments in the life of her fellow chorister. She must inform the police as soon as she received the promised phone number, she decided.

But as she waited for the kettle to boil, she heard a knock on the door. Wondering if a neighbour or a friend was calling on her, she went to open it. She was surprised when she saw the face of the unexpected visitor, smartly dressed in a brown jacket and blue trousers. For some reason, his unplanned presence flashed a memory into her mind of the night she saw Harry just before choir practice.

'Oh, Bethan,' the visitor said. 'I need to ask you a favour. Could I come in?'

She hesitated. The caller was not part of her social circle. Why was he there? There had to be some simple explanation.

'Well, I've only just come back and I haven't unpacked yet,' she said.

'I only want a quick word, my dear,' the visitor said imploringly.

'All right, come in,' she said. 'I thought you'd be busy today.'

The visitor followed as she led them from the hall into the sitting room. For a brief moment, her eye caught a glimpse through the far window of a robin on her bird table. She wondered if it was the same bird she'd observed before.

Suddenly, in the fleeting moments in which her back was turned, she caught sight of a cord or rope in front of her face.

She felt it being pulled tightly round her neck with brutal force until she was gasping for air. She felt the visitor's breath upon her neck as her fingers struggled to remove the ligature.

Bethan wanted to ask him why he was doing this to her. But she was unable to speak. For several seconds, she reached behind, scratching desperately at the attacker's face. But eventually she fell unconscious in front of the French doors.

Chapter 28

Tyler Brown walked up the path between the rose bushes and used the key he'd been given to open the cottage door. It was just after six o'clock and village residents were returning home from their working day.

He had left the Queensbridge Marina as early as he could as he was eager to see his partner, Bethan Thomas, again and hear about her holiday. But he'd been slightly delayed by rush-hour traffic leaving the town. He was carrying a box of chocolates for Bethan Thomas – a late Valentine's gift.

But, as he entered the hall, he immediately became concerned. There were no lights on, although it had been growing dark for a short while. Was she upstairs? Was she still in bed after her flight back from Geneva?

He switched the hallway light on and entered the living room. There was no one there. He was puzzled as to where she could be. He stepped into the new kitchen with its maple-coloured units and granite worktops. She was not there either.

Nor was she in any of the three bedrooms upstairs. He even checked the bathroom and, after unlocking the back door, took a stroll round the garden to see if he could see her or find any clue as to her absence.

The marina owner and former seaman was mystified as she'd arranged with him during a phone call from Verbier that she'd meet him there at 5.30 p.m.

Brown wondered if she'd gone to do some shopping as she'd have needed groceries after a month away. He took off his anorak and hung it on a hook in the hall. Then he sat down on the settee to watch television.

As he did so, he noticed a copy of that week's *Queensbridge Gazette* by the landline phone. It carried that week's date – which seemed to confirm she'd arrived back and been at the cottage.

The building was as cold as a Moscow winter. He went into the kitchen and switched on the gas boiler. As it flared into life, he took out his mobile and dialled her number, but her phone went straight to voicemail.

After leaving a brief message urging her to contact him, he called a few of their friends, but no one had seen her. Finally, he rang the rector, who explained how he'd met her at the bottom of Oxford Lane that morning. He mentioned she'd been considering making a report to the police about the night Harry Bowers went missing. He'd tried phoning her several times, but to no avail, the rector added.

This alarmed Brown even more. He decided to wait for two hours and, if she failed to return in that time, he'd call Queensbridge police station.

At 8.30 p.m., she'd still not appeared and he made the call. PC Derek Underhill was preparing to leave for the day after an eight-hour shift that had already turned into ten hours. But he gave up all thought of going home for the fish supper his wife had been preparing when Brown's call was put through to him.

'It's my partner,' Brown said. 'She came back from Switzerland last night and was around this morning, chatting to the rector. She arranged to meet me this evening but her cottage was in darkness.'

PC Underhill frowned. 'Have you spoken to her family? Perhaps she's visiting a relative or friend?'

'No. She's a very responsible person. She'd have left me a message if she'd been unable to meet me,' Brown explained.

'OK. What's the address, sir?'

'Rose Cottage, Oxford Lane, Norton Prior.'

Underhill had been gathering up some papers on his desk during the conversation. He stopped still at the mention of Oxford Lane like an army general who's spotted an enemy tank sweeping over the horizon. He'd seen the street name so often recently. It had featured on countless whiteboards in the station since Harry Bowers had vanished.

'Oxford Lane? I'll be over straight away,' he said.

* * *

Twenty minutes later, PC Underhill and a female constable, PC Vicky Denham, arrived at Mrs Thomas's cottage in a Vauxhall Corsa with police livery of white, yellow and blue. Brown greeted them at the door.

PC Underhill carried out an inspection of the ground floor rooms while his colleague looked upstairs. Afterwards Underhill took some notes. He wrote on his pad that Mrs Thomas's holiday clothes remained packed inside the two unopened suitcases in the main bedroom; there was no food in the kitchen fridge; and a copy of that week's *Queensbridge Gazette* was in the living room. He also took details of all Brown's phone numbers.

'This all seems very strange,' Underhill concluded, 'but there could be some logical explanation. I think it's best we leave this until the morning. She might turn up and it may well all end happily.'

'Yes, I suppose you're right,' said Brown. 'But what concerns me is she told the rector she'd got some information about Harry Bowers. I'm wondering if that might have had something to do with her going missing.'

'What do you mean, sir? That she might've gone to pass on this information – whatever it was – to Mrs Bowers or someone?'

'No, I was told Mrs Thomas was considering contacting the police because of something she saw the night Bowers went missing. I thought she might've gone to your police station to make a report?'

'I've been at the station all day, sir,' he replied. 'No one's come in to give us any information on the Bowers case, I can assure you. Look, sir, let's give it till nine o'clock tomorrow morning. If the lady's still missing then, call me and I'll alert Detective Chief Inspector Roscoe, who's in charge of the Bowers investigation. This is my direct line number. Can you call me at around nine tomorrow?'

'Yes, certainly. Sounds like a plan.'

'Perhaps, in the meantime, you could call her relatives. Obviously, try not to alarm them too much at this stage.'

'They're mostly in South Wales,' Brown said.

'Well, you never know. If a family member's suddenly been taken ill, she might've gone off.'

'I know what you're saying,' Brown said. 'But I'm sure she'd have let me know in that case. She would have phoned me at the marina or left a note.'

'OK, sir. Well, that's it for the moment,' the constable said. 'As I say, give me a call tomorrow and we'll look at the situation then. Good evening, sir.'

After the pair had gone, Brown made himself a sandwich with some tinned meat and bread defrosted from the freezer. Then he called Mrs Thomas's daughter and another relative in South Wales. Neither had seen her since the start of the year.

'Something terrible's happened to her. I'm sure of it,' he muttered to himself.

* * *

An hour later, at his home in Queensbridge, PC Underhill finally sat down to his meal of battered plaice, chips and peas that his wife had cooked. But he kept casting over in his mind the details of his visit to Rose Cottage. He thought again about Tyler Brown's words: 'Mrs Thomas had been considering contacting the police because of something she saw.'

Perhaps this added a sinister edge to the circumstances of her disappearance. Perhaps this was a matter that shouldn't and couldn't wait until the morning. He decided there and then to call Detective Inspector Andy Chadwick from Stratford CID for advice. The constable knew the importance of following police procedure to the letter or, as he and his colleagues described it, 'covering your own back'. Underhill had dealt with dozens of missing persons cases over the years. The individuals concerned usually turned up later. But, in the light of the Harry Bowers case, he wanted to make sure he acted by the book.

Chadwick praised Underhill for calling him and said the constable had acted 'absolutely correctly'. Then the detective inspector phoned Gavin Roscoe and briefed him on PC Underhill's visit to Rose Cottage. Roscoe, in turn, phoned his sergeant and the pair agreed to visit the cottage early the next morning.

Chapter 29

It was just before half past eight on the morning of Saturday, 16 February when DCI Roscoe's BMW came to a halt outside Rose Cottage. A few minutes later, his sergeant arrived in her car. They both clambered out and looked around while slipping their coats on.

'An idyllic spot, sir,' she observed as they gazed across the impressive expanse of open land that lay behind the cottage and to the side of it.

The roar of a red tractor spreading slurry across a muddy field could be heard in the distance. In the cottage garden, they spent a few seconds admiring the neatly kept borders with their vibrant pink cyclamen flowers and, here and there, some early white and yellow daffodils.

Across the lane, immediately opposite Rose Cottage, lay a field enclosed by a hedge and a padlocked five-bar gate. To the right, fifty metres away on the far side of the road, a long row of houses began that led all the way to the bottom of the lane.

Brown had stayed at the cottage overnight, but he'd only managed a few hours' sleep and he was at the door to greet the two detectives. He'd noticed their two cars draw up outside. Sunita was the first to walk up the pathway.

'Good morning, sir,' she said. 'Sergeant Roy. We met briefly at the marina three weeks ago. You'll remember my colleague, DCI Roscoe. May we come in?'

'Yes, of course,' said Brown. 'Mr Roscoe, we meet again.'

The DCI smiled. 'Yes, hello, Mr Brown. We hear you're concerned about Mrs Thomas. No news then?'

Brown, who was wearing a red, patterned shirt and blue jeans he'd worn the night before, looked pale and exhausted. The pair followed him into the sitting room as he began to open the front curtains.

'No, sadly not,' he said. 'I was meant to phone your PC Underhill at nine o'clock.'

Roscoe explained that the information about Mrs Thomas had already been passed onto the CID office at force headquarters and they'd decided to act on it as a matter of urgency.

'I've been in touch with Mrs Thomas's daughter in South Wales,' Brown explained. 'I tried very hard to dissuade her, but she insisted on travelling up here. She'll be arriving sometime this afternoon.'

'Let's hope her mother turns up in the meantime,' Sunita muttered.

As she spoke, Sunita cast her eyes around the oak-beamed room which, she estimated, was approximately eight metres long and four metres wide. There was a grey three-seater settee next to the cream-coloured right-hand wall with a matching armchair on either side.

On the opposite wall stood the impressive inglenook fireplace with a large piece of dark timber above it, decorated with horse brasses. A small table stood beneath the leaded light windows which overlooked the front garden of the cottage. The light-brown parquet floor was largely hidden by a green, patterned carpet which ended abruptly a few feet away from the far end of the room.

As Roscoe walked round, inspecting the furniture, he noticed a small wooden box under the table by the front windows.

'Out of interest, what's inside that box, sir?' he asked.

Brown shrugged. 'Oh, that's just Bethan's toolbox. I brought it into the house from the garden shed before Christmas to repair the downstairs toilet. I never got round to putting it back.'

'OK, that's fine,' he said as he bent down to examine it.

Sunita meanwhile walked slowly and thoughtfully towards the other end of the room and drew back the two large, beige curtains, revealing a pair of French doors. Light flooded in and she at once spotted a dark-brown coat lying on the floor between an armchair and the back wall.

Turning to Brown, she asked, 'Is this your girlfriend's coat, sir?'

'Good God! Yes, it is,' Brown said, rushing across the room to examine it. As he picked it up, he found her black handbag beneath it.

'She'd have never gone out without this coat,' he said, his face etched with worry. 'Let me check the contents of the bag. Her mobile's here and so's her purse.'

Sunita examined the phone. It had been switched off.

Remembering to lower his head to take account of the low ceiling, Roscoe strode across the room and joined the pair, who had stooped down in front of the double doors. He was becoming concerned but did his best to hide it.

'This suggests something's happened to her in the house,' he concluded while Sunita carefully examined the woollen coat.

Turning to her boss, she remarked, 'The sleeve's got a small tear on the left arm. It looks as if the coat's been snagged on thorns – maybe on the rose bushes outside. There's a trace of mud on the hem at the back.'

Roscoe bent down and took the coat from her hands. He too spent a few moments studying it. Then, by chance, he happened to glance down. He dropped to his knees and began to study the floor.

He turned to Brown. 'Was there a mat or rug here at some point?'

'Yes. Now you mention it, the Persian rug's missing.'

'Between the end of the green carpet and the French doors?' Roscoe asked.

Brown nodded.

'I see what you mean, sir,' said Sunita. 'There's an outline of where a rug used to be. Part of the flooring's been slightly discoloured by the sun, except for this rectangular area directly in front of the doors. So what happened to this rug, Mr Brown?' She too knelt down and studied the area around the doors.

Brown thought for a moment. 'Well, it was there at Christmas. That's very strange. I can't think of a reason why she would've moved it. It was there to protect the floor because we'd often walk in and out through the doors.'

As Roscoe stood up, holding his back, Sunita remained on her knees and became absorbed in studying the wooden beading at the threshold of the doorway.

'If I'm not mistaken, there are tiny spots of blood here,' she said, taking a closer look.

'You're right,' said Roscoe, squatting down at the doors beside her. 'At least three specks of blood there,' he said. He glanced up at Brown and noticed he'd become distressed.

'We need to carry out a thorough search of this house, Mr Brown,' Roscoe insisted. 'I'm afraid it looks as if something bad's happened. We don't know for sure until we've had the forensics team down here. Are you all right?'

As Brown buried his face in his hands, the DCI put his hand on his shoulder, consolingly.

'Do you want to sit down? This is upsetting for you, isn't it?' he said.

'This is my worst nightmare,' he murmured.

'We've got a very good family liaison officer, Pam Listers. I could arrange for her to call round...'

'There's no need. I'll be fine.'

Sunita hauled herself up from the floor. She stepped towards Brown, who was sitting in the middle of the settee with his head still in his hands.

'Mr Brown, I'm sorry to have to ask you this,' she said. 'Can you recall exactly what Mrs Thomas is meant to have said outside the newsagents?'

The tearful marina owner looked up. 'I've only heard about this third hand from the rector. He said Bethan had been thinking of calling the police because of something she saw the night Bowers went missing. That's all I know.'

Roscoe took his colleague aside.

'I need to go and see the rector immediately and find out exactly what was said,' he told her in a low voice. 'Will you be all right here on your own, Sergeant?'

'Yes, sir. Of course.'

'I won't be long. While I'm making my way down Oxford Lane, I'm going to call the office and get a team down here straight away. I'm declaring the cottage a crime scene and I want the whole place searched from top to bottom.'

Chapter 30

Sunita watched from the front window as the DCI walked away past the row of stone cottages and semi-detached houses. She was effectively in charge until he returned – only her fourth or fifth time in charge of a crime scene, she reflected. She wasn't overawed by the prospect. The whole team had a task to perform – an unpleasant and, no doubt, tragic task – and they simply had to get on with it.

Once the crime scene investigators and some of her CID colleagues arrived, she would be required to brief her team, but the crime scene manager would then take over responsibility for the building.

She cast her mind back to the discovery of the coat and handbag which had been lying in a corner of the living room, discarded by their owner and perhaps never to be picked up by her again.

By ten o'clock, there were six marked police cars and four unmarked police vehicles parked outside the property in Oxford Lane. The cottage and its gardens were cordoned off and a uniformed constable stationed at the gate.

The sergeant struck up a conversation with Brown until, ten minutes later, the crime scene manager ordered that the cottage door and hallway should be forensically examined.

Then the pair retreated to the rear garden, where they stood chatting until they were joined by PCs Brett Dawson and Omar Khalid.

* * *

While work was getting under way at the cottage, the DCI had arrived at St John's Rectory. He felt he'd built up a close personal rapport with the minister and believed he should interview him in person about the conversation Mrs Thomas was alleged to have had outside the newsagent's.

Revd Hughes glanced out of the rectory window and noticed the DCI walking up his gravel drive. He went to the door to greet him.

'My dear Chief Inspector, I was going to call you,' he said. 'Any news about Mrs Thomas?'

'No, not as yet,' the detective replied, shaking his head. He couldn't explain why, but somehow he liked and trusted the clergyman.

Hughes invited him in, but Roscoe declined. He was eager to return to Rose Cottage as soon as possible.

'Something's come up and we're very busy,' he told the churchman, taking out his notebook and pen. 'You met Mrs Thomas in the street yesterday, didn't you?'

The rector nodded. 'Yes. She'd just come back from a skiing holiday with friends in Verbier.'

'How exactly is it you know her – she's a regular churchgoer?'

'Yes. She's been in the choir since it was formed. She was present the night Bowers disappeared and, the very next morning, left for Switzerland. Then yesterday I saw her at the shop over the road and, of course, she'd missed all the news.'

Roscoe, who was writing in his notebook assiduously, asked, 'What time was this?'

The rector thought for a moment. 'Must've been just after nine o'clock. David Harrington was there too. Do you know him? Local farmer. Some other people were around as well.'

'What did she actually say?'

'Well, as far as I can recollect, she said she saw Harry near the lychgate with James Hockley. She was late for choir practice and the two men were having a fierce argument. I remember she used the words "Hockley was shaking his fist".'

The detective frowned. 'Is that the sum of what she said?'

'Yes,' said the clergyman. 'Oh, hold on. She spoke of someone hanging about in the shadows and it looked as though they were holding something. She thought it might've been the handlebars of a bike.'

Roscoe acquired the look of a worried headmaster. 'How bizarre. A bicycle? This is very important,' he said. 'Did she say anything else about this? Did she suggest who this other person might've been?'

'No, that was all she said. I didn't question her further. The main thing was the two men were having a fierce argument. I mean, this wasn't a total surprise to me because I'd seen Bowers and Hockley having words before, as I mentioned to you. It just seemed they'd taken their bad feelings one stage further.'

'Did she mention a time when this argument at the lychgate occurred?'

Revd Hughes said, 'Just after quarter past seven. After our conversation yesterday she headed back to her cottage and I promised to pass onto her your CID office number. She left us talking outside the shop at around nine fifteen. She should've been home well before nine thirty. But when I called her later to give her the number, there was no reply to her phone.'

Roscoe had been gazing round the rector's front garden during their conversation. But, after hearing these last few words, he gave him a solemn look.

'That could be very significant. What time did you phone her?'

The rector thought for a moment.

'Well, I don't know exactly, but I'd say it was between a quarter to ten and ten thirty,' he said.

'Is there any way we could be more precise?' he asked. 'Doesn't your phone automatically record the times of calls?'

'No, I've just deleted my call details – bit of a tidy-up. Phone housekeeping, I call it. But I had to be in Queensbridge visiting the hospital at 11.00 a.m. and it takes at least twenty-five minutes to get there. As I remember arriving there just after eleven, I'd say that, at the latest, I made the call to Mrs Thomas at 10.25.'

The detective, who was continuing to write all the information down, looked up at the churchman.

'Now,' he said, 'I need to know precisely who was listening when Mrs Thomas gave her recollections. Can you tell me again who was there?'

The rector paused as if to collect his thoughts. He said, 'As I say, there was David Harrington, myself and two or three others who'd popped into the shop.'

Roscoe glared. 'Can you be more precise? Was it two or three?'

'Oh, dear. No, I'm sorry,' said the rector. 'I didn't pay much attention. I was thinking about my sermon on Sunday, to be frank.'

'So they're the only people who were privy to this information?'

'Yes, that's right. Apart from James and Tyler, of course.'

The DCI's jaw dropped momentarily.

'James Hockley and Tyler Brown were there?' he asked.

'No, neither was actually there at the time,' the churchman said. 'By coincidence, James phoned me at the rectory just after breakfast yesterday.'

'What time was that?'

'It must've been just after nine thirty. He was inquiring about dates for the choir practice and asked whether Bethan had returned from holiday. I questioned him on whether he'd had a row with Harry on 8 January and he became a little annoyed.'

'Did you mention Mrs Thomas's remarks to him?'

'Just in passing,' he said. 'Much later, Mr Brown called me as he was worried about Bethan.'

'What time would that've been?'

'Between half past six and seven last night. I told Mr Brown she'd been thinking of making a call to the police because of what she witnessed.'

After putting all these details in his notebook, Roscoe thanked the minister and walked briskly back to the cottage. He was glad he'd spoken to him because the rector's words could have a huge bearing on the case.

He estimated, after the conversation outside the shop, it would have taken Mrs Thomas around twelve or thirteen minutes to walk home. As he strolled up the lane, he timed his own journey. It took him exactly eleven minutes and he was a quick walker.

That meant her arrival time at Rose Cottage would have been just after 9.25. He reflected it was therefore likely, if she'd been murdered, it would have happened after 9.25 and probably within an hour or two of that time.

But the case remained deeply puzzling. There was a string of potential suspects who'd all been made aware that the newly returned holidaymaker had some crucial evidence. It was beginning to look as though her honest but ill-considered remarks had inadvertently given someone a motive for murder.

Chapter 31

When Gavin Roscoe returned to Rose Cottage, he immediately put Sunita and Brett Dawson to work, setting up a HOLMES computer connection so information could be collected and collated.

Scenes of crime officers had contained the scene and arranged a series of rubber anti-contamination plates around the house and gardens so the officers could step around without disturbing any evidence. One of the force dog handlers was expected to arrive shortly.

Roscoe quickly assumed command, visiting every part of the house for an overview of what each member of the SOCO team was doing, taking care to avoid any risk of contaminating the scene.

At Sunita's suggestion, PC Dawson gently persuaded Brown to leave and return to his own house while police continued with their inch-by-inch search of the cottage.

Before he left, the marina owner confirmed there was no cellar beneath the house. He provided both the front and back door keys and informed police that neither the garden shed nor the wood store were regularly locked.

Ten minutes after Roscoe's return, Sunita joined trainee detective Omar Khalid in inspecting the garden shed, which was near the kitchen door and close to the neighbouring house. As she examined a collection of spades and shovels, she called out to Roscoe, who was by now standing just outside the French doors.

'Could you come and have a look at this, sir?' she yelled.

As the DCI's head peered in, she said in a low voice, 'There are traces of damp sand and soil on the bottom edge of this spade, sir.'

A forensic officer accompanying her, who was wearing plastic gloves, held up a three-foot-long spade to show him its nine-inch-wide stainless-steel blade.

'All the other tools are in pristine condition,' she revealed. 'It looks to me as though Mrs Thomas was the kind of gardener who cleaned her tools after use. If she'd used it before going away, the bottom edge would be dry by now. So I'm thinking someone else has used it recently and they've been digging in some damp sand.'

Roscoe beamed at her and nodded. 'Good work, Sergeant. There's a large sandpit at the bottom of the garden. Has anyone checked it out?'

Sunita shook her head. 'Not yet, sir.'

'Right. That's our next priority. I think we need the spaniel. And, while I think of it, perhaps our friend here from forensics can arrange to have this spade checked for any dabs.'

Roscoe surveyed the pit for any footprints or other disturbance. When he found none, he hurried out to the road. The dog handler had finally arrived.

'We need Millie's help in the back garden,' he announced to the young constable behind the wheel, who was stroking an attentive orange-and-white cocker spaniel.

Millie and her handler followed Roscoe into the front garden and then along a narrow path on the far side of the building, bordered by hedges and trees. Once in the rear garden, Millie was released from her lead. Her handler directed her to the giant sandpit, which lay at the end of the garden surrounded by high fencing.

Millie scampered into the pit, meandering around and sniffing the sand. Within seconds, she stopped still, pointed her nose at the centre of the sand and barked repeatedly.

'There's something there,' said the handler.

Roscoe nodded. 'Never takes her long, does it?'

As the handler rewarded Millie with a ball and guided her away, Roscoe beckoned Dawson and Khalid over. They crouched down by the side of the pit, casting their eyes around.

Khalid jumped up and turned towards the DCI.

'Guv, I'm seeing tiny traces of dark soil intermingled with the sand,' he said. 'A bit unusual.'

Dr Alice Ling, who was crime scene manager for the day, joined them at the edge of the pit. She bent down and burrowed with her hands in the trench. Her first discovery was a child's toy car and a stainless-steel teaspoon, which Dawson took from her and placed on the lawn. She continued to explore, this time ploughing her gloved hands deeper and deeper.

Roscoe and Sunita watched the activity from a vantage point on the patio in front of the French doors.

Finally, just after ten thirty that morning, Dr Ling discovered the gruesome fate of Bethan Thomas. She felt the rough texture of a carpet that was partly unravelled. Then she felt an object that seemed like the buckle of a woman's shoe. She dug further until she could feel the complete shoe. Inside was a foot, attached to a woman's body.

'It's a body, sir,' Dr Ling said quietly, rising to her feet and brushing some of the sand off her hands.

As Dawson stood on the edge of the pit, he could see part of a green skirt.

All the CSIs were alerted and, within minutes, a tent had been erected over the site of the sandpit together with lighting. Two of Dr Ling's colleagues then set to work, removing several small plastic containers of sand from around the body.

'Silas is on his way,' Roscoe remarked as he and Sunita exchanged solemn looks.

The pair didn't need to wait long. Just over an hour later, the familiar rotund form of the pathologist emerged through the open doors carrying his brown case. He immediately greeted the detectives like long-lost friends.

'Gavin! Sergeant Roy! I hear you've made a discovery,' said Dr Reynolds, who had already changed into a white lab coat and rubber gloves.

Within moments, he adopted a sterner demeanour.

'This is a terrible business. A truly terrible business,' he said. 'Right. Let's have a look.' He knelt down beside the shallow grave to make an initial assessment.

'The body appears to be partly wrapped in a carpet,' he said as he bent down.

'Is it a Persian rug, do you think?' Sunita asked.

The forensic specialist studied the material. 'Yes, my dear. I think it could well be. Why do you say that?'

'Because there used to be one just inside the living room, by the double doors, and it's missing,' she replied.

'Let's have a proper look at this body,' Dr Reynolds said. 'Could someone help me lift it out of all this sand?'

Dawson and Dr Ling lowered their hands into the pit and lifted the upper torso. As they did so, the blood-soaked Persian rug unravelled and slipped back down into the sand. The pathologist then took hold of the feet and together they hauled the body onto a piece of plastic sheeting that had been placed on the grass.

Dr Reynolds examined the body quietly for a few minutes as Dr Ling arranged for the Persian rug to be removed from the pit and placed next to the corpse.

'Well, it's a woman in either her late fifties or early sixties,' he said. 'Dark hair, hazel eyes and about five feet eight inches tall, I'd say. She's wearing a silver watch and silver necklace. She's got broken fingernails and bruises to her hands.'

Roscoe glanced at the pathologist. 'Any ideas on how she died, Silas?'

The doctor shook his head. 'Well, it's not totally clear, but the red marks round the neck suggest strangulation with a ligature.'

'Garrotted?' asked Roscoe.

Dr Reynolds frowned. 'You might call it garrotted, although, strictly speaking, that involves a noose with a rod inside, which is twisted round. Used to be a form of execution in Spain.' He paused. 'There's a clear ligature mark most of the way round the neck. The killer may have used a rope or cord. We'll take some photographs of the neck right away because any pattern in the skin will fade in the next few hours.'

Thinking out loud, he added, 'We must try and clear some of this sand away that's still covering part of the surface of the body.'

After a few minutes, he beckoned Dr Ling over. The pair placed a protective covering over the corpse before preparing for the task of putting it inside a body bag.

Rising to his feet, he told Sunita and Roscoe, 'Listen, it appears this lady's been strangled from behind as the ligature marks are consistent around the front and sides of the neck. Then, at the nape of the neck, there appears to be a cross-over point where the killer brought the two ends of the ligature together and overlapped them. Do we know who this poor woman is, by the way?'

'We believe the victim's Bethan Thomas, who lived here,' said Roscoe.

'Right,' the pathologist said. 'This lady's also been savagely bludgeoned. There's blunt force trauma to the back of the cranium – at least two injuries, probably caused by a claw hammer or axe. I can't think of much else that would cause that kind of injury. She's been the victim of a standard impact trauma injury caused by a weapon used with substantial force. I can't be sure until I carry out a full autopsy how many blows there were, but the victim's lost a bit of blood.'

Sunita interrupted to ask whether it was safe to assume that most of the blood had fallen onto the Persian carpet.

'Yes, my dear,' the pathologist said. 'I think the killer's wrapped the body in the carpet to contain the blood. He or she has then placed the whole shooting match in the sandpit in a bid to hide the evidence… or at least delay its discovery.'

'And the assailant would no doubt have been splattered with blood as well,' said Sunita.

'Undoubtedly. Are there traces of spillage anywhere?' he asked.

Roscoe nodded. 'Three specks of blood at the base of the French doors from inside the house.'

The forensic expert shrugged. 'This fellow – assuming it's a fellow – may have been a master of the clean-up. He's adept at hiding evidence away and clearing up after himself – which maybe tells us something about his character.'

'So let's get this right,' Sunita said. 'The assailant used two methods to kill his victim. It looks like he first came up behind her with a rope or a necktie…?'

'A rope,' Dr Reynolds insisted.

'With all his might, he tries to strangle her, but she puts up a struggle – which explains the broken fingernails and bruises.'

'Precisely.'

'Finally, he brings her to the floor half-conscious and she lands on the Persian rug by the French doors.'

'You've got it.'

'Because the strangulation was only partly successful, he grabs a hammer and deals the fatal blows.'

'That certainly seems to fit the facts, but we'd need to wait for the autopsy before we can be that specific,' the pathologist admitted.

'We must carry on looking for the rope and the hammer,' Roscoe murmured. 'They're missing and they're crucial. Silas, we've got an idea as to the time of death. The rector of the nearby church saw Mrs Thomas just after nine o'clock yesterday morning and she failed to answer her phone at about ten thirty.'

'Sir, her mobile's been turned off,' Sunita pointed out.

Roscoe nodded. 'So we can only assume she died sometime after about half past nine yesterday morning.'

Dr Reynolds nodded. 'That would fit in with the fact that there's been hardly any decomposition of the body – a process that would've in any case been slightly delayed by the corpse being immersed in sand on a mild winter's day.'

While the two detectives had been talking to the pathologist, Dawson and Khalid had continued sifting through the sand. They'd discovered that the plastic lining installed between the sand and the earth beneath had been cut away and some of the soil disturbed in order for the body to be buried more deeply in the ground. As Dawson' gloved hands burrowed into the sand at the side of the pit closest to the cottage, he made a discovery.

'Look at this, sir!' he urged the DCI.

Roscoe turned his attention towards the constable, who was holding a piece of rope about a metre long.

'Well done, Dawson,' he said. 'This could be the ligature that was used, Silas.'

The pathologist examined it.

'Yes, old fruit. It could well be. We'll have it bagged up and taken to the lab,' he said. 'Lots more tests are needed. It'll be interesting to see if this rope matches the one that was tied to the leg of the marina man.'

As Dr Reynolds spoke to members of the forensic team, Dawson, Sunita and Roscoe walked slowly back to the cottage. Roscoe patted the constable on the back.

'That was good work, Dawson, finding that rope,' he said. 'All we need now is the weapon.'

The sergeant reminded him that Mrs Thomas's daughter was due to arrive shortly from South Wales.

Roscoe nodded. 'Oh, that's a good point. Shall we station someone at the garden gate? That lady must be kept away until the body has been moved to the mortuary in Queensbridge. We must get someone sensitive to break the news to her gently. Dawson, perhaps you could arrange for Tyler Brown to be notified, as tactfully as you can. Better alert the coroner's officer as well.'

As the constable set off on his tasks, Roscoe and Sunita re-entered the house through the open doors, being careful not to hinder the crime scene staff. Sunita reminded him about the toolbox beneath the front window.

'There's a good chance the murderer took the hammer from that box during the attack,' she muttered.

'We can take a look, but if he took it out, I don't imagine he's put it neatly back,' Roscoe replied.

They tugged the sturdy wooden box out and searched its contents. Although there was a small hammer in it, they decided that was highly unlikely to have served as the murder weapon.

'We must ask Tyler Brown to look at the contents of the toolbox and confirm if there's a large hammer missing,' said Sunita.

Roscoe looked puzzled and was scratching his head.

'What do you make of all this, Sergeant?' he asked.

'It's a very strange case,' Sunita said. 'It obviously looks as if she's been targeted because of what she said in the street. It can't be a coincidence. One minute she's telling all and sundry she saw Bowers having an argument and the next minute she's meeting a grisly end.'

'We'll just have to carry on searching the cottage,' Roscoe concluded. 'I can't understand why there are no more traces of blood. The killer must've had blood on his hands and clothing. Yet all we found were three tiny specks. The SOCOs must be thorough and not overlook anything.'

As he tried to push the toolbox back under the table, he added, 'Do you know, Sergeant, what I can't understand is, why conceal the body? It was the same with the man in the Avon.'

Sunita thought for a moment. 'Well, there are some obvious answers to that, sir – to delay the body's discovery; to give the killer more time. Maybe the killer thinks his handiwork will never be uncovered if no bodies are found and he'll get away with his crimes.' She paused. 'And there's one more possibility. I read somewhere that sometimes a killer will conceal what he does in order to make the police look foolish. It's possible he wants us to look like idiots for failing to find Bethan Thomas's body straight away. All that suggests a strong personal hostility towards the police. I'm thinking this man who hides bodies may well have been in trouble with the police in the past and bear a grudge.'

Chapter 32

After their harrowing morning at Rose Cottage, Gavin Roscoe guessed that he and his fellow-detectives would appreciate an early lunch. This was quickly arranged in a phone call to his wife.

At half past twelve, he, Sunita and PCs Khalid and Dawson settled themselves round a table at the Apollo Tearooms.

'How nice to see you all,' said Helen, wiping her hands on a navy-blue apron which covered her slim-fitting black dress. 'You two boys I've met before – and you must be Gavin's new sergeant. I'm Helen.'

Sunita smiled and stretched out her hand across the table.

'Sunita Roy. Pleased to meet you,' she said as Helen shook her hand.

'You've come at the right time – just before the lunchtime rush,' Helen continued while handing out menus.

'I didn't realise you did lunches,' said Sunita.

'Nor me,' said Khalid and Dawson in unison.

'We only started doing them last year. Snacks really. Jacket potatoes, baguettes, salads, you know. But it's going very well, isn't it, Gavin?'

'The good citizens of Queensbridge seem to like it,' he replied. He quickly added, 'it's Helen's business and I try to stay out of it. Our daughter does a bit of waitressing.'

'Is that Melody, sir?' asked Dawson.

'Yes, that's right,' said Roscoe.

'Anyway,' said Helen. 'What would you all like?'

Twenty minutes later, Roscoe was demolishing a dish of jacket potato with cheese and bacon. Dawson and Khalid were tucking into baguettes, while Sunita, who was dieting to retain her trim figure, opted for a salmon salad.

Roscoe had invited Dr Reynolds as well, but the pathologist was keen to perform the autopsy as soon as possible and had declined.

'That man's totally devoted to his job,' Sunita muttered as she sipped from a cup of lemon tea. 'He'd rather be cutting up bodies in the mortuary at Queensbridge Hospital than enjoying a light lunch with us.'

'You're not quite right,' said the DCI as he devoured some bacon. 'I think he wants the job done so he can get home to his wife.'

'He lives some distance away, doesn't he?' the sergeant remarked.

Roscoe nodded. 'Shropshire. After lunch, I want to go back to Rose Cottage. I want to speak to Dr Ling and get some house-to-house organised.' He paused before adding, 'This meal is on me, by the way.'

Sunita smiled at Khalid as he grappled with his baguette.

'I hear you've been sent to the station to pick up Mrs Thomas's daughter this afternoon,' she said.

'Yes, Sarge. She was meant to be letting us know what time she was arriving.'

'She's coming from Tredegar. That's in South Wales, isn't it?'

'Don't ask me, Sarge,' Khalid replied. 'I know nothing about Wales. Until recently, I thought that well-known tourist place Betws-y-Coed was a mixed school.'

The team returned to the cottage after complimenting Helen Roscoe on their meal. Immediately, Dr Ling informed the DCI that microscopic samples of blood had been detected in the kitchen sink, where the killer may have washed his hands. They'd also found a microscopic trace of blood on the hallway floor and at the base of the internal front door handle.

As the DCI was being shown these locations, Sunita returned to the garden. She meticulously examined the brick patio outside the French doors.

After a few minutes, she yelled, 'Sir!'

Roscoe exited by the front door and followed the footpath round the side of the cottage. He found his sergeant in the back garden, bending down over the dark-red patio brickwork. The bricks, which were set out in a herringbone pattern, covered a rectangular area measuring approximately three metres by four metres. Sunita was studying a corner of the rectangle close to the double doors.

She told him, 'Most of the bricks here have moss growing around them, but the moss seems to have been disturbed on this group of bricks to the right side of the French doors. It looks as if these ones may have been raised recently and then put back. They're not exactly level with the other bricks either.'

Roscoe smiled. 'Well, let's have them up.'

The pair crouched down and began to remove the moss-free section. One by one, the bricks were easily prised up, leaving an area of loose sand and soil where woodlice and other insects were crawling around.

Sliding on the plastic gloves he kept in his coat pocket, Roscoe brushed the bugs aside and delved into the earth until he reached a hard object. Without a great amount of effort, he found he was able to scrape away the soil from around his find – which proved to be a bloodstained claw-hammer.

'Well done, Sergeant!' he said. 'It just shows what dogged determination can do. I'll pass this over to Dr Ling. With any luck, there may be some dabs on it and we might find out who this bastard is that's been striking fear into the heart of the community.'

* * *

Just after two o'clock, Sunita found PC Dawson drinking a takeaway coffee and watching the forensic team at the sandpit. She told him to put his cup down and follow her.

'Are you feeling fit? We're going to knock on a few doors,' she informed him after collecting a clipboard and some paper from her car.

'We've got a bit of a job on our hands here, haven't we?' he said as he put on his coat. 'It's a long road.'

'Well, we'd better begin straight away, Brett,' she replied as they began walking away from the cottage.

She stopped in her tracks, raised her right hand to her eyebrow and looked up and down at the houses and bungalows lying ahead of them.

'Shall we make a start here?' she suggested, pointing to the cottage next to the victim's home.

He nodded. 'Why not? Hey, Bowers is missing. Mrs Thomas is dead. Do you think the killer's making their way through the choir, one by one?'

She frowned. 'Bowers might not be dead and there's no suggestion the guy in the river was part of the choir – or that he has anything to do with the Bowers case. It's too soon for that sort of speculation. Come on.'

* * *

The next-door neighbour was a retired retail manager who lived with his wife, a former school secretary. The woman told Sunita she'd been in at around ten in the morning the day before, but she'd not heard anything or seen anyone.

'I'd probably got the vacuum cleaner on at that time,' she suggested. 'In any event,' she explained, 'the two gardens are separated by a high hedge and some trees. I noticed nothing unusual when I was hanging the washing on the line.'

They received equally unhelpful information from more than a dozen other householders they visited.

Finally, after forty minutes of door-knocking, the pair achieved a breakthrough. They came to a house which was situated a short distance from Rose Cottage on the opposite side of the road. It was the home of Brenda Taylor, a fifty-five-year-old shop assistant. She shared the three-bedroom Edwardian semi-detached house with her partner, a retired office manager.

When Sunita and Dawson first knocked on her side door, she was concerned they might be Jehovah's Witnesses.

Brandishing her warrant card, Sunita said, 'No, we're Heart of England Police. Sorry to disturb you. Have you heard what's happened?'

'About poor Mrs Thomas?' said Mrs Taylor. 'Yes, I just heard it on the radio news. I'll be honest with you, it's a bit frightening.'

Sunita smiled sympathetically. 'I can understand that,' she said. 'We need as much help as possible to catch whoever did this. Did you see anything strange or unusual sometime after nine thirty on Friday morning?'

Mrs Taylor thought for a moment. 'I'm not exactly sure where Rose Cottage is, dear. Is it one of the last houses? There's so many places round here with "cottage" in the name.'

Sunita pointed towards the blue and white police tape.

'It's that one a hundred metres away – the last house on the left, if you can see it.'

'Oh, I don't know the people there, dear. But there was a small car parked near there when I came back from the doctor's,' she declared. 'Do you want to come in?'

The two detectives had been losing heart as most of the householders they'd encountered on doorsteps had been unhelpful. Discovering someone who might've seen some suspicious behaviour raised their spirits. She led them into her small front room which contained a blue leather two-seater sofa, a matching armchair and a small table and chairs in the bay window.

The householder continued, 'It would've been somewhere near the last house. I can't be sure. I only saw a glimpse.'

Taking a seat on the settee, the sergeant pulled out a notebook from her jacket pocket. 'Do you mind if we just write this down. Now you're Mrs…?'

'Taylor. Brenda Taylor.'

Sunita wrote the details down. 'Your address is 223 Oxford Lane, isn't it?' she asked. 'Now, do you have any idea of this car's colour?'

'I think it was blue. A small blue car.'

'What kind of blue? Light? Dark?'

'I'd call it mid-blue, but I only caught a glimpse.'

'What time would this have been?'

'About ten o'clock as I left the doctor's at about a quarter to ten,' she said.

Dawson asked if she knew what make or model of car it had been.

'Oh, now you've got me,' she said. 'I couldn't say what type. I've never been good with cars. I noticed it because it was parked with the nearside wheels on the pavement. This part of Oxford Lane's fairly wide and people generally park on the road, a few inches from the kerb.'

Dawson, who was standing in the middle of the room, shook his head. 'I suppose you didn't take a note of the car's registration number?'

'No, I'm afraid I didn't.'

'Did you see anyone get in or out?'

'No. I just noticed it and then thought no more about it and came in here.'

Sunita stroked her chin. 'But you remember it specifically because of how it was parked? And it was blue?'

'Yes, dear,' said Mrs Taylor. 'I'm sorry. It was just a glance.'

'If we brought you some images of some cars, do you think it might jog your memory?' Dawson asked.

Mrs Taylor paused to think. 'Oh, I don't know. I don't think so.'

'We'll bring some round anyway,' said Sunita. 'You never know.' Standing up, she said, 'You've been very helpful. We'd better take your phone number before we go. We'd be grateful, of course, if you didn't talk about this to the press, if they come banging on your door, or anyone else.'

'No. I understand. Of course,' Mrs Taylor said.

After leaving the house, the pair stood outside for a few minutes chatting on the pavement. Sunita had been intrigued to hear the car was blue. She recalled from reading through the files on the Bowers case that James Hockley had a blue Toyota car.

The pair spent the next half hour knocking on doors along the street as they continued their quest for eyewitness evidence. But they couldn't find anyone else who had seen any suspicious behaviour.

'Maybe we should check the CCTV camera near the shop and see if we can find any footage of the blue car,' Dawson suggested as they knocked on yet another door.

Chapter 33

Revd Peter Hughes hauled himself out of bed early on Sunday, 17 February. He pulled on his slippers and stepped over to the front window.

He had slept fitfully, his mind burdened with the knowledge that one of his two missing parishioners had been found dead. He peered out at the cherry trees below. They provided visitors and passers-by with a beautiful display of colour when they blossomed in the spring. But at present their dark, spindly branches poked into the sky like outstretched arms and fingers, looking dull and uninspiring – sentiments he could relate to after his poor night's sleep.

As he gazed at the trees which dominated the garden and partly shrouded it from the prying eyes of passers-by, he tried to think forward to March and April when they would yield their pink blossom. He always regarded that as a harbinger of good fortune. They were God's sign that the community had beaten winter and the good days of summer were not far behind.

He often reminded himself of the words of the fifth verse of Jeremiah 29: 'Thus saith the Lord of hosts… build houses and live in them, and plant gardens and eat their produce.'

Revd Hughes was a firm believer in that message, which urged a patient acceptance of the present state. He was minded to write a future sermon on that theme.

It was 6.30 a.m. now. As clouds enveloped the Biddington Hills to the north of the village, he remembered it was his busiest day of the week and he would soon have to prepare himself for his priestly duties.

The rector, who was ordained in 2001 after studying for his Bachelor of Divinity degree at Cambridge University, had been deeply troubled to hear the previous evening of the death of Bethan Thomas. The chief inspector had phoned him with the sad news but had been loath to provide many details.

'We don't yet know for certain what caused her death,' Gavin Roscoe had said mysteriously.

He liked and respected the detective, whom he'd now met twice – though he privately suspected he was a non-believer or a man who'd strayed from God's path.

He felt this morning part of his role would be to reassure members of the parish that people like Roscoe were doing their utmost to catch the evil mind behind these unfortunate events. The death of the tramp at the marina had also caused alarm among villagers, but Bethan was one of theirs – a much-loved member of the community and a regular churchgoer. She had sometimes helped arrange flowers for the Sunday service. Her passing was bound to have a deep effect upon everyone.

Later that morning, at the church, he would say a prayer for Bethan, for the tramp and for poor Harry Bowers. He'd pray that the evil bringing fear and suspicion into the lives of the community would quickly be vanquished.

He went downstairs to the kitchen and cooked himself a breakfast of egg, bacon, tomatoes and toast. He'd got used to fending for himself since he became separated from his wife three years earlier. A cleaner visited twice a week and a gardener helped to tend the garden once a week, but otherwise he was solely responsible for the upkeep of the rectory and its grounds. He believed he coped very well.

Shortly after his meal, he left the rectory wearing his customary black clerical shirt and dog collar, grey jacket and matching grey trousers. The church bells began to peel as he walked down his drive and crossed the lane. He just had time to call in at the newsagent's to buy a Sunday newspaper. Then he'd settle down at home and skim through the news for half an hour before going over to the church.

He was served at the counter by Julie Carter, the short, brown-haired girl he had seen assisting there from time to time.

'Good morning, Julie. You're working hard these days,' he said.

'I know,' she said. 'I want to get some money together. I might be going to uni.'

'Oh, university, the chance to learn, converse with fellow peers and run up debts. It was all different in my day. *Sunday Times*, please, Julie. How's your grandad Jim?'

Revd Hughes's mind flashed back to the moment he'd once nearly had to ask the drunken farmworker to leave the church for disrupting evensong with his raucous hymn-singing.

'He's off work with a bad back.'

'Very sorry to hear that, young lady. And Mr Bailey?'

'He's into fitness again,' she said. 'He's taken up cross-country running. It's his New Year's resolution. Mr Bailey says he was spending too much time sitting around the shop over Christmas, putting on weight.'

'Good to hear. I know the feeling about putting on weight over Christmas.' He absent-mindedly tapped his own slightly inflated post-Christmas paunch.

'Have you seen the article in one of the papers about the murder?' she asked. 'It's only in one. Here you are.'

She showed him the second page of a Midlands Sunday newspaper. It had printed a short news item headlined, 'Murder squad find woman, 60, dead in garden'. The story said:

Heart of England police were called to a cottage in Norton Prior, Warwicks after a holidaymaker vanished just hours after returning from a skiing trip. The woman's body was discovered when police conducted a search of her home. The south Midlands coroner has been alerted. A police spokesman said the victim wouldn't be named until next of kin had been informed. He refused to give further details. No one's been arrested.

'I think it happened somewhere at the far end of the lane,' Julie muttered. 'Customers were telling me they saw lots of police up there yesterday.'

'This is terrible,' he said. 'I think I'd better have a copy of this paper as well.'

'Certainly,' she said, folding the two newspapers together for him and taking the money.

* * *

A few hours later, Gavin Roscoe cut short his Sunday with his family to call the force press office. He'd decided he would hold a 'press briefing' that afternoon and appeal for the public's help.

The female press officer on duty suggested he could speak to the media in the street outside Rose Cottage since a large contingent of reporters and photographers had gathered there for the second day running. Two hours later, he set off for Norton Prior.

Soon after three o'clock, Gavin Roscoe's car drew up a short distance from the murder scene. After a brief conversation with a press officer, the DCI stepped forward to address the throng of journalists.

Six reporters had been standing around and chatting on the pavement outside the house. But, as he signalled he was about to address them, a dozen more journalists and photographers emerged from parked cars and gathered round him.

'I'm glad you're all here this morning,' Roscoe told them. 'I'm appealing today for the public's help. As you know, there are currently investigations taking place into three major crimes – two murders and a missing person – and I can assure you that Heart of England Police are doing everything they can to bring the offenders to justice.

'We know some people in the village may be frightened and the Chief Constable has informed us that extra police patrols will be brought onto the streets for the time being to reassure the public. We particularly want to appeal to residents of Norton or visitors to the village. If anyone saw any suspicious behaviour in this area between nine thirty and ten thirty on Friday morning, 15 February, please contact the police – no matter how insignificant they feel that information may be. We've got the time and resources to investigate and something that might, at first glance, appear a minor matter could – in the context of the wider investigation – ultimately prove to have greater significance.

'We also need help in tracing a car. The vehicle concerned is believed to be a small blue car. It was seen here, outside Rose Cottage, on the morning of Mrs Thomas's murder. If the driver or anyone with information could come forward, that would hugely assist this investigation. It may be that the driver's got a totally innocent explanation for their presence here. If that's the case, it would nevertheless help us to eliminate them from our inquiry.'

Reporters began firing questions. One asked if Mrs Thomas might have interrupted a burglary, but the DCI revealed nothing appeared to have been stolen and there were no signs of a break-in. It seemed the killer or killers had been invited in and that Mrs Thomas therefore knew them.

John Singleton from Midlands TV said it was unclear to them how the woman died. Was she strangled or killed with a weapon?

Roscoe said he was unable to say anything more about this until he'd spoken to the Home Office pathologist and the coroner. He added they were also considering whether more than one person might have been involved.

Eventually, after twenty minutes, the force press officer stepped in. She exchanged glances with the detective and then announced, 'The DCI is not answering any further questions. Sorry.' She added, 'If you've got any other questions, please call the press office. You know the number.'

Chapter 34

The voice of the magistrates' clerk boomed out across the crowded courtroom on Monday, 18 February.

'Stand up. Are you Arun Halder?'

The computer technician rose from his chair in the dock, where he was flanked by two custody officers.

'Yes,' he said faintly.

The clerk of the Birmingham court continued, 'Do you live at 17 Elmfield Grove, Leicester?'

The defendant nodded.

'And is your date of birth 4 September 1991?'

'Yes,' said Halder.

The clerk, a grey-haired man in his fifties wearing a brown suit, went on, 'Arun Halder, you're charged with the abduction of Sunita Roy, a Detective Sergeant with Heart of England Police, on Friday, 8 February from Hall Green, Birmingham. Do you understand?'

Halder nodded again.

The clerk wrote something down before asking, 'How do you plead?'

The defendant replied, 'Not guilty.'

'Sit down!' the clerk demanded. Then he turned to the three magistrates sitting above him and consulted with them. He was explaining to them that this was the defendant's second court appearance since his arrest at Birmingham Airport.

Facing the court again, the clerk announced, 'I understand the second defendant in this case, Mr Ashok Halder, is unwell.' Gazing over his shoulder, he continued, 'If it please Your Worships, it's suggested his case should be adjourned sine die.'

The chairman glanced at his colleagues, who nodded in turn.

'Agreed,' he said.

Tom Vickers was sitting in the back of the court, only half-listening to the legal rigmarole. He had risen from his bed early that day to ensure he arrived at court in good time. His only concern was to see that Arun Halder should be denied bail.

The prosecutor then addressed the magistrates.

'If Your Worships please, I represent the Crown in this case. My friend, Mr Clifford-Jones, represents Mr Halder. This offence relates to an incident that happened on the evening of 8 February in Hall Green.

'The man in the dock once enjoyed a brief relationship with a lady who's currently working as a detective sergeant in the police. Despite her making it clear the relationship had ended and despite him being issued with a harassment warning, he has continued pestering her with messages and visits to her home.

'At just after five o'clock on the evening in question, he approached her near her home in Cateswell Road and threatened her with a gun. He then forcibly abducted her and drove her in his car to the city's airport where, fortunately, he was overpowered and arrested.

'In view of the seriousness of these offences, we're applying for the case to be transferred away from Your Worships' jurisdiction.'

The clerk then discussed with Mr Clifford-Jones whether he would be applying for bail. Vickers had, a few days earlier, discussed this issue with the Crown Prosecution Service, and it was agreed he should be denied bail. The clerk demanded then that the defendant should stand up again. Halder had to be hauled to his feet by his two attendants.

'Right,' said the chairman. 'Mr Halder, you'll be remanded in custody to a future date to appear at the Crown Court. You're denied bail in view of the serious nature of the offence.'

Pleased with the outcome of the hearing, Vickers slipped out of the court. He glanced round the lobby where other defendants were waiting with friends and relatives.

That man's looking at a long stretch, he thought to himself as he stepped over to the coffee machine and slid some money into the coin slot. He obtained a white coffee and found a seat on a nearby bench.

Then suddenly, as he was sipping his drink and contemplating his drive back to headquarters, he heard a commotion coming from the courtroom. It sounded as if someone had slammed a door twice. Then there were shouts of 'Oy! Oy!' Arun Halder had made a bid for freedom.

Alarmed at the prospect of being kept behind bars any longer, he had leapt from the dock, sprinted along the oak-panelled corridor and burst through the two heavy doors. He had then raced through the lobby like a whippet. Knocking into bystanders and fellow defendants, he careered out of the court building and dashed into the street. He was hotly pursued by two policemen and a custody officer.

Vickers put his coffee on the floor and followed them out of the building. He made an initial attempt to give chase, but the man who had caused his colleague Sunita so much anguish was lost in the distance by the time he reached the pavement. He watched as the three men who had pursued Halder walked back, shaking their heads.

How ridiculous he wasn't handcuffed while in the dock, he thought angrily to himself.

Later he phoned Sunita to inform her of the incident and assure her all officers working for West Midlands Police – the force responsible for the court – had been alerted to look out for the fugitive.

'The worst moment for any defendant is when they're told they're being denied bail,' he pointed out. 'It means more to them than virtually anything else.'

'Do you think he'll come looking for me again?' she asked.

'Unlikely. Not when he's got half the coppers in the Midlands on his tail. Don't worry, Sunita. He won't be on the loose for long.'

* * *

Gavin Roscoe was becoming gradually convinced that James Hockley and Margaret Bowers were behind the murders. It was clear from what his own daughter had told him that the couple were having an affair.

They'd been caught canoodling in Hockley's blue Toyota at the sports field in Oxford Park. Furthermore, Sergeant Roy believed she'd seen Mrs Bowers' coat inside Hockley's home. If they were lovers, they'd much to gain from Harry's disappearance.

But he needed concrete proof of their relationship. He decided to give PC Brett Dawson the task of maintaining an all-night watch on Heathwood House from a distance to see if Hockley was staying there. He would organise that immediately with the first watch timed for that night. If Dawson could obtain photographs of the couple together, so much the better.

There was also evidence of a disagreement between the businessman and the sports teacher. Hockley had been seen openly arguing with Bowers at least twice. And it was the second incident – the argument on the night of Bowers' disappearance and probable murder – that was crucial to the case.

Almost immediately after a witness to that event had started to reveal details of it, her life had been cut short in the most brutal manner. In his mind, this made Hockley a prime suspect in relation to both deaths – at least circumstantially.

Hockley had been informed by the rector about Mrs Thomas's testimony soon after she spoke out in Oxford Lane.

Not only that. The newly returned holidaymaker also told of seeing something else – a figure lurking in the shadows, watching the argument unfold.

Could that figure have been Margaret Bowers? Had she followed her husband on that fateful night to the scene of the argument and watched the two men in her life fighting by the lychgate? If this incident had led ultimately to her husband's death, where had she and Hockley hidden the body?

And what of the man who had been drowned and then dumped in the river? There was no clear link between the drowned man and Bowers. But all three cases were associated with the same small village. Had he also witnessed Hockley being involved in a criminal act and been silenced in a similar way – or had Hockley had some other motive for ending that man's life?

Everything seemed to be fitting into place. There was even an eyewitness account of a small blue car outside Rose Cottage around the time of Bethan Thomas's murder – and Hockley drove a small blue car.

All these thoughts were circulating through his mind as the DCI parked his car outside his office. He was in a buoyant mood, hoping that he would shortly be able to unmask the culprit. However, if he'd glanced over his shoulder, he might have noticed a few dark clouds were looming over the horizon.

Once inside his room, he took off his navy-blue coat and yellow scarf and placed them on a hanger. Then he left a message for Tom Vickers, asking him to call in as soon as he returned from court, and began reading through the morning's newspapers.

* * *

Half an hour later, the inspector knocked and poked his head round the door.

'Have you heard about the escape, guv?' he asked the DCI.

'What escape?'

'That Arun Halder guy broke out of the dock and did a runner.'

'Oh God. That's all we need.'

'I know, guv. We've issued an all-ports warning in case he tries to flee the country.'

'That's good. And West Mids have been alerted?'

'Yes, guv.'

'Good work, Tom. Must catch that guy. Sunita's abduction was all over the news when it happened and it doesn't look good, having one of our own officers kidnapped at gunpoint.'

'No, guv.'

'Other than that, are you fairly free at the moment?'

'Yes, guv.'

Roscoe smiled. 'Good, because I've got something else for you.'

Vickers interrupted him. 'Guv, you know you'd hoped to keep some of the gorier details out of the papers to protect the relatives? Well, I'm afraid things haven't gone our way. Two of the papers have got hold of the fact the body was found in a sandpit. I know we were trying to prevent that becoming public for a while in case we made an arrest and they'd got sand on their clothing.'

Roscoe gave a nonchalant shrug. 'Never mind. Let's have a look then,' he said.

Vickers pointed out one national newspaper which carried a frontpage banner headline saying, 'Serial killer hunt after gran, 62, bludgeoned to death'.

Then he flicked through a second paper until he found a page five headline which announced, 'Bludgeoned to death, then dumped in a sandpit'. He also showed the DCI a two-page spread in a third newspaper with a headline trumpeting, 'Murdered skier killed with claw hammer'.

Roscoe stressed how important it was that they made substantial progress on the case that week in order to placate senior officers.

'What do we know of Hockley's movements at the time of the Bethan Thomas murder?' Roscoe asked. 'I'm minded to pull him in, but, before we do that, we need to know where he was at 10.00 a.m. on Friday. We also need to account for Margaret Bowers' whereabouts at that time and discover who benefits from the deaths of Bowers and Thomas. Do you think that you, Sunita and two of our other people could get working on that?'

Vickers nodded. 'I can put in a call to West Warwickshire Academy this morning and find out about Hockley's attendance at school last Friday.'

'Oh, and one more thing,' said the DCI. 'When you get a moment, later this week, could you check the names of all the residents in Oxford Lane and nearby roads on the voters' list and the database? We need to see if any of them have previous convictions – particularly for offences involving violence. And the car, of course, which is probably our biggest breakthrough. I want details of everyone who owns a small blue car in Norton and for five miles around.'

'That's a tall order, guv.'

'I know it's a tall order, but it'll have to be done. That's how we often crack these cases – sheer hard work.'

Vickers was about to return to his desk when Roscoe called him back once again, saying, 'While it's on my mind...'

'Yes, guv?'

Roscoe smiled. 'Thank you very much for all the hard work you've been putting in, Tom. It's really appreciated. What are you doing tomorrow lunchtime?'

Vickers shrugged his shoulders. 'Nothing that I know of, guv.'

'Good. I'm thinking of taking you and the young sergeant out for lunch. I want us to get our heads together somewhere quiet and take some important decisions.'

'Away from the hurly-burly of the office, guv? I hear what you're saying.'

'All right, Tom. See you later.'

* * *

In the afternoon, Vickers was the bearer of some bad news.

'The school secretary says Hockley was taking a PE class of fourteen-year-old girls at 9.30 a.m. on the day of Mrs Thomas's murder,' he told the DCI in a phone call. 'He must've phoned the rector from the school between classes.'

Roscoe scowled. 'Can we be absolutely certain of that? Perhaps you should go and see the school secretary in person in case she's made a mistake. What about Margaret Bowers?'

'She doesn't have an alibi. She was at home on her own. The same goes for David Harrington. Only his son Michael can vouch for him, while Rashad Mahmood claims he was at a meeting in London, but we can't find anyone who can verify that.'

'What about the checks carried out into the wills?' asked Roscoe.

'Harry Bowers left everything to his wife, guv. Bethan Thomas's will was changed recently. Her property and assets are to be split equally between her daughter and Tyler Brown. Previously it was just the daughter who was to inherit.'

'So Tyler Brown stands to benefit? Very interesting, Tom,' the DCI said.

'That's not all, guv. Apparently, Mrs Thomas wasn't poor. She'd inherited two million quid from her husband when he died a few years ago, although you wouldn't think so – judging by her frugal lifestyle.'

'What about the CCTV at Norton News?'

'Dawson's checking through it, guv, but you wouldn't believe how many blue cars there have been travelling along Oxford Lane. Anyway he's taken note of all the car numbers he can decipher.' Vickers paused to cough. 'Sorry, guv. By the way, Sergeant Roy's come up trumps. She's discovered Tyler Brown's company, Royal Avon Marina, is in financial difficulties.'

Roscoe was heartened after hearing of these new developments in the case.

'Thank you for all that, Tom,' he said. 'First class work by both of you.'

Chapter 35

The Crown and Sceptre was a popular pub at the south-western end of the high street in Queensbridge.

Gavin Roscoe knew the venue would be busy on Tuesday lunchtime, particularly as it was market day. But he decided that, if he and his two colleagues met there at midday, they would be able to find a quiet corner for a summit on the Oxford Lane case.

Both of his colleagues had additional reasons for visiting Queensbridge that afternoon. Tom Vickers needed to visit Hockley's school, while Sunita Roy had to make an exhaustive search for any further CCTV film that might be available.

It was quiet in the main bar when the three detectives arrived. It was unlikely to remain so for long. By one o'clock, the bar would be filled with the hubbub of conversation as shop and office staff jostled with farmers, shoppers and tourists. But Roscoe felt this would give them enough time for a full discussion.

The building had a faded elegance often seen in England's former commercial hotels. The room had high ceilings with elaborate covings and cornices. It boasted grey upholstered perimeter seating with a range of dark-brown polished tables and upholstered chairs.

There were two couples drinking at tables close to the bar, so Roscoe headed for a table at the back of the room. Sunita surveyed their surroundings. There was a pool table nearby, but it was quiet and there was no music.

'I think this'll be fine, won't it?' said Roscoe. 'Let's just have a drink and see the menu.'

'Sounds good to me,' she said.

Vickers nodded.

A few minutes later, the group had settled themselves down at Roscoe's chosen table, which was next to a sash window. The men were each drinking a pint of QB Bitter, while Sunita had settled for an orange juice. They had also ordered sandwiches.

'Now the reason I wanted to have a word with you both is that I think I know who our murderer is,' Roscoe announced, as he sipped his drink. 'But I wanted to share my theories before I take the crucial next step. You've both been working hard on this case – particularly you, Sergeant. So I'd really appreciate hearing your thoughts.'

The DCI summarised all the latest progress made. He reminded them of the eyewitness report of a small blue car in Oxford Lane; the contents of Bethan Thomas's and Harry Bowers' wills; and reiterated details of Tyler Brown's financial problems.

'I think you'd probably agree we're looking for a man rather than a woman,' he said, 'and I think we can assume, at least for the moment, that all three cases are linked.'

Sunita nodded. 'It seems unlikely we'd have two murderers at large in a country village over the same short period of time.'

'That's right, on the balance of probabilities,' said Roscoe. 'We're looking for a man because they would've had to be strong enough to drown marina man and heave his body into the river. Strong enough to half-strangle a woman, bludgeon her to death and then bury her in a shallow grave. It's also someone who's highly secretive in the way they operate. All our hard graft so far points to Hockley being the killer with Margaret Bowers as an accessory.'

He also informed them that PC Dawson had struck lucky with his very first dusk-to-dawn undercover operation outside Heathwood House.

'He's got hazy photographs of Hockley under a streetlight – arriving at seven last night and leaving at eight o'clock this morning,' he said. 'To me, this confirms their relationship.'

As the food was delivered to their table, Vickers said he could understand him suspecting them since the pair were clearly lovers. But the CID team had to examine the lives of all the suspects, he insisted.

Sunita was encouraged by the inspector's refusal to accept Roscoe's theory without question. For she also had doubts about the involvement of Hockley and Margaret Bowers.

After biting into her sandwich, she leaned back on her seat and gazed across the table at Roscoe.

'Sir, we need to look at other possibilities as well. I think David Harrington can be discounted. Although he had a feud with the Bowers family and may have arranged the arson attack, it's hard to believe he would have launched a wholesale campaign of murder. But I believe we ought to consider Tyler Brown. He was desperate for money and stands to gain greatly from Mrs Thomas's will. He's got a clear financial motive, despite his apparent devotion to his partner.

'Another suspect must be Rashad Mahmood. He stands to gain in that he could now become sole director of the property firm set up by Bowers.'

The DCI nodded. 'That's true, of course, but his route to financial gain isn't clear-cut. Don't forget that Margaret Bowers would inherit a financial stake in that business if her husband were declared dead as she's the sole beneficiary of her husband's will.'

Sunita sipped her orange juice. 'I agree it looks bleak for James Hockley, sir. I can see why you'd consider him the main suspect, but there are several other factors we've got to look at. We've obtained samples of several suspects' handwriting and I think it's agreed that Margaret Bowers wrote the note herself – probably in an attempt to throw us off the scent. We've also got evidence she and Hockley were having an affair and had a lot to gain if Harry Bowers was out of the picture.'

Roscoe nodded. 'This is the reason why I think the two lovers are behind all this. It looks to me as if Harry Bowers got wind of their affair. He arranged to meet the teacher by the lychgate so he could tackle him about it. Margaret Bowers may have been hiding across the road as the two men fought. Bowers was killed and they found somewhere to conceal the body. That's how it appears to me.'

Vickers had been listening to the pair as he quietly ate his sandwich. Now he intervened to say, 'So is it your belief, guv, that, when Hockley found out that Bethan Thomas was a possible witness, he killed her as well?'

'It's possible,' the DCI agreed.

'There's only one problem with the case against Hockley,' Vickers continued. 'The school says he was taking a PE class at the time of Bethan Thomas's murder.

While I'm in the town today, I'm going to make further checks to see if that's correct.'

The DCI went to the bar and bought another round of drinks. Then, as he took a sip from his half-pint of ale, he returned to the conversation.

'We need to delve a little into Hockley's past life. For instance, has he ever been married? What do we know about his background? Sergeant, I'd like you to take on this research.'

'Happy to do that, sir,' she said. 'But I believe PC Dawson checked and couldn't find any details of a wedding.'

Roscoe raised an eyebrow. 'Strange, isn't it? He's thirty-four and one for the ladies. I'm wondering if he's changed his name. Can we check?'

'Yes, sir. I'll do that this afternoon. Sir, as far as the other suspects are concerned, we can almost certainly exclude the rector, Peter Hughes. But obviously there was a small group of customers talking to Mrs Thomas in the street. Anyone of them could've overheard what she said. And then again, maybe her death's got nothing to do with those remarks she made in the street.'

For the moment, Roscoe no longer seemed to be listening. He was thinking back to the moment he learned Hockley and Margaret Bowers had been seen kissing in Hockley's car. He was determined to have Hockley arrested, despite the misgivings of his two colleagues.

'Don't you both agree we need to have Hockley brought in and find out what he's got to say? We know he was with Bowers at the time he disappeared and it's vital to know for certain where he was at the time of the Bethan Thomas murder.'

'Yes, sir,' said Sunita. 'At the very least, it might give us the opportunity to eliminate him from inquiries.'

'I was just going to say the same thing,' added Vickers. 'Once he's arrested, we need to search his house and see if he's got any coils of rope, or sand on any of his boots.'

Roscoe nodded in agreement.

As the time approached one o'clock and the bar began to fill with customers, Roscoe decided to bring the conversation to a close.

'If it's all right with you, guv, I'm going to shoot over to the school,' said the DI.

'Yes. Good time to chat to school secretaries during the lunch-hour,' said Roscoe. 'Off you go, Tom.'

After he'd gone, Roscoe and Sunita left the pub and walked to the car park behind the building. Sunita harboured major doubts about the culpability of James Hockley, but at this point she didn't feel it was the right time to express them.

She accepted Hockley should be arrested and questioned under caution. People often became garrulous when placed under pressure in an interview room, she knew from her past short-lived experience as a detective constable.

'Thanks for coming, Sergeant,' said Roscoe. 'Good luck this afternoon and let's chat later.'

As she headed off in the direction of Norton Prior, Sunita began wondering what it was that turned a man into a murderer. Could a respected member of the community suddenly turn and take the life of another human being if they were under enough pressure to do so?

She believed, in some cases, this might happen. During her legal studies and experience of crime investigations, she'd been surprised by the diversity of characters and personalities that had been arrested, charged, prosecuted and found guilty of this ultimate crime.

There'd been rich, poor, young, old, educated and uneducated. Criminal profiling was helpful up to a point in determining whether a suspect showed the characteristics of a potential killer. But her personal experience suggested that not all murderers fitted the expected criteria.

Could James Hockley be one of these exceptions? Although he appeared to be an upstanding member of society, a schoolteacher tasked with educating young people about cultural and moral values, he'd at least twice shown aggression towards Harry Bowers.

However, she had real doubts about whether Hockley could've been involved in all three cases. To carry out a single murder was one matter. To carry out two, or possibly three, murders was different. The death of Bethan Thomas had been particularly brutal. This required a warped mind, she told herself.

* * *

Sunita had a rather fruitless afternoon. She couldn't find any other premises that had CCTV footage that could be of help to them.

She was about to set off for home when she unexpectedly received a call on her mobile phone from Tom Vickers.

'How you doing, Sarge?' he asked.

'Has Arun been caught yet?'

'Not yet. I'll keep you posted. He won't be able to last long out there. We're checking on all his known haunts. Anyway, I've had a wasted afternoon. None of the school secretaries I need to speak to have been around.'

'Wherever Hockley was on the 15th, Tom, I find it hard believing he could be a triple murderer.'

'I know what you mean, Sunita. You can imagine Hockley and Margaret Bowers having something to do with the husband's disappearance, but that teacher doesn't have the mark of a serial killer about him.

'His only previous convictions were for motoring offences as a young student. There's no history of violent offences. On top of that, he doesn't have the character and mindset of a triple killer.'

'I know,' said Sunita. 'His job requires him to help improve the physical health of children. That doesn't fit with someone who's killed three times over a few weeks. It just doesn't ring true.' She paused for a moment. Then she said, 'Do you know, Tom? One of the things baffling me concerns the timings that Hockley gave us for the night of 8 January.

'He says he was ten minutes late arriving for choir practice at the church hall. If he met Bowers at 7.00 p.m., he'd have only had twenty-five minutes at the most in which to kill him, dispose of the body and make it to the church hall. Is that enough time?'

'No. It isn't,' said Vickers. 'You're right.'

'According to other members of the choir, he turns up unflustered ten minutes after the choir practice started and sang his heart out as if nothing had happened.'

'No, there are doubts about his involvement, but as we both agreed at the pub, he's got to be brought in – if only to be eliminated.'

Sunita shook her head. 'I've a feeling we're looking at this all wrong,' she said.

* * *

Sunita Roy had been reading a new Preeti Shenoy romantic novel when the doorbell rang. She darted into the hall and unfastened the newly installed safety chain on her front door. Then she peered out into the dark February night. Through the gap in the doorway, she was delighted to see the smiling face and small, sharp, brown eyes of her older cousin Daniel.

'Daniel! How wonderful to see you!' she exclaimed, releasing the chain and throwing the door open.

They hugged earnestly.

'Come in! Come in!' cried Sunita as she led him into the living room.

'Rupa, you know my cousin Daniel, don't you?'

'Of course,' said Rupa without moving from her seat on the settee. 'Hi, Daniel. You're the one that went to Kolkata with Sunita, aren't you? I heard you ate too many pancakes.'

'Yes, that was me.'

Sunita laughed. 'Would you like some tea, Daniel?'

'I'm fine for the moment. I came round to find out how you are,' he said, sitting down next to Rupa. 'The family's heard about your problems with Arun Halder.'

'It's been a nightmare, Daniel,' said Sunita, settling herself into an armchair.

'I heard he pointed a gun at you at the airport.'

Rupa, who had an Indian travel book in her lap, beamed at him. 'Not for long. Sunita grabbed the gun, kicked him in the goolies and then pointed the gun back at him.'

'Well done, Sunita. So I hear he and his brother have both been arrested?'

'Yes.'

'But you haven't heard the latest, Daniel,' said Rupa, clasping her hands round her book. Sunita frowned at her. 'Sorry, Sunita. It's your story. You'd better tell it.'

'Thank you, Rupa,' said Sunita. 'Yes, Arun appeared at the court again and vaulted the dock to escape from the building.'

'What?'

'He dodged security staff and ran out of the court in the city centre. So he's now on the run.'

'Are you kidding me? Sunita, he could've killed you at the airport. What's to stop him coming back here again?'

'Nothing really.'

Rupa interrupted to say, 'Except half the West Midlands Police force are on his tail.'

Sunita nodded. 'That's right. One of my work colleagues, Tom, is keeping me updated and police have promised to step up patrols around here. So if he were foolish enough to call round here, he'd pretty soon feel a firm hand on his shoulder.'

Rupa laughed. 'Not to mention another firm kick in the groin from Sunita,' she said.

Daniel, who was slim with short, dark hair, smiled. 'So where does your friend Tom think he's gone?'

Sunita shrugged. 'He can't go home to his wife because the police might be watching the building.'

'He's got a wife?'

'Yes.'

'He's a crazy guy.'

'This is the problem,' said Rupa, becoming serious for a moment. 'He's so crazy he could do anything.'

Sunita frowned. 'A friend or relative must be harbouring him. He's got no access to money and his car's been impounded.'

'Let's hope they catch him before he does something stupid,' said Daniel.

'His details have been widely shared by all the Midlands forces,' Sunita explained. 'He can't get far. I'm sure it won't be long before he's safely back behind bars again.'

Daniel leaned back on the settee and stretched his legs out. 'Do you think I could have that tea after all?'

Rupa put her book down on the coffee table and stood up. 'I'll go and make it. Do you want one as well, Sunita?'

'Please.'

As soon as she had left the room, Daniel began speaking to his cousin in a low voice in Bengali.

'I wanted to mention that your parents are worried about you, and not just because of Arun. They haven't heard from you for such a long time.'

'Oh, Daniel. My life is different now. They've never forgotten the way I defied them over marriage.'

'Your father was very upset yesterday because he hasn't heard from you.'

'So you were delegated to visit me?'

'Oh, Sunita, it wasn't like that. I've always been close to you and, of course, wanted to see how things are with you. But your parents are concerned.'

'I'll give it some thought, Daniel.'

Chapter 36

Chief Superintendent Nicola Norris was dismayed when the latest edition of the *Queensbridge Gazette* was delivered to her on Thursday, 21 February. She at once summoned Roscoe to her second-floor office.

'Have you seen this, Gavin?' she asked as her chief inspector knocked and entered.

In truth, the DCI had only had time to glance at the front page and had not yet read it thoroughly. However, he was loath to let the chief superintendent know that. She might interpret that as a failing in addition to any other complaint she might have.

'I had a quick look at the frontpage piece, ma'am,' he said. 'It doesn't read well, does it?'

'No, it doesn't,' said Norris sternly. She started to read the article aloud.

> *Police under fire over botched murder probe.*
> *Heart of England Constabulary have been heavily criticised for alleged failings in their investigation into the Norton murders. Retired teacher Bethan Thomas was found strangled and her body buried in a children's sandpit after she was reported missing.*
> *A murdered man's body was recovered from the River Avon last month and a businessman is missing. Yet no one has been arrested. Police have failed to identify the dead man or locate the businessman. This newspaper today has got a message for Heart of England Police: Get your act together. The chairman of the Norton Residents' Association, local councillors and the Conservative MP for West Warwickshire have all joined in criticising the police over their lack of progress…*

'And so it goes on.'

The chief superintendent, who was in full police uniform as she was about to leave for an official function, glared at him.

'Now, as you know, Gavin, we don't take too much stock of what the press has to say. We plough our own furrow. But the assistant chief constable happened to stop at a petrol station near Queensbridge on his way to headquarters this morning. He spotted a billboard which said, "Police – get your act together". As you can imagine, he wasn't too impressed and he called me. So I was hoping you might have some news for me that can reassure us. If you don't, it's in his mind to bring in another detective to take over the investigation.'

Although he'd not been invited to do so, Roscoe slumped down on a chair in front of the chief superintendent's desk. He privately felt exhausted, as if all the lost sleep he'd been experiencing since January had finally caught up with him.

Then, with a hint of pride in his voice, he declared, 'Actually, we're on the point of making two arrests.'

'Good!' she said. 'That's what we like to hear. Who do you have in mind?'

'James Hockley and Margaret Bowers.'

'Hockley? Hockley? Isn't that the man who made a complaint to us?' said Norris, leaning forward across her desk and peering at the DCI like an owl watching a vole.

Roscoe confirmed that it was.

'Could you outline your reasons?' she asked. 'I need to pass on this news to the assistant chief constable.'

Roscoe then explained his rationale to her.

'So you're proposing to arrest the pair of them?'

'Yes, ma'am,' said Roscoe, who was careful to avoid mentioning the problem with Hockley's alibi for 15 February.

'Very well,' the chief superintendent said, scratching her short, grey hair with her chubby fingers. 'But some of the evidence is rather circumstantial. For instance, there are lots of small blue cars about. My next-door neighbour's got a small blue car.'

Roscoe nodded. 'I appreciate that, ma'am. But we believe we should get the pair in and interview them under caution. They may let something slip. We may even get a confession out of them.'

'Good. What's Tom Vickers doing these days?'

'He's just finished working on the Crows Wood robbery. We've got two guys for it.'

'Well, if he's free now, get him involved in the Norton case and see if we can't get it all wrapped up.'

Roscoe nodded.

Norris turned her wheelchair to the right and manoeuvred her way round to the front of the desk.

'By the way, how's your new sergeant making out? I was concerned to hear the brute who abducted her has gone on the run.'

'Yes, ma'am. Very regrettable. But she's a woman who can take care of herself. She snatched a gun from the fellow, after all. To be honest, ma'am, she's been incredibly helpful in the murder investigation. She found traces of blood at Mrs Thomas's home, traces of sand on a spade that led us to the discovery in the sandpit and she also uncovered the murder weapon. Like me, she wants Hockley brought in.'

Chief Supt Norris smiled. 'Good, solid detective work. That's what I like to hear. Carry on!'

On returning to his first-floor office, Roscoe found his sergeant waiting for him.

'Sir, you know you suspected Hockley changed his name?' Sunita asked. 'Well, he did.' Picking up her notebook, she continued, 'Hockley was born James Whelan in Tewkesbury, Gloucestershire on 18 July, 1981.'

'How on earth did you manage to find out Hockley wasn't his original name?'

'I called our family history researcher. He discovered Whelan changed his name by deed poll to Hockley after his father appeared in court on some sex offences. By all accounts, he was ashamed of his father and didn't want to continue with the family name. When he started at the school in Queensbridge, he introduced himself as James Hockley.'

'Well, that explains that. So has he been married?'

'Yes. I've got the wife's details. She lives in a small village in Gloucestershire.'

'Good. Go down there and take Dawson with you. Have you seen anything of Tom Vickers?'

'Yes, sir. He had to go to Birmingham. There's been a sighting of the guy who was stalking me. He was seen at a convenience store in Hall Green.'

'All right. Don't suppose he mentioned his school visit?'

Yes. I've saved the best news to last, sir. At the school, the secretary tried to stand by her initial claim that Hockley had been taking a PE class. But, as she was leading him out of the secretaries' office, they happened to bump into one of the fourteen-year-old girls who would've been taking PE at nine thirty last Friday. She informed him Hockley had called in sick and, at the last minute, a teacher called Mr Wood had had to take the class instead.'

Roscoe was delighted. 'So he could well have been in Oxford Lane at the time of the murder.'

'Looks that way, sir.'

Chapter 37

Tom Vickers had been looking forward to skipping off early and watching some of the afternoon's televised racing from Chelmsford and Sedgefield. But instead he'd spent three hours sitting in a patrol car with two colleagues from West Midlands Police – Detective Sergeant Nigel Martin and a force driver, PC Phil McKenzie.

'I fancied having a look at a horse running in the three fifteen at Sedgefield, Nigel,' he moaned. 'But it can't be helped. We've got to try and catch our friend before he causes any more mischief.'

'I was due to go late-night shopping with my girlfriend,' Martin replied. 'So not so much of a sacrifice for me.'

Vickers glanced at him. 'You might still get home in time,' he murmured.

PC McKenzie was sitting in the driver's seat of the Ford Focus car with Martin beside him.

'What about you, Phil?' the inspector asked.

'You mean, if I wasn't here outside the Tesco Express in Hall Green, enjoying the benefits of your conversation?' said the driver. 'I'd probably be on driving duties and then going home to clean out my garden pond. It's turned into a warm, sunny day – ideal for sorting out the garden.'

'I never touch our pond,' said the inspector. 'Always get one of the gardeners on our estate to sort it.'

'You're joking, aren't you, sir?'

The sergeant grinned. 'Of course, he's joking.'

'That's right. There's no pond on our estate,' said Vickers.

They all laughed.

'Nice young woman, that sergeant of yours,' said Martin. 'I can see why our Mr Halder was attracted to her.'

'She's bright,' Vickers remarked. 'She doesn't deserve to be hounded by that prat.'

'Why don't we go for a little drive round again?' Vickers suggested.

'If you like, sir,' said McKenzie. 'You say it's a red Volkswagen Polo we're looking for?'

'That's right.'

The driver travelled for a short distance along the Stratford Road before turning into Cateswell Road. The car, with its blue and yellow police livery, glided along the avenue with Martin's eyes gazing left and Vickers' eyes gazing right. There was no sign of their quarry.

Then the driver noticed a red vehicle heading towards them. It seemed to slow as it ventured near to Sunita Roy's address. The suspect car came to a halt more than a metre from the kerb.

'Come on, boys!' exclaimed Vickers. 'This looks like chummy.'

McKenzie slowed the car down as they approached. They could now see a man with short black hair and a black beard peering towards Sunita's front door. Vickers leaped out and ran towards the vehicle, but Halder spotted him and at once accelerated away towards the Stratford Road.

McKenzie quickly turned the Focus round in the middle of Cateswell Road, picked up Vickers and sped after Halder with his blue light flashing and siren wailing.

Using the car radio, Martin spoke to the West Midlands Police control room.

'Vehicle making off,' he announced. 'Failing to stop for West Midlands officers. Speed five zero miles per hour.' He explained who they were and that they were pursuing Halder, who'd escaped custody. He gave their location and requested back-up. 'He seems to be heading for the A45 Coventry Road. Any mobiles in that vicinity?'

Halder turned right at the junction and, after a short distance, turned right again into Reddings Lane, a narrow street of Victorian terraced houses. He was travelling at speeds of between fifty and sixty miles an hour.

'Who taught him to drive? Bloody Lewis Hamilton? He's going to hit some of the other cars if he's not careful,' remarked Martin.

Occasionally Halder hurtled onto the right-hand side of the road to overtake vehicles. McKenzie, despite years of experience as a fast-response driver, was battling to keep up.

The red car turned right into busy Warwick Road and then swept past shops and industrial premises in Acocks Green. A set of traffic lights ahead had just turned red, but Halder drove on – nearly colliding with an oncoming car – and turned left into Stockfield Road with McKenzie close behind.

'He's definitely heading for the Coventry Road,' said Martin.

Vickers nodded. 'Yes. He's maybe aiming to get on the M6 and head back to Leicester.'

The chase continued for another mile at speeds of more than sixty miles an hour through the district of Yardley with Halder frequently taking risks by overtaking slow-moving vehicles. After the Swan Island roundabout, the pursuit moved south along Coventry Road with Halder weaving in and out of traffic. McKenzie began to fall behind. A siren wailed in the distance behind them and a helicopter emerged in the sky. It hovered overhead as it appeared the promised back-up was finally arriving.

But then, suddenly, a pedestrian crossing light turned red and two vehicles in front of Halder stopped to give way, blocking the entire carriageway. Halder was travelling so fast he was unable to dodge the black Mercedes and white Transit van. His Volkswagen ploughed into the back of the van, shedding smoke and debris. Eyewitnesses later compared the noise to the sound of a gas explosion or a bomb. Glass and debris were strewn across the street.

With a screech of tyres and curses from McKenzie, the police driver somehow managed to bring his car to a halt several metres short of the crossing, which was close to a sub-post office and a parade of shops.

Vickers and Martin leaped out and raced over to the Volkswagen.

'You go to the passenger side,' the inspector told his colleague. 'Just in case he tries to escape that way.'

But Halder was in no condition to flee. The front of the Polo was a mass of tangled, smoking metal. As Vickers peered into the car, he could see the windscreen was shattered and Halder's head had smashed into it, rendering him unconscious. He had blood seeping from a head wound and the detective guessed he may also have chest, pelvis and leg injuries.

'Bloody fool wasn't wearing a seatbelt,' Vickers exclaimed as his colleague attempted to open the passenger door.

'We're going to need an ambulance – fast!' said the inspector as a crowd of onlookers gathered and two West Midlands Police cars drew up behind them, their blue lights blazing.

A man out with his wife dropped his shopping bags and ran to the car.

'I'm a doctor,' he assured them. 'Let me have a look.'

But despite his eagerness to tend to the victim, they were unable to get Halder out.

Vickers and Martin struggled for several minutes before they were able to prise the driver's door open. The doctor managed to clear the driver's airways, but he was still trapped by his legs in the wreckage.

A faraway siren told them the fire brigade were on the way. Twenty minutes later, three burly members of the fire crew managed to cut the driver free, and two doctors and paramedics then lifted him onto a stretcher. Halder was placed in the back of an ambulance and driven away under blue lights.

'Any idea where you're taking him?' Vickers asked the driver.

'Queen Elizabeth.'

'Heartlands is nearer,' the inspector pointed out.

'I know but the QE's the major trauma centre, sir.'

Vickers, Martin and McKenzie walked to a nearby cafe where they tried to unwind after experiencing the wide gamut of emotions that taking part in a high-speed chase over four miles can bring.

After a few minutes spent drinking coffee with them, the inspector stepped outside where, in the distance, he could see the wreckage of Halder's car being loaded onto a lorry.

Taking out his mobile phone, he phoned the hospital to check on Halder's condition. Then he dialled Sunita's number.

'Tom, how's it going? Any luck?' she asked.

'I'm afraid it's all ended in tears,' he revealed.

'Oh no. How?'

'Halder turned up in Cateswell Road and refused to stop for us. He hightailed it through the streets until we came to the Coventry Road when he ploughed into the back of a van stopped at a crossing.'

'Is he alright?'

'Not really. By chance, a medic was passing by and brought him back to life, but he's in a serious state in hospital, Sunita, and there's a good chance he's not going to make it.'

Chapter 38

Gavin Roscoe waved to the receptionist as he swept through the entrance hall at police headquarters and mounted the stairs. The feelings of fatigue from the day before had lifted. He was now enjoying an air of confidence.

Moments after his arrival at his desk, he used a red marker pen to ring that day's date – Friday, 22 February. Two little ducks, he thought. He strolled to the door, which was ajar.

'Sergeant Roy!' he bellowed. 'Have you got a moment?'

She approached the office door, smiling broadly and bristling with confidence.

'Any news from West Mids on Halder?' he asked.

'No change, sir.'

'Still critical?'

'Yes, sir. They've got a constable posted outside intensive care. The police conduct people, the IOPC, have already started interviewing officers involved in the chase. They're collecting dashcam and CCTV footage.'

'Yes, very unfortunate incident, but he failed to stop and then drove like a maniac. I hope you won't let this affect your day-to-day work with us.'

'Oh, no, sir. But I feel very sorry for Halder's wife, Rani, sir. I was thinking of paying her a visit.'

'That's the last thing you should do while there's an IOPC investigation going on, as I'm sure you're well aware. Now, onto other things. We need to know the whereabouts of both Hockley and Margaret Bowers as we're about to take them into custody.'

'Certainly, sir. I'll get onto that right away. Would you also like me to check on what the facilities are like at Queensbridge? You know, make sure there's an interview room available and the situation regarding the cells?'

'Yes, that would be helpful. Thanks.'

* * *

The DCI was scrolling through police reports on his computer an hour later when he received a call on his mobile phone from Dr Reynolds. The pathologist had some crucial new evidence about the death of Bethan Thomas, he told him, but he sounded like a street corner preacher with a megaphone. The DCI had to hold the handset several inches from his ear.

'Gavin,' he roared. 'We could be looking for a rock climber or a mountaineer, if my thoughts are on the right track.'

'Could you lower your voice a little, Silas? I'm finding it hard to hear you.'

'Is that any better, old fruit?' said Reynolds more quietly.

'Fine.'

'I've just finished the post-mortem on Mrs Thomas's body. The provisional cause of her death is blunt force trauma. Tests have confirmed the killer used the victim's own claw hammer. They failed to strangle her because this lady was a fighter. She put up a hell of a struggle, which explains the broken fingernails and bruises to her hands.'

'Good for her,' the DCI mumbled, standing up and gazing out of his window towards the park.

'But the ligature eventually rendered her unconscious, whereupon the killer struck her with two blows of the hammer, leading to her death. By the way, there was no sign of any sexual assault.'

'Have you been able to carry out tests on the blood that was found?' Roscoe asked.

'Dr Ling and her colleagues are still performing tests. We may have some more information on that later. They're also looking at the microscopic debris recovered from the victim's fingernails. She may have scratched his skin. So we may find the killer's identity that way. But here's the interesting thing: we've carefully examined the rope marks which dug into her neck. The line of the ligature crosses immediately below the prominence of the larynx and passes back to the nape of the neck. The indentation in the skin was undoubtedly made by the rope we found. I believe it might be a climbing rope – you know, the specially made, rather elastic rope used by outdoor fanatics like rock climbers.'

Roscoe was pleased to hear this. 'I'm looking into questioning a sports teacher later today, so this could be vital information,' he said as he resumed his seat at the desk.

'Yes, old fruit,' said the forensic expert. 'You could be looking at a sportsman, rock climber, ex-serviceman – you know, someone who follows outdoor pursuits. But listen to this, Gavin. It's exactly the same kind of rope that was tied to the man we hauled from the river. Examination of both ropes show they almost certainly came from the same coil.'

'Brilliant. That clearly links the two murders then,' said Roscoe. 'Well, thank you very much, Silas. That helps immensely.'

'It's a pleasure. By the way, you know the inquest was opened and adjourned by the coroner, don't you?'

'Yes, a few days ago, wasn't it?'

'On Tuesday,' Dr Reynolds said. 'The coroner postponed the full hearing until your investigation's finished.'

'But we still don't know who he is.'

'We don't.'

* * *

After dabbing some lip gloss round her mouth and straightening her hair in the ground-floor ladies' washroom, Sunita Roy went looking for PC Dawson. She suspected she knew where she'd find him – and her guess proved right. He was standing by the coffee machine, chatting to an attractive blonde girl from the payroll office.

She coughed diplomatically. 'Sorry to interrupt.'

'Just a minute,' he murmured on seeing his colleague.

'Catch you later,' the girl replied, walking off with her coffee.

'We've got an urgent job,' Sunita informed him.

'Sorry, Sarge,' said the constable, breaking into a smile. 'Where are we off to?'

'Gloucestershire. I'll tell you on the way.'

'Let's get going then.'

As they passed through CID and strolled out of the building, she explained they were visiting James Hockley's former home.

'And you say there's a woman listed at the address?'

'Yes,' said Sunita. 'We think she's his ex-wife.'

'This should be an interesting couple of hours then.'

'Sorry to drag you away from your little chat with Julie from payroll.'

'We were only talking about soccer. She's a West Brom fan. They got lucky and beat us on Saturday.'

'Maybe you two could go to a match together sometime.'

'She's just a friend, Sunita. And anyway, she's got a boyfriend.'

Within a few minutes of leaving St James Street, they were speeding down the M42 motorway in Sunita's car through leafy countryside. After twenty minutes, they joined the Evesham road, entering the heart of a vast market gardening region, before passing through a string of quaint Cotswold villages.

'So Hockley was born with a different name?' said Dawson.

'Yes. He changed it in his late twenties. The story is that his father brought disgrace on the family with a court appearance. He sought a new life in Queensbridge and chose Hockley as it was his mother's maiden name.'

After meeting traffic in Broadway, a quaint town with red chestnut trees and historic honey-coloured limestone buildings, they finally arrived in the hamlet of Stretton Heath.

Sunita knew little about the isolated rural community, except it had a church, a shop, a pub and a small river running through it. The landscape was flat with farms and farm labourers' cottages appearing here and there. She wondered what sort of lives the people here led. She assumed most of them spent their time tilling the fields or herding cattle and sheep.

The pair asked at the inn, the Six Bells, for directions to Home Farm Cottages in Stream Walk. A barmaid said she believed a single lady lived there.

'The place is half a mile down the road on the left-hand side. You can't miss it,' she assured them.

Home Farm Cottages consisted of four brick-and-flint terraced properties located on a straight, narrow country lane surrounded by fields. They'd been built in the early part of the nineteenth century to accommodate farm labourers and their families.

In recent years, the red and grey cottages with small front gardens had been sold many times over and no longer housed farm workers.

Sunita wondered whether James Hockley would have enjoyed living in such a remote spot. The only change in scenery would have been the odd passing car or bleating sheep being herded home across the fields.

She parked by the roadside and the pair got out. As her car door slammed, a crow from a nearby tree was disturbed and flew above them, squawking in the cold February air. She opened the partly rotten wooden gate to the second cottage and walked up the red brick path, followed by her colleague. She knocked on the black, wooden door.

At first there was no reply. Then a young woman in her late twenties wearing a burgundy-coloured sweater and brown jeans opened it a few inches.

'Did a Mr Hockley live here once?' asked Sunita.

The householder looked surprised. 'Yes, a long time ago.'

'Police. Need to ask you a few questions,' said Sunita, showing her warrant card.

'You'd better come in then,' said the woman, rather begrudgingly.

The pair bowed their heads before walking directly into the small, dark living room. They found it contained a small green sofa, a table and three chairs, and was decorated with white wallpaper covered in tiny red flowers.

'You know Mr Hockley then?' Sunita continued.

'Yes, I know the swine,' she said. 'I should do. I'm married to him. Why the interest anyway?'

The two detectives were shocked. Sunita's face turned whiter than snow.

'You… you mean you're still married to him?' she stammered.

The pair tried to retain their composure as they stood in the centre of the room.

'Yes. I suppose this is about Harry Bowers, is it?'

'Just routine inquiries,' Dawson explained. 'Mr Hockley was the last person to see Bowers alive in Norton Prior.'

'I'd heard something about that. I'm Caron, by the way. Caron Whelan.'

Their hostess was a slim, dark-haired woman who was about five feet three inches tall. Sunita thought her rather plain-looking, but she'd an easy-going nature and, after her initial hesitancy, seemed resigned to answer questions.

The pair sat down on the sofa. Caron made them tea and, after examining Sunita's warrant card, sat down opposite them at the table.

'Yes, I've seen on my laptop about the missing man and the murders,' she said. 'We're going through a divorce, so I'd better watch what I say. But I can tell you he's been a pain in the backside.'

Sunita took out her small notebook. 'How long have you been married?' she asked.

'We got married in Gloucester in 2008 and we've got a little girl who's now nine called Molly.'

Sunita drew a quick breath. 'You've got a little girl?'

Their host nodded.

'Did you live here with your husband throughout the marriage?'

'Yes. My parents live just up the road and James got a job in a school in Cheltenham. But he was hardly ever at home. He was always at the school or playing football or organising a sports team. It wasn't a marriage, and, when I complained, he used to hit me. He beat me with a cricket bat three times. Once he struck me so hard I had to go to hospital. The nurses were suspicious, but I just said I'd fallen downstairs.

'My dad had to kick him out in the end, six years ago, and I've not seen him since. He pays me money for Molly, but it's not a great deal, and, if it weren't for my parents, I don't know how I'd be managing.'

Sunita was diligently taking notes. 'Have you got a job?' she asked.

'I work part-time as a cleaner in a school. It's hard raising a child on your own.'

Dawson looked into her anxious eyes. 'Having the cops round every now and then must've been a pain,' he remarked.

'The police only came once in 2011. My father called them out. I didn't want to make an issue of it. Look, he was a bastard to me, but if you're trying to link him to these events in Norton, I've got doubts. I'm not sure he could beat a woman to death and hide the body in a sandpit. That sounds like someone with mental health problems.'

'Did you know he was involved with Margaret Bowers?' Sunita asked.

'Yes,' said Caron. 'I'd heard rumours. He's probably only after her money.'

'Is that you and James above the fireplace?' Sunita asked, after noticing a colour photograph of a couple standing by a church door.

'Yes, that was our wedding day. I've only kept it there for the sake of Molly. She takes it down and looks at it from time to time. She used to cry and cry when he first left.'

'When was that?'

'Summer 2012.'

'So you've been separated for four years?'

'Yes, that's right.'

'So when did you discover he'd changed his name?'

'I didn't hear anything from him for two years. Then I got a letter out of nowhere saying he'd taken to using his mother's maiden name.'

Dawson was intrigued by the name switch. He leaned forward. 'Did he give any reason?'

'He said his dad had been taken to court. He wanted to break all ties with his family and started calling himself Hockley.'

Sunita wrote down Caron's phone number and then the pair set off back to the CID office.

'I hope the DCI will be pleased with our morning's work,' she remarked as they passed Evesham and headed back towards the motorway. 'We know a little bit more now about our Mr Hockley.'

'Yes, bit of a swine to his wife. I can see he'd have been more than ready to use his fists if someone provoked him.'

'I'm going to carry out some checks on the name James Whelan when we get back. I'll look into his dad's case as well. I wonder if he really changed his name because of his dad.'

'How do you mean?'

'Well, some people change their name after a spell in prison.'

Chapter 39

There was a strange stillness about the night. As Sunita stared out of the car window, she could see countless stars twinkling above her. But there was no sign of the crescent moon, that mistress of the night sky, who'd slipped into hiding – camouflaged by the clouds. The young policewoman was peering through the windscreen and front passenger window of Roscoe's BMW as the DCI drove them ever closer to the village of Norton Prior.

After leaving Birmingham's leafy suburbs, their journey had passed through dark country lanes before they reached the well-lit streets of Queensbridge with their mix of modern and medieval buildings. Soon afterwards, they were plunged back into the gloom for the final stretch of their journey.

They passed between open fields and meadows with just a few trees, here and there, to break up the monotony of the landscape. Now and then, they would see a bright glow as they passed a streetlight illuminating a row of shops or a terrace of farm cottages. Then the interminable darkness would return.

Finally, at just after eight, they arrived at their destination, Heathwood House, on the village outskirts. Sunita was slightly in awe at the gravity of their mission. She was also a little excited. They were there to arrest Margaret Bowers.

Roscoe had arranged for PC Underhill to meet them outside the gates to the house with four other officers.

He'd also arranged for Tom Vickers and three other colleagues to call at James Hockley's home in Norton Hill in a simultaneous raid. Forensic teams had been alerted and were on their way to both addresses.

Sunita got out and peered through the iron gates at the impressive house at the end of the drive. Her eyes drifted past the wisteria and rose bushes towards the leaded light windows. The house was in darkness apart from one light flickering in the hallway and another shining from an upstairs window. For a moment, she thought she spotted a face appear at the curtains. Roscoe took out his mobile phone and called Vickers.

'Are you all set, Tom?' he asked.

'Yes, guv. We've stopped a hundred metres from the house and have the place under observation,' the inspector replied.

'Right. All units, go,' said Roscoe before ending the call.

Outside Heathwood House, the DCI pushed the button on the wall to open the electric security gates.

'Who is it?' asked a sleepy woman's voice.

'Police,' replied Roscoe.

'I hope you've got some good news,' the woman replied as the gates began to swing open.

Roscoe and his sergeant swept up the drive. The uniformed officers followed in two Vauxhall Astra estates.

Striding up the steps, Roscoe pressed the doorbell several times. Eventually, Margaret Bowers, wearing just a white nightgown, pushed against the leaded light window above and thrust her head out.

'What is it? What do you want?' she demanded. 'Oh, it's you, Mr Roscoe.'

The detective nodded. 'Could you come downstairs, please? We need to talk to you.'

Within a couple of minutes, Margaret appeared at the door in blue jeans, a white top and grey cardigan to be confronted by Roscoe and the three uniformed constables.

Roscoe scowled at her.

'Mrs Bowers, are you on your own here?' he demanded.

'That's not really your business, is it?'

'I'm afraid it *is* my business. Everything's my business.' He glanced round at his colleagues before returning his gaze to her. 'Margaret Bowers, I'm arresting you in connection with the suspected murder of Harry Bowers. You don't have to say anything but, if you do, it'll be taken down and may be used against you in a court of law.'

'This is preposterous,' she said.

'We're taking you to Queensbridge police station, so please gather up a few personal effects you may need. We'll want the keys to the house as we're going to carry out a thorough search.'

PC Underhill asked, 'Do we need to handcuff her, sir?'

'No, that won't be necessary,' said Roscoe. 'I think she's going to cooperate.' He glared into Margaret Bowers' face, which had turned pale.

'Should we arrange for someone to take care of your daughter?'

The arrested woman shook her head as she pulled on her fawn overcoat. 'She's staying over with friends.'

As Underhill escorted Margaret towards his police car, Roscoe's phone suddenly rang out. It was Tom Vickers.

'The whole house here's in darkness, guv,' he said. 'We've tried the door. There's no response. What shall we do?'

'Stand by for the moment. We'll see if we can ascertain from Mrs Bowers where her boyfriend might be.'

Sunita had been keeping a careful watch on the upstairs window and noticed a shadow appear and then disappear. She walked over to the DCI, who was standing on the front steps.

'Sir, I think there may be someone in the upstairs bedroom,' she said. 'I've seen movement.'

While PC Underhill sat Margaret in the back of his car, Roscoe ordered two of the other constables to search the upper floor of the house immediately.

As a Transit van arrived in the driveway containing forensic staff, the two officers ran up the stairs and caught James Hockley on the first-floor landing. The sports teacher was wearing just a pair of brown cotton trousers. Roscoe climbed the stairs.

'I'm afraid you're under arrest, sir,' he told him. Then he turned to the two constables, saying, 'Get a shirt on him and then we'll formally caution him.'

'I wish I knew what the hell this is all about,' yelled Hockley as he was led down the corridor.

A few minutes later, now wearing a shirt and cardigan, he was taken downstairs.

Roscoe warned him, 'James Hockley, you're under arrest on suspicion of the murder of Bethan Thomas. You don't have to say anything, but, if you do, it'll be taken down.'

Hockley looked astonished. 'This is absolutely ridiculous. You haven't got any evidence against me. Do you think I'm the kind of person who'd do that?'

Roscoe snapped. 'Take his keys off him and any sharps. Then you'd better cuff him.'

As the forensic team mounted a thorough search of the house, he phoned Vickers back. He explained that Hockley's keys, found in his pocket, would be handed to one of the forensic team working at Heathwood House. If the inspector called round, he could collect the keys and then enter Hockley's home without force in order to conduct a search.

Roscoe and Sunita followed the two other police cars to Queensbridge police station, where both suspects were due to be interviewed.

Chapter 40

The interview room at Queensbridge police station had been newly decorated. But no amount of paint in the world could have removed its dated look. It would have served as an ideal interrogation room for a 1940s war film. Situated at the end of a long, dingy corridor on the first floor, there was just one window, which was barred and overlooked the vehicle yard.

While the walls were a plain magnolia, the floor was covered in a red linoleum which had been in vogue decades before. The only sign of the modern age were the cameras and digital video recording equipment fitted to a shelf in the far corner.

Roscoe planned to interview Margaret Bowers first. Days before, he'd come to realise that Hockley must have been the main protagonist in the events that had taken place. He would be forced to rely on all the skills he'd acquired during his twenty-nine-year career in the police for both these crucial interviews.

Hearing what Margaret had to say might give him extra ammunition to use against Hockley. He also realised that, as they were lovers, Hockley would be concerned about his partner. He blatantly planned to use this as psychological pressure, if need be, to try to wheedle a confession from the teacher.

However, his thoughts became disorientated when Margaret was escorted into the room just after ten o'clock on that Friday evening. Her make-up was smudged where she'd been crying. She appeared tired and pale as though lacking sleep. Without being asked, she slumped into a chair by the window and stared out. A few minutes later, her tall, bespectacled lawyer, Roger Sims, the duty solicitor, appeared at the door, followed by Sergeant Roy.

'Come in, Mr Sims,' said Roscoe. 'Have you had a chance to speak to your client?'

'Yes, we've had a few words,' said Sims, taking a seat next to her at the table. He peered at the detectives over the top of his glasses.

'Right, let's get going,' said Roscoe as he announced everyone's name for the benefit of the recording. 'Can I remind you, Mrs Bowers, you're still under caution. You've a right to silence, but whatever you do say could be used in a criminal court. If you fail to mention something now which you raise in court later, a judge might well wonder why you didn't bring it up at the first opportunity. Now I think you know why you're here.'

'I was hoping you had some information about Harry, but then, back at the house, you arrested me for his murder, which is ridiculous,' she said, glancing at her solicitor.

'We haven't found your husband, Mrs Bowers,' said Roscoe, taking a seat next to his sergeant. 'But we believe you're involved in his disappearance and probable murder.'

'How do you make that out?'

'Well, the message that you handed to police, for one thing.'

'Chief Inspector,' said Sims. 'Are you talking about the note found at Heathwood House on January the 9th?'

'Yes. The one that begins with the words "I just can't take any more".' Roscoe gazed back at his suspect. 'The fact is you wrote it, didn't you?'

She glanced at Sims, who was shaking his head.

'No comment,' she said.

'You wrote it to make police think your husband had gone away voluntarily to begin a new life. To cover over the fact that he'd been murdered.'

She sighed. 'No comment.'

Roscoe tutted. 'We've had a handwriting expert examine samples of handwriting from every suspect in the case. This expert believes the note was written by you. Four of the letters, the *j*, *y* and two *g*s, had larger than usual loops that sweep back up and nearly touch the preceding letter. Not only that – the letter *g* on the envelope was written in the same style. We've also seen sentences written by your husband. His writing was significantly different. You concocted it, didn't you?'

Margaret's face turned red as the DCI scowled at her like a bird of prey. She'd never been able to hide her feelings easily, but she hated being the subject of accusations.

'No comment,' she insisted.

Roscoe persisted. 'Mrs Bowers, we believe you were involved in arranging the death of your husband. You'd embarked upon an affair with James Hockley and your husband wouldn't give you a divorce. You wanted him out of the way so that you could continue your affair.'

Margaret shook her head and looked down at the table. 'No comment.'

'Where were you on the night of January the 8th at seven o'clock in the evening, Mrs Bowers?'

She glanced at Sims, who nodded.

'At home with my daughter.'

'Can anyone vouch for that?'

'Only Rachel.'

'You didn't follow your husband to Oxford Lane?'

'No comment.'

'All right. I can see we're not making much progress for the moment. I think we'll stop there and resume in the morning.' Turning to the two female constables at the rear of the room, he said, 'Could you take Mrs Bowers back to her cell?'

Roscoe and his sergeant exchanged glances.

'Hockley next,' Roscoe whispered.

The sergeant got up and watched from the doorway as their prisoner was led away.

Suddenly Margaret must have caught a glimpse of Hockley being led up the stairwell from the basement cells.

'James!' she cried. 'Are you all right?'

'Yes, Maggie. You OK?'

They were both ordered to be quiet. Hockley was then briefly returned to the custody suite until Margaret had been securely locked in her cell again.

Roscoe was not too annoyed when he discovered the pair had fleetingly met on the stairs. He hoped that, since they'd seen each other in what was – to them – the rather alien environment of a police station, it might put added pressure on them to answer questions honestly.

Within a few minutes, Roscoe and Sunita resumed their seats.

'Mr Hockley, you're still under caution,' said the DCI. 'You've a right to be silent, but whatever you say might be used in a court of law.'

The teacher nodded and looked down at the table.

After knocking, solicitor Mr Siddiqui, a short, plump man in a dark-green suit, put his head round the door and strode in.

'Welcome,' said Roscoe. 'It's good of you to come out this evening at short notice. I take it you've had a word with your client?'

'Yes, we had a little chat a moment ago,' said Mr Siddiqui.

After announcing their names for the recording, Roscoe said, 'Mr Hockley, you're here first of all in connection with the disappearance of Harry Bowers. You're also here on suspicion of involvement in the murder of Bethan Thomas.'

'Bloody ridiculous,' Hockley said. 'You've no evidence.'

Mr Siddiqui frowned at him and put his finger to his lips.

'Well, let's start with Harry Bowers,' the detective said. 'You were twice seen arguing with him in public – first on Christmas Eve while coming out of church.'

'No comment,' Hockley declared.

'We've a reputable witness who saw you exchanging words,' said Roscoe. 'Then, according to Bethan Thomas, you were arguing with Mr Bowers by the lychgate in Oxford Lane on the night he vanished. You were – to quote her – "wagging your finger and shaking your fist."'

'No comment.'

His initial confidence had drained away like soapsuds down a sink. He turned to the lawyer.

'Look, I want to clear this up. I know this may annoy you, Mr Siddiqui, but I'm an innocent man and I want to give the officers a proper explanation.

'I'll be honest with you, Mr Roscoe. Bowers and I were friends for a short time, but that quickly changed. We argued about where we stood during choir practice. We argued about how particular stanzas should be sung.

'Then he discovered I was seeing his wife. You're right. I did have a big row with him just before going to the church hall on that Tuesday night. But he was the one being aggressive. And I didn't hit him and I didn't kill him. I walked away. I'm a teacher. I didn't want an assault charge going on my record. I went to the choir practice and I was surprised, like everyone else, when he failed to turn up.'

'I should leave it there!' an exasperated Mr Siddiqui told him. 'The police should be satisfied with that.'

A stern-faced Sunita asked Hockley, 'You didn't think to ask members of the choir or the choirmaster about why he hadn't shown up? You'd seen him just a short distance from the hall and he was clearly intending to make an appearance.'

'No comment,' Hockley replied.

She shook her head and the DCI shrugged his shoulders.

'How long have you had a relationship with Margaret Bowers?' Roscoe asked.

The teacher glanced hesitantly towards his lawyer. 'No comment.'

Roscoe's voice became louder. 'You were seen behaving in a threatening and aggressive way towards a man. Since that moment, that man's not been seen. So I've got to ask you this: Did you kill Harry Bowers?'

Hockley leaned back in his chair with a look of contempt and disgust on his face.

'I've already said I didn't kill him.'

Throughout the brief interview, Sunita had been studying the suspect's features and demeanour. She had seen that three of his knuckles appeared to have been injured.

'You've got red marks on your right hand, Mr Hockley,' she said.

The accused man turned towards Mr Siddiqui.

'May I?' Then, turning to Sunita, he said, 'I fell off a stepladder and hurt myself while taking down Christmas decorations.'

Roscoe was more interested in asking him about the written message found at Heathwood House. 'Did you get your girlfriend to write a note that purported to be from Harry?' he asked.

Hockley's face looked blank. 'What note?'

The DCI persisted. 'The note saying Bowers had gone and his wife shouldn't try to find him.'

Hockley shook his head.

'May I ask a question, sir?' Sunita asked. Turning to Hockley, she said, 'We've searched your house and found examples of your handwriting. The only person who could've written it was Margaret Bowers. But we believe she may have been pressured into writing it by you.'

'I'm sorry. I haven't got a clue what you're on about.'

'Now we come to the car,' said Roscoe. 'A blue car like yours was seen outside Rose Cottage in Oxford Lane, Norton at 10.00 a.m. on 15 February. What were you doing there?'

The teacher looked puzzled. 'I was a mile away at Heathwood House. The Bowers' gardener will vouch for me.'

'What time did you leave Heathwood House that morning?' he asked.

'No comment.'

'We know a blue car was outside the cottage at about the time Bethan Thomas was murdered,' said Roscoe, calmly.

'No comment.'

Roscoe glared. He felt they were making no progress.

'OK, we've got other inquiries to make,' he said. 'I think we'll leave things there for the moment.'

'Can you tell me how much longer my client is likely to be kept here?' Mr Siddiqui asked.

'Mr Siddiqui, your client faces possible murder charges. We intend to hold him for twenty-four hours and may apply to hold him for longer.' While he spoke, he could feel the teacher's resentful eyes boring into him like two lasers.

After Hockley was escorted back to the cells and his lawyer left, Roscoe and Sunita sat and talked together. Then, after more than twenty minutes, Mr Siddiqui re-appeared in the doorway.

'Together we've drafted a further statement,' he said. 'My client's been thinking about what you were saying, and, although this isn't necessarily the way I would've dealt with things, he believes he owes you an honest statement of the facts.'

'All right. Bring him back,' Roscoe said.

Hockley and Mr Siddiqui resumed their seats.

The lawyer glanced at the two detectives before reading out the statement. It said:

> *I am a teacher, helping with children's development and moral choices in the formative years. I am also a Christian. It's just not in me to take another person's life.*
>
> *Mrs Bowers and I went to bed late on Valentine's Day and I overslept. I got her to phone the school and say I was sick. I phoned the rector that morning because I'd forgotten when the next choir practice was and wanted to make sure it was definitely on for the following Tuesday. I didn't have the choirmaster's number.*
>
> *The rector mentioned to me in passing that Mrs Thomas had seen me and Bowers arguing. I did have an argument with Bowers in Oxford Lane. I'm afraid I lost my temper and hit him with my fist, but it was only once and he was alive when I walked away from him. That's the end of the statement.*

'It's in your best interests to make a full admission,' Sunita insisted. 'We carried out a search of your house. We need to know why you had rope in your garage and why there's sand in your car and sand on your garage floor. Do you go rock climbing or mountaineering?'

Hockley shook his head. 'No, never. I took my sister and nephew to the seaside during the summer. I tied the boy's bicycle to the roof rack with rope as there was no room in the boot of the car.'

'Mr Hockley, you're a liar,' said Roscoe. 'I think you're as guilty as hell. I've got to put it to you that you killed Bethan Thomas and buried her body in her garden.'

'No, of course I didn't kill poor Bethan,' said Hockley. 'And you've got no evidence I did.'

'You killed her because she'd seen something happen between you and Harry Bowers – something incriminating!' Roscoe shouted across the table.

Sunita touched her boss's shoulder, concerned that he shouldn't lose control and breach interview rules.

'You tried to strangle her,' Roscoe continued, 'and, when that failed, you savagely battered her to death with her own hammer!'

Hockley sighed and shook his head. 'No, that's ridiculous. Bethan was a lovely woman. I wouldn't have hurt a hair on her head. Look, if you want a suspect, try talking to Rashad Mahmood. He hated Bowers and has been rowing with Maggie over money.'

After Hockley was taken back to his cell again, Roscoe remained in the interview room, discussing the case with his sergeant.

'We ought to find that gardener and speak to him,' said Roscoe. 'I think, when we visited Mrs Bowers in January, she mentioned his name was Jeff Williams. Could you find him and have a chat with him? We need to see if he can give Hockley an alibi for the time of Bethan's death.'

'Yes, sir.'

'If he can confirm Hockley was at Heathwood House all the time between half past nine and half past ten on the morning of the murder, I think we may have to let Hockley go. But we need to ascertain what time Hockley arrived, what time he was in the kitchen and what time he left Heathwood House.'

Chapter 41

It was unusual for Helen Roscoe to rise in the morning before her husband. But Saturday, 23 February was an important date in her calendar. The president of Queensbridge and District Bird Fanciers' Society had booked a table for ten guests to enjoy a high tea that evening. Many of the other venues were booked up solidly because of special school half-term deals, but the president was a personal friend of Helen's and had insisted they book a table at her tearooms.

She rose from their bed and left her husband sleeping at six thirty. She put on a long-sleeved blue checked top and some jeans. Then she descended the stairs to the kitchen, put on an apron and began preparing and printing menus.

An hour later, Roscoe trudged downstairs in his dressing gown, moaning he'd not had a good night's sleep and that he'd been woken by the sound of the dishwasher in the kitchen. He was feeling despondent after failing to secure a breakthrough in the Oxford Lane case and he was not looking forward to having to face Margaret Bowers in the interview room in a few hours.

'You're up a bit early, darling,' he told Helen.

She was engrossed in folding up menus and didn't look up. 'Some of us have work to do. It's going to be a really busy day.'

He stepped over to the sink and, while rinsing some plates, gazed out of the picture window to the farmland beyond. Fields, crisp, barren and brown, stretched out to the horizon beneath a dove grey sky.

'Come on,' said Roscoe. 'I'll give you a hand with those menus.'

It was a cold, cloudy morning and he felt a few spots of rain as he climbed into his car and drove to Queensbridge police station, although it was forecast to be warm and sunny later. While he was disheartened at the lack of progress with the case, Roscoe was determined to bring the perpetrators to justice. He firmly believed Margaret Bowers knew far more than she was saying and he was resolved to seek answers.

Smartly dressed in a charcoal-grey suit, he made his way to the first-floor interview room, where his sergeant was waiting patiently for him.

She smiled. 'Good morning, sir.'

'Good morning. Everything OK? Did you find the gardener?'

'Yes, sir. He confirms that Hockley was at Heathwood House at around ten o'clock on the morning of the woman's murder. He doesn't know what time he left, but he'd just made two cups of coffee for himself and Mrs Bowers at the time. The guy didn't hear him drive off but believes Hockley must've been there until at least twenty past ten – maybe longer.'

'Is it feasible he could've left there and gone to Oxford Lane?'

'I suppose it's possible. The guy was digging at the side of the house and didn't see him after he'd spotted him in the kitchen.'

'So Hockley could still be in the frame,' said the DCI. 'Have we heard back from Dawson?'

'Yes, sir. Hockley does have a sister and nephew. They live in Tewkesbury.'

'So he's got a sister as well as a wife and daughter.' He paused. 'We know that Hockley's wife never wanted to press charges after he attacked her. I've been thinking about this violent streak he's got. I've noticed during the interview with him he gives off an air of arrogance and he's been staring at us in a rather insolent way. All that points to a violent nature.'

'Yes, sir.'

* * *

Fifteen minutes later, at eleven that morning, Margaret Bowers was escorted into the room by two female officers. Wearing the same clothes as the night before, she looked weary and dispirited. She was followed moments later by Roger Sims, immaculately dressed in a dark suit and blue tie.

'Good morning, Mrs Bowers. Mr Sims,' said Roscoe.

'My client wants it known she'll do her best to answer all your questions, unless I indicate otherwise,' the solicitor said.

After announcing their names for the recording, Roscoe asked why it had taken Margaret a week to report her husband's disappearance. She stared into Roscoe's eyes.

'For several days, I wasn't worried. He'd gone away on his own before and turned up later. In any case, I had a note saying he'd gone. But, as the days passed and my daughter Rachel kept asking where he was, I decided I'd better inform the police.'

Roscoe shook his head. 'That was very strange behaviour, taking a week to report it. It was also strange the way you walked out of the press conference. A wife would normally be very concerned when her husband goes off suddenly and would want to help publicise his absence. I was very surprised you didn't want to help get the maximum publicity.'

Margaret looked embarrassed.

'I'm afraid ours wasn't a normal marriage, Chief Inspector, and I stopped caring for Harry long ago. He was having affairs with other women and I suppose I turned very cold towards him. It was only a matter of time before we got divorced.'

'Your whole attitude's wrong,' Roscoe continued. 'You've never shown emotion about your husband's disappearance. You've not made inquiries of the police since reporting him missing. The only ones making constant inquiries have been your husband's parents. Try and see it from our point of view, Mrs Bowers. A man's missing. The wife shows no emotion. She's got a new relationship. There's a patently bogus note that seems to have been written by her, and she's been making inquiries about her husband's life insurance. It all leads us to think you and Hockley arranged Harry's death in a joint enterprise.'

Margaret glanced at her solicitor. 'That's completely wrong,' she said.

Mr Sims whispered in her ear. She nodded back at him.

'I'm not prepared to help you any further,' she said. 'Your questions are utterly ridiculous.'

Roscoe glared at her.

'Let me take you back to the night of January the 8th,' the DCI said. 'You told me, when I first visited you, your husband came home just after 6.00 p.m. You rowed over money, then he stormed out.'

'No comment,' said Margaret.

'You followed him to the church hall, didn't you – along with your boyfriend, Hockley?'

'No comment.'

'You were nearby when Hockley confronted your husband. You were watching the encounter from across the road. It was you that Bethan Thomas reported seeing lurking in the shadows.'

'No comment.'

The DCI was gradually beginning to lose his temper. It occurred to him the damn woman's attitude was as perplexing as a Mongolian crossword puzzle.

He raised his voice. 'You were watching as your lover attacked your husband and killed him. That's what happened, isn't it, Mrs Bowers?'

Nervous and jittery, Margaret glanced at Mr Sims and then shook her head.

'What happened to the body, Mrs Bowers?'

Both her eyes glistened with tears as she whispered, 'No comment.'

'Are you all right, Mrs Bowers? Do want a break in proceedings?' Mr Sims asked.

'I'll be all right,' she said, wiping her eyes with a white handkerchief.

'Chief Inspector, I must protest,' the solicitor whined. 'You're questioning style has become unnecessarily aggressive.'

Roscoe tutted. 'Mr Sims, we believe your client's boyfriend is involved in both the disappearance of Mr Bowers and the murder of Bethan Thomas and that your client's been complicit in at least the first of these events. This man, with whom she's now associating, has a history of violence. Hockley's wife ended up in hospital on at least one occasion.'

Margaret glanced at him in surprise.

'Wife?' she said. 'He's married?'

Sunita interrupted to tell her, 'Yes, he's still married in the eyes of the law, although they're estranged. She's raising his child.'

Margaret became tearful again as this new revelation brought fresh anguish.

Roscoe turned towards the solicitor. 'Mr Sims, I need to tell you I'm considering bringing a criminal charge against your client at the very least of perverting the course of justice. We're convinced the note Mrs Bowers claims was written by her husband was written by her. This is supported by a handwriting expert. We believe its intention was to muddy the waters – to mislead the police into believing Harry Bowers had gone off on his own accord.'

Mr Sims frowned. 'I see. Could I have a few minutes to confer with my client?'

Roscoe agreed that the solicitor could spend a few minutes discussing the case quietly with Margaret. The pair were led to a private room. He hoped the solicitor would make the woman see sense.

The two detectives walked along the corridor to the coffee machine where they both purchased hot drinks.

'Are you charging them both, sir?' Sunita asked in a low voice.

Roscoe frowned. 'I'm not sure at the moment. We'll have to see what she says when we go back in. Did you see the expression on her face when I mentioned perverting the course of justice?'

'Yes, she looked very upset. It was the same gloomy look when you mentioned Hockley's wife,' the sergeant said. 'It appears she didn't know he had a wife.'

'Time's running out. I'm inclined to let them both go for the moment. There's not enough to hold them.'

At that moment, Mr Sims appeared in the corridor and signalled Mrs Bowers was ready to return to the interview room.

'My client would like to make a brief statement,' he told the detectives as they resumed their seats.

Margaret had a haunted look as Mr Sims read from a sheet of paper: 'I want to make my position absolutely clear. I didn't write a note and pretend it was from my husband. The note's genuine and I had absolutely no involvement in his disappearance. I'm absolutely sure that Mr Hockley isn't involved either.'

Roscoe was shocked that, despite their strong evidence and the colossal pressure she was under, Margaret was still refusing to admit the truth. He sighed and shook his head.

'OK, I'm proposing to release both you and Mr Hockley after we've taken fingerprints, photographs and

DNA samples from both of you. But our inquiries are in no way concluded. We're going to release you on police bail. You'll have to return to this police station for more questioning when we ask you to. Do you understand?'

Mr Sims looked at Margaret, who indicated by nodding that she would agree to this.

'Yes, Mr Roscoe,' said Mr Sims. 'My client understands perfectly.'

* * *

At around three o'clock that afternoon, as both Margaret and Hockley travelled back separately to Heathwood House after spending nearly eighteen hours under arrest, the two detectives continued to discuss the case over a sandwich lunch in the police canteen.

Roscoe frowned. 'All we can do is carry on.'

She smiled. 'It'll be interesting to see what develops between the pair. She now knows Hockley's technically still a married man and that he's got a child. That all seemed news to her.'

'She's sticking to her story about the note like a barnacle to a boat,' moaned Roscoe. 'I'm sure she's only doing that to defend her bloody boyfriend. She knows in her heart of hearts that he murdered her husband and she may have written the note in the mistaken belief it might protect him. But, now she's learnt he's still married, I've a feeling their cosy, romantic little relationship may not prove so cosy and romantic after all.'

* * *

That evening at eight o'clock, Roscoe was watching a quiz programme on television at his home when Helen arrived back from an exhausting day at the tearooms. He revealed they had had to release the two suspects.

'I'm sorry if things aren't working out for you, dear,' she said while unbuttoning her coat.

'What did the proud members of the Queensbridge and District Bird Fanciers' Society think of their meal?' he asked. 'Did you receive any feedback?'

She beamed. 'The function went well and Mel had to help out in the kitchen. Twelve bird fanciers arrived in the end – so we needed to make two extra places.'

Her husband beamed. 'And what did they choose from your menu?'

Helen said, 'They nearly all went for the chicken.'

His smile faded. 'Chicken? I thought they were bird-lovers?'

'No one can resist my chicken with garlic and rosemary – not even bird-lovers.'

Chapter 42

Exhausted and emotionally shattered after her interviews, Margaret Bowers was relieved as she travelled back to Heathwood House by taxi.

As the car travelled along the country road, she believed her life would never be the same. The whole experience had taken a heavy toll. On the Friday evening, she'd been placed in a small, uncomfortable cell with just a small bed containing a hard mattress.

She'd tried to sleep but had only managed to doze for a few hours. She'd been woken by the cold and by the sound of doors slamming. Every few hours an officer had looked in on her through a small service hatch in the door as if she were on suicide watch.

The police questioning had been relentless and, at the end of it all, her solicitor told her that, although she'd not been charged, she might be called back at a later date. He warned her that police might charge her with perverting the course of justice or a lesser charge – wasting police time.

She'd been under an unbearable strain. But she was most of all aggrieved at discovering during her second police interview that her lover, James Hockley, had told her lies. She'd learnt from the mouth of a police officer that he had a wife and child that he'd never mentioned. How devious and deceitful some men were, she thought. After all the moments they'd shared, after all the love she'd given him, had his approaches been genuine and sincere? Had he been simply using her to console himself while living apart from his wife? Had he been using her in the short term just to fulfil his manly needs?

When at last the taxi arrived at her home and she was able to climb the front steps and close the door behind her, matters only became worse. After calling the friend who'd been caring for Rachel and asking if she could be brought home, she found a message from a journalist on her phone's answering machine. The woman's voice politely asked if James Hockley was there and asked him to phone her.

Margaret realised at once what that meant. It almost certainly meant the local newspaper would be carrying an article about James's wife and child. It meant that, in addition to the news of her arrest, she'd be burdened by this further shame.

Shortly afterwards Hockley arrived at the house. His dark, ginger hair looked unkempt and his blue shirt and jeans dishevelled. He walked somewhat warily into the hallway, knowing that Margaret would be upset after her ordeal. He was about to discover how deeply upset.

'Maggie! Maggie!' he called.

'I'm in the sitting room,' she called back.

As he walked in, he found her crouching by the inglenook fireplace. He wanted to kiss her, but the atmosphere was icier than an Alaskan winter.

'You all right?' he asked tentatively.

'What do you think?' said Margaret, who by now had showered and changed into fresh clothes.

'That chief inspector puts you through the mill, doesn't he?' said Hockley. 'They'd got absolutely no evidence against us.'

Margaret had decided she was not going to mince words.

'James, why didn't you tell me you were married?' she demanded.

'I kept meaning to, but I never found the right moment,' he said. 'Anyway it ended years ago. A divorce is going through.'

She glared. 'You also didn't tell me you had a daughter. How many other secrets have you hidden from me?'

'It wasn't a secret. It was part of my past that was over. I worried that, if I mentioned it, it might spoil things.'

Margaret covered her face with her hands. When she removed them, Hockley realised she'd been crying.

'How long have you been married?'

'We married in 2008. Molly was born two years later. Listen, my marriage was an empty shell. Caron is self-obsessed and never gave me any support in my teaching career. I became depressed and then decided I'd had enough. I managed to find myself a job up here and moved to Norton seven years ago.'

His words did nothing to assuage her pain. She began crying again.

'To think that I lied for you!' she screamed.

'What do you mean?'

'That bloody note. The police kept going on and on about it. I wrote it to protect you.'

Hockley put his hands to his face. Gradually, the truth was emerging. She had written the message on his behalf. But why?

'What was this note exactly?' he asked her.

'I thought you might've been involved in some way in Harry's disappearance,' said Margaret. 'So, to support you,

I looked at some of Harry's handwriting and concocted a few words. It said something like "I've gone away. Don't bother looking for me." I thought the police might take it at face value and stop looking for him. Thousands of people around the world disappear every year and they don't have snoopy coppers going to the ends of the earth to track them down.'

Hockley frowned. 'I see why you did it, but it wasn't the cleverest thing you've ever done. You didn't really think I could've had anything to do with your old man going missing, did you? I know we laughed and joked about how wonderful our lives would be if your husband wasn't around. But that's all it was – laughs and jokes. I was raised a Christian and I could never take a life.'

'I didn't know for sure. I mean accidents happen. It was so strange him disappearing and I've seen you fly off the handle. I didn't know if you'd acted in fury. A small part of me believed you might've had something to do with it. I was worried for days. I didn't see you for a while after he went missing. I didn't know what had happened to Harry and I didn't know what had happened to you.'

'So you wrote a few words and posted it to yourself!' Hockley said.

'Yes. I did it for you,' she said. 'I realise now it was a stupid thing to do. Look, James, I've been through hell and worse is to come, I'm sure of it. Your wife's going to be in the paper and all my neighbours are going to know you're married. We'll have to have a break. Just for a while. Till all this passes over.'

Hockley shook his head and looked down at the floor. He felt as though the hand of God had reached down and snatched his heart away. It was devastating to hear she wanted to call time on their affair, albeit temporarily.

Just for a while. What does that mean? he thought to himself. Was her heart set on a permanent rift? Was she trying to sever their connection forever without him causing a major scene?

'You're going through a bad time. I can see that,' he said.

'Just for a while. I'll phone you.'

At that moment, they heard a noise outside. Rachel had arrived home. Margaret wiped her eyes and went to open the front door.

'Mummy, you're back,' said Rachel. 'Is everything all right?'

'Yes, dear,' said Margaret. 'James is just going.'

Hockley knew he had to leave as he stared at Rachel, standing beside her mother in the hall. He reached over to give Margaret a peck on the cheek, but she moved her head away. He wondered if this would be the last time he'd see her. He walked towards the front door.

'Don't forget to call me,' he whispered.

'Don't worry. I'll give you a ring in a little while. When the dust's settled,' she told him.

Chapter 43

Fog shrouded the streets around Queensbridge like a wispy white curtain as the chief inspector woke early on Sunday morning. Trees beyond the lane were bathed in a silvery glow while the nearby fields were masked by the haze. From time to time, Roscoe would hear the sound of a car passing along the main road at the end of the lane. He didn't envy the drivers trying to navigate their way across the misty terrain.

Roscoe had slept fitfully after his gruelling day interviewing the two suspects. He was still uncertain whether Margaret Bowers and James Hockley were behind the disappearance. But if they weren't responsible, who was?

He made himself some breakfast and cleaned the kitchen before the family rose from their beds. When they did, Helen set off on a shopping expedition. George went to visit his friend Ryan in Norton Prior, while Melody decided to go horse riding with her boyfriend, Alex.

Roscoe thought he would relax on the settee and try to unwind after his busy week. He switched on the television but couldn't find anything he wanted to watch and, half an hour later, switched it off with the remote.

He took his black, lace-up shoes off and brought his feet up. Perhaps he could catch up on his lost sleep. But somehow he couldn't clear his mind of the investigation. Details of all the suspects, their possible motives and their alibis kept floating through his tired mind. Why was this quest to find Harry Bowers so challenging? Fear was building within him that, if he failed to make a breakthrough, he'd have to face the full wrath of the chief superintendent. Could he cope with the shame of being removed from the case?

As a cloak of exhaustion and sleep began to drape itself upon him, he contemplated whether Hockley and Margaret Bowers were really guilty. The evidence was too neat, too orderly, too circumstantial. Hockley's friends spoke highly of him and he didn't fit the profile of a serial killer, although hearing of his rough, abusive behaviour towards his wife had surprised Roscoe.

Aspects of the entire case filled his consciousness as he drifted in and out of sleep. He was on the train with Sunita travelling to London. She was smiling at him. Then he was in the mansion block with Gillian McLeod. She was smiling at him too.

For some reason, he also kept recollecting the interview Sunita had conducted with the sacked maid, Tessa Griffiths. She'd asked her about the note on the table and the words in her witness statement kept swirling through his mind.

Tessa had been absolutely certain that the note had first appeared at Heathwood House on 9 January. She'd said, 'I remember because my brother Richard, who's a gravedigger, got took bad the day before and had to go home early from work in the middle of his job.'

Why did these words remain so vividly in his thoughts? Perhaps partly because of the ungrammatical phrase 'got took bad' instead of 'got taken ill'. Why did he consider this so important? Her brother clearly worked as a gravedigger at the church of St John – the only church in Norton Prior. The terms 'got took bad', 'loved you madly', 'gravedigger' and 'climbing rope' swirled around his head like phrases in a stream-of-consciousness novel.

Suddenly Roscoe realised he was not alone. He wasn't travelling on a train with Sunita or in the elegant London mansion block. He was on the living room settee.

'Oh, I must've fallen asleep,' he said out loud.

George had knocked and walked in. Roscoe glanced at the mantelpiece clock. It was half past one. He'd slept for at least an hour.

'Come on, Dad. Mum needs help in the kitchen,' he said. 'Are you all right, Dad? You look as if you've got something on your mind.'

Roscoe put his feet on the floor and turned to look at his son with watery eyes.

'Yes, George. We've hit a brick wall in the investigation. I've had to let Hockley and Margaret Bowers go without charging them.'

'So the mystery goes on,' said George. 'Police have searched high and low for Harry Bowers and yet they don't have a clue. It's as if the earth's just swallowed him up.'

Roscoe's eyes remained focussed on his son. Gradually an air of realisation swept over him. George observed a look of excitement develop in his father's face. Finally, Roscoe punched the air with his fist.

'Do you know, that's the most perceptive thing you've said in a long time.'

Chapter 44

It was a bitterly cold Monday morning. Roscoe, who was wearing his thick navy-blue coat and scarf, had heard on the radio, before leaving home, that temperatures were likely to fall to minus one that day. It was even possible they'd see some snow.

He arrived at the village hall car park, close to St John's churchyard, just before ten. He rubbed his hands and stamped his feet for a few minutes before he spotted Sunita Roy's Peugeot travelling into the lane. She parked beside him and got out.

'Good morning, sir.' She beamed.

'Morning, Sergeant,' he murmured, as he pulled his scarf more tightly round his neck. 'If this theory of mine proves right, we could be on the way to finally putting this case to bed.'

'Let's see, sir,' she muttered back as she buttoned up her grey coat. 'I was very impressed when you explained your thoughts.'

Earlier that morning, Roscoe had been making a few discreet inquiries. He'd discovered that, on the very same cold January day when Harry Bowers vanished, there'd been a funeral service at St John's Church. A woman had been buried in a plot close to the lychgate where the tycoon was last seen alive.

Tessa Griffiths' brother Richard had been taken ill – or, to quote Tessa's words, 'got took bad'– and had failed to complete his burial job. Following George's chance remark that it was as if the earth's just swallowed Harry Bowers up, the chief inspector had been drawn to a striking conclusion – that the body of the missing man may have been placed inside the grave, along with the coffin of the deceased woman.

If that was how it happened, the two detectives could finally be on their way to solving the mystery that had been baffling them for so long.

Roscoe was naturally keen to visit the graveyard as soon as possible. But he wanted to ensure they would be alone. He didn't want to be pestered by church visitors, inquiring about their presence.

He had phoned his new friend the rector to alert him that they'd be making a brief inspection of his graveyard. He'd also contacted Richard Griffiths at his Norton home and asked if he'd be kind enough to meet them there. Roscoe had arranged for a police vehicle to collect him.

The DCI was a non-believer and his sergeant followed the Hindu religion, but as they approached the churchyard at the bottom of the lane, they were both rather in awe of the sixteenth-century church. The building towered above them like a huge stone citadel rising from the ground – a bulwark against the licentious, the wrongdoer and the disbeliever.

While men and women of the parish had spent their lives living in its shadow, this light-grey edifice had stood unmoved – a symbol of Christian faith for more than five hundred years.

When the pair reached the lychgate, with its roof constructed from darkened timbers, Roscoe paused for a moment. He gazed ahead at the twelve lime trees that stood like ghostly figures either side of the red-brick path leading to the church's Norman door.

Then his eyes veered to the left where there was a set of graves. One of them, the closest to the gate, was so new that no turf had been placed upon it and no headstone erected. The two detectives walked over and bent down to inspect it. Neither spoke as they read the inscription on a small plaque fixed to a wooden cross above the mound of soil. It said simply, 'Daphne Cruickshank. Aged eighty-six'.

'From speaking to the rector, I've discovered Mrs Cruickshank died at Christmas,' he told her. 'Her coffin was buried in this plot on January the 8th.'

'Rather sad, sir, that all that marks her final resting place after such a long life is this plaque on a stick.'

Roscoe nodded in agreement.

As the pair stood over the grave, a Vauxhall Corsa police car drew up and Richard Griffiths stepped out, dressed in a bright turquoise shirt and a scruffy pair of blue jeans.

'What's this about then?' he asked them as he walked through the lychgate in. 'My neighbours are probably wondering what's going on – seeing me picked up by a cop car.'

'There's nothing for you to worry about, Mr Griffiths,' Roscoe replied. 'We just wanted to ask you about January the 8th – the day you went down with the flu.'

Richard nodded. 'Yes, I went home early that day. I hope I'm not in any trouble.'

'You're in no trouble. We just want to ask you a few questions. Did you fill in the grave after the funeral of Mrs Cruickshank?'

'To be frank, sir, I was feeling very bad. I made sure there was enough soil in the grave so the coffin was well covered. Then I scarpered.'

Sunita interrupted them to say, 'According to Church of England rules, the coffin would've been buried at a depth of six feet. Is that right?'

'Yes, ma'am,' Richard said. 'It's a traditional grave. It allows for the husband's coffin, when he goes, to be placed above hers.'

'Is that right?' said Roscoe. 'So this plot was intended for two interments?'

'Yes, sir. The rules lay down that, after the mourners have left the graveside, the grave should be entirely back-filled and made tidy. Work's also meant to be finished on the day of the burial and coffins shouldn't be left uncovered overnight. But honestly, sir, it weren't left uncovered. I put at least another two foot of soil in before I went.'

Sunita interrupted them. 'So you left large mounds of earth piled up at the sides, did you?'

'Yes, ma'am. But it was only for the night. They got a gravedigger over from Biddington to finish the job the next morning. I wasn't back at work till 22 January.'

The two detectives nodded.

Sunita gazed down at Mrs Cruickshank's grave and then glanced at the gravedigger.

'How much space would've been left at the top of the grave when you went home?' she asked. 'Would there've been enough room, for example, to hide something – money, guns, a body?'

Richard was startled by the suggestion. He peered towards the grave.

'Now you come to mention it, ma'am, I suppose there would,' he said. 'But it was only overnight. I left at four as it was getting dark. I found out the job was finished by nine in the morning.'

'All right,' said Roscoe. 'That's all we need to know, I think. Unless you have any further questions, Sergeant?'

'No, I don't think so,' she said. 'You've been very helpful, Richard.'

'Oh, thank you,' the gravedigger said. 'By the way, how did you know I got took bad and didn't finish it?'

Sunita grinned. 'Oh, we bumped into your sister, Tessa, and she mentioned it.'

Richard's eyes lit up. 'Oh, so one of you must be connected with the tearooms.'

Roscoe nodded. 'My wife.'

'Yes, our Tess did some waitressing.'

'That's right,' said Roscoe. 'Thanks once again for all your help.'

As Richard returned to the waiting car and was driven away, the two detectives spent a few minutes gazing across the churchyard. Daphne Cruickshank had been laid to rest in one of ten graves that had been positioned in a row. Behind her grave there were two other similar rows before the pattern of graves became less perceptible.

Here and there, the detectives' view towards the church was interrupted by the sight of a tomb rising majestically from the ground or a yew tree – that reddish-brown symbol of the immortality of the human soul.

The pair were silent for a minute. Then Sunita become stern-faced. 'It would've been so easy for the killer,' she said. 'He could have murdered Bowers by the lychgate. Then he just had to drag the body a couple of metres to the Cruickshank grave. Piles of soil stood on either side. He simply had to heave the body into the burial plot and sweep in enough earth to cover it. Job done!'

The DCI nodded. 'It explains why it was so easy for the body to be disposed of. The killer must've had a smile of satisfaction on his face. Poor old Bowers was piggybacked into the grave. So I'm wondering where we go now, Sergeant. We might need to get a coroner's order.'

Roscoe knew, from his years of experience in the force, that the coroner had powers under the Home Office for a warrant to examine a grave if a criminal act was suspected. The police would inform relatives of Mrs Cruickshank – in this case, her husband Graham – and the diocesan authorities, as a matter of courtesy.

But he was confident that, in a short time, they'd be able to open the grave. Hopefully, there'd be no need for an exhumation of the poor lady's body.

Then he noticed his sergeant had strolled over to the cemetery wall and was examining an object on the ground. She picked it up. It appeared to be a three-foot-long metal rod which she'd seen lying on the grass. She'd also seen a house brick which had been dumped a short distance away. She picked both items up, in turn, and walked back to Daphne Cruikshank's grave, where her boss was standing.

'I don't suppose this is something you'll find in any police manual!' she said. 'Could you hold onto me, sir?'

With Roscoe holding her left arm, she leaned over the burial plot.

Looking around carefully to ensure no one was watching, she then gently pushed one end of the rod into the centre of the grave. Finally, with all her strength, she slammed the brick down onto the top end of the rod and drove it into the ground. When it had travelled some distance into the earth, the rod came to an abrupt halt.

'Here. Let me try,' said Roscoe.

He also leaned across and tapped the rod as far as it would go while Sunita supported him.

'There's definitely something in the ground which isn't too far beneath the surface,' she concluded.

Withdrawing their makeshift probe, she estimated that it had travelled for a distance of just two and a half feet.

'That's far too near the surface for the coffin,' she said.

'Unless that's a stone we've struck,' said Roscoe.

'You could be right, of course,' she admitted. 'Only opening the grave will tell us for sure.'

At Roscoe's suggestion, the pair then walked round to the rectory so they could inform the rector, as a matter of respect, that they'd need to arrange for a coroner's warrant so they would have the authority to reopen the grave.

Moments later, they found Revd Peter Hughes in a thick green pullover and dark trousers, tending his vegetable garden.

'I was just having a look at my carrots, Chief Inspector,' the rector said as they approached him. 'I'm going to have to protect them with a cloche. It's so cold at the moment.'

Roscoe smiled. 'Good to see you find time to look after your garden as well as your parishioners, sir.'

'Just taking a break from my normal work,' the churchman replied. 'I've got to prepare a sermon in a minute or two. I noticed you over by the lychgate. Is everything OK?'

'I'm afraid we may at last have discovered what happened to Mr Bowers,' he said.

The minister stood up with a confused look, rubbing his hands together to remove some earth.

'Yes?' he said. Then, for the first time, he noticed the detective's colleague.

'You're helping the chief inspector, are you?'

'Let me introduce Sergeant Roy,' said Roscoe, slightly flustered. 'This is Revd Hughes, Sergeant.'

The pair shook hands.

'We've spoken on the phone,' she said.

'Apologies if my hands aren't too clean. I can't find my gloves. You look very young, my dear, to be helping the chief inspector.'

'She's proved a real asset,' the DCI murmured. 'Look, this is strictly confidential, sir, but we're going to have to apply for a coroner's order to reopen the upper part of Mrs Cruickshank's grave.'

'Oh, is that really necessary?' the rector asked. 'She's only just been buried. Graham would be so upset.'

'I'm afraid it'll be necessary if we're ever to find out what happened to Mr Bowers,' he said.

'You think Harry's been buried there?'

Sunita nodded. 'A few hours after Mrs Cruickshank, sir.'

'You mean...?'

'One theory we're pursuing is that his body might've been hidden in the earth above her coffin,' she admitted.

The rector gave a surprised look. 'I'll have to have a word with the diocesan office. You see, once someone's body's been committed, a grave's a sacred place. I've never had an exhumation before.'

'To reassure you, sir, it won't be necessary to disturb the coffin at all,' said Roscoe. 'We're not requiring an exhumation. If you speak to Mr Cruickshank, you can explain that to him. You can put his mind at rest on that score.'

Chapter 45

A column of police vehicles wound its way through the deserted streets of Queensbridge at six o'clock in the morning on Friday, 1 March. They trundled on between the fields and meadows of the Warwickshire countryside until reaching the village of Norton Prior and its final destination of St John's churchyard.

Most residents slept on as five police cars and a black Ford Transit van drew up at the bottom of Oxford Lane. But, here and there, curtains were twitching as anxious householders peered out from the upstairs windows of terraced houses to spy on the visitors who were gathering in the misty dawn air.

Officers cordoned off Oxford Lane between the church hall and the junction with the main road. Then members of the forensics team erected a small canvas tent over the grave of Daphne Cruickshank and set up arc lamps.

Ten minutes later, Gavin Roscoe's BMW swept into the lane followed shortly afterwards by two other cars, driven by Sunita Roy and Brett Dawson. They were all waved through the police cordon as they travelled to the church hall car park.

Sunita had been taking a few days' break to visit estate agents in Warwick, where she was thinking of buying herself a one-bed flat.

'Any luck with your flat hunting?' Roscoe asked as he stepped from his car.

'Not so far, sir,' she said. 'Everything I want is too expensive.'

'Always the way. Tom's had some news about that guy Halder. Apparently his heart stopped twice during surgery following the crash and scans have revealed a serious brain injury. It's still touch and go whether he'll live.'

'It's terribly sad, sir. I'm trying not to think about it.'

'Yes, that's probably the best way.' He glanced at PC Dawson, who was emerging from his car. 'Good morning, Constable.'

'Good morning, sir. A bit colder today.'

'That's right. Well, come on.'

The three detectives strolled down the lane and passed through the lychgate, where they came to a halt and watched the forensic team at work among the stone memorials.

Sunita's eyes dwelt briefly upon the grave of Daphne Cruickshank and then gazed across the graveyard as far as the fluted trunks of the yew trees at the far side.

A few minutes passed. Then the person they were all waiting for, Dr Silas Reynolds, roared into the lane in his silver Porsche Cayman sports car.

'Good morning, Gavin. Good morning, Sergeant,' he mumbled as he approached them in his hallmark dark-green blazer, pale green shirt, black trousers and black boots. 'Bit of an early start. Never mind. We can get this little lot sorted out and then get on with the rest of the day.'

The forensic team had already removed a shallow layer of earth. After greeting the pathologist, the senior officer began to remove more soil with his spade.

As they toiled, Sunita observed Revd Peter Hughes leaving the rectory through the back door. He followed the path that crossed his vegetable garden until he reached the wooden gate. There he stood for several minutes, appearing to cast a reluctant eye over the proceedings. Then he walked slowly across the churchyard and watched as the team of men – who included a police exhibits officer, an official photographer and the coroner's officer – stood in a huddle nearby.

* * *

It had taken Roscoe longer than he would have liked to obtain all the permissions required to excavate the top section of the grave. The senior Warwickshire coroner had willingly provided a warrant for the task because it was a case involving suspected homicide and because of the matter's urgency.

He'd consulted with the police and Home Office before issuing the warrant. The church authorities had also been notified as the grave was on ecclesiastical ground.

Graham Cruikshank, the widower, had at first been horrified and upset at the prospect of his dearly departed wife's grave being disturbed. But, after a few days, the grieving husband had come round to accepting the matter. The couple had always planned to be buried together in the same plot. He consoled himself that, if another body had been buried there through a criminal act, it should be removed as soon as possible and the grave restored to its original state so that, one day, his remains could join hers in their final resting place.

Roscoe, who was wearing a dark-blue, woollen coat, had arranged for the excavation work to take place early in the morning in the hope of keeping this delicate police operation as private as possible.

If the sergeant's theory was proved correct and the missing man's corpse was found, Harry Bowers' father, Joseph, had agreed he would travel to the mortuary at Queensbridge General Hospital to identify it.

* * *

After more than fifteen minutes of gruelling work, the forensic officer inside the tent put down his spade. He'd reached a depth of eighteen inches and it was time to take a different approach. He and Dr Reynolds began filling plastic bags with earth. Each one was passed from the tent by hand. Deeper and deeper they delved into the ground. Eventually, around two feet below the surface, they uncovered a piece of transparent plastic.

'Gavin! We've got something here,' the pathologist exclaimed.

An air of excitement spread among the ranks of waiting police and civil staff. The pair continued scooping out earth until they could see a black coat concealed beneath the plastic.

Dr Reynolds called out to Roscoe, 'What sort of coat did you say our man was wearing when he went missing?'

'A long, black overcoat,' he yelled.

'Well, I think we could be in business then, old fruit.'

* * *

An hour later, as the sun rose over the sleepy village, the body of Harry Bowers was removed from the earth. The coroner's officer, who'd worked for Heart of England Police before taking up a full-time post with the coroner, had driven to Oxford Lane in a black cargo van. The body was due to be placed in the back of the van and would shortly afterwards be taken to the mortuary so the pathologist could carry out an immediate autopsy.

After emerging from the tent, Dr Reynolds took Roscoe and the sergeant aside.

'It's a white man, five feet eight inches tall with black hair and hazel eyes. He's wearing a white shirt and tie, blue jeans and a black coat with navy-blue trainers. The body's been placed inside a large, see-through, plastic bag. It looks like he's tried to defend himself because there are lacerations to the arms and hands.'

Roscoe shook his head. 'Good God! The poor man,' he said. 'But why the plastic bag, Silas?'

Reynolds shrugged. 'We obviously don't know for certain that this chap here has been a victim of the same killer as the other two. But let's assume, for the sake of argument, that he was. As we now know, the killer is a person who's meticulous in their attention to detail. He may have placed the body in a bag to prevent blood leaking onto the ground and leaving us a trail. But ironically, in his efforts to prevent traces of evidence from being released, he's actually preserved it for us.'

Roscoe was shivering in the cold morning air. He pulled his canary yellow scarf more tightly round his neck.

'So you mean that, by surrounding the body in plastic, he's done himself a disservice, Silas – allowing forensic evidence to be retained?'

'Precisely, old fruit,' the pathologist said. 'Not only that – he's tied the bag with some string round the opening, which means the body was completely sealed. We need to get him officially identified, but, presuming this is Harry Bowers, he's been dead for two months. The body won't have decomposed too quickly at this time of year and we've got a good chance of finding out all we need to know.

'I can tell you already he's been stabbed a number of times. Unluckily for him, it seems his coat was unbuttoned at the time of the attack and the knife's penetrated his shirt. It appears to have been a very violent, passionate assault.'

Sunita asked him whether there were any other signs of injury to the body.

'I'll need to examine the corpse carefully, of course,' the pathologist said. 'But it appears he's also suffered from a periorbital haematoma.'

She frowned. 'A black eye?'

'Well done, my dear. Yes, a black eye. At some point, ante-mortem, he's been viciously punched in the face.'

Dr Reynolds set off shortly afterwards for the mortuary, promising to phone Roscoe as soon as he had more information.

The rector had been keeping himself in the background until this moment. But, as the body was removed from the churchyard and placed in the van for the coroner's officer, he walked towards the detectives.

'Good morning to you both. I'm very sorry you had to come here this morning,' he said.

'So are we,' said Roscoe sensing a tension in relations between church and state. 'I can think of better ways of spending a freezing cold morning than digging about in a country churchyard.'

'Yes, so you got what you wanted then?' he asked.

Roscoe nodded. 'Sadly, it looks that way.'

'Poor Harry,' said the rector. 'I hope he finds peace. The Lord giveth and the Lord taketh away.'

Sunita found it a strange comment for the churchman to make regarding one of his parishioners.

'I'm afraid we cannot officially confirm whose remains they are,' Roscoe said. 'We need to get a positive identification before we can reveal anything.'

'Of course,' said the rector. He wandered away, muttering to himself.

'Right,' said the DCI. 'Who fancies some breakfast?'

His suggestion was greeted with roars of approval.

* * *

Half an hour later, he, Sunita and Dawson were enjoying breakfast at the Apollo Tearooms.

'I'm glad we've found what happened to Mr Bowers,' said Dawson as he tucked into eggs, bacon and mushrooms. 'I thought it would become one of the great mysteries of the world – like the Ark of the Covenant or the Marie Celeste. Did you know, when the Celeste was found floating off the Azores–'

'I think that's enough, Constable,' said Roscoe. 'If you were more sensitive, you'd realise that the sergeant here has been really shaken up after that experience in the graveyard.'

'It's all right, sir,' she replied. 'Yes, it's been a shock – particularly since my guesswork played a part.'

'Finding the gravedigger's sister and prodding the grave. A not insignificant part, Sergeant,' said Roscoe.

'I just feel so sorry for Joseph and Sheila Bowers and for Harry Bowers' daughter, Rachel.'

Roscoe nodded. 'Yes. It's going to be tough for all of them.'

After Dawson had returned to St James Street, Roscoe admitted he no longer viewed James Hockley as the prime suspect in the murders.

'While you were visiting Warwick a few days ago, I had a call from Dr Ling in forensics. The sand found on the floor and in the car at Hockley's garage was a completely different type from the sand in Bethan Thomas's garden. On top of that, the rope in the garage didn't match up with the rope in the sandpit. So it looks as though you were right all along about Hockley.'

'I always had some concerns about him, sir. But he was definitely a person of interest.'

'Well, I think we can almost certainly rule him out now.'

Just then Helen emerged from the kitchen to collect the breakfast plates.

Sunita beamed at her. 'Thank you so much for such a lovely breakfast, Mrs Roscoe.'

Helen smiled back. 'The eggs, mushrooms and asparagus were to your liking?'

'Yes, definitely.'

'You're keeping all right, are you? It's just that Gavin was a little concerned about the question of your security.'

'It's all been resolved, Mrs Roscoe.'

'That's good. You must come round one evening and have a meal. It'd be lovely to see you. I'm very interested in the spicy teas that come from India.'

The sergeant nodded. 'I'd be happy to tell you about them. Masala chai is my favourite.'

* * *

After breakfast, Sunita set off for the mortuary, which was two miles away on the other side of town. Roscoe had to visit a shop but promised to join her there later.

As she drove through Queensbridge, she considered all the potential murder suspects. Whoever had killed Bowers must've had a strong motive, she thought. The pathologist had described the attack as a 'very violent, passionate assault'. They were looking for a man of violence who was also a man of passion.

But she recalled that when Dawson had initially examined police records, he had been unable to find anyone in Queensbridge or Norton Prior with convictions for serious crimes of violence.

So was the killer a newcomer to the area? Was he someone who, for some reason, had never been in trouble with the police in the past, yet had suddenly turned to violence? Or was he someone with a criminal background who'd somehow been missed or overlooked? She decided she would thoroughly check the records herself at the first opportunity.

Chapter 46

Just after 11.30 a.m. that morning, Margaret Bowers was watering her jasmine and primula houseplants when she heard her intercom buzz. She immediately recognised her visitor's softly spoken voice.

'Could I have a word, Mrs Bowers?' the caller asked.

As the automatic gates opened, she watched PC Underhill's Vauxhall Corsa car with its white, yellow and blue livery glide up the driveway.

'Now what?' she moaned to herself.

After he had parked outside, she led the constable into the hall.

'Would you like to come through?' she asked, indicating the living room.

'No, it's all right. I won't, if you don't mind. Mrs Bowers, I'm sorry. I'm so, so sorry. I've brought some sad news with me.'

'Is it Harry?' she asked. Memories of their once happy times together flashed through her mind, blocking out, for the moment, more recent memories of their furious arguments.

'Yes, I'm afraid so,' he said. 'We've found a body and your father-in-law is going to the mortuary in Queensbridge to make a formal identification. We should hear back from the mortuary shortly.'

'Oh my God. So he's dead.' She moved from the door and sat down on the stairs. 'Forgive me. It's a shock,' she said as she began to weep.

'Mrs Bowers, there are lots of questions about how he died and the body won't be released for a funeral until these have all been resolved.'

For a fleeting moment, Margaret was not paying attention. His words echoed around the hallway as if devoid of meaning.

She'd for weeks been consumed with bitterness towards her husband. So much anguish and resentment had built up inside her over his affairs with other women. As a result, she felt she'd become a woman of steel, immune from any sympathetic thoughts towards her husband – towards the man she once referred to as 'My Harry'.

She thought all the happy memories had been hidden away or forgotten. But strangely now, after officially hearing of his probable death from the mouth of a policeman, thoughts of happier times returned. Now, when it was too late. How strangely the human mind performed.

Harry's engaging smile as they danced at the student ball; wine-filled evenings at their Birmingham flat; joyful days playing with their young daughter. These reminiscences flitted across her mind and a tear trickled down her left cheek.

'I'm sorry,' she said. 'I think I need to sit down. Oh my Lord. How am I going to tell Rachel?'

The teenager was at school, but at half past four she'd be returning home – ready to raid the biscuit tin and watch cartoons on the television. How was Margaret to explain her daddy was dead? Underhill helped Margaret into the living room and settled her down on the settee.

'This is obviously a big shock for you,' he said. 'Can I get you anything?'

'No, no. I'll be all right,' she said, recovering her composure.

'DCI Roscoe asked me to come round. The body was only found earlier today, but he asked me to tell you immediately. He wanted me to pass on his personal condolences.'

'Do you know what the man was wearing when he was found?'

'White shirt, blue jeans and a long black overcoat.'

'Thank you, officer,' she said as tears continued to form. 'That sounds like Harry. May I ask where his body was found?'

'In St John's churchyard. It had been buried on top of a woman's coffin, as I understand it, and then covered over with soil.'

'In the churchyard? So he didn't go far from where he was last seen?'

'That's right.'

'And may I ask how he died?'

The constable thought for a moment. 'It's still being worked out. The post-mortem will take place soon.'

'But can you give me an idea? Was it a peaceful death?' she asked.

'No, not peaceful, but I can't really say any more. If you want further information, the DCI might tell you.'

As more tears welled up in her eyes, she walked to the front door with the constable.

'Are you sure you'll be all right?' Underhill asked.

'Yes. I'll be fine,' she said. 'It's very hard though.'

'Of course,' he said, handing her a piece of paper with a handwritten message. 'If there's anything else, here's my name and number. Please give me a call if you need to.'

She glanced at the name on the card.

'Thank you very much, Derek,' she said, closing the door behind him.

* * *

Sunita Roy had little experience of visiting hospital mortuaries. She'd been inside one twice before while working, but she'd not enjoyed the experience.

As soon as she entered the building at the rear of the nineteenth-century Queensbridge Hospital just after midday, she was first greeted by the unwelcome smell of chemicals wafting towards her from the corridor ahead. Then a bearded assistant asked her to put on a white gown. She felt awkward, despite realising the need to maintain standards of hygiene.

She saw the body of Harry Bowers immediately after pushing her way through the double doors that led to the examination lab. It was lying on a stainless-steel table in the centre of the room under gleaming lights. Less than four hours earlier, the search for him had finally reached its tragic conclusion in the peaceful churchyard.

Dr Reynolds was bending over the corpse in his white overalls with a dome magnifier, peering across the dead man's face. His freshly cleaned chisels, knives, forceps and scissors stood lined up in pristine order along a nearby bench.

Sunita was gradually remembering all her previous misgiving about mortuaries. This was a cold and uninviting place. There were six metal tables arranged at intervals across the room, which was well-lit with fluorescent lighting. There was space for the pathologist and his staff to walk round each table with ease. On the far wall were a series of chrome sinks and draining boards – a pair for each table.

'I'm so glad you're here, my dear,' he told her, standing back from the body and smiling towards her. 'Joseph Bowers has just turned up at reception. Could you possibly go and fetch him?'

The sergeant immediately agreed. She followed direction signs into the main part of the hospital until she reached the reception desk.

She recognised the retired bank manager straight away and at once shook hands with him. He looked tired and haggard.

'Better get this over with,' he muttered as she led him through the maze of corridors that led back to the mortuary.

By the time they returned to the examination room, the DCI had arrived.

Joseph Bowers' visit was a brief and tearful experience. When the white sheet was raised, he immediately recognised his son's face, despite extensive bruising round the left eye, which had turned purple. The dead property tycoon had a pale, haunting look which his father said he'd never forget. The visitor quickly looked away and then broke down in tears. He had to be comforted by Dr Reynolds and Sunita.

'Yes, that's Harry,' he said. 'Who could take the life of someone who was so loved? He didn't even reach his fortieth birthday.'

Roscoe touched him on the arm consolingly. 'We're so sorry for your loss, sir.'

Dr Reynolds clasped the visitor's hand. 'Try to take comfort in the fact he enjoyed a good and successful life.' The sergeant then escorted the elderly man back to reception.

When she came back, she overheard Roscoe praising the pathologist for his work at the churchyard.

'Silas, you did a grand job of work up there,' he was saying. 'Now I'd be very interested to hear what you've discovered since.'

Reynolds informed the pair Bowers had been stabbed altogether fourteen times. He'd received three slash wounds to his left arm and two slash wounds to his right hand.

'Some of the stab wounds to the chest penetrated deep into the left pleural cavity and the lung parenchyma,' said Dr Reynolds. 'Unfortunately, one of the stab wounds penetrated right to the heart and death would've been fairly instantaneous. He's also been punched hard in the left eye, as I mentioned before.'

She noticed that Dr Reynolds had arranged Bowers' clothing on a separate table, along with the contents of his pockets.

'May I have a look?' she asked timidly.

'Of course, my dear, but don't touch anything – obviously,' he said.

Roscoe kept her in his sights as she wandered across to the second table. She peered at the dead man's black leather wallet. Next to it lay three banknotes adding up to thirty pounds along with some silver and copper coins. She could see his house keys and car keys. A photograph of a ginger-haired teenage girl had been inserted into the fob of the car keys. She also saw some typed lyrics, which he'd been learning in preparation for the choir practice, and a packet of unopened peppermints.

She looked up to find her boss was beside her.

'Whole business is very sad,' he murmured.

She pointed to the key fob. 'That's obviously Rachel's photo.'

He nodded.

On the far end of the same metal table, Dr Reynolds had arranged Bowers' clothing: his blue Levi jeans; his heavily bloodstained shirt; a light-blue tie, also bloodstained; his navy-blue trainers; and his blood-splattered black overcoat.

As they stared at the garments, Reynolds put his dome magnifier down and strolled over.

'Gavin, I've made an interesting discovery that I've been meaning to mention. My assistant and I found that microscopic fibres from a different coat have become lodged in the fabric of the dead man's coat.'

The detectives immediately became intrigued.

'Excuse me, Silas,' said Roscoe. 'Are you saying that tiny fibres from another coat – possibly worn by the murderer – became embedded in Mr Bowers' coat during the assault?'

'Exactly,' said Dr Reynolds. 'We've examined the fibres from the victim's coat and compared them with the new fibres, which came from another black coat which was of a poorer quality. Part of the reason this has happened is that the microscopic fibres on the lower-quality coat were looser and thus very likely to travel onto another item of clothing during any sudden motion.'

'So we're looking for a murderer with a cheap black coat?' he said.

'Precisely, old fruit,' the pathologist said. 'He's a murderer who needs to get a better tailor. Seriously. Although it's not my job to suggest to you both how you run your investigation, here's my suggestion, for what's it's worth. You collect up the coats of all the main suspects. Find the coat which left these black fibres and you've got your man.'

Chapter 47

Later that Friday, Sunita Roy was adjusting her hair in the ground-floor ladies' washroom at police headquarters when a young slim woman with long, dark hair came in. She immediately recognised her as DC Hopkirk from Tom Vickers' office.

'How are you, Wendy?' she asked as she continued gazing into the mirror above the row of basins.

'Looking forward to chilling over the next couple of days after the week I've had,' Hopkirk moaned. 'I don't imagine you're feeling too bright either after what's happened.'

'You're right. Mortuaries aren't the most cheerful of places.'

'I wasn't referring to the Bowers case. I was talking about... Oh, don't you know?' She glanced into the sergeant's eyes. 'You don't, do you?'

'I don't know what?'

'Haven't you heard about your stalker, Mr Halder?'

'No. What's happened?'

'I'd better not say any more,' said Hopkirk as she peered at the cubicles, wondering if anyone could overhear them.

'Come on, tell me.'

'Well, you didn't get this from me, but he's died in hospital.'

'Oh God, no!'

'I'm not sure I should've told you, but I was chatting to a friend who works for West Mids. He died last night.'

'That's terrible, Wendy. His poor wife. Thanks for telling me.'

'You're welcome,' Hopkirk replied as she went into one of the cubicles.

By the time she'd returned to her desk five minutes later, Sunita was visibly upset. PC Dawson informed the DCI that he had seen the sergeant crying at her desk and thought he ought to know. Roscoe called her into his office.

'You all right, Sergeant?' he asked.

'I've just heard about Arun Halder, sir,' she mumbled.

'Yes, I was informed a few hours ago. I was going to tell you but with all the business at the mortuary, I couldn't find the right moment. Are you going to be OK?'

'Yes, sir. I'll be fine. Sir, I was just wondering. Do you think I could go round the office and collect money for Halder's family?'

'Very noble gesture,' muttered Roscoe as he sat down behind his desk. 'Not sure the guy deserves it after what he put you through.'

'I know, sir. But I just feel some kind of obligation to help them.'

'Very fine sentiments, and if you want someone to set the ball rolling, here's my contribution.' He handed her a ten-pound note. 'Now are you sure you're going to be all right?'

'Yes, sir.'

'Would you like a cup of tea?'

'Yes, please,' she said, drawing up a chair from the side of the room and sitting down.

While he went to the vending machine to get two teas, she looked around. How disorderly his desk appeared compared with hers. Newspapers, files and letters were scattered about. She wondered how he managed to juggle all the cases for which he was responsible.

Once they had begun sipping their teas, she smiled across the room at him. 'By the way, sir, it was a brilliant suggestion that we check the graveyard for Bowers' body.'

'My son gave me the idea,' he explained. 'He was chatting about the mystery of the man's disappearance and suddenly said, "It's as if the earth's just swallowed him up." It immediately crossed my mind that the body might've been literally hidden under the earth. Put that together with the cleaner's words about her brother, the gravedigger, going home in the middle of his job, and it suddenly made sense to see if the body had been buried in the most recent grave.'

Sunita beamed. 'If you think about it, a grave's the perfect hiding place for a body – a dead man among the dead.'

They both took sips from their drinks.

'By the way,' he said, 'I'm organising a major operation tomorrow to find the black coat thought to have been worn by Bowers' killer. We're going to call on all the main suspects in the case and, if they've got a black coat, seize them and have them forensically examined.'

She nodded. 'It's a tall order, but I reckon we can do it. Sir, there's something I want to show you. I'll only be a minute.'

She left the room and returned two minutes later with a document in a plastic, see-through wallet.

'What've you got there?' he asked as he leaned back in his chair, sipping his tea.

She placed it on his desk before sitting down again. He glanced at it.

'Isn't this the love letter Bowers received from a mystery woman? The one Gillian McLeod gave us in London?'

'That's right, sir. What really puzzled me was why it appeared to be unsigned.'

The DCI shrugged before peering again at the handwritten words. 'If it's a secret love letter, then you might expect the sender to leave it unsigned.'

Sunita shook her head. 'But it wasn't secret – not in the way that, for example, Valentine's cards are often secret with the sender leaving a question mark or simply writing "Guess who?"'

'It was clear that the recipient, in this case Harry Bowers, knew the sender's identity. It was a letter primarily to thank him for some gift or other. It didn't make sense the sender left their name off it. Then I realised they'd not left their name off it at all. There it is for all to see at the end of the letter.'

Roscoe raised an eyebrow. 'I'm sorry. You've lost me. What do you mean?'

Sunita stood up and walked towards his desk. 'The final words of the letter are: "Every moment with you is cherished. Loved you on day we met in Stratford. Loved you madly since year dot." Then there's a cross to indicate a kiss. It was hastily written by someone who doesn't write their vowels clearly.

'What the letter actually says, I believe, is, "Loved you on day we met in Stratford. Loved you madly since. Your Dot." The phrase "since the year dot" has become so well-known that, on reading it for the first time, you easily jump to the conclusion that that's what the writer's saying.'

It gradually dawned on Roscoe that the words in the letter could be interpreted exactly as his sergeant was now suggesting.

'You mean that the sender was a woman called Dot?' he said.

She smiled. 'That's exactly what I mean. It comes from a woman called Dot, which, of course, is a short form for the Christian name Dorothy or Dorothea. It means that, a few months before he was killed, Harry Bowers received a love letter from a woman with that name.'

'You're right!' said the DCI. 'Well done, Sunita. That's very interesting. Unfortunately, I'm not sure, at the moment, how much further it takes us. We may have here the name of a secret admirer – possibly one of several women in Harry Bowers' life. But who was she? She could live anywhere in Britain. And even if we managed to identify her, will it lead us to the killer's door? I have to say I believe Silas Reynolds' suggestion of finding the killer through the coat is far more likely to bear fruit.'

Sunita nodded. 'I take your point, sir. But, if you could give me a day or two, I'd like to have a go at finding this woman.'

Chapter 48

James Hockley glanced at his bedroom clock. It was still only 7.00 a.m. on Monday, 4 March. Why does time pass so slowly when you're unable to sleep? he wondered. The sports teacher felt more alone than ever in his three-bedroom house now that his lover didn't wish to see him. He was still in a state of shock after hearing her ominous words. He still couldn't erase them from his mind.

'We'll have to have a break. Just for a while. Till all this passes over,' were the heart-breaking words spoken by the woman he loved. The dreadful words he kept remembering.

His life was entering an uncertain phase. He felt he'd been thrust into an unreal world in which hope and despair seemed locked in an endless battle. Should he cling to the belief the fading embers of their love might be rekindled? Or should he gracefully surrender to the prospect he might never see his love again?

He'd never been arrested and interrogated by the police so rigorously before. He'd never been called in by a headmaster before and questioned about his private life. This had all proved a chastening experience. But those matters seemed rather insignificant now – compared with the fears besetting him over his future with Margaret.

These fears had been passing through his mind all night, and he'd been forced to accept these feelings of despondency would consume him for a while. Finally, in a desperate attempt to raise his spirits, the teacher – who'd been given leave of absence from his school on compassionate grounds – took a decision. He had to get out of the house. He had to go for a run and try and gain a fresh perspective.

He'd read somewhere that depression and anxiety symptoms were often relieved by resorting to strenuous activity. Sprinting round the village might help to ease the tensions in his head. He slipped on his blue tracksuit and white trainers. Then he put his keys in his trouser pocket and shut the front door behind him.

The weather was bitterly cold as he darted past a pair of neat semi-detached houses. A woman opened her front curtains in one of them as the teacher appeared. She was getting their twelve-year-old son ready for school. She had probably seen Hockley's face in press reports. They'd probably read all about his arrest and, over the coming days, would hear about his secret marriage. They'd probably heard the rumours about his affair with the murdered tycoon's widow and formed their own opinions.

This morning, he was fighting to disregard such thoughts. He vowed to adopt a more positive mindset as he made his way down Norton Hill.

At the bottom of the incline, he turned into the sports field and jogged round the perimeter. Past the changing rooms, past the clump of trees and past the swings and slides. Past three villagers who were waiting at a bus stop on the main road. Past the Victorian cast-iron road bridge that spans the River Avon. On he ran.

A few minutes later he found himself at the bottom of Oxford Lane, close to the lychgate where he'd had his infamous encounter with Margaret's husband. How he wished now he'd never confronted him and had gone quietly to the choir practice without an exchange of words.

He'd struck his rival in the face with a ferocious punch and left him sprawling on the ground, despite initially telling the police he'd not resorted to any violence. But he couldn't have killed him. Could he?

That morning, on the TV news, it was revealed the body of a man – believed to be Bowers – had been found in a shallow grave at the churchyard. He found that most perplexing. Who'd have gone to the trouble of killing Bowers, digging into the ground and hiding his body beneath soil? It simply made no sense.

The teacher continued up Oxford Lane, past the now deserted Rose Cottage, until he reached the open countryside. After three miles, he arrived at the village of Biddington with its array of black and white timber cottages. Finally, he took the right fork, crossed the humpback bridge over the Avon and followed the road back to his home on the Tree Tops estate.

As he came round a corner and his house came into view, he could recognise two police vehicles parked near his home along with a white minivan and a blue BMW.

He thought he recognised the man in the navy-blue coat and yellow scarf standing by his front door as the detective who'd arrested him ten days before. He was accompanied by four officers in uniform.

Oh no, he thought, not the cops again. When will this nightmare end?'

Gavin Roscoe appeared agitated as he approached. He was staring up at Hockley's first floor windows. His facial expression turned to relief when the teacher, red-faced and perspiring, came jogging up the driveway.

'Mr Hockley. We're sorry to trouble you again,' he declared with an apologetic expression on his face.

'I'm not sure you are,' he replied, panting after his run. 'It feels like you're hounding me.'

'Look, this won't take a lot of your time, Mr Hockley. I believe you may own a black coat.'

'That's right.'

'Did you wear it on the night of January the 8th?'

'I can't remember, to be honest. Why's this so important?'

Roscoe persisted. 'We need you to go and find it.'

Hockley glared. 'This is so intrusive.'

'If you don't want to cooperate, we could easily get a warrant from the magistrates to search your house again.'

'Oh, very well. I'll fetch it. It's still in the wardrobe.'

As Hockley unlocked his front door, the DCI beckoned to a young constable standing nearby.

'Can you follow him?' whispered Roscoe.

The officer pursued Hockley upstairs to his bedroom. A large black Italian-made woollen coat appeared as soon as the teacher drew back the wardrobe door. The officer stored it in a large plastic evidence bag, which he then carried downstairs and placed in the back of the minivan.

After confirming with Hockley that it was the only black coat he owned, Roscoe said simply, 'That'll be all, sir,' and stepped away.

In return, Hockley muttered sarcastically, 'Oh, what a shame. You could've stayed and had some breakfast.'

Roscoe glanced back with a stern expression. 'Look, chum, don't try and be funny. You're still on our radar.' He walked to the end of the drive. 'We'll bring your coat back in a few days,' he yelled. Then he climbed into his car and they all drove away.

* * *

The sun was struggling to appear from behind the clouds as Gavin Roscoe arrived at his office later that same morning. He shivered in the cold air as he made his way past the reception desk and climbed the stairs to CID.

He noticed immediately that Sunita Roy and Brett Dawson appeared to be on the phone. He wondered, as he often did, whether someone had tipped them off that his car had drawn up. Had they been idly gossiping before he arrived?

Shortly after hanging up his coat and scarf, there was a knock on his door.

'Good morning, guv. Could I have a word?' DI Vickers asked, opening the door a fraction.

'Of course, Tom. What is it?' the DCI replied as he glanced over the headlines of that morning's national newspapers. 'Why don't you come in?'

The inspector stepped inside and closed the door.

'Guv, I've been making some inquiries about Revd Peter Hughes. I heard you mention his name the other day. I know it's a fairly common name, but it jogged my memory, so I made a call to a police colleague who now works in Wolverhampton and he confirmed what I thought.'

'You seem to be talking in riddles, Tom. It would help if you got to the point,' said Roscoe. 'I've a lot of work this morning and, on top of it, I've got to see the chief super.'

'Well, it's like this, guv,' said Vickers, as he sat on a chair by the wall. 'A few years ago, Peter Hughes's elderly parents owned a cottage in the village of Knowle, with breath-taking views across the countryside. But a property company gained planning permission for a development – a small estate of twenty homes at the rear. As a result, tens of thousands of pounds were wiped off the value of their home overnight.'

'Are you sure it's the same Peter Hughes?'

'Yes, definitely,' said Vickers. 'The rector's father suffered a lot of stress and died from a heart attack within months. Then his mother, unable to cope alone, was moved into an old folks' home. Their cottage had to be sold and a lot of the money went towards her care bills. Harry Bowers was behind the development. My mate, who was in the fraud team at the time, suspected a corrupt relationship between the planning chairman and Bowers. But he was unable to prove anything and the case was shelved.'

Roscoe leaned back in his chair, surprised at the DI's revelation. Did this mean his friend, the rector, had been harbouring a secret grudge against Harry Bowers? How was it this information had not come to their attention before?

'Well done, Tom,' he said.

'When his name first came up, I thought nothing of it. It was only yesterday, for some reason, that it set bells ringing.'

Roscoe smiled. 'Wasn't church bells, was it?'

'Good one, guv.'

'Great work, Tom. That's very useful. Can you write me a brief report on it? Then we'll have to consider paying our man of the cloth a little visit.' He paused and then said, 'Tom, can you get the whole team together for a meeting here at midday? We'll need uniformed branch to assist.'

'Yes, guv. No problem. Midday, you say?'

'Yes. I had a call early this morning from the forensics people. They've tested Hockley's coat and ruled it out as being the one that was in contact with Bowers.'

As the words emerged from his lips, Roscoe realised at last that the cloud of suspicion that had hung over the teacher for several weeks had now been completely lifted.

'So we're going to have to check out the coats of all the other possible suspects.'

Vickers nodded and rose to his feet. 'A major task, guv.'

'Yes. But let's hope that, by doing this, we can flush out the killer. Because, if we don't have any luck with this, you know what the only other option is, don't you? We might have to resort to inviting all men living in Oxford Lane and the surrounding area to hand us their coats.'

'Let's hope it doesn't come to that,' he murmured.

Vickers arranged for all the CID and uniformed officers he could deploy to attend the noon meeting. Then he fixed photographs of all the main murder suspects on the large whiteboard on the wall. Finally, he wrote the suspects' names next to the photographs in capital letters with a black marker pen and added brief profile details beside each one.

Roscoe took a moment to look over the inspector's shoulder at one stage and to examine the list of the 'persons of interest': David Harrington; Michael Harrington; Rashad Mahmood; and Tyler Brown.

'Because of the great initiative you've shown this morning, I think we should definitely add the rector's name. It seems he might have a motive.'

'What about the six other men in the choir?'

'Yes, but forget the choirmaster. Several witnesses have confirmed he was at the church hall at twenty to seven and never left the building until all the choristers had departed at eight thirty.'

* * *

By midday, all the officers notified by Vickers had gathered together in the CID office. Roscoe peered round his doorway to see Vickers, Brett Dawson, Omar Khalid, Wendy Hopkirk, three other detective constables and seven uniformed constables huddled together around the desks, chatting and laughing.

He walked across to the whiteboard before turning to address them.

'Thank you all for coming. It's good to see so many of you here this morning. Now you lucky people have been chosen to join our coat patrol. We've got to visit each of these suspects on the board to see if they've got a black coat. The object of the exercise is to find out who owns the coat that came into contact with our murder victim on the night he was killed. We can eliminate our key suspect, James Hockley. We're now engaged in a blitz on all the remaining suspects.

'I want you all to liaise with DI Vickers, who'll split you up into individual teams. Each team will go to a known address. Don't take any nonsense. If any suspect plays up, we'll just have to return later with a warrant. But warn them it's in their best interests to cooperate. We've got to catch this killer before he strikes again.'

He glanced across at Sunita, who was watching proceedings from her desk in the centre of CID.

'Sergeant Roy, you won't be involved in the visits because of your special assignment. OK. That's it. Let's move!'

One by one, the officers approached Vickers to find out which addresses they'd been allocated to visit. Gradually, they all left the office and set out on their mission.

Chapter 49

The village of Norton Prior was eerily quiet as Sunita Roy drove her car along the main road past a series of streetlights which were gradually flickering out with the approach of daybreak.

It was six o'clock on a bitterly cold Thursday morning. Here and there, she noticed an upstairs light as a householder prepared for the morning ahead. She passed a milkman in his noisy van on the way to make deliveries. Birds were singing in the trees to herald the start of another day as she reached the village green and recognised her boss's car. He had parked in the lane close to the Coach and Horses inn. She parked in front of him.

As she slipped her grey coat on and walked along the pavement towards him, she began to wonder whether that day would finally mark the end of the crimewave that had brought fear to the village.

A light came on in a nearby house as Roscoe switched off his ignition – he had been running the heater to keep warm – and stepped out of the car to greet her. For some reason, he had chosen to wear a bright red scarf with his coat.

'This is the second time this week I've had to get up at this wretched hour!' he complained. 'I'm starting to understand why some of my old colleagues opted for early retirement.'

Sunita smiled. She recognised he was a person who used humour to mask his nerves.

'You may as well get in and I'll whisk us up to Oxford Lane,' he said. 'No sense taking both cars.'

As she took her place in the passenger seat, his thoughts immediately became focussed on the job in hand.

'Could we just run through it again before we go?' he said. 'You told me yesterday that you searched local addresses and found a Dorothy Bailey in Oxford Lane?'

She nodded. 'That's right, sir. There were several Dorothys in the Queensbridge area, but this one stood out because she lives in Oxford Lane, close to the lychgate. She was listed along with her husband, Edward Bailey. He's the newsagent who runs Norton News.'

Roscoe's eyes lit up as she continued, 'Everything now appears to fit into place. If this man found out his wife was having an affair with Bowers, that would give him a motive for murder. He could also be responsible for the death of Bethan Thomas. If the shop door had been open, he might've overheard her outburst in the street. To be honest with you, sir, I'm annoyed we didn't think of him before. After all, he was one of the last people to see Bowers alive. That should've rung alarm bells before now.'

Roscoe nodded. 'We're all at fault for not considering him. But since you may have discovered the identity of Dot, I've started to believe that Bailey's our man and I've obtained a warrant from magistrates to search the premises. So shall we go? We're meant to be meeting the others at the church at six thirty.'

Sunita nodded. Roscoe started the engine and the car glided out onto the main road.

'What happened about all the coats?' Sunita asked as they crossed the river and approached the bottom of Oxford Lane.

He glanced across. 'We bagged up six black coats from suspects. Dr Ling's desk in forensics looked like the coat counter at Primark. To avoid cross-contamination, they were all taken away and tested separately by comparison microscopy for blood, hair and fibres, but, in the end, they were all ruled out.'

'That was quite an operation, collecting all those coats. Did anyone cause a fuss?'

'David Harrington gave us a bit of grief. But he played along in the end.'

DI Vickers had parked his car beside the churchyard wall, close to the yew trees, when Roscoe's car drew up. PC Derek Underhill and three other uniformed constables from Queensbridge were parked behind him, along with Brett Dawson and Omar Khalid.

Sunita walked beside the stone wall until she reached the junction with Oxford Lane. She could see the lychgate and the walls of the church hall but the street was cloaked in darkness, waiting for dawn to caress the morning with its golden glow. The only prominent light was streaming from the front of the newsagent's shop, which was three buildings from the junction. It was a sign that the premises were open for business and that Bailey was almost certainly there.

'Come on then,' said Roscoe. 'Let's go and see how the land lies.'

He asked Underhill and one of his colleagues to go down the driveway next to the shop. Their role was to watch the rear of the premises in case the shopkeeper should try to flee out of the back door. Then, accompanied by the other team members, Roscoe and Sunita entered the brightly lit premises.

The shop had a large counter covered with neatly arranged newspapers and packets of sweets. Tins of groceries lined shelves on the right-hand side, while refrigerators containing drinks and a freezer laden with frozen food stood on the left.

Bailey, untidily dressed in a purple shirt and blue corduroy trousers, was busy cutting open a bundle of newspapers behind the counter with a six-inch knife as the police arrived. He glanced towards the doorway as he heard footsteps approach.

'We're not open yet,' he muttered. Then he stood up fully and observed the police uniforms of the constables gathered on the pavement outside.

Roscoe glared at the proprietor. 'Are you Edward Bailey?'

The shopkeeper raised his upper lip in a sneer. 'That's what it says on the front of the building.'

'I'm afraid you're under arrest.'

'What for?' he demanded.

Roscoe stared into his eyes. 'For murder. I'm DCI Gavin Roscoe of Heart of England Police. I'm arresting you on suspicion of the murder of Harry Bowers and Bethan Thomas. You don't have to say anything...'

Bailey scowled. 'You don't have nothing on me, copper.'

'…but it may harm your defence if you don't mention, when questioned, something which you later rely on in court. Anything you do say may be given in evidence. We also have a warrant to search these premises.'

On hearing those words, Bailey ran through the door behind the counter and fled into his back garden. Sunita, who'd been watching from the shop entrance, had mentally prepared herself for such a reaction and ran out into the street. She sprinted down the steep driveway, calling out to Underhill as she ran.

'He's coming your way, Derek!' she called. 'Take care. He's got a knife.'

Sunita reached the end of the driveway and discovered a back garden cluttered with junk. At the rear of the house stood an old Bedford van; two old fridges; a metal storage tank full of murky, green water; a disused washing machine; and plastic stacking trays. On the far left, beside an uncut hedge, lay a pile of old cardboard boxes. She also noticed an old cricket bat and a pile of rope beside the concrete path which extended along the right-hand side of the garden.

The air was thick with the stench of rotten vegetables which seemed to come from three dustbins. Further down the garden lay an untended lawn and a neglected vegetable plot. Beyond them stretched an overgrown plot of land and then the river.

As Sunita's eyes absorbed the view, she spotted the shopkeeper running as fast as he could towards the water's edge, pursued by a policeman. Then, to her horror, she heard a moaning sound and realised PC Underhill was lying on the ground just a few metres to her right, close to the wooden boundary fence.

The front of his torso was drenched in blood and he was clutching his shoulder. Sunita rushed to his side as Tom Vickers and Omar Khalid caught up with her.

'You all right, Derek?' she asked.

'Bastard stabbed me,' was all the constable managed to say.

'Better call an ambulance!' Sunita yelled, as she then raced down the garden in pursuit of the fleeing shopkeeper.

Behind her, Khalid began tending to the injured constable while the inspector used his mobile phone to make emergency calls to the ambulance service and police control. Vickers could be heard on his phone saying, 'IC1 male reported with a knife. On the run near to Norton Bridge.'

Moments later she caught up with Bailey and the pursuing constable beside the riverbank. The officer had managed to delay Bailey's escape by grabbing his purple shirt in his fist from behind. But the shopkeeper had retaliated by spinning round and goading the officer with his weapon, threatening to cut open his face with the knife.

'Come on, then!' he screamed at the constable.

As Sunita approached, Bailey extended his invitation to both of them.

'Who wants some more of this?' he yelled. The pair advanced upon him together, each trying to tackle him from a slightly different direction. The constable bravely grabbed Bailey's right arm and, simultaneously, Sunita grabbed his left arm. For a few seconds, Bailey appeared to relax. It was as if he was finally surrendering. But it was just pretence.

Summoning up all his strength, he suddenly snatched himself away from them, brutally knocking the constable to the ground as he did so. Sunita realised a small rowing boat was moored by the bank beneath a willow tree and that he was heading towards it – presumably in the hope he could flee down the river.

But as the newsagent dashed towards it, Sunita was behind him like a hound and rugby-tackled him to the ground. They then scrambled around on the muddy bank for what seemed like half a minute.

Bailey staggered to his feet first. He rounded on the detective, who felt the man's rough left hand gripping her neck. Bailey forced himself down on Sunita's body and lunged at her with his knife, brandishing it in front of her eyes. The detective grabbed her attacker's wrist and, for several seconds, they grappled on the ground by the water's edge.

Bailey seemed determined to stab her and, for several terrifying minutes, his knife was poised just inches from her face.

Sunita wondered how much longer she could restrain her wiry attacker. But then she felt the weight of Bailey's body being suddenly dragged away from her and hurled to the side.

DI Vickers, an ex-rugby player, had come to her aid. He'd brought with him the old cricket bat she'd seen in Bailey's garden. Before the shopkeeper could spring into action again, the inspector struck him on the head with it.

He acted with such force that Bailey dropped the knife and ended up flat on his face beneath the willow tree.

'Are you all right, Sarge?' asked Vickers.

Sunita blinked and took some deep breaths. Her clothes were covered in mud. Some of it had worked its way into her nose and mouth. She turned away from the inspector and spat some of the brown dirt onto the ground. She could detect a strong, unpleasant smell of river sludge about herself, but the ordeal was over and she'd survived.

'Yes, Tom,' she spluttered. Then she added, 'I just couldn't get a grip on him.'

'I heard you took down a knife maniac on a plane a couple of months ago.'

'That's different, Tom. I wasn't skating around on a mudbank.'

As she staggered to her feet, Vickers and the constable handcuffed the newsagent and marched him back to the shop.

DC Khalid had meanwhile removed PC Underhill's blood-splattered shirt and tunic. He'd pressed on his wound with the shirt to stem the flow of blood until two paramedics came and took over. A few minutes later, the injured officer was placed on a stretcher and whisked off to Queensbridge General Hospital.

A forensic team arrived shortly afterwards and carried out an inch-by-inch search of the shop and the newsagent's flat above. They found a black coat, which was bagged up and taken away to be examined.

Two officers were sent to Stratford railway station to inform Bailey's wife, Dorothy, of the arrest. She immediately closed her kiosk and returned home.

* * *

Roscoe was delighted that Bailey had been caught, but he was concerned that an officer had been injured. Once Bailey had been driven off to Queensbridge police station, he made a personal call to Underhill's wife on his mobile phone.

'Your husband's unfortunately been stabbed, Mrs Underhill,' Roscoe told her. 'I wanted to let you know personally and to explain that he acquired his injury in the course of his duties. He bravely tackled a suspect who was armed with a knife.'

'Whereabouts was he stabbed?' she asked.

'In the shoulder. It's not life-threatening and Derek's expected to make a full recovery. I'm going to arrange a car to collect you and take you to hospital'

He found an old blanket in his car boot. He placed it on the passenger seat so his sergeant could travel with him in her mud-splattered clothing.

After ending his call, Roscoe glared at her.

'Bloody hell, Sergeant,' he said. 'What have you been doing?'

'It's the river mud,' said Sunita, in a feeble attempt to explain away the stench.

'Let's get you back to your car as quickly as possible,' moaned Roscoe. 'Open your window. By the way, I haven't been idle. While you and Tom were by the river, I had a good look round the garden. There's a metal water tank at the rear of the house full of rainwater. I imagine it once stored water in Bailey's loft.'

'I noticed it myself, sir.'

'It's full of green water. I'm going to ask forensic to take samples from the water in case that's where marina man was drowned.'

Sunita nodded.

'Are you all right?' he continued. 'You look exhausted. Bailey led you on quite a chase, didn't he?'

She smiled. 'Yes, sir. I'm OK. I fell over in the mud as I tried to snatch his knife, but Tom came to the rescue. Did we manage to retrieve Bailey's knife?'

Roscoe nodded. 'Yes. It was found on the riverbank and will be sent to the lab to be examined along with the coat. It's the same knife he was using to cut through his bundles of newspapers.'

Sunita's smile faded. 'I doubt whether it's the knife that killed Bowers. He's probably hidden that one away.'

Chapter 50

Edward Bailey was feeling sorry for himself. After five years without the police meddling in his affairs, they were back and threatening to derail his new life in the country.

The custody suite in Queensbridge had not unsettled him. His cell measured only two by three metres. It contained a hard mattress on a low-level bench with a single pillow, grubby sheet and blanket; a high window; and a rudimentary toilet in the corner. But it was luxury compared with the small cell he'd been forced to share with another inmate years before in Winson Green.

Soon, he thought to himself, he faced endless questions from nosy coppers about that bastard Bowers, who'd seduced his wife, and that interfering bitch Bethan Thomas.

Shortly after ten o'clock, he heard a knock on his door's metal hatch.

'Bailey, there's someone to see you,' the custody sergeant announced.

'I'm not seeing anyone unless it's my wife,' he shouted back.

Who the hell's this? thought Bailey, who was still wearing the same purple shirt and blue corduroy trousers he'd worn when arrested a few hours earlier.

A man in a black pin-striped suit thrust his head round the door.

'Mr Bailey? I'm Roger Sims, the duty solicitor. Could I have a word?'

'Suppose it won't do no harm,' said Bailey.

The visitor was carrying a wooden chair as well as a briefcase. He placed the chair on the floor and tried to make himself comfortable.

Then he smiled weakly. 'They won't let me take you to an interview room, so we'll just have to make the best of it here. What I'd like to know is whether you'd be happy for me to represent you?'

'Yes,' said Bailey. 'You look a reasonable bloke. I'm in a spot of trouble. Maybe you can help me.'

'Right, as you know, you're facing two charges of murder.'

Bailey nodded, sweeping his straggly grey hair towards the back of his head with a swipe of his right hand. 'I know, but it wasn't me.'

'Good.' Sims took a writing pad and pen from his briefcase. He wrote, 'Edward Bailey, aged forty-five. Not guilty.'

Bailey watched him like an owl studying a mouse. The solicitor was around six feet tall, bony with a long jaw and had mild grey eyes which matched his hair colour. His glasses rested upon a long thin nose. He was smartly dressed with an aura of respectability. He was the kind of advocate a judge would listen to, Bailey thought.

'Right, well, I gather you're going to be brought in for interview shortly,' Sims continued.

'Yes, they're taking their time, aren't they? It's about ten o'clock now, isn't it?'

'It's just gone ten fifteen. I don't know the reason for the delay. My advice to you is to make no comment – at least, to begin with. We want to hear what they've got to say.'

'That suits me. I weren't going to say much anyway. Listen, can you get a message to me missus? Can you tell her I'm being framed by the cops and I hope to see her very soon?'

'I'll do my best to get the message to her,' Sims said as he prepared to leave. 'But I'm afraid I'm an extremely busy man at the moment. Yours isn't my only case.'

'You're a good fella. Just do your best.'

* * *

An hour later, Bailey was brought up to the interview room by two burly officers. He was ordered to sit on a chair in front of the desk. A few minutes afterwards, Roscoe and Roy arrived, followed by the solicitor.

'Good morning, Mr Bailey. Mr Sims,' said Roscoe with a faint smile.

'Good afternoon, more like it,' muttered Bailey.

'Let's get started,' said the DCI, ignoring Bailey's remark and turning on the recording equipment.

'OK. This is your first interview, Mr Bailey. Also present are Sunita Roy and Roger Sims. Just to remind you, you're still under caution after we arrested you earlier today.'

Sitting down beside his sergeant, he gazed directly into the shopkeeper's eyes in his first opportunity to study him since his capture by the riverbank. Bailey stared back with an expression that smacked of defiance.

'Now I want you to cast your mind back to seven o'clock on the evening of Tuesday, 8 January this year. You were behind the counter at your business, Norton News, when Harry Bowers came in.'

Bailey frowned. 'No comment.'

'He bought a packet of mints, which I gather is something he often bought from your shop.'

'No comment.'

'Oh, it's going to be like that, is it?' said Roscoe sharply. 'You're not doing yourself any favours, you know.'

He paused. 'Now you told DS Roy here in January that Mr Bowers had called in earlier than normal as if planning to meet someone. This was designed to implicate someone else in the events of that night – to implicate James Hockley, wasn't it? After Bowers left your shop, you saw him in the street talking to Hockley, didn't you?'

'No comment.'

'You watched as Hockley punched Bowers in the face near the lychgate, didn't you?'

'No comment.'

'You stood at the top of the alley and looked on from the shadows as Bowers lay recovering on the ground from the punch and Hockley walked on to the church hall. You thought you'd be able to frame Hockley for what you were planning to do, didn't you? You stood motionless, holding the hand trolley or barrow you use for shifting bundles of newspapers.'

Bailey looked down at the table and shook his head.

'The next thing that happened was that Bethan Thomas walked down the lane from the direction of her home. From a distance, she saw the two men arguing. She also saw you and thought you were holding the handlebars of a bicycle. But she entered the hall as she was late for choir practice. No doubt she was unaware that Bowers became injured at the hands of Hockley and she simply decided he must have changed his mind about coming to choir practice for some reason.'

'No comment,' said Bailey.

'You seized your chance and, when the street was deserted, stabbed Bowers to death with a knife. You placed the body in a plastic bag to avoid spillage of blood and wheeled him on your trolley to the unfinished grave.

You'd noticed in fading light from your window earlier the grave was only partly filled in. You quickly spread earth over the body and wheeled the trolley back.'

'No comment.'

'More than a month later, on 15 February, you were working at your shop when you overheard a conversation outside. Bethan Thomas was speaking unguardedly about what she'd seen. You heard her words because the shop door was open, despite the cold. You couldn't take a chance. She'd got information that could implicate you and she had to be silenced.'

'No comment.'

'You drove to her cottage in your blue car and, because she knew you, she let you in. While her back was turned, you used some of your brother-in-law's climbing rope in an effort to strangle her. When that failed, you grabbed a hammer from her toolbox and battered her to death. You then hid the body in the sandpit. You were lightly splattered with blood, which you attempted to wash off. Traces of blood found at the cottage match your DNA.'

'No comment.'

'You've possibly been wondering why you had to wait so long today before being interviewed.'

'I thought you'd taken time off to go shopping.'

Roscoe ignored Bailey's cocky remark. 'Our forensic people have been working hard on the case. They carefully examined under a microscope your black synthetic coat and found some of the fibres became transferred onto Bowers' coat during your attack on him.'

'Do things like that happen? That don't sound likely to me.'

'Whether it sounds likely to you or not, it's a fact and we believe it's the final piece in the jigsaw that'll convict you before a jury.'

The DCI warned Bailey that he faced being jailed for life for the two murders.

'The evidence against you is overwhelming. I strongly suggest you give yourself a clear conscience and use this opportunity to tell us the truth.'

Bailey leaned back on his chair and glared at him. 'No comment.'

Sunita had been watching Bailey's denials, his exasperated groans and his dismissive hand gestures throughout the interview.

'We've made several important discoveries while searching your premises, Mr Bailey,' she said. 'We've found earth on the wheels of the trolley which match earth samples taken from the grave. We've found your blue Honda – which was spotted outside Mrs Thomas's cottage by a neighbour – in a garage near your shop. We've found a coil of climbing rope in your garden that matches the rope used to attack Mrs Thomas. It's all looking very bad for you and a jury might draw an inference if you fail to give any explanations.'

Bailey looked perturbed for the first time. A shimmer of doubt flickered across his face.

'Do you mind if I get a word with my brief?'

Roscoe nodded in agreement, allowing Bailey and Sims to hold a short, whispered conversation while leaning away from the table.

Then, turning back to face Roscoe, Bailey said, 'No comment to all that.'

'Right. You're to be formally charged with the two murders,' he told him. 'You'll appear before Queensbridge magistrates tomorrow morning. Do you have anything else to say?

'No.'

Sunita interrupted to say, 'Mr Bailey, we should point out it's also possible you'll be further charged with the murder of the man found in the River Avon on 24 January; with assault on a police officer; and with resisting arrest.'

Sims raised an eyebrow. 'This is the first I've heard about these offences. Can someone fill me in?'

'Mr Sims, there's a possibility Mr Bailey may be charged over the death of the man whose body was found at Queensbridge Marina on 24 January,' said the DCI. 'We're still making inquiries. The alleged assault relates to one of our officers who was seriously injured yesterday in the course of arresting Mr Bailey.

'Because of the seriousness of the offences and the risk he may commit further offences or fail to appear, we'll of course be opposing bail. All right. We'll call a halt there.'

Chapter 51

Daylight was fading and a gentle rain falling as Sunita Roy's car reached the outskirts of Queensbridge on Tuesday, 12 March. She'd been given directions to Woodside Way, but the address was still proving hard to find.

At last, she saw a narrow lane flanked on the left by a row of ash and beech trees and knew this must be the turning. Open fields, newly ploughed and exuding a rich, reddish-brown colour, lay to the right.

No sooner had she stopped her car to re-read the directions than a light-blue car appeared behind her and its driver flashed his lights. She lowered her window after recognising Tom Vickers was behind the wheel.

'All right, Sunita?' he asked after jumping out of his Volkswagen Golf and approaching her window. 'You look a bit lost. Don't worry. I've been here before. It's not far down here. Do you want to follow me?'

She nodded as the rain began to ease off. 'That's a good idea, Tom. Do you think I look all right? This green saree was all I could find. I don't go out in the evening that much at the moment.'

Vickers grinned. 'You look very nice.'

She glanced at him. He was wearing a dark-grey suit with a blue tie. He'd shaved off his dark, ginger moustache and she'd never seen him looking so smart, but passed no comment.

'Does the boss often invite members of his team round to his house?' she asked.

'Not very often. I guess this is a special occasion. Oxford Lane was a tough case to crack. The boss wants to celebrate. He's back in Niggler's good books.'

'So he's told me. Thanks for your contribution to the funeral fund, Tom. I sent off the money. It was nearly two hundred pounds.'

'That's great, Sunita. Did you know Arun Halder's funeral was today? I've seen some pictures online. Here you are.'

He fiddled with his mobile phone. Then a photo of the weeping widow and her aging parents flashed up on the screen. Sunita was moved to see them with their heads bowed over the coffin. She still felt partly to blame for what happened to Arun. Vickers sensed she was upset.

'You know you've got nothing to blame yourself for. That guy just got a crazy idea in his head – that's all. He's entirely at fault for what happened to himself – no one else. Come on. I'll show you where The Willows is.'

A few minutes later, after they had parked in the drive of their boss's home, Roscoe and his wife welcomed them both inside.

'You must be cold. Come in and warm yourselves up,' said Helen, who was wearing a mauve dress with a halterneck top. 'Has it stopped raining?'

Sunita nodded. 'Just a few minutes ago.'

'Let me take your coat and show you where the loo is,' said Helen, leading her away.

Roscoe, who was looking uncomfortable in an unfamiliar brown suit, took the inspector aside.

'I had my reservations about Sunita to begin with, but I'm glad to say I've been proved wrong. We wouldn't have cracked the case without her. I must say she's looking very elegant this evening.'

'Yes, guv. That's a dazzling dress your wife's in, if you don't mind me saying.'

Roscoe smiled. 'A friend once told me, "When your wife's set her heart on a particular dress, a wise man says nothing." I've always tried to follow that advice.'

Soon after seven, the group moved into the dining room, which contained a long mahogany table and six high-backed chairs. An ornate chandelier hung above the centre of the table. A painting of two bay horses hung above the marble fireplace.

'Lovely room, sir,' remarked Sunita.

'Glad you like it, Sergeant,' he replied as they all sat down.

Helen had prepared starters of prawn salad or melon. This was followed by a main course of chicken in white wine with roast potatoes, carrots and broccoli for the men and herself. She had cooked a spiced lentil and spinach pie for Sunita. Roscoe opened a bottle of white wine and filled four glasses.

Sunita normally declined alcohol, but felt she could have one as it was a special occasion.

As they ate, Roscoe was reminded that it was five days since Edward Bailey's arrest. Since then the newsagent had appeared in court and been remanded in custody. His next court appearance was due to take place the following Friday.

Roscoe was relieved they'd caught the man. He'd seen tensions and suspicions growing among the local residents because of the murders. Now the police had identified the perpetrator, a sense of calm was beginning to return to people's lives.

During the meal, they talked about the Roscoes' children, events in the town and the increased trade Helen was enjoying at the tearooms.

But after desserts of fruit and cream, the conversation turned inevitably to the team's success in solving the case.

Vickers glanced at Roscoe. 'How on earth did we manage to overlook Bailey, guv? I gather he'd been in prison for armed robbery and had a record for violent offences.'

'Quite simple,' he said. 'It was a police records blunder. He was on the database under the wrong spelling. He was listed under B-A-Y-L-E-Y instead of B-A-I-L-E-Y. That one-letter mistake made such a huge difference.

'Bailey had a tragic childhood, you know. He was brought up by a cruel stepfather and got into trouble with the law from the age of thirteen. He was in and out of young offender institutes as a young man – sometimes for crimes of violence – and got to see quite a bit of prison as he got older. He tried to go straight with a new life in the village running a business after inheriting money, but his old demons came back when his wife began an affair with Bowers.

'He loved his wife Dorothy – or Dot, as she often called herself – with a passion. She was the only thing in his life he really cared about. He developed a deep resentment against the property developer when he discovered the affair and became determined to kill him. He felt forced to kill Mrs Thomas when he feared she'd blab to us.'

Sunita interrupted to say, 'Isn't it highly likely he also killed the man in the marina?'

Roscoe nodded. 'Yes, it looks that way. Bailey's got an old water tank at the back of his place he uses for watering the garden. Silas carried out tests on the water and samples proved a match for the microscopic particles found in the drowned man's body.'

'So he drowned him in the tank and then dumped the body in the river?'

'That's how it looks. It turns out the man was Dorothy Bailey's brother, a former squaddie called Colin Knight. He couldn't find anywhere to live after leaving the army and ended up sleeping in a tent in the woods. He stayed at the Baileys' flat above the shop for a time, but he resented the way Bailey sometimes spoke to his sister and the two men didn't get on. One evening Knight came back to see Bailey. The shopkeeper lost his temper with him and drowned him. He wasn't reported as missing to police because Dorothy simply assumed he was sleeping rough somewhere. We're just getting all the evidence together and Bailey's going to be charged with that murder as well.'

Sunita turned to face Roscoe. 'The coil of rope in Bailey's back garden linked Mrs Thomas's murder to Colin Knight's murder.'

'That's right. Knight learned rock climbing in the army and became an enthusiast. Bailey tied some of his victim's own rope to a heavy rock in an effort to keep the body submerged in the river. It was exactly the same rope used on Bethan Thomas. Bailey's a highly devious, self-obsessed man who hasn't shown a shred of remorse for his evil conduct.'

Roscoe stretched himself back on his chair and beamed at Sunita. 'You've done a wonderful job, and we're blessed to have you as part of our team.'

She smiled. 'That's very kind, sir.'

'It's true. Do you know this case supports my long-held belief that, when tackling even the most evil criminal mastermind, the law will always triumph – so long as we use our brains and have the resources?'

Sunita nodded. 'I agree with you, sir. Murder won't stay hidden and men like Bailey can't cheat their karma.'

Vickers leaned across the table towards the DCI, who was sitting opposite him. 'Will you be taking any action against Hockley and Margaret Bowers, guv?'

'I don't think so,' he said. 'We're fairly certain now that Hockley remonstrated with Harry Bowers and punched him but then left him, still alive. We also know Margaret Bowers' note was written by her because, at the time, she believed Hockley may have been the killer and wanted to defend him. But, at the end of the day, we've got the real killer and we don't think much would be gained by charging those two with any offence.' Roscoe looked down at the floor and grinned. 'Do you know I never trusted that man Bailey since the time we lived in Norton and he delivered the wrong Sunday papers two weeks in a row?'

Helen and their guests smiled.

As she rose from the table, Sunita glanced at a small, oak sideboard behind her. In the centre, surrounded by china ornaments, was a framed photograph of Roscoe and his family.

'May I, sir?' she asked.

'Of course. That's Melody on the right. She's at college studying hospitality and catering. George is on the left. He's a year older and works as a barman at the moment. He doesn't really know what he wants to do.'

'Often the way at that age, guv,' remarked Vickers.

Sunita couldn't take her eyes off the picture. It was a traditional, happy family portrait. Everyone was smiling. How much it contrasted with the Leicester photo of the Halders she's been shown earlier.

* * *

As Sunita drove away from The Willows, she reflected on how much she had enjoyed the evening. Roscoe was a kind, considerate boss. Helen had been an amiable hostess who had shown genuine interest in her. Tom Vickers was a jovial and supportive companion.

But she had become unsettled on seeing the image of mourners at Arun Halder's funeral and, later, the photograph of the Roscoes. There was an emptiness in her life, she realised, and she had felt that even more strongly this evening.

While her mind was engrossed in this way, she drove in the direction of her home and found, to her surprise, she was travelling into Queensbridge. She was unsure how it happened. Perhaps she'd failed to pay enough attention to the road signs.

The town centre was ablaze with lights. She stopped her car in the middle of the high street. It was barely ten o'clock. Was it too late in the evening to disturb someone? A group of drinkers were huddled outside the Crown and Sceptre. A drunken man was weaving his way along the opposite pavement. Some late-night shoppers were loading their cars with groceries under a lamp post.

She removed her phone from her handbag and dialled the number she had been for so long averse to calling. A man's voice answered. Her hands were trembling. Then she spoke softly.

'Hello, Papa.'

THE END

If you enjoyed this book, please let others know by leaving a quick review on Amazon. Also, if you spot anything untoward in the paperback, get in touch. We strive for the best quality and appreciate reader feedback.

editor@thebookfolks.com

www.thebookfolks.com

More fiction in this series

THE CROSSBOW STALKER (Book 2)

When a serial killer armed with a crossbow terrorises the West Midlands, Chief Inspector Gavin Roscoe suspects a motive of jealousy and revenge. But as the number of victims increases, the connection initially established between them wears thin. DS Sunita Roy has a different theory and resolves to pursue her own instincts, come what may.

MURDER OF A DOCTOR (Book 3)

Police search for the identities of people seen near the scene of a doctor's murder. And it seems like an open and shut case when a father with a grievance against him can be placed nearby. But DS Sunita Roy wants to dig deeper, and with an internal affairs investigation ongoing, she'll have to tread carefully.

OUT FOR REVENGE (Book 4)

There's a noticeable change of atmosphere in the city when a dangerous prisoner is released. He has plans to up his drugs business. But someone will quickly put an end to that. Detective Sunita Roy has the unenviable task of hunting down the gangsters who were likely responsible. But when the cops close in, they'll have an even bigger problem than they first imagined.

All FREE with Kindle Unlimited and available in paperback.

Other titles of interest

THE SILENT QUARRY by Cheryl Rees-Price

The first title in an immersive mystery series set in Wales

Following a fall and a bang to the head, a woman's memories come flooding back about an incident that occurred twenty years ago in which her friend was murdered. As she pieces together the events and tells the police, she begins to fear repercussions. DI Winter Meadows must work out the identity of the killer before they strike again.

AN EARLY GRAVE by Robert McCracken

The first title in a thrilling mystery series set in Liverpool and Belfast

A tough young Detective Inspector encounters a reclusive man who claims he holds the secret to a murder case. But he also has a dangerous agenda. Will DI Tara Grogan take the bait?

THE LONG DEAD by John Dean

The first title in a gripping mystery series set in northern England

When a routine archaeological dig turns up bodies on the site of a WWII prisoner of war camp, it should be an open and shut case for detective John Blizzard. But forensics discover one of the deaths is more recent and the force have a murder investigation on their hands.

All FREE with Kindle Unlimited and available in paperback.

Printed in Great Britain
by Amazon

18255833R00181